DOUBLE PLAY

SEATTLE CASCADES
BOOK 5

C.M. KANE

COPYRIGHT

~

Editing & book design by Maggie Kern @ Ms.K Edits

Cover art by Golden Czermak @ FuriousFotog

BOOK FIVE

DEDICATION

For my mom, who listened to me telling her stories my whole life, and always asked the questions I didn't know I had to answer.

PROLOGUE

Ariana…

"It's cute you think I care what you think," I said. "The fact is, I can do whatever the fuck I want, and there really isn't anything you can do about it."

"Well, then, you can just fuck off," Reggie said. "I don't need a bitch like you around. There's plenty of pussy out there for me to have any time I want. You're a loser, anyway, and no one wants to fuck you, so get lost."

"Pretty sure my name's on the deed," I said. "So the one who needs to get lost is you."

"Fuck you," he said, then stomped like an angry toddler toward the door, opened it, stepped out, and slammed it behind him.

He didn't really have much of anything at my place, since he never wanted to live together, so I went to town, bagging up his shit just to get it out of my space. The fights had been getting worse, and I really didn't want him around me anymore. I'd decided that I was going to start putting things up in my house that suited me, not him, and remove the shit he thought was "so nice" and "a perfect piece for us." How anyone would think that the dogs playing poker was a fancy piece of art, I would never understand, but it was what it was, and it didn't matter anymore.

It only took an hour or so to find everything he'd left, and I put it all in a couple of those giant black trash bags so I could drop it off at his mom's house. Oh yeah, he still lived with his mom, and she was just a peach. The woman never liked me, didn't like that I "disrespected" her baby boy by telling him he had to get a job before he moved into my place, and that I wasn't gonna pay for anything if he didn't. Her precious boy was too sensitive to have to do actual work, like something that paid him more than minimum wage. Even those jobs were too much for him.

My brother had told me to kick him to the curb months ago, and I should have listened. I was too far up my own ass to notice the giant red flags he was waving around. My brother, Demetri, knew him from back in the day, but Reggie had promised me he'd changed. He did that love bombing thing, getting me flowers all the time, little things that felt like he was actually paying attention to what I liked, but it turned out it was all his mommy. Fucking loser didn't even bother to hide that after a while, and I still didn't see the issue. I just saw that he was being resourceful.

Now, though, it was blatantly obvious that the dick was just that, a dick. And he didn't even give good dick, which was even worse. When we first started dating, he was pretty good at making sure I got off before him, but after a couple of months, he slowed that down, told me he was having a hard time with something, and just needed to get off first. Why I let him get away with that was beyond me, but I did. Entirely too much time had been given to him, and when the first anniversary of our dating came around and he didn't even bother to show up to the dinner I made him, I knew it was over.

Thankfully, I could throw myself into work. Doing remodeling with my brother and his best friend was physical, but worth it. We made good money and were always busy. During the winter, we had to do more indoor jobs, but sometimes the outdoor ones would come along. I actually loved working in the rain, but concrete didn't exactly like that, so we tried to make sure those jobs were done in better weather.

Thing about Seattle, and the surrounding areas, was that it did rain, but not all the time. No, mostly we had cloud cover rather than sunshine, but the rain wasn't bad. I mean, Honolulu had more rain per year than Seattle, if that said anything about it. I guess if you were in Hawaii, rain wouldn't be that big of a deal, but I didn't know from personal experience.

My phone pinged, and I checked to see that it was a text from Reggie. When I opened it, it was a picture of him fucking someone else, so I blocked his number. I'd drop the trash at his mom's house late tonight when I knew he'd be asleep or out fucking some bitch he picked up at a bar. Either way, I'd be done with it. I'd take a photo, send it to him after unblocking, then delete him from my life. If I could delete the last year and change from my brain, I'd be happier, but that wasn't how that worked.

My phone rang, and I looked and saw it was Demetri calling.

"Hey," I said upon answering.

"What the fuck did you say to Reggie?" he asked.

"I kicked him out of my house," I said.

"Good for you," he said. "But now he's telling people you did it without reason. Said something about you cheating on him, and he went to you begging to work things out."

"I could send you the picture he just sent of him fucking someone," I said.

"Oh, no," he said, and I could hear the terror in his voice. "I believe you, not him, but thought you should get ahead of things if you were of a mind to."

"I don't even care," I said. "His shit is bagged up, and I'll drop it off at his mom's tonight after she's gone to bed. I'll take a picture of it all, send it to him, then block him for good."

"Need help with it?" he asked.

"If you've got nothing better to do, sure," I said.

"Brad would be down to help, too," he said.

"There isn't that much shit," I said. "But if we want to make it a company outing, and you bring your truck so he doesn't recognize my car if he's home, I'm down for that."

"Brad is gonna be stoked," he said. "He's been trying to figure out why you were with him. I kept telling him to just hang on, 'cause eventually you'd figure it out. I'm sorry it took over a year, but I did warn you in the beginning."

"Yeah, I know," I said. "And the 'I told you so' is well earned."

"Whatever," he said. "What time do you want us there?"

"Give me half an hour and I can be ready," I said.

"See you soon," he replied, and I could hear the smile in his voice.

CHAPTER ONE

S pencer...
"I just want to get something to put in the living room," I said. "It's fucking cold in there, and I want a carpet to put down."

"It's dumb to go to the hardware store for this," Billy said. "There's a fucking Wally World down the block. Why don't we go there? It'll be cheaper."

"And will wear out faster," I replied. "Besides, I'm paying, so I get to pick."

"Whatever," he said as he climbed out of the truck.

We made our way into the store, weaving through the aisles to find the carpet and flooring section. I grew up living in a home decorated by Wally's, and I fucking hated it. Everything was completely disposable, and it didn't last nearly as long as it should have. Billy was more middle class, so he didn't understand the shit that the folks who worked there went through.

I did a stint working there for a whole month one summer, and I fucking despised it. Shit pay with shit managers who didn't do shit but fuck around on their phones and bark orders. Never shopped there after that, even though my mama wanted to. I explained everything to her, but she just didn't get it.

As soon as I made enough money to not care where I shopped, I promised myself I would always buy quality over price if I could manage it, and that's just what I'd done. The house was technically mine, but Billy lived with me. We each had our own rooms, but we needed to get some things fixed, so our private rooms were big enough that we could each get away if needed. As it was, I had what was technically the master suite, and he had the guest room. Both had their own baths, but his was smaller, a point he always liked to bring up.

I also wanted to add an upstairs, if I could, over the garage, so we had a true and proper playroom. We shared women and liked to get our kink on, but there really wasn't a place to do that in the house. We had to sort of pull shit out of the storage area if we were feeling a particular type of way. It was a pain in the ass if we were mid-fuck and wanted to spice things up, so we always had to plan ahead. Having a room dedicated to it was definitely the way I wanted to go, and he seemed to be game. We just had to figure out who to hire and get it done.

"I'd tap that," he said.

I looked down the aisle to see a fucking stunning woman. She was in shorts, which was odd for November, and had a tank top on with a zip-up hoodie over the top. Her hair was long, nearly to her waist, even though it was up in a ponytail. It wasn't quite black, but was super dark brown, and had just enough curl at the end to show that it would have waves if it were shorter. Her ass was round, the way some women were, with enough cushion for the pushing, which was just how we liked them. I couldn't see her tits, but that didn't really matter.

She was on her toes, reaching up to a shelf that was just out of her grasp. She was trying to pull some flooring or tiles or some shit down, and damn if I didn't want to walk up behind her and press my cock against her ass. I wouldn't, obviously, but I'd be lying if I said I didn't think about it.

Billy started toward her, and I followed him. I wasn't sure what he had in mind, but he could get a girl to fuck him just about any time he wanted. It was like this magic thing he did that I didn't understand.

"Need some help?" he asked her.

"Yeah," she said, stepping back. "I need three boxes of that flooring right there, but I'm too short to pull them down. I didn't want to stand on the cart and didn't want to bug someone to get them. But since you're here, would you mind?"

She was talking a mile a minute, and honestly, it was kind of adorable. Billy had this sort of smile he gave women, and they would just fawn all over him. It kind of pissed me off sometimes, but he shared his wealth, so that made up for it.

He reached up and pulled one of the boxes down. I went behind him and pulled the other two, needing to show I was just as impressive as he was. It was a fucking dick-measuring contest, but I had absolutely no fucks to give.

"Thank you guys so much," she said. "I hate asking for help, and normally my brother comes and gets this kind of thing, but he's deep in the middle of putting in a surround shower and didn't want to stop mid-install. So I was the lucky one to make the trip."

"No problem," I said. "We're happy to help. Say, you said your brother was doing an install of a bathroom?"

"Yeah," she said, shoving a loose strand of that deep chestnut hair behind her ear. "It's our company. Both his and mine. Dad handed it down to us when he got sick, so we've been running the show since. It's been really great. God, I'm sorry. I'm just blabbering all over the place right now."

"No, it's fine," Billy said.

"We actually were just looking to do an addition onto my house," I said. "I wasn't sure how to go about finding someone, and here you are."

"Oh, wow," she said. "I don't know about a whole addition right now. We are kinda swamped, but I could definitely see if we could put in a bid."

"That'd be great," I said. "It's an older home, but I think we can add a second story to the garage area. Could be completely wrong, too, so we'd need someone to come take a look at it."

"Oh, sure," she said. "I suggest you get more than one bid, just because it's your money you're spending, but I'd be happy to have someone come take a look."

"Would you be willing to do the bidding?" Billy asked, and I saw a fleeting emotion run across her face.

"With your brother," I added. "You know, so you both would be able to tell us what to expect. I wouldn't want to put you in a position where you wouldn't feel safe."

"Definitely," she said, shoving her hand in her shorts pocket and pulling something out. "Here's my card. Send us an email and we can set up a time to come take a look. Like I said, we're kinda swamped right now, but we could give you a ballpark as to when we might be open to doing the work, if you chose to go with us."

"Thanks," I said, taking the card from her hand.

They were working hands, which I could appreciate. My dad worked his ass off, so I knew they meant she earned her money honestly, and I was all for that.

"Anything else you need help with?" Billy asked.

"I think that's it," she said. "Thanks again."

"Thanks for the card," I said, holding it up. "I'll get an email out to you soon."

"Have a nice day," she said, then began to push her cart down the aisle.

"Damn, can't wait to pound that ass," Billy said.

"She's gonna do work for us," I said, slapping his chest. "Until she's done that, we need to keep our hands and dicks to ourselves. You fuck up the remodel, I'm kicking you out."

"Says the man who wants to fuck her just as much as I do," he said.

"Yeah, well, we'll see when we get there," I replied.

Ms. Carington,
We met at the hardware store yesterday and you gave me your
card. I wanted to see what I could do about scheduling a time
for you and your brother to come out and look at the project I
want to do at my house. As I said, I want to add a second floor

*to my garage area, and I think it is doable. I'm completely free
until mid-February, so any time, day or night, will work for an
inspection.*
Spencer Adams

I PUT my phone number and address at the bottom of the email and
hoped she'd get back to me soon. Billy was right. I wanted to fuck her.
But more than that, she actually seemed like a cool person, and I
wanted to get to know her. Usually, we would find a bullpen bunny,
bring her home, fuck her, then send her on her way with a consolation
prize and no other contact. This girl, though… Well, I didn't want to
treat her that way for some reason.

"You send it?" Billy asked as he walked into the office.

"Just did," I replied.

"Good," he said. "Now, let's go find someone to fuck tonight."

"Go ahead," I said. "I'm not feeling it."

"You cool if I bring her back here?" he asked. "I'll let you know and
you can tap in if you're of a mind to."

"Sure," I said, but really wasn't thinking I wanted to.

I simply couldn't get Ariana Carington out of my mind.

CHAPTER TWO

Ariana...

"Hey, Ari," Demetri shouted. "Got an email that's addressed to you."

"Oh yeah?" I asked.

"Yeah," he said. "Some dude named Spencer."

"I have no idea who that is," I said, coming into the office area of the shop.

"Says you met him yesterday at the store," he said.

"Oh, yeah," I said. "Couple of guys helped me get the flooring down from the shelf and said they wanted to do some remodeling, so I gave them my card. Figured that more work is better."

"I mean, yeah, it is, but still," he said. "Says something about adding a floor, and we've never done that before."

"Dad has," I said. "He can tell us what to look for, and what we need to keep in mind."

"You know this will mean hiring out for an architect, right?"

"I know," I said. "But if we want this business to grow, we need to start expanding outside just bathroom remodels and dishwasher installations."

"You're gonna do the talking," he said. "And you're gonna take Brad with you. You cool with that?"

"As long as Brad knows he's there for the job and not me," I said. "He thinks that now that I've become single, he's next in line. He needs to know that I do not, at all, see him that way. Besides, these guys gave off some serious money vibes, so I don't want him to fuck it up."

"Who am I gonna fuck up?" Brad asked as he came into the office.

"No one," I said. "I think I'll take Dad. It will do him some good to get out. Besides, he's the one who's gonna know if it's something we can handle or not. Not to mention, he'll know who to get to help with the drawings and shit."

"You eat with that mouth?" Brad asked.

"Not you," I said, then turned and walked out.

Brad had been crushing on me since I started getting boobs. Nothing I did or said could convince him that he was basically an older brother to me and there would never be anything going on between us. I think on some level he knew, but he kept on pushing. It was really starting to piss me off. I'd told Demetri to keep him on a short leash, and if he was gonna work with us, then he had to keep his mouth shut about anything to do with me. I guess I was gonna have to talk to Dad about it and see if he could knock some fucking sense into his son. My words were having no impact on him.

"Hey, pumpkin," Dad said when he answered the phone.

"Hi, Daddy," I said. "We have this possible job and I'd like you to go with me to the first meeting."

"Why don't you have Demetri go with you?" he asked. "Or Brad?"

"Dee is doing something else," I said. "And you know how Brad gets when he thinks no one is paying attention. He isn't the right person for the job. Besides, it's more complicated than anything we've done since you sold us the business, and I really want this to go well."

"Do I need to talk to Brad?" he asked.

"Not yet," I said. "I shut him down for now, but if something happens that I need your help with, I'll let you know."

"Okay, pumpkin," he said. "When are we doing this meeting?"

"I wanted to make sure you could do it before I set it up," I said. "I'll send an email over to the guy now and set something up. He said he's basically open whenever, so if there's anything you have that I have to work around, let me know."

"I've got nothing but time, sweetheart," he said.

"Okay," I replied. "I'll let you know when it's set up. I'll pick you up on the way."

"Just let me know," he said.

"Will do," I replied, then disconnected the call.

"What did you mean when you said that you might have him talk to me?" Brad asked, and I jumped.

"What the fuck are you doing?" I asked him.

"What?" he asked. "I just want to know what you meant when you said that."

"Okay, first of all, don't sneak up on me," I said, hands on my hips. "And second, I told my dad that you have been creeping on me since forever and it needs to stop. Pretty sure Dee told you to stop it, and I've told you entirely too many times. If you don't knock it off, you may have to find another place to work."

"So, now I can't be nice to you?" he asked.

"That's not what I mean, and you know it," I barked. "I don't want to go out with you. Don't want to date you. Don't want to fuck you. You are like a brother to me. I don't want to do any of those things with Dee, so why would I want to do them with you?"

"But I'm not your brother," he argued.

"Doesn't matter that we're not related by blood," I said. "You have known me for forever, and you only started seeing me as more than a sister when I started to get tits. There's no fucking reason for you to try to deny it now. I am not, nor will I ever be, interested in any kind of relationship with you."

"Jesus, take a chill pill," he said. "I guess I won't talk to you anymore."

"That'd be fine with me," I said, then turned around and walked down the hallway and to my own desk.

I sat down at my desk and turned on the computer, waiting for it to boot up. Once it was working, I logged on and went to our email server to find the email from the guy from the store. He didn't seem like a Spencer to me, but what did I know? I hit the reply button and started typing out a response.

> *Mr. Adams,*
>
> *Thank you for sending the email to our office. We are pleased you chose to ask us for a bid on your construction project. I am looking at the next few days to see if we can find a time to meet and look at what you want done. I understand it is an addition above a garage. While this is a larger job than our small firm normally handles, I would be more than willing to see if it is something we can accomplish. I would suggest we set aside about half an hour to an hour to look at the space and get some idea of what you want. I would be available to come to your place on either Tuesday or Wednesday morning, say around 10:00 a.m. Would that be convenient for you? I will be bringing another member of our team with me, as he is more knowledgeable about this type of work and would be helping to ensure we do the project right the first time. I look forward to hearing from you soon.*
>
> *Ariana Carington*
> *Carington Construction*

I reread the email a dozen times, making tweaks along the way to be sure it sounded professional. No need to fuck the job up before it even starts. I had no idea what we would need to do, or how much we should even charge for this type of thing. I knew that my dad would know, and he'd be there, so I wouldn't mess anything up, underbid, or overbid. I was actually looking forward to being the manager on this project. I'd done a few before, but this would be the first big one I handled. If I could do it, then it would help to show Dee that I was truly a partner, and not just here because Daddy wanted us to share the company.

Sending the email, I took a big breath, held it for a minute, then let it out slowly. I'd done this breathing technique for years, ever since Mom got sick. It was my way of connecting to myself, finding my center, and being ready for whatever came next. Mom was really good at those sorts of things. When she started to fade, she let me sit with her and we would do the breathing thing together. It made me feel closer to her, since I was the only one she did it with. Dee was way too cool to do something so stupid, but I knew it was just his way of pretending Mom wasn't sick.

When Dad's health started to fade, and he asked if we wanted to run the company, Dee said he'd be in charge, since I was a girl and didn't know that much about it. Daddy reminded him that I was the one who worked with him first and knew almost as much as he did. If Dee wanted to be a part of the company, he would be partners with me, not my boss. He still, occasionally, tried to boss me around, but we had found a happy medium where we were both fine with the balance of power. I pretended to be subservient until he pushed too far, then I'd flex the muscle I had as half-owner, and he'd back down.

I pulled out my phone and sent a text to Dee, letting him know that Brad was on very thin ice, and that one more fuckup and I was gonna fire him myself. I knew they were best friends, but his behavior had gone on long enough. I was shutting it down now. One more lewd comment, one more backhanded compliment, one more anything, and he was out the door. I reminded him that Daddy knew about it all, and that he would back me on it. Dee was going to have to make Brad mind, or I was gonna terminate him.

My computer pinged, and I looked up to see a response to my email. It was quick, and I wondered what the guy's job was that he was able to email during the day like that.

Ms. Carington,
Tuesday at 10:00 a.m. will work fine. We want to add a second
story above the garage, but if that isn't feasible, then we can
look at other options while you're here.
Spencer Adams

He had his address below his name. I did a quick search of the area to see where he lived, and what we might be looking at as far as the project was concerned. Once the images came up, I let out a slow whistle. I was right about him having money, 'cause that neighborhood was definitely in the high price range. Thankfully, I didn't have to try to fit in with the crowd, just had to do a good job on the remodel to make some bank. I picked up my phone and called my dad.

"That was fast," Dad said.

"Yeah," I replied. "He was pretty quick with an answer. We're going out on Tuesday at ten. We'll have to leave around eight, though, to make sure we're not late. It's gonna be a bit of a drive."

"Where does he live?" Dad asked.

"Juanita," I said.

"Not bad," he replied. "Wait, where did you say you met this dude?"

"At the hardware store," I replied. "I was picking stuff up for a job in Highland Terrace, and this was probably the closest one to them."

"Oh, I see," he said. "You sure he's the actual owner?"

"Daddy," I said. "You're going with me, and we'll be fine. He looked like a nice guy, but if you want, I'll search his name and make sure he isn't wanted for being a serial killer or anything, okay?"

"I'd feel better if you did," he said. "I'd actually feel better if you brought your brother or Brad with you."

"I can do this," I said. "I need to do it. Besides, neither of them will be able to tell me if it's a job we can do. I need you for that."

"Just know that I'm not gonna be around forever," he said.

"Daddy, don't talk like that," I said. "If you die, I'm gonna resurrect you and kill you for it. I can't have you both gone. Not yet."

"I'm sorry, kiddo," he said. "I just want to make sure you guys are set, and you can't be set if you can't figure this kind of stuff out on your own."

"I will be able to," I said. "I just haven't had the experience yet. I'll get that on this job, so the next time this comes up, I'll know what to do."

"All right," he said. "But know that I believe in you."

"I know you do," I said. "And I love you for it."

"Did you talk to your brother about Brad?" he asked.

"I talked to Brad about Brad," I said. "Told him to back off and knock it off or he was gonna end up without a job. I told the same thing to Demetri, too. I think they finally heard me, so hopefully it'll stop. Otherwise, I'll bring you in and you can remind them that I own half the company, and if they don't shape up, you just might give me your ten percent to make me the majority owner."

"Don't put this on me," he said. "I know you're right, and they do, too, but I'm not gonna give one of you the bigger share just because the other one is being stupid."

"I know," I said. "But it might not hurt to threaten them. I mean, boys are dumb. It's why I throw rocks at them."

"Your mother always loved that phrase," he said.

"I know," I replied. "That's why I said it. She was right, too."

"That she was," he said. "Okay, I'll remind the boys that they need to shape up, but we can do that Tuesday after we do the bid."

"Okay," I said. "Thanks, Daddy."

"You're welcome, peanut," he said, then disconnected the call.

I knew I could count on him to make sure everything would work out. I just wish Demetri would get his head out of his ass and realize what a dick Brad was.

CHAPTER THREE

B illy...

"Tuesday morning," Spencer said.

"Okay," I replied. "She coming alone?"

"No," he said. "She's smart and bringing someone with her. Said it was another person who worked with them, so I don't know who it is. I'm betting it's a big, burly dude who makes her feel safe."

"Or it's her boyfriend," I said. "And he's gonna come and try to intimidate us."

"That is a possibility," he said. "Either way, we gotta make sure we're ready and know what all we want."

"You gonna have them build furniture, too?" I asked.

"No," he said. "We just need to know what we're gonna need up there. I'm thinking we should have it broken down into two rooms, with a bathroom in each room."

"With a big fucking shower and a giant tub," I replied.

"In one of the rooms, sure," he said.

"We could put the shower in one and the tub in the other," I said.

"That might work," he said. "First thing we gotta figure out is if we can even do it."

"Do what?" I asked.

"The addition," he said. "Adding a second story is kinda a big deal, so we may not even be able to do it."

"What if we can't?" I asked.

"Then we figure out what we can do," I said. "Might have to look for another house. Who knows? We'll just have to wait and see."

"I fucking hate waiting," I said. "I need some pussy."

"Good God," he said. "Is that all you can think about?"

"It's the off season," I said. "It's the best time to fuck around. Once we return to training, it's gonna cut into our social life something fierce."

"Go ahead," he said. "I'm gonna see if I can figure out exactly what I want and see if there is anything I need to get cleaned up before they get here."

"Dude, that's like cleaning before the cleaning lady comes," I said.

"Yeah," he said. "I don't like to live like a pig, so I try to make sure the cleaning lady actually cleans things that I can't do. Which reminds me, would you pick up your shit?"

"Fine," I said and grabbed a mug that was sitting next to the couch.

It was a love-hate relationship we had. I fucking loved sharing women with him, but he could sometimes get a bug up his ass about the weirdest shit. I guess it didn't matter, though. We were good together, both on and off the field. I loved the infield, he loved the outfield, and both of us loved to fuck women.

CHAPTER FOUR

Spencer...

I don't know why it bothered him so much, but it was like dealing with a teenager sometimes. Granted, I was a good six or more years older than him, and was pushing thirty, while he was still in his early twenties. Still, we worked well together with most things. He'd been better about not leaving his shit all over the place, but sometimes I had to nag him, which just pissed me off. I wasn't his parent, and I shouldn't have to remind him to clean up after himself.

Now, he was off to wherever to find someone for himself. He sometimes liked to go solo, which I understood. I sometimes liked to be one-on-one with someone as well, but definitely enjoyed the play with him too. Now, though, all I could think about was little Ms. Carington and that fine ass, that long, long hair, and those lips that just needed to be wrapped around my cock. I'd be lying if I didn't admit to wanting her, but I knew that you didn't shit where you ate. And right now, I had more important things I wanted her to do.

Instead of wallowing in self-pity, I decided to get some stuff done around the house, so I didn't have much to do once Tuesday rolled around. I started in the kitchen, emptying the dishwasher before loading it again. Then, I made sure that all the pots and pans were clean and put away. Next, I tackled the fridge, which desperately needed to be cleaned. It was a lot of little things that just added up to one big mess, and finally, by the time Billy was rolling in with a broad on his arm, I had finished the kitchen, as well as taken the trash and recycling out.

"Hey," he said as he walked through the door.

"Hey, yourself," I said.

"Hi," the blonde on his arm said. "Are you his roommate?"

"I own the house," I said. "So, he's my tenant, technically. But yeah, we're roommates for all intents and purposes."

"He said you guys liked to double team girls," she said, and the smile that was on her face told me she was definitely in the mood.

"Sometimes," I replied. "But I'm beat tonight. You two enjoy yourselves, though."

Her pout told me he'd talked us up as a team all the time, and she was looking forward to enjoying both our company. He sort of glared at me over her head, silently telling me to get on board and take one for the team. I just didn't have it in me.

"See you tomorrow," I said to him, not her, and then walked past them and down to my room.

"I thought you said he would be fine to do it," she whined, and that just sealed the deal on not wanting to partake in that particular flavor of strange.

Instead, I shut my door, turned the lock, and headed in to take a shower. Knowing I'd likely hear her, because she seemed like the type that would be loud, I wanted to get to sleep before they began. It probably wasn't gonna happen, but I could hope.

As I turned the water on in the shower, I could hear her already moaning, which said she was fake as fuck and worth staying away from. Billy was that way, though. He'd damn near fuck anyone if they offered. I was surprised he didn't have any random kids out there or didn't have any sort of disease with the number of times he'd go raw.

That was not my thing. No, I always suited up, wrapping my cock every time I dipped it into someone. I wouldn't mind going without, but I hadn't met anyone who made me want to take that chance.

My clothes were on the floor, and I was under the spray, getting my hair wet to wash it. It was starting to get long, and I was definitely gonna need a cut before the week was out. Maybe I should plan that for Monday, so I'd look my best for our guest who would be here on Tuesday morning. The thought of her, stretching up to pull those boxes from the shelf made me hard, and I couldn't help but palm my cock, wondering whether she would prefer it in her mouth or her pussy. Either option made me want to find out sooner rather than later, but I knew I needed to keep myself in check. If I wanted to have her, I had to play it slow, keep my cool, and not jump in before the timing was right.

Of course, that's about the time I heard the bimbo Billy brought in start her wailing. It was as if he was skinning a cat or something, the high-pitched whine she was emitting. I wondered if I would soon hear the cats in the neighborhood join her in their own chorus of howls. With the way things were with him, he'd probably fuck it up right from the get-go. Maybe I needed to make sure he was out of the house on Tuesday. How I'd get that to happen, I had no idea.

The more the woman wailed, the softer I got, which only pissed me off more. I tried to drown it out by shoving my head under the running water, but it did nothing for me. Instead, I just showered and got out, drying myself in the towel from the rack. Looking around the bathroom, I saw that it could use an update as well. Maybe I'd just keep finding projects to keep her around. It was as good an excuse as any, honestly, and one I'd use.

I scooped up my clothes and took them with me into my bedroom, dropping them one by one into my hamper. I pulled my wallet and keys out of my jeans and made sure I didn't have anything else in any of the pockets before they were in the spot for wash day, which was coming soon. I'd hired a housekeeper, but she mostly did the deep cleaning chores, the ones I didn't want to do. Sure, she came around during the season and did more, but in the off season, she was mostly just there to make sure we didn't end up with the deep grime on anything.

When I bought the house, Jonathan Bridge, one of the players who used to be on the team, suggested I get someone to come in and do the heavy lifting. It was a great idea, and he even recommended someone who was now a regular in our house once a week during the season, and every other week, late October through mid-February. I always let her know when we were heading down to spring training, and she'd come in the day after we left to do a deep dive into every single room in the house.

She was good at keeping our secrets, too. She knew the one closet she wasn't to go into and had never indicated that she had seen what was in there. It was more a storage room than anything and had a door that we locked. I'd told her it was where we kept the things we hadn't figured out where they went, and she never questioned it. The fact that it was in the garage helped, as she didn't really do anything in there, anyway.

Thinking of her, I had to figure out how we were gonna deal with the room I was hoping to add. Did I just tell her it was a private space we added that we didn't want anyone to go into, or would it be better to let her know exactly what the space was? I would likely need her to clean the bathrooms we planned to put in there, so I guess it was going to be a kind of awkward conversation to have with her once we got there.

The woman had quieted some and was doing more moaning and less wailing. Either Billy had shoved something into her mouth, and knowing him, it was likely, or she was worn out. Either way, I was thankful she'd quieted down. I pulled some shorts out of my dresser and pulled them on, then headed from my room out to the kitchen.

I came around the corner and had to stop in my tracks. The fucker had her up on the counter, naked, legs open with a spreader bar, and hooked to the rack for our pans.

"What the actual fuck?" I asked.

Billy, who was on the other side of her, cock in her mouth, stopped and looked at me.

"I didn't think you were joining us," he said, not bothering to stop his motion.

I looked back at the woman. She had something in her pussy, but I wasn't exactly sure what it was. As I got closer, I realized that he'd shoved an eggplant into her, covered, thankfully for her, with a condom. It had something shoved through the end of it to keep it from getting lodged in her, so at least he thought ahead. She hadn't moved, really, from when I'd first walked in, and I wondered how he had her bound at the other end.

He liked to control women, while I preferred to let them choose what, and how much, control we had over them. Every time we started, he wanted to go straight to straps and restraints, but I wanted to give them time to warm up to us, tell us what they wanted, and let us have a dialogue of where things would go. I'd almost always have to rein him in, which was a bit annoying, to be honest.

"Check this out," he said, shifting slightly.

I walked around the island the woman was trussed up on and saw that he'd hooked her hands into straps he was standing on, so she was bent pretty far over the edge of the counter. It looked uncomfortable. I looked at her face, but she wasn't showing any signs of distress, so I had to trust they'd had a conversation about this prior to him bringing her home.

"I got tits right here," he said, squeezing her breasts. "She's in the perfect position for me to fuck her mouth. And she's got something shoved in her that's bigger than me, so she's getting enjoyment out of it all."

He'd started moving his hips again, and she did seem to be enjoying the attention, but it wasn't doing anything for me.

"Just make sure you clean this shit up when you're done," I said, walking past him to the fridge to pull out a bottle of beer. "I don't want ass prints on the counter, or your cum all over the floor. Also, toss that eggplant once you pull it out of her. I'm not eating it."

"She's gonna eat it," he said, his grin wide and feral. "It's something she said she wanted to try, and I'm more than willing to give her what she wants. Ain't that right?"

She didn't really move, and couldn't really respond, as he had her completely controlled. She did sort of nod her head some, her mouth smiling around his cock, and the emotion reached her eyes. I had to take his word for her agreeing to all this beforehand, but still, not something I wanted to be a part of. At least not tonight.

"Still," I said as I walked past them. "Clean your shit up, pots and pans included. I don't want to know which ones you used. You need to make sure you send them through the dishwasher a couple of times. Got it?"

"Yes, *Dad*," he said, something he'd started doing off and on whenever I told him to do something.

"Fucking moron," I muttered as I headed down the hall to my room.

Maybe I needed to move him out. Let him get his own place where he could fuck and eat whatever he used all the time and live in his own mess for a while. I wouldn't do it, but I thought about it at that moment, knowing he could afford it. Still, at least the woman was quiet, and I didn't have to hear the sounds coming from her anymore.

I walked into my bedroom, shut and locked the door, then turned on the television to find something to watch that would take my mind off what I'd just seen in my kitchen. It'd be a lie to think I wasn't going to thoroughly clean that island off, as well as wash every single pot, pan, and dish in the kitchen, twice.

CHAPTER FIVE

Ariana...

The weekend went by in a rush, and before I realized what had happened, Tuesday morning had dawned. I stretched when my alarm went off, knowing I had to get up and be ready to do a bid on that dude's house. I hopped into the shower, washing my hair, and then braiding it once I was out. It was gonna still be wet when I got home, but having it braided was better than having it free flowing. Nothing like getting shit into it that you simply couldn't get out.

Mom had wanted me to have long hair, but I fought it for a long time. Then, I realized that having it was something that gave me pride. That in-between stage, where I was trying to get the bangs I insisted I needed in seventh grade to be long enough to tuck behind my ears, was a nightmare. But it had all been worth it in the end.

Now, I took very good care of my hair, and putting it in a braid was the easiest option on a day like today. Some days were buns, some were ponytails, but today felt like a braid day. Once I was dried off, and my braid was tightly in place, I headed to my bedroom to get dressed. Pulling out everything I needed, I threw it on the bed and went to start the coffee. I needed that almost as much as I needed a shower, both working together to get me to that awake state I needed to function.

Back in my room, I pulled on a pair of panties, then my socks, before pulling on a pair of dark jeans. They were snug but fit well. I'd been in shorts the day I'd met the guy, and I really wanted to ensure we got the bid, so I wanted to dress better than that. Once my jeans were in place, I pulled my bra on, then a tank top over that before pulling one of our logo shirts over my head.

Dad had thought the shirts were a bit over the top, but once he saw them and realized it was a branding decision, he insisted that everyone wore them while they were working in someone's home. Whether it was an install or a complete overhaul, we needed to be sure we presented ourselves as the company.

I was wearing a polo, which had a more business feel to it than the tee shirts or jackets, but I had one of those, too, and planned to wear it to the meeting. It was still November, so it was bound to be cold. Hopefully, it wouldn't snow until we got the concrete poured at the Henderson place. That was a simple patio, but it required a tear-out, along with all the prep work to get it ready for the pour. We were set to do that on Thursday unless the weather changed.

Today, though, was all about meeting a new client, getting the information for the addition he wanted, and making sure we could actually get it done. I slid into my steel-toed boots, pulling the laces tight and tying them off, before pulling the legs of my jeans over the top of them, then headed to the kitchen to get my travel mug ready to go with my coffee mixed up just right.

I'd told Daddy that I'd be picking him up around eight. It was already pushing close to that, so I had to get this ready and out the door before I was late. The fact that I was going to have to drive up 405 through Bellevue wasn't lost on me, and I hated doing that in the trucks from the company. Thankfully, my little Camry had the logo on the door, so we were gonna take that. Save gas, and not have to try to do anything with a big-ass truck. It was a win-win.

I locked my door, climbed into my car, and shot a text off to Dad to let him know I was on the way. Then I plugged the address for the house into my GPS and got it ready to roll once I picked him up.

Backing out of my driveway, I headed toward the main road to head on over to get my dad.

"That was quick," Dad said when he climbed into the car. "Not that you'd speed or anything, but I expected it to take at least another ten minutes to get here."

"Dad," I said, rolling my eyes. "It's a five-minute drive to get to your house on a bad day."

"You know I'm yanking your chain, right?" he asked.

"And I'm giving it back to you," I said, a smile on my face.

"All right," he said as he shut the door. "Let's get this party started."

I pressed the button on my phone and my GPS started giving me directions to the house. I got us onto the freeway, then crawled along in rush-hour traffic with all the other nuts who had to drive into their offices, or wherever they were going, before pulling off and onto 405, only to crawl along there as well. Finally, after entirely too long, we got to the exit my phone indicated, and we pulled off.

By the time we got away from the freeway, traffic was minimal, and we were able to actually drive the speed limit, getting to the area with a good twenty minutes to spare. As I drove along the side streets, my dad looked out the window. He gave a slow whistle.

"This is some money," he said.

"Yeah," I replied. "The guy looked like he had money. At least the one I talked to did."

"There was more than one?" he asked.

"Yeah," I said. "There were two of them. The one that talked to me was older than the other one, and I have no idea what their situation is. Maybe they're brothers or something. Could also be roommates, but I have no idea."

"Seems weird a couple of guys living together," he said.

"Maybe they're a couple," I replied.

"Pfft."

"What?" I asked. "They could be."

"Maybe," he said. "Still seems weird."

"Dad," I said, slowing down and pulling over to the side of the road. "If they are a couple, I need you to be cool with that. Every-

27

one's money is green, and if they are willing to pay, then it doesn't matter."

"I just don't understand all that," he said.

"Dad," I said, and waited until he looked over at me. "I need you to be okay with the fact that these guys might be gay and a couple. If you're not, then you can stay in the car while I speak to them."

"I don't care about any of that," he said, but I wasn't so sure. "Trust me, I don't have any issue with what someone does in their own bedroom. I just don't wanna hear about it or see it."

"Fine," I said. "But you better be on your best behavior. If you mess this up, I'm not gonna be happy. Hell, these guys might be super wealthy, and if we do a good job, it could mean getting more jobs from people they associate with. It could mean the business could grow. Isn't that what you want?"

He inhaled, then blew out a breath before saying, "Yeah, I guess."

"Good," I said. "I just want to make sure you're gonna behave."

"I promise, pumpkin," he said.

I waited a minute, just to make sure he wasn't gonna add something to his statement. When he looked at me confused, I put the car in gear and continued to the house.

We pulled up in front of a single-story rambler in the midst of several homes that were both single-story and two-story, all of which were well outside my price range, even if the company was mine alone. Dad gave that low whistle again and nodded his head. I could see the wheels turning as he looked it over, and judging by what I saw, he thought this might work.

I shut the car off, and unbuckled my seatbelt, opening the door and stepping out with my keys in hand. I opened the back door and pulled out my portfolio, which had my notebook, some pens, and business cards. It was basically my walking office when I had to bid on jobs like this.

"You ready?" I asked as my dad got out of the car.

"Ready as you are," he said, and walked around the front of the car to join me as I walked toward the front door.

As we stepped onto the porch, the door opened, and the man who had done most of the talking stood there, looking entirely too enticing for my mind to handle. I sort of just stood there waiting for him to say something.

"I'm Spencer Adams," he said, reaching out to shake my dad's hand. "You must be the one who knows all the things."

"I don't know about *all* the things," Dad said. "But I do know construction."

"Then you're the one we need to have in this first meeting," he replied with a smile. "Ms. Carington," he said to me, sticking his hand out. "It's a pleasure to see you again."

"Likewise," I managed, finding my voice. "I understand you're looking to add a second level above the garage, right?"

"To start with," he said. "But I've found that there are some other things I wouldn't mind having upgraded as well. Depending on costs and your availability, of course."

My dad was standing close enough to be able to reach out and slap my side with his hand without it being obvious, and I nearly jumped out of my skin.

"I'm happy to look at all your projects," I said. "Lead the way."

He stepped back and allowed us into his home, which was actually nicely furnished. Not that I thought it wouldn't be, but I wasn't actually sure what to expect. The living room, which is where we stepped into, had a leather sectional separating it from the kitchen and dining areas. There was a large fireplace with an insert that I was pretty sure was gas, and above that was a large screen television. The dining room had a nice table with chairs around it, and the kitchen had an island in the middle, with plenty of counter space to cook many dishes at once. It was something I wished I had in my house, but that wasn't something I needed to worry about at the moment.

"The garage is this way," he said, walking through the kitchen toward the side of the house the garage was on.

We'd seen it from the driveway, so knew it was that direction. Dad hadn't made any comments about anything, which was good, but also worried me. I wasn't sure what he was thinking, and sometimes the not knowing was worse than something that might fall out of his mouth. He'd never come across as anything other than respectable, but the comments he made in the car were niggling at the back of my brain.

"I want to add a couple of bedrooms," Spencer said. "Each with their own bathroom. Maybe even a kitchen, but that's not an absolute."

"So, like a mother-in-law suite type of thing," I said.

"I guess you could call it that," he said, looking at me.

"You got a mother-in-law?" my dad asked, and I wanted to slap him.

"No," he said. "Just a roommate, and he's not here right now. He's sort of staying here until we can find a good place for him. It's just worked out that we can share the space."

"Oh," Dad said. "You work together?"

"Dad," I whispered, hoping he'd shut the fuck up about whatever he was going on about.

"It's quite all right," Spencer said. "And yes, we do work together."

"I see," Dad said, and I could tell it was in relief.

"So," I said, trying to get the conversation back to the possible job. "You want a second floor. Do you just want it above the garage or are you wanting it to go over part of the house?"

"I hadn't thought about it," he said, looking at me. "I guess it will depend on how things figure out. I'm not an expert, so I'm going to defer to you on those kinds of things."

"It's really gonna depend on how much room you want," I said, looking at the space. "You said two bedrooms, each with their own bathroom. Do you want a living room type space? I know you were thinking maybe a kitchen, too, but weren't sure."

"I wouldn't at all be opposed to making it a fully functioning second space," he said. "I just want to be able to have company stay over, and not feel like we're all cramped in the house. I have quite a few teammates, and we do sometimes get together. When we do, sometimes we end up needing to have a safe space for everyone to crash. Having a couple of extra rooms would be convenient."

"Nothing like having a bunch of folks sleeping on the living room floor to show you that you need more space," I said.

"Exactly," he replied, and his smile was dazzling.

He'd had this brooding sort of look on his face, but the moment I suggested something he liked, he lit up like a Christmas tree, and it changed his whole image.

"Let's take a look at the structure," Dad said, walking over to the wall opposite where we were standing. "Looks like it's good construction. Fully able to add a second floor if it's all like this. What's in this room?"

Spencer stiffened, and I saw a bit of hesitation on his face. It wasn't like he was afraid of being found out, but more like he would be embarrassed about what was in the room.

"We'll have time to assess that once we get closer to actually doing construction," I said, and the relief I saw on his face made me wonder what was in the room, too.

"The whole garage has the same walls," he said. "This room was here when I moved in, and it's basically just a storage closet."

"Ah," Dad said, leaving it be.

I didn't know if Dad really wanted to see into the room, or if he was oblivious to the conflict that was running through Spencer. Either way, he was done with asking those questions, it seemed.

"So," he said. "What other projects were you looking at?"

"Dad," I said. This time my admonishment was louder.

"Oh, no," Spencer said. "It's totally fine. I'm thinking of redoing the kitchen, as well as the bathroom in the master suite. There's nothing wrong with them, just thinking an update might be nice to have."

"The kitchen is fantastic," I said. "But if it's something you want me to look at, I'm happy to do that."

"That would be great," he said, then looked over at my dad. "Did you want to come and look at it, too?"

"Nah," Dad said. "She knows what she's doing. I'm gonna sit in the car. You two figure things out."

I looked at my dad, completely confused. He looked at me with some sort of look, and I wasn't sure what it meant. He reached out, and I handed him my keys, then he went out the front door, shutting it behind him.

"He's a lot of help in keeping you safe if he's sitting in the car," Spencer said.

"Yeah," I replied, still looking at the closed door. "Anyway," I continued, turning back to the man. "Let's go look at what else you want done."

CHAPTER SIX

Spencer...

I damn near shit myself when the man asked to look in the closet in the garage. That wasn't gonna happen, at all, and if I knew he would want to see that, I'd have moved everything to my own closet. It would have been a tight fit, but worst-case scenario, I'd shove some of it into Billy's room.

"The kitchen is more of a want than a need, but my bathroom is pushing a need," I said. "Which do you want to look at first?"

"Let's start here," she said, pointing to the kitchen. "From what I can see, it's pretty well laid out. Was there something specific you wanted to change?"

The island, I thought.

"Just thinking an update might be nice," is what I said, though. "Maybe update the counter tops. A new island fixture. Not really sure."

"Do you mind if I take some pictures?" she asked. "It'll be something I can reference to come up with some ideas for you."

"Sure," I said.

She pulled out her phone, aimed it at the kitchen as a whole, and took a shot. Then she walked around and took closer shots of each of the areas. She knew what she was doing, for sure, and she was thorough. She pulled on the countertops, then made some notes in her notebook that she'd been writing in the whole time we'd been talking.

I watched her move, the way she was simply gliding along the floor, feeling the backsplash on the wall, the countertops, the doors of the cabinets without opening them. Each movement was clean and concise, no extra steps or unnecessary movements. It was like watching a dancer, and all I wanted to do was see her do it all day, every day.

"Okay," she said, and I startled, but held myself without much reaction. "I think I have what I need for the kitchen to give you a good estimate. I'll give you several different options for everything, from basic to over the top, and everything in between."

"Sounds good," I said.

"Want to show me the bathroom?" she asked.

"Yeah," I said. "This way."

I walked down the hall, and it felt weird to be walking to my bedroom with a beautiful woman, knowing that I wouldn't be seeing her naked, or even close to it. Opening my bedroom door, I was glad I'd cleaned up in there, making the bed and putting away all my clothes.

"It's in here," I said, walking across the room to the bathroom door.

When I opened it, she let out a little gasp. I turned to her, and she was staring, mouth open. I looked in the room to see what she was looking at and couldn't figure out what was so shocking to her. She moved past me, as if in a trance, and stepped over the threshold to the shower surround. Running her hands along the tile, she was reverent in her touch, as if she were looking at something that was so important, she didn't want to disturb it for fear of it breaking.

"When was this house built?" she asked, turning her dark eyes to me.

"No clue," I said. "Is this something I should be worried about?"

"On the contrary," she said. "You should be happy that this Calcatta marble is still intact. Replacing it would cost a fortune."

"Really?" I asked, and she turned her face to me.

"This is the first time I've ever seen it in person," she said. "I'm kinda sad Dad's in the car, 'cause he would go nuts over this."

"I didn't realize it was that impressive," I said, looking at the white tile with golden marbling through it. "It came with the house, and it seemed fine when I moved in. I never really thought about it."

"I wouldn't want to remove this," she said. "I would feel like I was raping the room. Taking its perfection from it."

"Then, I guess, we don't change that," I said with a sort of laugh.

"No," she said. "I won't touch that area at all."

"What about the rest of the room?" I asked, and she finally turned to look around her.

The bathroom was bigger than most, with the shower being the biggest feature. I had the other normal things a bathroom had—a double sink, and the toilet was in its own room. Everything else was a boring white, which seemed off now that she mentioned the tile of the shower. I kind of wanted to tell her to match the tile from the shower and redo the bathroom with that in mind.

"We can definitely make some improvements," she said. "It's structurally sound and knowing I don't have to modify the shower will save a lot of both time and money for you."

"Money isn't a problem," I said.

"Still," she said. "If I can keep from spending your money, I will. I'm frugal, but not cheap, so you'll get quality work, but at a fair price."

"I appreciate your honesty," I said.

"Pictures okay?" she asked.

"Sure," I said, then stepped out of the room to let her get whatever shots she wanted.

I sat on my bed, thinking of the house in its entirety, wondering whether I could find enough to keep her here forever. I mean, obviously it would be better to keep her here with me under better circumstances, but maybe we started with just the remodeling.

"Done," she said as she stepped from the bathroom.

"Great," I said, standing up.

"Anything else on your list?" she asked.

"Nothing I can think of at the moment," I said. "Let me know what you can do, give me some prices, and we'll work it out."

"You need to get at least one more bid," she said. "I don't feel right being the only contractor you check with."

"I trust you," I said. "I don't want to work with anyone else."

"Why does it feel like you're hitting on me?" she asked, and I could see the concern in her eyes.

"Your competent," I complimented. "You seem to know what you're doing. You brought in an expert, even if it was a smoke screen to keep yourself safe in a stranger's house. From what you've asked, and the notes and pictures you've taken, I feel confident in your ability to get this job done and done well. I don't want to work with anyone else."

She blinked at me, like she wasn't used to hearing good things about herself, and that made me a bit sad. I wondered whether she always put on a front, acted tough, just to keep up with the rest of the guys in her field. It couldn't be easy to work in such a male-dominated field as a woman, but she knew what she was doing. And everything I'd said was the truth. I trusted her to do the job right, and not to screw me over.

We stood there, staring at each other. I wasn't sure whether she actually heard what I had said, or if she was so surprised that I said it, that it was taking time to register. Finally, after quite a while, a slow smile crossed her face.

"I'm going to bring my brother with me when I bring over the plans," she said. "I'm going to need you to tell him everything you just told me. He needs to know that I can, and will, run this business, or take my half and walk away and make my own. My dad should hear it, too."

"Absolutely," I said, feeling good about her response. "I assume your dad is the one sitting in the car right now."

"He is," she said, her smile brightening. "I'd ask you to go tell him now, but I think he'd think I put you up to it."

"When you bring over whatever it is, bring them both along," I suggested. "Tell them that you're not positive I'll take the information you give me as good enough without having them here. Are you all owners of the company?"

"It was my dad's first," she said. "He gave half to each of us but kept just enough that neither of us own more than the other. I've told my dad how Dee treats me, and how the rest of the guys see me as more of a glorified grunt than an actual partner, so it would be nice to have them knocked down a peg."

"Then don't tell them I want them there for any reason other than I want to ensure I'm talking with the owners," I said. "When you start to present, if either of them interrupt, or if they try to do all the talking, I'll shut that shit down. Sorry," I said, realizing I was swearing.

"Fuck that noise," she said. "You can swear as much as you want. Believe me, working in construction taught me all the best phrases."

"Good to know," I said. "Anyway, you can say whatever you want to get them here, just do it. Let them take the lead, or you can do it to see if they interrupt. Then I can bitch-slap them because it's you I want to work with."

Again, she gave me a slow blink, but her smile was quicker to come this time. It was like she was seeing someone she could use to get what she wanted in life, at least her business life. I was happy to let her use me in any way she wanted, especially if it meant I could be around her. This seemed like a win-win situation for us, and I was happy to be part of it.

CHAPTER SEVEN

A riana...

"Took you long enough," Dad said as I climbed into the car.

"What's that supposed to mean?" I asked.

"Just wondering what you were busy doing in there," he said. "Doesn't take that long to look at a couple of rooms."

"Dad," I said. "I wanted to get pictures of the rooms he wants to remodel. You taught me to make sure to get more than what I need, because more is better. That's what I did. He's looking at remodeling the kitchen and a bathroom right now. That's on top of the addition."

"He gonna do the little ones first?" he asked.

"I don't know," I said. "I'm going to make some recommendations for the two smaller rooms, and I'm gonna need you to put me in contact with someone who we can work with on the addition. I don't want you doing it. Just give me a name and a number."

"I don't know that they're gonna want to work with you," he said. "Maybe your brother should handle this."

I opened the door to my car and went back up the steps to the front door and knocked.

"That was fast," he said as he opened the door.

"Come with me," I said, reaching out and grabbing his hand. I walked him to the car, opened my door, and said, "Tell my dad what you said to me before."

"Before?" he asked.

"Yeah," I said. "When I suggested you get a second bid on the project."

"I told you I didn't want a second bid," he said. "I want to work with you. You're the reason I'm even looking at doing any of this. You are competent, well spoken, took notes and pictures, and I anticipate that you'll come back with a reasonable plan with options that I can decide on. My guess is you will have everything from the bare bones to as lavish as anyone could imagine. That's what I expect, and that's why I want to work with you."

"She suck that good?" Dad asked, and I froze, my face blooming red.

"Sir," Spencer said. "If you weren't her father, I would slap the taste right out of your mouth. The fact that you are her father just makes me disgusted with you. It was a rude thing to say about any woman, but the fact that you thought your daughter would prostitute herself out for a job is just awful. In fact, I'm not sure I want you involved in this project at all."

"Whoa," Dad said, obviously realizing that this wasn't his best moment. "I was just surprised you said all that shit without some sort of incentive."

"The incentive is I want the job done," he said. "I want it done and done right. I think your daughter can do that, which is why I am hiring her. I'm not hiring the company, it's her that I'm hiring. One would think that by the time someone got to be your age, they would have been taught better manners, but I guess there are still some folks who can't get out of their own way."

My dad was flustering in the car, and I almost laughed out loud. No one, and I mean absolutely no one, has put my dad in his place like that before. For that reason, I knew I was going to do this job to the best of my ability, and I was gonna do it on my own, without help from either of the other men in the business. For all I cared, they could go fuck themselves.

"Thank you," I said once I had my mouth under control. "I'll email you to set up a meeting when I have something to show you."

"Take my number," he said.

"Sure," I replied, grabbing my notebook and pen.

He rattled the number off to me, and I thanked him again, promising to be in touch. I climbed into the car, shut the door, and started it up. He'd stepped back and away from the car but was still outside and watched as we drove away.

"You know he just wants to fuck you, right?" Dad said when we were on the way out of the neighborhood.

"If that's all you think about me, then you can get out and walk home," I said, not looking at him. "But tell me now, so I can pull over before I shove you out of the car."

"It's so obvious," he said, and I pulled the car over and put it in park.

"Dad," I said, turning to look at him. "You have two choices right now. You can either shut up and let me drive you home, or you can keep going on this misogynistic bullshit, and can get out and walk or call Dee for a ride. I am an adult who knows how to take care of myself. I also know how people are, and yeah, he probably does have some designs on maybe getting into my pants. But, as an adult, that would be a decision I would make. Also, it's not something I would do while working for him. That's crossing a line, and I won't do that. You might. Dee might. Brad definitely would. But not me. Now, what's it gonna be?"

"I'm sorry you took offense," he started, but I cut him off.

"You are not apologizing, you're excusing yourself," I said. "An apology is admitting you've done something wrong, then changing your actions. Can you do that? Can you realize that everything you've said since I walked out of his house has been horrible? Or do you want to pretend that you're the man and know better than some little girl?"

"What has gotten into you?" he asked.

"Dad," I said, and looked at him. "Answer the question. Do you want to get out now, or shut the fuck up?"

"I'll shut up," he said, but I knew he didn't want to. No, the only reason he said it was because there was no way Dee was gonna come bail him out, and he didn't want to figure out another way home.

"That's what I thought," I said. "While you're shutting up, you should think about what you've said. Honestly think about it. If someone else said what you did about me, how would you react? Because if you wouldn't punch a motherfucker in the mouth for it, then I don't know whether I want to be around you at all anymore."

I put the car in gear and pulled back out onto the road. The entire trip back to his house was silent. He was fuming, but I was feeling so fucking proud of myself. I'd never stood up to my dad like that, but I never felt the need to. He'd gone too far, though, and he needed to remember that I was the one in charge. If he couldn't see that, then we were not going to have a very good relationship moving forward.

By the time I pulled into the lot at the office, I'd settled some but was still mad. I walked in and Dee stomped out of his office.

"What the fuck did you do?" he asked.

"What are you talking about?" I asked.

"Did you fuck that guy for a job?"

"How dare you," I said, my hands on my hips. "I have never, nor would I ever, do anything of the kind. If you got the call from Dad saying that, then you need to hear what actually happened. If you're just gonna believe Dad over me, then I'm done and you can buy me out."

"Wait, what?" he asked.

"You want to know what happened?" I asked.

"Fuck," he said, running a hand over his face.

"Yeah," I said. "Dad decided to walk out of the house after we looked at the garage. Spencer said he wanted me to look at a couple of other things he was thinking of doing, so I stayed and looked. He's looking at a kitchen and a bathroom remodel. Dad thought I took too long looking at two little jobs and assumed I'd fucked him or sucked him off to get him to agree to use us."

"Did you?"

"I swear on Mom's grave, I will slap the shit out of you if you ever accuse me of that," I said.

"Okay," he replied, holding his hands out in front of him in surrender.

"I looked at the jobs," I said. "Took a shit ton of pictures and notes. That's what took time. Does he want me? Who the fuck knows. I don't even care. I'm doing the job. Just me. Not you, and not Daddy."

"What do you mean?" he asked.

"I mean," I began, and Brad came in from the yard with a couple of the other guys, so I stopped.

"Someone die?" Brad asked.

"Fuck you," I said, and went to my office. "I do not have the fucking time for any of this."

I slammed my door and sat down at my computer, booting it up. I had work to do and didn't need a bunch of stupid boys to try to figure out whether I'd fucked a guy to get a job. Would I? Maybe. I mean he was hot, in that rugged kind of way. But I didn't know him, other than the short interaction we'd had. A whole lot can hide in someone if you didn't get to know them well.

Once my computer was up, I logged on and started searching through our records for who we'd used for architectural stuff before. While we hadn't done a ton of jobs since we took over from Dad, there were a couple. We still had Dad's list of contacts, so I was sure I could find someone.

After about fifteen minutes, Dee knocked on my door.

"What's up?" I asked.

"Can we talk?"

The way he asked made me wonder if there was something wrong. I wasn't sure what he wanted to talk about, but we did need to finish our conversation from earlier.

"Sure," I said, and he stepped in and sat down.

I had the smaller office, but that's because we put his name first on the door. The company was originally called Carington and Sons, but Dad took the "sons" part off when I was born. Demetri was the older one, but when Mom had me, she reminded Dad that he had two kids, and we weren't both boys, so he needed to treat us equally. There were days when I missed her ability to play mediator with us all. Not that she ever took sides, more that she made us all sit down and listen to each other if shit was going sideways.

"I'm sorry about earlier," he said.

"Okay," I replied. I was still salty about it, so I didn't just want to give in.

"I shouldn't have said what I did," he continued. "It was wrong of me to assume that you'd debase yourself like that for a job. I know you're good at what you do, and if I'd been there and Dad had said that, I'd have been pissed, too."

"Good," I said.

"You really want to run this one, don't you?" he asked.

"Yeah," I said. "I know I can do it, and I want to prove it to Dad. He won't trust me if he doesn't see that I can actually do the work."

"It took him a while with me, too," he said.

"Yeah," I agreed. "But he gave you more of a benefit of the doubt than me. He thought I wouldn't want to get my hands dirty."

"You loved to get into shit," he said. "Still do."

"Painting, mudding, tile work, all the messy things," I said. "It's my happy place."

"Meanwhile," he said. "I prefer to make sure the structural part is sound."

"You do you," I said with a smile. "I'll do me. We work well together."

"We do," he said.

"I should probably have your help on this," I said. "At least the addition. I can do the kitchen and bath, no problem. The addition, because of all the structural stuff, is gonna need your eye. You good with me being the boss?"

"As long as you're not a hard-ass," he said.

I smiled at him. He really was a good guy, and I didn't say that lightly.

"Can you do something about Brad, though?" I asked. "'Cause his shit has got to stop."

"I already talked to him," he said. "He's been told that one more word to you that isn't actually about a job will be the end of him here."

"I don't want him to lose his job," I said.

"He knows he's on thin ice," Dee replied. "He's been doing some other shit that needed addressing, too. I just put it all into one big basket of bullshit that needs to end. He does anything, says anything, that is out-of-pocket, you tell me. I will happily let you fire him, but if you don't want to be that bitch, tap me in."

"Thanks," I said. "I'm sure we'll be fine."

"What do you need to get this project figured out?" he asked, and just like that, we were back to business.

CHAPTER EIGHT

Billy...

It sucked when Spencer was in this type of mood. He was always the one to get things going, move things along, and make sure that everyone was safe and taken care of. Don't get me wrong, I fucking loved banging chicks with him, but sometimes I wanted to try to strike out on my own.

The other night was off, though. I mean, the bitch was fine, and willing to do whatever the fuck I wanted to do, but it wasn't right. Spencer must have just known. It was like he had this fucking radar inside him that could figure out when a woman was gonna be good and when she was gonna be needy and bitchy.

I hadn't even finished with her. I mean, when Spencer walked away, I sort of just shut down. I got her up, untied, and pulled the fucking eggplant from her pussy. She wanted to cook it up and feed it to me, but by the time I had her disassembled, I was done. The fucking bitch asked me to pay her when she was leaving, too. Like, nah, bitch, you didn't indicate this was gonna be a transaction. You said you were up to play.

Guess I had to live and learn. She left pretty easily when I reminded her that asking me for payment meant she was a prostitute, and that I could call the cops on her. Whatever, I never got my nut, and that kinda pissed me off.

He'd sent me on some wild fucking goose chase Tuesday morning, and by the time I got back, the contractor chick was gone.

"So," I said, drawing the word out to indicate that I wanted him to give me details.

"She's gonna give me a bid on the addition," he said.

"She gonna fuck you?"

"Fuck you," he said.

"Well, I'll go first if you want," I replied.

"No," he said. "I mean that's not what we talked about. I need this work done, and I figure if she spends enough time here, she'll get to know me and we might move the needle in that direction."

"You gonna share?"

"Dude," he said, and I could hear the tone. "We need work done. I need to make sure that it gets done right. I don't need to fuck it up by hitting on our contractor, especially when she brings her dad with her to do the bid."

"Whoa, she brought her dad?"

"Yeah," he said. "Making sure she was safe, like I had suggested in my email. That's why I didn't want you here. I didn't want her to feel like I was just hitting on her. It's not like I'm hiring her for sex."

"Ain't you, though?"

"No," he said, and it was a bark more than a word.

"Okay," I said, holding my hands up in surrender. "I just thought you were doing it so we could get laid. Guess I have to do that part myself."

"Look," he said. "You're young and inexperienced with this kind of thing. You did that fast rise to the bigs and never had to actually work to get women. Kinda like Beckett when he first came up. You two were about a year apart, so you had to deal with it without the benefit of someone taking you under your wing by force."

"No," I said. "You just pulled me aside and said you had something to offer."

"Not exactly," he replied. "I asked if you were interested in sharing that chick in the first year. You jumped on it and sort of invaded my space and life."

"You want me to move out?" I asked.

"That's not what I'm talking about," he said, and ran a hand down his face. "Look. Let's just let her do the job I'm paying her for. Once she's done that, if things progress naturally, then we'll see. I do not want you hitting on her at all while she's here. Do you understand that?"

"Fine, *Daddy*," I said in a mocking tone. "Whatever you say, sir. I'll be your good little boy and follow the rules."

It was something he fucking hated. I mean, he was fine if we dominated women, but he hated being called Daddy, and absolutely didn't like me trying to play a role I wasn't built for. His face said it all, which was that he was gonna shun me for a week, not let me even talk to him, which was fine. I was kinda sick of his shit right now.

I turned away and headed to my room to pack a bag. If he wanted to be a bitch, I was gonna go and get me some pussy. I'd use my good looks, my boyish charm, and fuck every woman I could find. If he didn't wanna play, he'd be the loser.

CHAPTER NINE

Spencer...

As soon as he walked away, I knew he was gonna go on one of his benders. Not like drugs or booze, but he'd go get a hotel room, tap every woman he could, just to prove he could, and come back feeling like shit. I'd end up consoling him, coddling him, and making sure he was okay. It was the cycle we went through, and it was annoying, but it made sense.

He'd never opened up to me about anything in his past, but I knew something happened. I didn't push, 'cause I didn't want to make him feel like he couldn't trust me. Eventually, he'd be willing to share. I didn't know if it was abuse or torment from other kids, or what, but something happened to make him insecure. He was a fucking genius on the field, but off the field, with women, he was a train wreck.

I didn't really have time to babysit him, though, 'cause I had to figure out exactly what I wanted Ariana to do. There were the things we already discussed, but I wondered whether it would be good to have other projects. I mean, I was sure I could keep her busy with projects from now through the next few months, but after that, I didn't know what I would do to keep her here if I hadn't made a move.

That was the other thing. I didn't want to push her away, or make her feel uncomfortable while she worked here, so it was gonna be a delicate dance to get to the point where we might move things from business associates to actual friends, and from there to something more. I swear to all that is holy, if Billy did something to fuck it up, I might just ship him off to someone else's place. Maybe Beckett could knock some sense into him.

I was lost in my thoughts when my phone rang. I answered without checking who it was.

"Hello?"

"Mr. Adams," the woman said. "It's Ariana Carington from Carington Construction."

"Please, call me Spencer," I said. "Mr. Adams is my dad, and that is definitely not me. What can I do for you?"

"I was wondering if you wanted me to start with the smaller jobs you suggested," she said. "I mean, we may be waiting a while for permits and drawings on the addition, so I thought it might be nice to knock those other projects off the list, first."

"That's actually a good idea," I replied.

"Oh, great," she said. "I thought I might come over so you could look at some of the ideas I've come up with. If you have time, that is."

"Sure," I said. "I'm pretty much home all day, so any time you want would be fine."

"Okay," she said. "I'll figure out what I need to bring with me, pick up the samples I'm thinking of using, and then let you know when I'm on the way. Would this afternoon around three work for you?"

"I will actually make that work," I said. "Everything I need to do is here at the house, so I'll be here, anyway."

"Great," she said. "See you then."

"See you then," I replied, then disconnected the call.

I looked around the kitchen and realized that I needed to get some dishes washed and do a quick clean up. I also wanted to shower and rub one out so I wasn't sporting a chub the whole time she was here. I decided that a shower first would be better, which reminded me that I should ask her about the hot water issue we had. We could both shower, but if we did dishes or laundry, we had to wait. Yeah, that would be another project I could ask her to do.

"Keep making a list, dick," I said to myself. "Eventually you'll get to the item on the list you want most, which is her."

I undressed once I got to my room, throwing my sweats and shirt into the laundry basket, followed by my boxers. I was already hard, so I knew it wouldn't take much once I started imagining her getting me off. When I turned on the water, I looked at the tile in the shower. Actually looked at it with a more critical eye and saw what she'd meant by it being good quality. Each tile was large, and the golds and blacks flowing through them was truly remarkable.

I stepped into the space, ducking under the spray. The way the shower was laid out, there was a glass brick wall by the shower head which kept it from spraying all over the place, but the rest of it was open. There wasn't a door or anything that I had to move around. I liked that feature and felt it was something that I wanted to make sure we did when we added the bathrooms in the addition.

Thinking of the addition, I wondered exactly what I wanted up there. I'd told her two bedrooms, each with a bathroom, and perhaps a kitchen or kitchenette of some sort, but other than that, I wondered if there was anything else I should have. The garage was decent sized, being it was a two car, plus an extra section. It was also deep, which gave me more space to work with. Honestly, I could probably put a whole mother-in-law apartment up there for guests who might want to stay, or players who needed an in-between crash pad until they could get their own housing.

Hell, I could even set it up so that Billy could just live there and do his own thing. That would give me the whole of the main house to myself. I could make his room a spare bedroom, which would make the second bedroom above the garage perfect for putting all the pieces we owned that currently lived in the garage storage room.

Thinking of those pieces, I wondered whether Ariana had ever experienced anything on the kinkier side of the sex scale. Maybe she was in a relationship already and wouldn't be interested in me at all. She hadn't been wearing a ring, but that didn't mean anything. Most construction folks didn't due to the possibility of getting it caught in or on some piece of machinery or something.

I had to stop getting ahead of myself with all my what-if's and just worry about the problem at hand—to get myself done in the shower so I could be ready when she got here. I poured some shampoo into my hand and washed my hair, then rinsed, before grabbing the bar of soap to clean the rest of me.

After I was clean and rinsed, I shut the shower off, grabbed a towel, and dried off before heading into my room to pick out something to put on. I didn't want to come off as too snooty, but I also didn't want to look like a slob. I grabbed a pair of boxers and pulled them on, then pulled out some jeans from my closet, tugging those on as well. I looked at a few of the button-up shirts in my closet but opted for a plain gray tee shirt.

I decided to go barefoot instead of putting on socks and shoes. The house was plenty warm, even though it was November. It was one of the selling points I loved about it when I first bought it. The floors were heated, which was another thing I was gonna ask her about for the addition. Things were just piling up on what I wanted to talk to her about, not that I minded. It just meant I'd have more time to spend with her.

Heading to the kitchen, I put the dishes that were left in the sink into the dishwasher, then dropped a pod into it before starting it up. I grabbed my broom from the pantry and swept the floor, dumping the dustpan into the trash before putting it all back. Wiping down the counters, I noticed there was something stuck to the edge of the island, so I pressed the rag harder, but it wasn't coming off.

Grabbing the spray we had under the sink, I hit it with a blast to let it sit for a minute before continuing the rest of the way around the island. By the time I got back to the spot, it wiped up easily. I didn't know what it was, but it was on the end where Billy had tied up that woman, so I'd have to remind him to clean better when he finished. Honestly, that was something I had to do way more often than I needed, which just solidified the fact that I wanted to move him to the addition once it was done.

There was a knock at the door as I was starting the washing machine, so I finished and headed to answer it.

"Hey," she said when I opened the door.

"Hey, yourself," I replied. "Need help with that?"

She had her hands full of what I presumed were samples and plans for the smaller projects.

"That would be great," she said, and I grabbed some of the stack from her arms. "Normally I have a cart I can put them in, but I didn't want to take the truck out here with the way your driveway is shaped. I wasn't sure if there would be room for anyone to get in or out while I was here. Besides, it's a pain in the butt to drive and maneuver, so I only take it if I absolutely have to."

She was rambling as we walked from the front door to the dining room table. I set the stack of tiles and such on the top, then pulled out a chair so she could sit after setting her own pile down.

"Did you want to look at the designs or the product first?" she asked as I sat next to her.

"What's the best way to go about this?" I asked.

"I guess we could do the designs first," she said. "Then we can determine whether some of the materials are worth even looking at. Yeah, that's probably the best. Do you want the kitchen or bath done first?"

"Let's start with the bath," I said. "But speaking of kitchens, I've thought about it more and think putting a kitchen in the addition is something I wanna do. My roommate is beginning to get on my nerves a bit, and I think I might make the addition one he can move into as soon as it's done. Get him out of my hair and give me more space in my own area to do what I want."

"Living with people can be a pain," she said. "I did that for a bit, but not now, thankfully."

"You live alone?" I asked, then realized it was creepy. "I mean, without roommates? No, wait…"

"It's fine," she said, and I must have been blushing because she took pity on me. "Yes, I live alone. No, I don't have roommates. I did for a while, but it was just too much work. I was much more mature than anyone who lived with me, which meant I was cleaning up after them constantly."

"That's the biggest thing with me," I said.

"Really?" she asked. "'Cause your place looks great."

"I actually just cleaned," I said. "My roommate left for a little space, which was what brought up the idea about the kitchen in the addition. I think that if I rent him the whole space up there, then I don't really have to worry about whether he cleans up or not."

"Be careful," she said. "I had someone who rented out a place, and the guy she rented from didn't clean the kitchen in his area, and she ended up with bugs all in her stuff. It was gross."

"Yeah," I said. "I'd make sure he had a housekeeper who he paid to make sure that the basics were done. He can afford it, or hell, I'd even pay if that was an issue. I have to figure out exactly how I'm gonna tell him, 'cause he's a little touchy about some things, which is why he's gone for right now."

"It's amazing how moody some people can be," she said. "My brother is that way. He thinks he knows everything, but when I explain something to him, he gets butt hurt that he didn't think it up himself. I had to remind him that I was going to be in charge of this project, and that he would be working for me. Thankfully, we'd already had a big blowout and I'd threatened to leave the company and make him buy me out, so that wasn't a big deal."

"You guys are equal partners, right?" I asked.

"Yeah," she said. "We each have forty-five percent. My dad has ten percent. It was something Dad wanted to do to make sure that we didn't mess everything up."

"I guess it's good he's looking out for you both," I said, and she laughed.

"Yeah, that's not what it's about," she said. "He holds that ten percent over our heads like it's the biggest portion. We let him think he has more power than he does, and sometimes I push to have him give it up, but he did this forever. We know he'd be pissed if we broke the company up, so we behave, especially around him."

"He seemed pretty young," I said. "If you don't mind my asking, why did you guys take over the company?"

"He had a fall a few years ago," she said. "Messed his back up something fierce. He spent a good month between the hospital and then rehab. His doctor told him that if he kept going like he was, he might end up paralyzed. That was enough for him to give us the option to take it over."

"That's a rough hand to be dealt," I said.

"Yeah," she replied. "Came shortly after my mom died, too, so it was like a double blow."

"Oh, man," I said. "I'm sorry."

"Thanks," she said. "It's been a minute, so I'm good now. Sometimes something makes me sad, but I mostly can handle it."

"That's good," I replied.

She sat there, looking at me, her deep brown eyes so full of life and, my God, did I want to reach out and touch her. It took everything in me to keep from doing it. Even just to brush her hair back, but I couldn't risk it. Not this early in the game. It was like trying to steal home in the first inning. It just wasn't done.

"Anyway," she said, breaking eye contact and shaking her head a bit. "Let's start with the bathroom. I figure if you're gonna want to redo the kitchen, and you want to do it after your roommate moves to the new section, then we should do the bathroom first to give us time to get the add-on done and get him moved."

"Sounds like a solid plan," I said.

"Good," she replied, pulling out her little notebook and opening it up. "Let's start with the centerpiece, which is, of course, that gorgeous shower."

CHAPTER TEN

Ariana...

It took everything in me not to make an absolute fool of myself sitting at his table. He was so close to me, and whatever the fuck shampoo, soap, or cologne or whatever he had on just enticed me to no end. I couldn't stop babbling, and then I couldn't stop spilling every fucking secret I had.

He was hot. Like, cover-model, sports-star, superhero type hot. It was probably good I did the meeting by myself, 'cause I know that if Dee or Dad came with me, they'd have made a complete ass of me. Either that, or they would never let me live it down. I was glad when we went from talking about me to talking about work, 'cause that I could concentrate on.

He liked almost everything I showed him with respect to both the bathroom and kitchen. There were some questions he had, which I anticipated, and then when we went to start picking tile and fixtures. He wanted to see them in the light they were going to be used in, so we headed back to his bathroom to lay them all out.

"I think I like the combination of these two," he said, looking at a smokey gray slate tile and a white marble one.

"They do look good together," I said. "Unfortunately, they're completely different types, which means using both together won't work. I can see if I can find one that is similar to either one, depending on which you like better."

"Oh," he said. "Hadn't thought of that."

"Don't worry about it," I said. "That's my job. I probably should have asked what type of material you were looking at so I only brought things that worked together."

"I'm glad you brought different types," he replied. "I wouldn't have known what to tell you if you'd asked that question."

"Okay," I said. "Of these two, which do you like better? Or do you want me to talk about the qualities of them so you know which one would work for what you want?"

"Why don't we do that," he said. "Honestly, this is well outside what I know anything about, so you're probably gonna have to hold my hand the whole way through."

"I can do that," I said. "Do you want to talk here or should we head back to the kitchen?"

"Either one is fine," he said.

"Let's go talk specifics," I said. "Then I can show you what fits the parameters of what you want. That will be easier."

"Great," he said, picking up the tiles from the counter.

"I can get those," I said.

"I got 'em," he replied, walking from the bathroom, holding them all.

It wasn't like they were super heavy, just sort of awkward. I actually liked that he did it. Most guys would just make me do it, especially Brad and Demetri. They liked to pretend they were busy with something else when we had to pull big boxes in. I could do it, that wasn't the problem. The issue was, they could do it easier and faster, but they wanted me to "feel like one of guys" so I didn't feel like I was left out.

We get to the kitchen, and he set the tiles on the table where they'd been before.

"You want something to drink?" he asked. "Soda, water, beer?"

"Water would be great," I said.

"Tap okay?" he asked. "Or do you want a bottle?"

"I've got ice and a water dispenser in the fridge that's filtered," he added, and I smiled.

"That sounds great," I said.

He pulled a glass out of the cupboard and walked to the fridge, angling his body so I could watch him put the ice and water in it, always keeping the glass in my eyeline, which was a really nice thing to do.

"Here you go," he said.

"Thanks," I replied, taking a drink. "Also, I appreciate you making sure I could watch you do everything. It's a little thing, but I appreciate it, being I'm a woman in your home."

"Absolutely," he said. "I want you to be comfortable here. Both now, and while you're doing the work. If you ever have an issue, or feel like you're not safe, feel free to walk out, or call me. I don't want you to have any issues."

"That is really a nice thing to say," I said, and it was. "Most people don't even think of me as someone who has to worry about that. Of course, most of the time, I'm not at a house alone. This is something special, though. I kinda feel bad not telling you this before now, but this will be my first project as lead."

"I have no problem with that," he said. "I'm honored you feel confident enough to tell me. I never would have guessed you hadn't done it before, what with your poise and knowledge."

"I appreciate the confidence you're putting in me," I said.

"I mean it," he replied. "I do have to tell you that I did call you more because I liked how you took charge in the hardware store when we first met. Don't take this wrong, but you exude power and grace."

I blushed. I could feel the heat rising up my chest and into my face. It also wasn't the cute blush some girls got. No, my whole face turned so red it was like I was having a heat stroke or I had been sitting in the sun all day with no sunscreen. It was that lobster red that happens and I was so unlucky to have that be my natural reaction to blushing. I fucking hated it.

"Did I embarrass you?" he asked, a smile on his lips. "Because I didn't mean to. It's just that I see amazing things all the time in my job. True athleticism in action. And you were just beautiful to watch in that moment. Honestly, I wanted to just ask you out on a date right then and there but felt a bit awkward about it."

"You did?" I asked.

"Yeah," he said. "I do want the work done on the house. That's not a lie. But I wouldn't want to put that kind of pressure on you if you wanted to walk away from this because of my feelings."

I shook my head and had to laugh.

"What?" he asked.

"My dad asked me if I..." I looked at him and my face turned so red it hurt. "Well, he asked if I *pleasured* you to get you to give us the job."

"I'm so sorry," he said. "I don't want this to be weird, so if you want to walk away, or have someone else be in charge of the project, I completely understand."

"Fuck no," I said, then slapped my hand over my mouth.

"You can swear," he said. "I don't mind at all."

"Oh, thank God," I said. "I kind of have a mouth."

"Probably comes with being in construction," he said.

"It's like you know," I said, feeling more comfortable. "Anyway, I wanted to prove them wrong and show them that I can do any job they can, even if I am a woman."

"Then this conversation never happened," he said.

"Oh, no," I said. "You're not getting out of it that easy. That portion of the conversation will be edited out of any discussion I have with the guys about this meeting, sure. But you and me, we are definitely having a conversation about that. Believe me."

"I just don't want you to be put into a position where you feel like you can't just be who you are," he said. "I want you to be comfortable while you're working here. We can push all that other shit off to the side until we get going on this."

"You know," I said, realizing something. "You never did tell me what you do for a living."

"Oh," he said with a smile and, my God, did he look fucking gorgeous when he smiled. "I'm a baseball player," he said, and I had to blink and think.

"I'm sorry, what?"

"I play baseball with the Seattle Cascades professional baseball team," he said, laying everything out so nice and neat.

"No way," I said, my eyes wide and my mouth hanging open.

"I do," he said. "I'm an outfielder. Left field, to be exact, but on the roster it's listed as outfield."

"Shut up," I said, pulling out my phone. "I gotta look this up, 'cause this is gonna make my brother flip the fuck out."

I opened the phone, pulled up the internet browser and did a search for the team's website. Once I was there, I went to the roster to see the names of the guys. It was the off season, yeah, but they still had rosters up. It would shift up until spring training started, but I should be able to find him. I scrolled down to the bottom of the page for the roster and there was the name *Spencer Adams*. Clicking on the name, it pulled up his information, and sure as shit, it was him.

"Holy fuck," I said, then looked up. "Sorry, I can't control it when I'm excited."

"Totally fine," he said. "Like I said, I don't mind."

"This is like the weirdest shit I've ever had happen to me," I said, stumbling over my words. "You're a real-live baseball star."

"I think star is going a bit too far," he said.

"Bullshit," I replied. "Look, you might think it's no big deal, but for us common folks, this is huge. Shit, what if I don't tell Dee? What if I let him figure it out on his own? Oh, yeah, we need to keep this on the down-low, 'cause I want him to actually discover it on his own."

"I'm cool with that," he said.

"So, is your roommate a player, too?" I asked.

"Yeah," he said. "He plays second base."

"Oh," I said. "So, wait, he rents a room from you? Like, doesn't he make like a million dollars a year or something?"

"He makes enough to have his own place," he said, but there was something he didn't say that I wasn't sure I wanted to know.

"So, are you two like a couple or something?" I asked. "Because that's totally fine with me. It's just, what you said before, and this," I added, waving my hand between us. "I'm just... I'm confused."

"You seem like you have a pretty open mind," he said, and I nodded. "And you are comfortable with alternative relationships, I'm assuming." Again, he looked at me, and I nodded. "So, we have a unique relationship," he continued. "We are not a couple, nor will we be a couple. I do not swing that way, nothing wrong with it, just not my bag. We do, however, share women."

I looked at him, confused, and it was clear on my face, I was sure, because he just waited for me to get what he was saying. It took entirely too long for me to realize exactly what he meant, and I wasn't sure what to say.

"Okay," I said, because nothing else seemed to work. "I kinda want to ask a bunch of questions, but I don't want to offend you."

"How about I give you some information?" he said. "Then, if you have more questions, you can ask. Does that work?"

"Yeah," I said, because now I really wanted to know.

I didn't really remember the guy he was with, but that's probably because I saw the two of them for all of half a minute. Maybe I could look him up later, but I had to pay attention to the here and now and worry about the rest of it later.

"We are both heterosexual," he said. "We enjoy our time with women. Sharing isn't always something we do, but we will if we're both in the mood and the woman is willing. I would never push someone to do something they weren't comfortable with, because that's not only wrong, but not how I get my rocks off, if you get what I'm saying."

"Oh, I get that," I said, and the thought of him and me, and sex, kinda made me feel some type of way.

"Anyway," he continued. "If the woman is willing, we offer several options for the interaction to go. As I'm sure you know, there are many, shall we say, *positions*, that one could find themselves in with a partner. When you add another person into the mix, it changes things up a bit."

"I'm sure," I said, fascinated by this conversation.

"I did not intend on having this conversation with you today," he said.

"That makes two of us," I said.

"Anyway," he said, continuing the discussion. "We will never do anything the woman doesn't want to do, including sharing. If she is only interested in one of us, the other bows out gracefully. Doesn't matter which of us it is. In fact, he's out at a hotel, likely hooking up with several women as we speak. He gets a bit off sometimes, so he needs to clear his head. He's found the best way for that is to, well, enjoy several women's company."

"I assume you both use protection," I said.

"Absolutely," he replied.

He was shifting in his seat, which caused me to look down, and yeah, he was hard, and that turned me on. The fact that he was just having this casual conversation, talking about sex without using any of the actual words that should be used when talking about it, and seemed so controlled while still hard, well, that was some serious focus.

"'Cause, that would be a must if I were to ever get involved," I said, and I couldn't believe I said that. That saying of don't shit where you eat was important, and me fucking one of our clients seemed like a really bad idea.

"I wouldn't let you join while you were doing repairs," he said, as if he'd read my mind. "But I wouldn't be opposed to it after you'd finished. At least with the big addition. That must be done before we even think about entering into any sort of relationship. It would be bad for you, and I won't put you in that position."

"Trust me," I said. "It would be bad, and I'd never hear the end of it. I won't let it happen, either. I'll be doing the smaller parts of the jobs, and my brother will be doing the framing, roofing, and other, larger portions. I know how to keep secrets and know how to make it seem like I am not at all involved with someone. Trust me."

"Oh, really," he said, his interest obviously peaked. "Do tell."

"There was this guy in high school," I said after taking a breath and blowing it out. "He really liked me, but he was the kind of guy who couldn't be with someone of my socioeconomic status, as in, he was rich, I was poor, or at least solidly middle class. God, I can't believe I'm telling you this."

"You don't have to," he said.

"No, I do," I replied. "I need you to understand that I know how to be discreet. Anyway, he slid a note into my hand as he passed me in the hall. I tucked it into my pocket, then went to class, a class we shared, that he was doing horribly in, by the way. Anyway, I caught him looking at me a handful of times, and I sort of glared at him, making him think that I didn't like him. At lunch, I went into the bathroom, read the note, which was basically, I like you, here's my number. I sent a text to him, telling him who was texting him, and that if he needed to keep this secret, then we could set up a tutoring schedule for cover."

"So," he said. "You're beautiful and brilliant."

"Can you not right now?"

"Sorry," he said, and I felt bad.

"No," I said. "It's fine, it's just, this is kind of weird."

"I get it," he said. "You can tell me whatever you want to tell me, or nothing at all. I'm good with that."

"So, anyway," I said. "He texted back that he would like that. That night I asked my dad if he would mind if I tutored one of the kids in my class, because he was struggling, and that he would pay me for it. It felt a bit cheap to ask the guy to pay me to tutor him, but if we were gonna do this, it had to look legit. It didn't matter, though, 'cause he had to have some help anyway.

"So, it started out as tutoring," I continued. "My parents were none the wiser, which was mostly because my mom was starting to get sick then. My brother was oblivious to anything that wasn't his preferred flavor of the week. The only one who thought something was up was Brad, and he only thought that because he had the hots for me."

"Didn't you say you worked with someone named Brad?" he asked.

"Yeah," I said. "Same guy. I've told my brother that one more word from him and I was gonna fire him, so he's on a short leash right now."

"Okay," he said, though there was something behind the word I couldn't place.

"Anyway," I said. "Cut to the end of my semester and the boy wants to actually date. Like, out in public, not behind anyone's back, fully date me. We'd done a ton of shit together already, so it wasn't like we weren't actually dating. We just weren't out if you know what I mean. I told him he had to make it public and do everything in front of people first, or I would brush him off like I thought he was an idiot. He pushed and pushed until I finally said to him that I was done."

"Done as in…"

"Not sleeping with him," I said. "Not tutoring him anymore. Not being his hidden girlfriend, or even his out-in-the-open girlfriend. Ended up blocking him on everything when he started spreading lies about me. Well, not everything was a lie, but I was able to get it all turned back on him. Even my brother stood up for me against him and his cronies. It was quite the scandal, let me tell you."

"Should I be worried?" he asked.

"Not unless you plan to fuck me over," I said. "And I mean in the not cool way."

"That's not gonna happen," he said. "I don't play that way. Although, we would need to keep it quiet until you were ready. I'd prefer to not move forward until after the big addition was done, though."

"Completely fine with me," I said. "I prefer to actually get to know people before I push past the most basic of things."

"I'm hoping we'll be able to do that while you're working on my house," he said. "Completely platonically, of course."

"Oh, of course," I said.

He was really nice, and really good at talking, and getting me to talk, too, which, yeah, that was a feat. Whatever situation he and his roommate had, I wasn't sure what that was, and I wasn't sure I wanted into it. I'd just have to wait and see how things shook out.

CHAPTER ELEVEN

Spencer...

We talked for quite a while about damn near everything under the sun. She was so open and honest, and it was refreshing that she was just normal around me. Sure, she had that moment when she found out my profession, but she sort of just glossed over it for the most part and kept on going. I swore we could have talked for days and not run out of things to talk about.

Finally, though, we got back to the real reason she was at my house, which was the remodel. She went over every item she brought, told me the pros and cons of each, and helped me pick things that would work for what I wanted, went together with what we were keeping, and were reasonably priced.

When all was said and done, I had picked out the tile for the floor, countertops, and a new sink and cabinet for the master bath. We ended up running out of time, so we didn't get to the kitchen, which was fine. It meant she'd be back.

I walked her to her car, carrying the things she brought to show me. After she'd gotten in and driven away, I went back into the house, down the hall, pulled my clothes off and got into the shower. I'd completely forgotten to take care of myself before she got there, but I don't know that it would have mattered. She was so damn beautiful, and when she blushed, my God, she turned the brightest shade of red I'd ever seen.

Talking to her was so easy, and she didn't balk at the fact that Billy and I shared women. Instead, she seemed intrigued. It was weird to have that type of conversation with her without him there, but I was glad he was gone. If he'd been there, things probably wouldn't have gone the same way.

The water was hot, and I ducked under it, grabbing my cock, and closing my eyes. I thought about her in this space, the way she talked about things that needed to be done, her ideas, and the confidence she exuded. I'd have never guessed that this was her first time being in charge of a project. She seemed to know exactly what needed to be done and wasn't shy about going over things when I didn't understand something.

As we'd sat at the table initially, I wanted to touch her. She smelled like springtime, sunshine, and fresh blooms. At one point, I almost reached out and brushed her hair back. She'd had it up in a sort of bun type thing, folded over and twisted, but secured at the top of her head. I wondered what it would feel like to let all that hair fall down her back, see it spread across my sheets, fist it in my hand as I held her in a position to make sure we both felt so good we exploded into a billion pieces. Just the thought of that had me losing my load, the water washing it from my hand and cock as I imagined what it would feel like to touch her.

When I finished, I washed up, cleaning myself before shutting the shower off. I toweled off, the second time that day, and went to put some sweats on. Heading to the office, I turned my laptop on and waited for it to boot up. Once I logged in, I found the email exchange we'd had and sent a new one to her.

Ms. Carington,
I forgot to discuss with you while you were here, but I believe
my water tank may be in need of replacement. We tend to run
out of hot water faster than we'd like, so if you have any

suggestions on that issue, I would love to discuss them with you.

I look forward to more details on the bathroom remodel, as well as the addition we're looking at. I assume someone will need to come out and do a structural test at some point to ensure the second story can be added, so let me know when that needs to happen.

As we discussed, I am in town until early February, and would love to have the addition completed by then, if at all possible. If not, then it may be complicated to get it done while I am working. I tend to be out of town quite often, and my work hours might be an issue for construction.

Please let me know if you need any additional information, or if you need to swing by the house to get any measurements of any kind.

Sincerely,

Spencer Adams

I read it over several times and wasn't sure how I could make it any better, so I hit the send button. Hopefully she'd get back to me with some answers to my questions. If she had to come over, I would not be upset about that, either. While I wanted to enjoy her company in the most intimate of ways, I also wanted to be true to my word and not push that aspect of any relationship until after the addition was done. That was the most important thing, and once that was done, she would likely be able to do everything else herself.

CHAPTER TWELVE

Billy...

"Dude," I said when I came home. "There are some seriously crazy bitches out there."

"I'm sure there are," Spencer replied, and he looked distracted.

"What's up?" I asked, setting my suitcase down.

"What?" he asked. "Oh, nothing. I just have to figure out where to keep the stuff when they do the measurements and start the project. My guess is we'll have to have that closet empty for a few weeks at least."

"You could always get a storage locker," I suggested. "I mean, not ideal, but it would keep our stuff safe, and out of prying eyes."

"Yeah," he said, but he still seemed off.

"What happened?" I asked.

We didn't usually do the mushy, buddy talk, but he seemed like he wanted someone to listen to him, so if that was what I had to do, I'd do it.

"I'm just trying to figure out how we're gonna swing this whole thing," he said, looking up at me from where he was sitting at the table. "We've got three months, give or take, until we have to head to Arizona. In that time, we have to figure out the addition, move our shit so no one finds it and outs us and our kinks, and also get into shape so we aren't fucking turds when we get on the field."

"I was afraid you were gonna talk about working out," I said with a laugh. "I mean, you need it cause you're old, but I'm fit as a fucking fiddle."

"Trust me," he said. "Everyone needs to work out and get ready for the season. Even you."

"Yeah," I said. "I know. It's just fun to fuck with you."

"Did you figure your shit out?" he asked, and I sort of looked away. "Don't tell me you fucked something up out there."

"No," I said, sliding a chair back and plopping down on it. "Just, it isn't the same."

"I don't know what you mean," he said.

"I used to be fine with doing chicks solo," I replied. "I mean, I'd been doing it since I was way too young to have been doing it. But since we've started sharing, it's not nearly as fun without you. Please don't think I've fallen in love with you or anything, it's just... I don't know. It's like something is missing."

"You sure that's it?" he asked, and I almost immediately got defensive.

"Look," I said. "I know you think I'm young and dumb and don't know anything, but seriously, it's not the same."

"You're saying you don't want to fly solo anymore?" he asked, and I had to stop and think about it.

On the one hand, having a woman to myself was nice. But then, working with Spencer to play a woman like a fucking song was something else. The way he knew how to make sure we were working in tandem, no matter what way we were working her, seemed like just the perfect way to do it.

"I guess I just miss it," I said. "It's been a minute and a half since we've done anything. Why don't we go out and find someone?"

"I was actually thinking of holding off," he said, and something about the way he said it made me look at him.

"You already hit her?" I asked, jealousy bubbling up.

"No," he said, and seemed offended that I'd even asked.

"Because you've got guilt written all over your face," I said. "I mean, if you did, fine, but I thought we were gonna do that together."

"I talked to her," he said, and I waited, knowing he'd spit whatever it was out when he was good and ready. "She wasn't offended by it or disgusted by us."

"Well, that's good," I said, leaning back in my chair.

He'd been sitting so still it was weird.

"I told her we'd wait until after they finished the addition," he said. "I just don't want to fuck that up, you know?"

"I get it," I said. "But that doesn't mean we can't hit someone else in the meantime."

"I don't want to," he said. When he looked at me, there was something there, just behind his eyes. "I think I want to wait for her."

"Okay," I said, drawing the word out. "Does that mean I'm stuck as a monk until you hit her?"

"No," he said, almost laughing. "You couldn't hold out that long."

"Damn fucking right," I said. "But we could maybe tease a bit with her, couldn't we?"

"No," he said, a demand almost.

"Fine," I said, my ire rising. "I'll figure some way to get my fun, and you can sit around and sulk until you're man enough to hit it."

"I don't sulk," he said, and I just smiled at him, because we both knew that was bullshit.

"Anyway," I said, getting up from the chair. "I gotta get my laundry done and take a shower, but not in that order. Speaking of which—"

"I sent an email about the water heater," he said. "Figured I would put it on the list of things she can figure out."

"Cool," I said. "I'm off. See you when I'm out."

"Okay," he said, but stayed sitting at the table. Yeah, there was something off about him.

CHAPTER THIRTEEN

riana...

It had been a few days since I'd met with Spencer, and he'd sent me an email about their water heater issue, so I'd been in research mode. I'd also scrounged around the old files to find a few architects that Dad had worked with in the past, and started reaching out to them to see what their availability was, and whether this was even something that could be done.

The other thing I'd done was look up his roommate on the team's website. It took a bit to figure out exactly which infielder he was, but when I did, it was weird. I wasn't sure what I was expecting, but this guy was young. When I saw his picture, I remembered him, though he had longer hair when I saw him. He was young, like stupid young. Not that I was old by any stretch of the imagination, but I was older than him by a few years. I'd looked back at Spencer, too, and he was older than me, but just barely.

When he'd first talked about what they did, the sharing thing, I wasn't sure I was interested. But the more I thought about it, the more intrigued I was. I'd had a decent amount of sex in my life. I wasn't a slut, but I'd been active. I mean, I was nearly thirty, so one would hope

I'd at least done the horizontal dance a time or two. Having been with Reggie for a year, my sex life had slowed, and I was definitely ready to get some action. Still, two at once seemed a bit daunting, and I wondered if we'd start slow, or just wham, get at it.

I jumped when Demetri knocked on my office door.

"Shit," I said, my hand to my heart. "You fucking scared me."

"'Cause you're sitting there, daydreaming again," he said. "Who you thinking about?"

"What?" I asked, but I couldn't lie. No, my body gave everything away when that fucking blush creeped up my neck and into my cheeks.

"I knew it," he said. "Which one of the guys is it?"

"What?" I asked, this time actually confused.

"Ain't there two guys that live there?" he asked.

"Oh, yeah," I said. "But I've only met the owner. The other one is a roommate, so he doesn't make any of the decisions. At least according to the owner."

"So, you were thinking about him," he teased.

"I was trying to figure out which architect to go with," I said. "You know, since that's my job and all."

"Then why did you turn red when I asked?"

"Because it was weird," I said. "You surprised me, and I was uncomfortable about being caught thinking hard without noticing the world around me."

"Just keep lying to yourself," he said. "I'll see for myself when we go over to get the measurements."

"I need to pick an architect first," I said. "Can't really do anything until we nail someone down for that part of the job. That's what I'm figuring out right now."

"Bullshit," he said. "I can get the measurements at least, and get a rough idea of what he wants in the addition—"

"I am the lead," I reminded him. "I want to nail down an architect first."

"How are you gonna know if it's the right guy if you don't know what the dude wants?"

"I know what he wants," I said.

"It's you," Dee said, and I threw a pen at him.

"Shut up," I shouted. "I know the needs he has—"

"From you," Dee said, and I threw another pen at him.

"Keep this up, I'll find something bigger to throw at you," I said, and his smile fell.

"You don't have to be a bitch," he said. "I was just trying to treat you like one of the guys."

"Except that's not how you'd tease a guy," I replied. "You would not be accusing Brad of wanting to fuck the client, nor would you accuse him of being a target of the client. You're doing it to me because I'm a girl, and I'm fucking tired of it."

"Fuck," he said, shaking his head.

"Yeah," I said, knowing he realized I was right. "So, can you quit being a fucking prick and listen to me?"

"Okay," he said, sliding into one of the chairs in my office. "What does he want?"

"It's basically gonna be a mother-in-law suite," I said. "Two full bedrooms, each with their own bath, plus a living space that will include a kitchen. I asked about just a kitchenette, but he wants to go all the way in, so full kitchen on top of the rest."

"He knows it's gonna cost a pretty penny, right?"

"I think he'll be fine," I said.

"Oh, you think so?"

"Shut up," I said, but I was smiling. "Now, I need to get back to work and figure out who I want to talk to about this. Can I do that?"

"Yeah," he said. "Besides, I gotta go check on Brad. He's on a site right now, and I'm not sure I trust him to behave."

"Fuck," I said. "If he fucks our reputation up, he's gone. Friend or not, he is messing with our livelihood, and our future."

"That's why I'm going," he said. "That's what I came in here to tell you. You want me to lock up?"

I looked at the clock on my computer and realized that I'd been sitting there for entirely too long.

"Yeah," I said. "I'm gonna take some notes, send a few emails, and then head home. Might see if I can get some sketches down, too. I really want to do a good job with this one. It's important to me."

"Because of the client?" he asked. "Or because it's your first one?"

"It's my first one," I said, although the client had a lot to do with it, too. I wasn't gonna tell him that, though.

"Okay," he said. "See you tomorrow."

"See you," I said as he got up and walked out.

I heard the front door open and shut, then heard him throw the deadbolt, so I knew I was locked in. I pulled up the app for the alarm for the building and armed it to stay. I wasn't going anywhere for a bit, and I felt better when the alarm was actually on.

I'd narrowed the list of options for an architect down to three, so I sent emails out. I told them the basics of the project, that it was an addition on top of a garage that would be a full suite, and that we were looking to start as soon as possible. I wanted to make sure they had room on their calendar, and that we wouldn't pick them, only to find out they couldn't do anything for a few months. I wanted specs nailed down before Thanksgiving, and we were pushing close to that already.

I got a response immediately from one of the firms thanking me for the email, and that they would get back to me within a week. Not the best option, but maybe one of the others would be better. No auto reply from the other two I sent, so I was hopeful that was a good sign. Either that, or they weren't smart enough to set up an auto reply on their email server.

Grabbing my tablet, I tucked it into my bag, along with my notebook, and set my computer into locked mode. I could remote into it from home if I needed to, so I didn't want to shut it down. Most of the stuff I could do on my own laptop, but I preferred to be able to get files and such direct from the server, and remoting to my office computer made it easier to find.

Slinging my purse over my head, I put my jacket on, then grabbed my bag before turning the light out in my office. Dee had left the light on at the front but had flipped the sign to closed. I pulled my keys out, hit the alarm to get it armed for away, then opened the door and headed to my car.

Being as it was November, it was already dark, but we had decent lighting in the parking lot, so I never felt like I had to be concerned. I did, however, keep my eyes open, and didn't get distracted by my phone or anything else. My focus was on my surroundings and getting to my car and in it to head home safely. Thankfully, tonight was like every other night, and I clicked my fob to unlock the door, climbed in, and locked myself in before starting it up.

The drive home was boring as usual, with the normal traffic. I'd plugged my phone in and was listening to a podcast when I got a call. Without looking, I went ahead and answered it.

"Hello," I said. "This is Ari."

"Um, hi," a man said.

"Hello," I replied. "Can I help you?"

"I didn't expect you to be a girl," the guy said.

"Sorry to disappoint you," I replied. "But I'm a woman. Now, is there something I can do for you?"

"I got the email you sent asking for an architect," he said, and I was a bit confused.

"I specified that I would like to be contacted by email," I said, not bothering to hide the annoyance from my tone. "Is there some reason you called instead?"

"Well," he said. "I just, well, I don't like using email. I prefer to talk to people, get to know them, and decide if I want to work with them."

"Which firm are you with?" I asked, getting creep vibes from the dude, and I couldn't even see him.

"I don't want to say," he said. "I don't want to put you off our firm because I didn't do the email thing."

"Is that so," I said, realizing that I was not going to use whoever the fuck this was, no matter what else they had going for them. "What if I told you I already knew who you were with? Would that change anything?"

"You can't," he said emphatically. "There's no way you can know who I am."

"K, bye," I said, then pressed the disconnect button on my phone, the podcast I'd been listening to just a few seconds earlier than when it was cut off by the phone call coming back on.

I didn't normally get creeped out by guys, having been around large and scary men all my life, but this dude gave me serious pause to wonder exactly how the call had even started. I'd figure it out when I got home, which was now going to take longer because I was going to have to drive around and around, using alternative routes to get there. Fuck assholes who think it's cool to call women and freak them out.

CHAPTER FOURTEEN

S pencer...

I'd been low-key waiting for a call or email saying they were gonna come out and need access to the whole garage, so I'd had Billy help me move the bigger pieces we had from the storage unit in the garage into the office. There wasn't much in there that I needed access to, and I could definitely keep folks out if the need arose. I figured that would be the best spot to stick the stuff until we had a more secure spot to put them, or the closet was available again.

It wasn't like we had a whole dungeon or anything, just a couple of larger pieces that worked well for what we liked to do. There was nothing wrong with what we did, and if someone was butt hurt about it, they could figure their own shit out. One cross and a spanking bench were nothing to get all up in arms about, but some people just didn't understand how consent worked. If everyone was willing, there wasn't an issue.

I'd leave the dresser in there that had all the smaller things, but I didn't want to explain to anyone, let alone someone from Ariana's family, why I had those bigger items in the garage. She seemed cool with it, even excited to think about it, but I wanted to hold off. I knew I could get her to play if I tried, but I really did want to respect the business relationship first and foremost. It wouldn't do to have our secrets out there, and I didn't want to have to threaten legal action if it came to that. Holding off was the right thing to do.

"What's up?" Billy asked when he came home from his trip to the gym.

"Thinking we should move the cross and bench into the office," I said. "Don't want her daddy finding them and thinking bad things about us."

"Yeah," he said. "Wouldn't want to give him the wrong impression, now, would we?"

"Nope," I said.

"Okay," he said. "Let me shower and I'll come help."

"You don't want to do it first?" I asked. "Shower after?"

"Oh," he said, as if the realization that manual labor may cause him to sweat dawned on him. "Good idea."

I headed to the garage, opened the door, and walked to the storage closet. The door was locked, but we each had a key. I pulled mine out and opened the closet door, yanking on the chain for the light in there.

"We should have them do a proper light in here," he said, following me in. "You know, with a switch and everything."

"Not a bad idea," I replied. "Actually, might not be a bad idea to do an overhaul of the whole garage. Maybe add some storage places along the side so we can actually make more room for the cars."

"I like it," he said. "Too bad it won't be in time for any snow we might get."

"Yeah," I replied. "Don't like the snow, and my car isn't exactly made for it."

"Which is why you should have gotten a Jeep," he said. "Those fuckers can go damn near anywhere."

"Four-wheel go is only so good," I replied. "You need four-wheel stop, too."

"I know," he said. "We should put a gym in. You know, so we don't have to leave in the winter when we can't get out. Besides, fucking on some of the equipment might be fun."

He reached past me and grabbed the bench, pulling it toward him. I took the other end, and we walked it out of the space, across the garage to the door to the house, then up the couple of steps and into the kitchen. It was something we did often enough that we pretty much had it down to a science. Once we reached the hallway, he set his end down and opened the door to the office.

"You sure you want this in here?" he asked.

"Why?"

"Come look," he said.

I set my end of the bench down and walked past it to the door of the office. I realized what he meant when I looked at the mess in the room.

"Shit," I said.

"Yeah," he replied.

"I guess it'll go in my room for now," I said.

He picked his end up again, and we walked further down the hall, turning to go into my bedroom. It was a bit awkward, but we managed to make it work every time we brought it in here. We slid around the corner without much hassle, setting it near the end of my bed.

"Good enough?" he asked.

"Good enough," I agreed.

"You want to wait on the cross?" he asked.

"Unless you want it in your room," I said.

"I'd rather not," he said. "I have no problem using it, just don't want it lording over me while I sleep."

"Okay," I said. "I'm gonna see what I can do in the office. Maybe we can get it in there tonight or tomorrow morning."

"They coming out?"

"Call it a sinking suspicion," I said.

"Ah," he said, as if it was clear as day. "You're afraid big brother or Daddy are gonna come out and find your kink room and ban the pretty girl from your house, aren't you?"

"Maybe," I said. "But that's neither here nor there. I do know that we need to get it out of there, so doing it now makes sense."

"Whatever makes you sleep better," he said with a laugh, then went into his room.

I heard the shower start and now had time to figure something out for the office. I decided to start with the top of my desk, file what I could, get things put where they needed to be, and work my way around the room.

By the time he'd finished his shower, I had pretty much gotten the desk in order, but there were still things around on the floor. Looking at them, I realized that it was all Billy's shit that he'd sort of just stuffed in here instead of finding a home for it. His suitcase for longer trips was sitting in the middle of the floor, and there were cleats and other bags scattered around as well. I swore, it was like having a teenager hanging out at the house instead of an adult.

"Billy," I shouted when I heard his door open.

"What's up?" he asked, looking over the mess.

I sort of spread my hands around the room, indicating pretty much everything. He looked around, then back at me.

"What?" he asked.

"Most of this shit is yours," I said. "Your suitcase, cleats, and other shit I have no idea what it is. How hard is it to put shit away?"

"Sorry," he said, but sounded anything but. "Didn't know I had to clean everything up all the time."

"You're a fucking adult," I said, and it came out harsher than I wanted. "Look," I continued, lowering my voice. "I know you are young, but you're still an adult. Adults need to clean up after themselves. I shouldn't have to tell you to pick your shit up, or wash your dishes, or do your laundry. Those are all things adults just do."

"You don't need to nag me," he said.

"Apparently, I do," I replied. "I'm not your parent, but they either didn't teach you this, or you didn't consider it was something you had to do. Either way, you need to figure your shit out."

"Fine," he said, and turned around and went back to his room.

"Fucking child," I mumbled, noticing that he didn't even bother to pick anything up to take with him.

I started wondering what his room looked like, but I couldn't go in there now and see without it looking like I was watching him. I'd go do it the next time he headed out of the house. I was almost afraid of what I'd find.

CHAPTER FIFTEEN

illy...

B I fucking hated it when he treated me like a child. Sure, I didn't do everything perfectly, but it wasn't like I was pouring shit out on the floor or anything. I just left a few things lying around. He could've just picked it up and put it away himself, but *no*, he's gotta make a big deal about it.

Maybe it was time for us to live apart. I didn't want that because I really liked Spencer. He'd taught me so many things, and not just with sex. No, he'd been the one to help me set up all my banking and shit, not to mention the investment accounts and making sure I didn't blow all the money I made on stupid shit. For that, I would be eternally grateful.

Looking around my bedroom, I realized that it was, in fact, a total mess. I had shit all over the place. I mean, not making my bed wasn't a big deal, but the clothes that hadn't gotten to the hamper didn't need to be there. I had a handful of used condoms sitting on the floor and realized that was pretty gross. Maybe I was stupid and didn't know how to take care of myself.

Instead of wallowing in self-pity, I decided that I'd try to be the adult Spencer believed I was. I grabbed my hamper and started throwing clothes in it. Turned out, I had way more than just one load. How the fuck did I have so many dirty clothes? Either way, I decided that today was gonna be about getting my room shaped up, or at least enough room for me to bring in the shit I'd shoved into the office.

In that respect, Spencer was right. I had just sort of tossed stuff in there without thinking or worrying what was up with it. First order of business was to get all my clothes loaded up and ready to do the laundry. Thanks to my roommate, I knew that I couldn't just throw everything in the same wash, so I started piles, one for the darker clothes, one for whites and light colors. Once that was done, I shoved all the lights into the hamper and headed to the laundry room. Spencer wasn't around, or if he was, he was in his room, 'cause I didn't see him anywhere.

Throwing my clothes into the wash, I added the soap and fabric softener to the tubs in the drawer, then shut the door and turned it on. I took the hamper with me and loaded it up with the rest of my clothes, taking it back to the laundry room so I could wash them next.

After that, I figured I had enough room to pull my shit out of the office and at least bring it into my own room to figure out. I was actually surprised at how much was in there, and a little embarrassed, if I was telling the truth. Spencer was right. I was a fucking adult, and I should be able to clean up after myself.

I knocked on Spencer's bedroom door, and he yelled at me to come in.

"Hey," I said. "We can move the cross if you want. I've got my shit out of there. I've got a load going in the washer, and another ready to go in when it's done, unless you need it."

"Nah," he said, getting up from his bed. "Let's get the cross moved, and I can lock the door."

"You sure you don't want to move the dresser, too?" I asked.

"It's a dresser," he said. "If someone looks in there, it's their own fault for what they find. Don't snoop. You might not like it."

"All right," I said, deferring to his judgment on that.

We went back to the garage and grabbed the cross. The fucker was heavy, and it always took both of us to bring it out. Once the addition was done, I hoped we wouldn't have to lug it around all the time, and we could find a home for it to live. Maybe that's what the bonus room upstairs would be for.

Tugging the cross, we slid it onto the wall by the hall, just to the left of the door. It wouldn't be obvious there and could easily be hidden. Besides, no one would likely be going into that room, and if we were concerned, we could always lock the door.

"You wanna move the bench in here, too?" I asked.

"Not right now," he said. "I want to get back to the emails from Ariana. She's sending me options for what we can do, and I want to go over them thoroughly to make a decision."

"You need help with anything, let me know," I said.

"Thanks," he said. "And thanks for getting that room picked up. I appreciate it."

"No problem," I said.

I went across the hall to my room, shutting the door behind me. There was still a lot of shit I had to do in there. It was really starting to bother me now that I'd looked at it from his perspective. I mean, messy was okay, but this was outright gross.

"Time to grow up, Billy Boy," I said to myself, and got back to work.

CHAPTER SIXTEEN

A riana...

Spencer had been quick to get back to me after I'd sent him the sketches. I also heard back from both the other architects, and one had room to do the job. It wasn't like it was a big thing, but those fucking drawings were a must in order to get a permit. I sent an email asking him when we could come over and measure for the addition.

Everything was moving pretty quickly, which was nice, but with Thanksgiving coming up in a little over a week, I knew I had to get shit in so I didn't miss the window for requesting the permit. I likely wouldn't get it approved until after that, but if I could get it to the top of the pile, then the rest would likely fall into place pretty quickly.

As I pulled up to the house, I saw two vehicles in the driveway. One was the car that had been there the few times I'd gone over, but the other was a Jeep I'd never seen before. Demetri was coming from a job site, and said he'd be here closer to the time the architect was planning on arriving. Since I knew Spencer, and felt comfortable meeting with him, I grabbed my bag and headed up to the door.

"Hello, gorgeous," the man said as he opened the door.

"Um, hello," I said, completely thrown off. "Is Spencer here?"

"Oh, yeah," he said, then looked behind me. "Spencer," he shouted after turning back to the house. "Our beautiful guest has arrived."

I blushed, furiously, and felt so embarrassed I wanted the ground to open up and swallow me whole.

"Jesus, Billy," Spencer said as he came around the corner. "Are you a fucking moron?"

"What?" Billy said. "She's by herself, so no harm, no foul."

"I'm sorry," Spencer said to me. "He's not quite housebroken, yet. Please, come in."

He sort of shoved Billy out of the way and opened the door for me to come in. Billy had a pained look on his face, like Spencer had just told him to go to his room, which, from what I'd heard about him, explained the look.

"The architect and my brother should be here in a few minutes," I said. "Dee is coming from a jobsite, and the architect is likely coming from his office."

"So, we have time for a little fun," Billy said, and Spencer answered with a glare. "Geez," Billy said. "Didn't know you were so hung up on rules and shit."

"It's not rules," I said. "It's common courtesy. When you meet someone for the first time, you should be polite. It's not that hard."

"We already met," he said. "And Spencer said you were down. I don't know what's up your ass about it now."

"Dude," Spencer said, but I put my hand on his arm, and he looked at me.

"Billy," I said, trying my best to sound patient, but likely failing. "There is a time and a place for everything. While I may have had a discussion with Spencer about things of a more personal nature, that conversation didn't include you. As such, what I may or may not have agreed to with him has no bearing on this current situation. I am here as a contractor for the remodel of the home. As such, you will treat me with the respect I deserve. Do I make myself clear?"

He stood there, sort of blinking, and I couldn't read the expression on his face. I continued to stare at him, waiting for him to answer my question. When he hadn't for entirely too long, I decided to prod him a bit.

"Did you not understand the question?" I asked.

"No," he said, and as I went to explain it again, he said. "I mean, yes, I understood the question. And yes, you made yourself perfectly clear."

He shifted on his feet, and I glanced down at them, noticing that he was erect inside his gray sweatpants. Oh, so he was that kind of boy. Well, this might work out well for me, then.

"Good," I said when I looked back at his face. "Now, would you mind fetching me a bottle of water while Spencer and I talk?"

"Yes, ma'am," he said, scurrying off to do as I asked.

"And please don't open it," I said as he went by.

Spencer looked at me, then toward the kitchen where Billy went, and back at me, confusion clear on his face.

"He likes to be told what to do," I said simply. "He needs someone to be in charge, and it can't be him."

"How did you…"

"I just sort of know these things," I said.

I didn't want to get into all of my history, but I'd had a boyfriend in high school who had some serious mommy issues. He liked being told what to do, how to do it, and would acquiesce to my every demand. It was fine at first, being able to control him and make him do whatever I wanted, but it got old after a while.

"We're gonna have to break him of some of this," I said. "But not until I know his history and where this comes from. Could be bad, just so you know. Do you know anything about his growing up?"

Just then, Billy came back with a bottle of water, the cap securely in place, just as I'd asked.

"Thank you," I said.

"You're welcome," he replied, a soft smile on his face.

"Would you mind taking these?" I asked, handing him the stack of papers I had in my hands. "We'll be sitting at the table until the rest arrive. Then, we'll need to be able to get into the garage and take the measurements we need."

"Okay," he said, taking my stack and walking away.

Spencer stood there, completely confused, and I smiled at him, patted his arm, and said, "Don't worry. He'll be fine."

CHAPTER SEVENTEEN

S pencer...

I didn't know what to think. I'd never seen Billy react that way. It was like she'd flipped a switch in him, turned him on, but made him as complacent as a baby. I'd have to talk to her about that, but as she'd said, this was neither the time nor the place for that.

We followed Billy to the table where he set the stuff she'd given him down and pulled out a chair for her. She thanked him, then sat, and he went to stand in the kitchen. It was like he was afraid of her, but it wasn't quite that. No, he was so turned on it looked painful.

"Hey, Billy," I said, and he looked at me as if I'd slapped him. "Why don't you go take care of yourself. We can handle this."

He looked at Ariana, but she smiled and did this sort of shooing motion with her hand, and he headed to his bedroom.

"What the fuck just happened?" I asked her once he was out of earshot.

"He likes to be told what to do," she said. "It's quite normal and might be a product of his upbringing. I'd love to chat about this, but I don't want to start a deep conversation that I know isn't gonna be finished, so let's talk after everyone else is done and gone."

"Um, okay," I said, still completely baffled.

I'd no sooner agreed before there was a knock on the door.

"That's Dee," she said. "The architect would ring the bell, see how it sounds."

I looked at her confused as I got up to grab the door.

"Hello," the man at the door said. "I'm Demetri Carington. I believe my sister is here. The architect called while I was on the way saying he would be a few minutes late."

"Yes," I said, pulling the door further open. "It's nice to meet you."

I stuck my hand out, and he shook it, but was looking at me, confused.

"You look really familiar," he said. "Have we met before?"

"I don't think so," I replied, closing the door behind him. "Ms. Carington is at the table. This way."

I walked toward the dining room where Ariana was seated, and she stood up.

"Did you say the architect was running late?" she asked him.

"Yeah," he said. "Like ten minutes. I figured I could get started with the measurements while we waited if you didn't mind."

I smiled and nodded just as the shower from Billy's room turned on.

"It's right this way," I said, heading through the kitchen toward the garage. "We haven't really cleaned it up, much, but can definitely do that before we head out in February."

Opening the garage door, I flipped on the light, then stepped down onto the main floor, giving room for both of them to come down as well.

"Will you hear the bell if we're out here?" Ariana asked.

"Yeah," I said. "It actually comes to my phone, too, so no need to worry about him standing on the porch."

Demetri had walked further into the garage, checking the walls and what not, as well as the closet we had in the back.

"Will you be keeping this here?" he asked. "I know we're gonna need to get in there to check the walls out behind it, so thought I'd check."

"We haven't decided whether we'll need to keep it, yet," I said.

"It'll depend on how much room the addition gives us. I can open it now, though, if you need that."

"That'd be great," he said. I walked over and unlocked the door.

"We also thought that if we do keep this, we'd like to put a regular light up," I said. "This is just the temporary one that was here when we moved in."

"So, the room was here before?" he asked.

"Yeah," I said. "Don't know what they used it for, but we just stick stuff in there that we aren't using. We pulled a couple of things out, figuring you guys would need to get in there."

"You probably didn't have to move them," he said. "But it does make it easier, especially if the room was pretty full."

"It was," I said. "We thought it might be better, so we just did it preemptively."

"Cool," he said, stepping into the room.

"I think the architect is here," I said, feeling my phone vibrate in my pocket. "I'll let them in, unless you need me here."

"Nah," he said, looking at the wall at the back of the room.

I went back up the steps and into the house, walking to the front door as the chimes finished ringing from the bell. I guess Ariana had been right when she said they would ring it.

"Hi," I said after opening the door. "You must be the architect. Won't you come in?"

"Thank you," he said.

He was an older guy, closer to my parents' age, or even older, if I had to guess, but he was well put together. He was wearing a button-down shirt with a jacket over it. No tie, and the collar was loose. He had jeans on, but they were stiff, like they'd been pressed, and a pair of bright white tennis shoes.

"The home is lovely," he said as he looked around. "I can see some nice touches in here. Are you just doing the addition or are you remodeling anything inside?"

"We're starting with the addition," I said. "But we're open to additional changes. I just have to plan it out with my work schedule."

"And the budget," he said with a smile. "So, are the contractors here? I saw a truck out front."

"Yeah," I said, walking toward the kitchen. "They're in the garage, where we're adding the second floor."

We walked to the door and I opened it, allowing him to precede me down the stairs.

"Demetri, Ariana," he said as he saw them. "It's good to see you continuing your dad's work."

"Hey," Demetri said. "It's been a while."

"Oh," Ariana said. "Hey."

"You're all grown up," he said, looking at her. "Last time I saw you, I think you were in middle school or something."

"Probably," she said with a smile. "Spencer, this is Mr. Hancock. Mr. Hancock, this is the owner, Spencer Adams."

"Nice to meet you, officially," he said with a smile. "So, what do we have?"

"I think it looks pretty solid," Demitri said. "Walls are fine for adding a second floor, I think. Might have to add some beams for support in the middle, but it should be good. We just need to measure and figure out what he wants."

"Well," Mr. Hancock said. "I do need to see a few things, first. Do you mind?"

He looked at me and I nodded, holding my hand out to indicate he had free rein of the space.

"So," he said, as he walked toward the front of the garage. "What do you want for the second floor? Do you want the entrance to be from the garage, from the exterior, or from inside the house?"

"I hadn't really thought that far ahead," I confessed. "It's gonna be a separate living space for my roommate, mostly, but I may end up heading up there at times, too. Would it be possible to have an exterior entrance as well as one from inside the house?"

"We'll see what we can do," he said. "I'll have to look inside again, figure out where we would need to put the staircase, but I think we might be able to make that work."

"That's definitely something I'd like to check," I said. "I know that he'll want an entrance that doesn't come through the house, but I want him to still have access to the house as well."

"Would you want to have the entrance between the main house

and the guest area separated by a locking door?" Ariana asked. "Or would you leave that open for the time being? Or, you might want to have adjoining rooms like they have in some hotels. You can lock the door from either side."

"Oh, that's an idea," I said. "See, this is why I'm paying you guys. You come up with the answers to questions I didn't even know I needed to ask."

She blushed, and it was wonderful, but I hoped her brother didn't get any idea that we'd had some conversations that were absolutely *not* business related. He gave her a funny look, but didn't seem too upset about it, which I was thankful for.

CHAPTER EIGHTEEN

Ariana...

Thankfully, Dee knew I would blush at damn near anything, but especially a compliment like what Spencer gave me. Otherwise, he may have questioned what was going on. The architect took notes, Dee and I took measurements, and once we'd finished in the garage and had a good idea of what we were looking at from that side of things, we went back into the main house to find Billy standing at the sink, washing up a coffee cup.

"Hey, Billy," Spencer said. "Why don't you come meet the team who will be doing the addition for the house."

He turned around with this devil-may-care smile, charming yet devious, and wiped his hands on the towel next to the sink.

"Hi," he said, reaching his hand out to the architect. "Billy Swift. I'm the roommate that's getting the new digs."

"I'm Richard Hancock," he replied, taking Billy's hand.

"Demetri," my brother said, taking his turn next. "My sister, Ariana, and I, own the company with our dad."

When he finished shaking Dee's hand, he turned to me.

"Ariana Carington," I said, taking his hand, even though we had already met unofficially.

"Brains of the operation, I'm sure," he said to me, and there was dancing in his eyes, which was an expression I'd never understood until that very moment. "Does that make him the brawn?"

"Not hardly," I replied, taking my hand back. "We both work both sides of the business, although I do take more of the finishing work. But that's because I prefer that portion. I've been known to throw some wall board in my time."

"How very interesting," he said. I wasn't sure I liked his tone, so I gave him a look that sort of made him shut up, which was nice.

"Anyway," I said. "We had a few questions that we wanted to ask you about the space, since you're the one that will be occupying it."

"Shoot," he said, leaning his hip against the counter.

"If I could," Mr. Hancock said. "Would you mind letting me look at the area outside the garage so I can make some notes about what would be needed to add an entrance from the exterior?"

"Sure," Spencer said, then gave a look to Billy that clearly told him to behave.

They left, and Dee stayed with Billy and me. It was awkward, because I really didn't know him that well, but he seemed quite comfortable with me.

"So," he began. "What do you want to know?"

I was relieved he went straight to the question I needed him to, instead of making it even more awkward. Although, the smile he trained on me told me he wanted to make me uncomfortable. Instead of taking the bait, I pulled out my notebook and pen and began asking questions.

"Spencer said you might want an adjoining door from the upper addition to the main house," I said. "Do you think you might want to do something like they have in hotels for adjoining rooms? Or will you have it be an open door between the two spaces?"

"Hadn't thought about it," he said. "What do you think?"

"I'm thinking either the double door type situation or a landing that has a door on either side," I said. "It really is up to you whether you think you'll need a locking door between the spaces."

"I mean," he said, his smile growing. "We do hang out together a lot. But then again, I do like my privacy. Add to that the fact that he may end up having to sell the place, and I'd think something that could be locked from either side would be best. I like the idea of a landing, though. Something you could come up to and get into, then knock to be let in."

"That was my thinking," I said. "The staircase could either have the door at the bottom, or the top, and would serve as a barrier between the two living spaces. Then, if one or the other of you were going to the opposite part of the house, you could get there and wait for the other person to let you in."

"Or we could text or call and say we're coming over," he said. "And the other person could unlock the door."

"That would work, too," I agreed.

"Say," he said, looking at Dee. "What do you think of those electronic door lock things? Like the ones that have a code you can open, but you can also open them with your phone. Are those secure?"

"I mean, they are," Dee said. "It really depends on the door and the jamb. Those are gonna be the bigger issue, no matter what kind of lock you use. We usually use decent doors and jambs, but it really depends on the price range you've got. If you don't have a decent budget, we can't just give you a higher priced door or jamb. We'll do our best to get you the best option, but you get what you pay for."

"Sounds about what I thought," he said. "So, they're just as secure, depending on the door and shit?"

"Sure," my brother replied. "So long as you can make sure you get one that's decent. Again, price is everything, so plan accordingly."

"Cool, cool," Billy said.

"I know that Spencer said two bedrooms, both with full baths, and a living space that includes a kitchen," I said. "Do you know what else he might want up there? Is there anything you want us to incorporate when we start making serious plans?"

"I'm sure Spence has a plan," he said. "He's always got a plan."

He said the last directly to me, and I wondered whether he was talking about the house or the other things I'd discussed with the homeowner. I didn't have to fret, though, as Spencer and Mr. Hancock came back in at that moment. I was very happy that Billy had been quiet about our alternative discussions.

"I think we'll have to put the staircase inside the garage," Mr. Hancock said. "You'll lose some space, but I think in the long run, it will be a much better option. Now, we just have to figure out how to get up there from inside."

"That's gonna be the big issue," I said. "I mean, your space is pretty well laid out, so things are gonna have to shift and adjust."

"Would it be something we could incorporate into the kitchen remodel?" Spencer asked. "Or could we use the laundry room area as part of it?"

"Now, that's a good idea," I said. "What do you think?"

"Your kitchen is pretty good sized," Mr. Hancock said. "Using the laundry room, or doing a combination of both, would probably work well. Let me have you measure a few things and we'll see if we can make that happen."

"We talked about what would be best for the door between the two spaces," I said. "We're thinking of a landing at the top of the stairs with a door on either side. Or we could do a door at the bottom of the stairs for this side of the house."

"Definitely something we can play with," Mr. Hancock said.

He, Spencer, and Demetri went to the door that led to the laundry room, and I was left alone with Billy. His smile grew, and I knew I was getting red, so I turned to look away from him, moving some of the paperwork around on the table.

"What's wrong, Angel?" he asked, his voice low so it didn't carry.

"Don't call me that," I said.

"Why not?" he asked.

"I don't like pet names," I said.

"Ariana seems so formal," he said, and I could tell that he'd moved closer to me.

I looked up, and he was standing next to me, barely any space between us, but he wasn't touching me. I could feel the heat radiating off him, and it did things to me I wasn't proud to admit. I wanted to pretend he didn't affect me, but I'd be lying.

"I can smell you," he whispered, his breath at my ear.

Closing my eyes, I took a deep breath, but that was a mistake. Whatever cologne or body spray he was wearing rushed into me, and I felt my panties get wet. I hadn't been this aroused in entirely too long, and I wasn't sure whether that was a good thing or not.

"I'll keep it a secret," he said, and moved away just as the rest of them walked back into the kitchen.

"…and we should be able to make that work," Mr. Hancock said.

I sat down in the chair, nearly falling, and ducked my head down, trying desperately to get my stupid face to quit blushing. They were looking at me, but I just studiously worked on the notebook I'd been taking measurements and jotting down things that had been discussed.

"Ready?" Demetri said, and I looked up at him.

"For what?" I asked.

"We're done here," he said, and looked at me like I'd sprung a second head.

"I wanted to go over a few details with Mr. Adams and Mr. Swift," I said. "Things like trims and flooring."

"There's plenty of time for that," he said.

"True," Mr. Hancock agreed. "It's going to take me at least a week, maybe two, to come up with some sketches to run by them. No need to get ahead of yourself, dear."

"This was for the bathroom," I said, finally feeling like I had myself under control.

"Yes," Spencer said, and I nearly sighed in relief. "I had been meaning to talk to you about those tiles you brought last time. I might want to change my mind on the one we initially chose."

I wasn't sure if he could tell I was feeling put off, or if he actually wanted to talk to me. Either way, I was grateful that he'd spoken up.

"Suit yourself," Dee said. "I'll see you back at the shop?"

"I should be back there, soon," I said. "I have a few things I need to wrap up here, but then I'll head back to pick up anything that I need before tomorrow."

"Tomorrow?" Dee asked.

"I have that other job," I said. "It's the Simpson job."

"Oh, right," he said. "You're finishing up the details, then getting a schedule set, right?"

"Right," I said.

"See you when you're back," he said, but the way he said it told me he wanted to talk to me, and without the other men in the room.

"See ya," I said, trying to sound completely calm.

He gave me a once-over, then turned and shook the guys' hands, promising to work hard to get everything done as soon as possible. Once they were gone, I let out a sigh, and slumped in the chair.

"You okay?" Spencer asked.

"I don't know," I replied. "I think Dee suspects something, but I can't be sure."

I felt the heat behind me before Billy set his hands on my shoulders. It wasn't the first time he'd touched me, but I felt the electricity from that minute connection rush through my body.

"Our little angel is anticipating our first interaction," he said. His mouth was near my ear, as I felt the rush over my shoulder.

"I said don't call me that," I muttered, but there was no weight behind the words.

"She doesn't like pet names," he said, his voice soft. Before I knew what was happening, he placed his lips just above the collar of my shirt.

I shuddered under his touch and, my God, did it make me want him, which was really weird, because this was the first time I'd met him. It could have been the fact that Spencer was across from me, his eyes dark, and his lips turned up just enough that I could tell he was pleased. Oh, God, was I doing this?

"You taste good," Billy said, his warm breath brushing over the spot he'd just kissed. "I want to taste every inch of you."

"Billy," Spencer said, and I felt him turn to look at the other man, the one that I was watching so closely.

Spencer did it for me, looks-wise, but Billy had that boyish charm that sort of made me question whether I should be with one, the other, or both. I didn't have an answer to that question, nor did I even want to try to find one. Where Spencer had the classic good looks, Billy was more of a free-spirit type person, at least in the looks department. His hair was tousled, longer that Spencer's by a bit, and he was clean shaven, looking closer to the age I presumed he was, maybe even younger. I hadn't taken the time to look him up, because, honestly, I couldn't remember his name. I had no idea how old he was, but Spencer had said he was about six years younger, so I had an approximation, at least. Spencer had that almost permanent five-o'clock shadow on his sharp jawline, and the darker hair made it stand out against his skin. Where Billy's eyes were blue, Spencer's were somewhere between brown and that weird hazel that couldn't decide what color it wanted to be.

I didn't know what to do. I mean, I did want them, but this job was really important to me. I didn't want to fuck it up. I had to stay focused on what would help me in the long run, not what I could gain in the short term. But that short-term thrill was sorely tempting.

"I think we should let you go," Spencer said, and I hadn't realized he'd moved so close. "You're showing all the signs that you won't leave unless we make you, and we promised to behave during the addition. In order for us to keep our word, we're gonna need you to not be here. Do you understand?"

I nodded my head, my thighs clenched together at the deepness in his voice, along with the heat that was radiating off Billy at my back. Every fiber in my body wanted to just say yes, fuck everything else and take me. But I knew Spencer was right. If I didn't get out of there soon, I would likely succumb to my desires, which would put me at a severe disadvantage.

Billy backed away, and I missed the heat. Spencer helped me to stand and gathered up the papers and such that were on the table. There were fewer now, since I'd given the blueprints of the original house to Mr. Hancock, but there were still quite a few.

"Let's go, Angel," Billy said, and I couldn't even muster enough anger to ask him to stop. The term wasn't something I aspired to, but the more he said it, the more I started to like the fact that he called me that. I wasn't sure it would last but, for now, I couldn't argue.

They walked with me to the door, near me, but not touching me, and I was dying to feel their hands on me, even just on my arm or shoulder—anything. But they were right. I had to leave and leave without letting myself get swept away with the hormones rushing through my body.

When Billy opened the door, he looked at me with a smile that clearly said he wanted me. Spencer walked out the door, carrying the paperwork I'd have to take with me back to the shop.

"Let's go," he said, holding a hand out to me.

"Okay," I replied, almost robotically.

He walked me to my car, held the door for me as I got in, then handed the stack of papers to me so I could set them on the seat beside me.

"Behave," he whispered in the car before standing back up.

He shut the door and turned to walk back up the driveway. I shuddered again, but not from the cold. No, I was entirely too warm.

CHAPTER NINETEEN

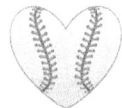

Billy...

"What the fuck was that?" Spencer asked as soon as the door was shut.

"What?" I asked.

"You know exactly what I'm talking about," he said. "We promised her we would keep our hands to ourselves until the addition was complete. Then you go and fucking kiss her?"

"You missed more when you were in the laundry room," I said, and God did I want to rub it in his face. "She couldn't look at me, and when I got close to her... Mmm, she smelled so fucking good. She was wet and ready to go, I promise. It wasn't anything she didn't want, so there's nothing wrong."

"Except we promised," he said. "And when we go back on our word, it makes us unreliable. That is not what I want for her."

"You calling fucking dibs or something?"

"I'm telling you to think before you act for once," he barked. "Her brother was right fucking there. I know he noticed something because she was a fucking lobster. I'm sure he knows you said or did something. Why do you think he was trying so hard to get her out of here?"

"He's a fucking tool," I said.

"Who owns half the company that's doing the work," he said. "That means we need to play nice with him until we get the majority of the work done. You think he's gonna be cool with her coming over all the time if he thinks all we're thinking about is fucking her?"

"Just cause we're thinking about it, doesn't mean we're doing it," I said, getting angry. "Besides, she's a fucking adult and can make her own decisions. You saw how she responded. She was ripe, man. Like, ready to be plucked. I can't wait to taste her nectar."

"Do you even hear yourself?" he asked. "You sound like a fucking teenager with his first fucking crush. It's almost like you've never even had sex. I've never seen you like this. I'm not sure what is driving it, but you better figure your shit out, or you're gonna fuck this all up."

"Don't tell me what to fucking do," I shouted. "It's not your job to boss me around."

"I know," he said. "But it seems like you can't figure your shit out unless someone is giving you instructions."

"I have no problem with her giving me instructions," I said.

"I noticed," he replied.

"But you cannot tell me what to do," I continued. "I am not your child, not your subordinate, and certainly not your minion. I'm a fucking adult, and I'll do whatever the fuck I want."

I turned around and stomped into my room, pissed at Spencer, but more pissed at myself. I knew it was wrong to kiss her, but I couldn't stop myself. She was right fucking there, sitting and waiting on me. And that smell, my God, I was still hard even after the fight with Spencer.

"Fucking dammit," I shouted.

Yanking my shirt over my head, I tossed it onto the bed. I finished taking my clothes off, knowing I needed to be punished for what I'd done. I had never let Spencer know what I did when I wasn't doing what I was supposed to. He'd have a fucking field day with it, I was sure, but there were some things that were private, and this was one of them.

I reached under the bed, pulling out my bag that no one ever saw, and took it with me into the bathroom. The things in the bag were only for me, no one else, and I wouldn't share them, or tell anyone about them. My secret had to stay safe, and if anyone knew... well, I didn't want to think about what would happen if someone found out. That's why I didn't do this unless it was absolutely necessary. And today, it was.

CHAPTER TWENTY

Ariana...
When I pulled into the parking lot and turned off the car, I was worried about what my brother would say to me when I came in. I took a deep breath, blew it out, then opened the door to my car. I wasn't sure, but I figured I'd be fine. I mean, I was an adult, and it wasn't like I hadn't had boyfriends before.

"Why didn't you tell me who they were?" he asked as soon as I stepped into the building.

"What are you talking about?" I asked.

"Seriously?" he asked me, and I looked at him, confused. "They're baseball players."

"Oh," I said, realizing what he was talking about. "Yeah, they are."

"That's all you've got?" he asked.

"I mean, what do you expect me to say?"

"You could have told me," he said. "I could have been better prepared when I got there."

"To do what?" I asked. "'Cause last time I checked, the occupation of the client really wasn't any of our business."

"You know Brad's gonna want to go with us," he said.

"That isn't happening," I said. "He's dumb and will fangirl all over the place."

"He can behave," he said, and I stuck my hands on my hips and glared at him. "Okay," he finally said. "You're right. I just feel like a dick not letting him know."

"Well, that's too fucking bad," I said. "He isn't involved in this job. Not just because of how he'll behave when he realizes who they are, but also because of how he behaves around me. I'm sick of his shit, so I don't want him on my jobs. Got it?"

"You've never complained before," he began, but I cut him off.

"Bullshit," I said. "We were literally just talking about this last week. How much he pushes, the rude comments he makes toward me, and just, everything. I'm done."

He rolled his eyes, but he knew I wasn't fucking around. I walked to my office and grabbed my laptop, taking the cord with me.

"I thought you had work to do," he said.

"I'm going home," I said. "I'll work from there."

"Brad's gone," he said.

"I know," I said. "I don't care. I'm still going home. I'm tired, my body is trying to get sick, and I don't need to add that on top of every-thing else."

"Whatever," he said, turning to go back to his own office.

"You want this locked?" I shouted, but he didn't answer. I walked to his office and looked at him, waiting for him to look up. When he did, I sort of just waited.

"What?" he asked.

"Do you want me to lock the front?" I asked.

"Oh, yeah," he said, and I looked at him for a minute.

"What's up?" I asked.

"Nothing," he said.

"Oh, no," I said, moving in and sitting down. "You've got this look on you, and something's wrong. Tell me what it is."

"I said it's nothing," he barked, and I held my ground, waiting him out. He ran a hand down his face, then blew out his breath. "Some-thing happened," he finally said. I didn't say anything. He would tell me when he was ready. "Remember that one job we did," he said, massaging his temples. "It was at that house way up in Bellingham. Where there was a dude who was making all the decisions, wouldn't let his woman talk, and they had a teenage daughter?"

"Vaguely," I said.

"The girl messaged Brad," he said.

"Which girl?" I asked. "The mother or the daughter?"

"The daughter," he said.

"Should I be concerned that Brad is gonna end up in jail?" I asked.

"No," he said. "Brad asked me what to do, so I suggested he ask what she wanted. Turns out, the dude isn't her dad but her mom's boyfriend. I guess he's been pretty shitty to the mom, and the mom has had quite a few 'accidents' since they moved in with him."

The way he said accidents, and the fact that he put air bunnies around the word, told me that the mom wasn't actually accident prone, but the dude was abusive.

"What's he gonna do?" I asked.

"He called the kid's school," he said. "Turns out, the girl hasn't been going. Kept being sick, so they sent out a social worker to the house, and the dude said they didn't live there."

"What the fuck?"

"Oh, it gets worse," he said. "The social worker just left."

"I'm sorry, what?"

"Yeah," he said. "Our great child protection services at their best. I mean, yeah, they've got a shit ton of cases, but to just take the dude's word for it that she doesn't live there anymore?"

"Did the girl message again?"

"She did," he said. "But it was cryptic as fuck. She sent a message that said something about not being able to go out to the movies 'cause she was grounded or something."

"Did she know she was texting Brad?" I asked.

"He asked the same thing, and she said she did," my brother said. "Anyway, Brad's gone out to Southcenter to talk to a friend who knows some people who might be able to help."

"Help what?" I asked, confused.

"I guess they're the kind of people who know how to make bad shit happen to bad people," he said. "As in, don't ask questions, just be thankful they exist."

"Okay," I said, drawing the word out. "What does that have to do with anything?"

"I guess he's gonna see if they'll help get the girl out," he said. "Or the woman, or both. I don't even know at this point. It also means he may not be around for a bit just in case he needs to help out in some way or another."

"So, he's bailing," I said. "Perfect."

"I don't think so," he said. "I just think he needs to see this through. He'll be back soon enough, though."

"Well, he's your problem," I said. "I don't want him on my jobs."

"I know," he said. "I also know that I've been kind of a shit brother for the last bit. I'm sorry about that."

I sort of just blinked while I looked at him. I mean, Demetri Carington did not apologize. Ever. So, the fact that he had made me a bit uneasy.

"Is that all that's going on?"

"Yeah," he said. "I mean, we gotta make some money soon, so I'm really glad you've got those rich boys wanting you. It means they'll be paying for damn near anything you say."

"I'm not fleecing them," I said.

"Not what I meant," he replied. "I just mean that they're gonna come up with any excuse they can to get you back out there to do another project. I kinda feel bad about wanting you to get close to them, to be honest. Feels like I'm using you."

"Don't worry about me," I said. "I can definitely take care of myself. Promise."

"I know," he said, again running his hand down his face.

"How bad are we?" I asked. "Like, are we in danger of losing the company?"

"Oh, no," he said. "We're fine that way. I just, with Brad gone until he's not, and you running this project with the baseball boys, I feel a bit like I've got the whole company on my shoulders."

"We have other employees," I said. "I mean, they're all ones we hire on as needed, but we've got regular guys we work with. What do you need?"

"I kinda wanna ask Dad to come in a few days a week and look things over," he said. "I know we should be able to do this on our own by now, but I…"

"Hey," I said, reaching across his desk. "It's okay to ask for help."

"I just feel like a failure," he said, his voice hoarse.

"You're not," I insisted. "I would have run us into the ground if I'd been in charge, and you know that. You are the smarter of the two of us. We'll figure it out. If you need Dad to come in, call him in. He'd probably love to be back in the saddle."

"I just don't want to disappoint him," he said.

"I don't think you could," I replied. "Besides, it would be good to get him out of the house a few days a week. You know, get him away from all the memories and shit."

"Yeah," he said, sniffing. "Okay. I'll call him tomorrow."

"Good idea," I said. "If you need me, let me know. And don't keep this type of shit secret. We're partners in this, so I need to know where things stand."

"Think those boys of yours would be willing to pay in advance?" he asked. "You know, for the whole job? You could throw in a little something extra for their generosity?"

"Ha, ha," I said. "You're a regular comedian."

"Seriously," he said. "If we could get them to pay a bit in advance, I think we'd be fine."

"I'll write up the bid tomorrow," I said. "Then, I'll swing by, offer to get to work right away on the bathroom if they give us a deposit for the addition."

"You do like them," he said.

"Shut up," I replied, my face once again the color of a lobster.

"It's fine," he said. "They seem like nice guys. Well, Spencer does. That other guy kinda freaks me out. His eyes got something wrong with them."

"I'm not going to do anything until we have this job done," I said. "Promise."

"Yeah," he said. "Let's not fuck up one of the potentially biggest jobs we could have."

"I won't," I said. "You good?"

"Yeah," he said. "Thanks."

"Anytime," I replied, then got up. "Lock up?"

"Yeah," he said.

I walked out of his office, through our tiny building, and out the front door, locking it behind me. I climbed into my car and wondered what I was going to do. I mean, if we're needing money, I'm sure I could convince Spencer to let me start on his bathroom right away. I just didn't know if it would be enough. I wasn't sure how I would go about getting him to pay something toward the addition when we didn't even have the drawings, yet.

"Problem for another day," I said to myself as I got onto the freeway. "Any other day."

CHAPTER TWENTY-ONE

S pencer...

Billy had gone to his room after our fight, and I didn't hear from him for a couple of days. I mean, I heard him come out and go to the kitchen to get food and shit, but that was it. He was practically a silent ghost. I didn't mind, though, because I had to retreat to my own room and get myself under control. One thing was certain, though, we could not be trusted around Ariana.

I'd sent an email to her, letting her know that we would be available when she had more information about either the addition or the bathroom remodel. I also asked whether the stairwell would be put in before or after the addition, as I wanted to make sure we were good with clothes before they came in and tore the room apart. She'd sent me a tentative schedule which included the bathroom, the addition, and the stairwell inside the house. I hadn't realized how long it would take and was concerned that it might overlap with our leaving for spring training.

The other thing I did was send her a text to let her know I was sorry about what had happened after her brother left, that it wasn't my decision, and that Billy would behave moving forward. She'd sent me a text back thanking me for the apology but reminding me that she was open to the things we'd discussed earlier. Her text got me to wondering whether the number she gave me was a work number or her personal cell, so I sent a text to ask her.

Personal. I purposefully didn't give you the work number. All work discussions should happen through email.

I was thankful that was the response I got, because I didn't want to think about her brother coming across these exchanges. Like Billy said, she was an adult, and could make her own decisions. But, as I'd said, we needed to play it cool around her brother, as he may push to have her removed from all the projects at the house, and that wasn't what we wanted at all.

After about a week, when we were just gearing up for Thanksgiving, she sent an email to let us know that the architect had pushed to get the plans done so we could put in for the permits, and wondered whether we were available to meet and go over them. I was glad I hadn't planned on going home this year.

My sister had just had a baby, and my parents were doing the doting grandparent thing, so I suggested they do their own thing and I do mine. Mom hadn't been too happy about it, but I reminded her that I was an adult, and very capable of handling these things. She said she didn't want me to be alone for the holiday, but I reminded her that I had a roommate, and sometimes liked to be alone. Finally, between my sister and me, we were able to get her to let go of me going home, so I was gonna be around.

Billy had decided to go back home, and had left just before I got the email, so it would just be Ariana and me looking over the plans. I actually liked that thought. Not that I didn't want to share her, but she seemed to be entirely too reactive to Billy, and I had to admit that I had a bit of jealousy showing its head.

We'd set a meeting for Monday, late afternoon, as she said she had several things she needed to handle before the meeting. I was actually glad she put me at the end of the day. That way we could see if things moved along in a more non-work direction. As much as I wanted to get to that, I knew that we had to play it carefully, especially since things weren't signed and sealed. I didn't want to jeopardize my addition, or her career, but I so wanted her.

I'd asked what she liked to eat, so that I could order in or make something. She'd declined, saying she didn't want to mix business with pleasure, which I respected, even though it frustrated me. It wasn't one of those things where I couldn't contain myself, but more that I just wanted to see whether we were compatible, or not. That might change everything, and I wanted to know before I got myself invested further.

The addition would happen, and so would both the bathroom and kitchen remodels. What happened between Ariana, Billy, and me wouldn't change that. I'd been thinking about it before we even stumbled upon her at that hardware store, and the more things went on with Billy, the more I was glad I'd made the plunge and gotten it moving.

As the time grew closer, I started to have a little anxiety. I wasn't anxious about her, but more worried that her brother would be with her, or someone else, and we wouldn't be able to have an actual talk about things outside the plans. If she had someone with her, I'd be fine, but it was the not knowing that was bugging me. It was like I was going on a first date back in high school, and I was afraid the girl would bail at the last minute. It was an unreasonable thought process, but it was there, so I just tried my best to ignore it.

When the knock on the door came, I headed there, hoping to just see her. Thankfully, she seemed to be alone. I was pleased.

"Hey," she said.

"Hey, yourself," I replied. "Come on in."

"Thanks," she said, stepping inside.

It had been raining off and on all week, and the temperature was turning colder. I wondered whether there would be snow in the next few weeks.

"You by yourself?" I asked.

"Yeah," she said, so I closed the door. "I brought a few of the concept drawings that the architect did. He has some ideas that might work better than others, but everything is feasible. It's more of a preference thing than anything else."

We'd walked to the table where she'd set everything down. I held the chair out for her, and she slid into it, not looking at me. I wondered what that was about but didn't want to push for an answer.

"Have you picked the one you think is best?" I asked.

"I wanted to see what you and Billy wanted," she said.

"Well," I said, sitting down next to her. "He's gone home for the holiday, so it's just me."

"Oh," she said, looking at me. "Should we wait until he gets back to make the final decisions?"

"My house, my rules," I said. "Besides, he won't really care. As long as he's got a room with a bathroom attached, and a place to put his food, he'll be fine. Everything else is really just for me, and for the resale value if and when I have to move."

"You're moving?" she asked.

"Hopefully not soon," I said. "The issue with my business is that I could be traded at a moment's notice and end up on the other side of the country. It won't happen before we get this finished, but by mid-season, depending on how the team's doing, how I'm playing, and what the market looks like, it's possible."

"That would be awful," she said, and I was sure she was talking more about any relationship we got into and less about the remodel we were working toward.

"It happens," I said. "We had a guy who was just traded this week, so it's possible that it might happen at any moment."

"Why does that sound so unstable?" she asked. "Like, I wouldn't want to have to be told to move at any point, but it just seems cruel to do it when you're not even playing."

"Worse in the middle of the season," I said. "At least with this, you can figure out your housing and getting your shit moved. Middle of the season, you may end up in the middle of a game, getting pulled, and have to jump on a plane."

"I guess that would be worse," she said.

"Thankfully, I'm pretty safe," I said. "My contract is good through the next couple years, and I've got a good spot on the team. Not that it couldn't happen, but it's not very likely. Besides, I'm getting old, and I can just retire if they want to ship me off somewhere."

"I'm sorry, you're old?" she asked.

"In baseball terms, yeah," I said. "Not super old but getting up there."

"You're not even thirty, are you?"

"Not yet," I said. "But where baseball is concerned, you hit middle age at thirty, and everything over that is on the downhill slope. That's why I want to get this done before I get there. I've been pretty good about minding my money, and it's invested fairly well. Add to that the fact that I live on a pretty small budget, and I've got plenty held over for when I retire."

"That just seems so weird," she said. "I don't even have retirement stuff set up."

"You should," I replied. "The sooner you start, the faster it builds. If you want, I can set up an appointment with my investment banker. He can talk to you about all the things you need to know, and how to get started."

"I just don't think I have the funds for that," she said. "It sounds like something rich folks do, but not us regular middle-class people."

"We'll get you going," I said. "I would hate to see you having to work somewhere in your old age when I could help you plan for it now."

"Why would you do that?" she asked.

"Why wouldn't I?"

She shook her head, clearly confused as to why I'd help her with this sort of thing. I mean, it wasn't exactly the top thing I'd help with, but if I could get her to a place where she was saving, even just a little, I think it would be great for her. Of course, I didn't really know her financial situation. I mean, she was part owner of the company, but other than that, I didn't know much.

"How about we table that for now?" she said.

"And we can start talking about the drawings," I added.

"Exactly," she said.

She pulled out a few packets of paper, then started unfolding them. They were pretty big, much bigger than I thought they'd be, and I wasn't sure whether they were all together on one sheet, or if each sheet had its own plans. Once she finished unfolding the first, I realized that each packet she had was a different drawing.

"This one is a pretty basic one," she said once she got the first one open. "It's got everything you asked for—two bedrooms, each with their own bathroom, a kitchen, and a living space. Nothing spectacular, but decent to start with."

"Okay," I said, looking over the lines and notes all around it, and not making much sense out of the jumbled mess.

"The next one is one that I think will work well for you," she said, unfolding another packet. "It's got those things, but the space is laid out fairly well, with a more open concept for the living space. There's a breakfast bar that separates the kitchen from the rest of the area, and with the small space you've got, I think that will help to make it feel bigger."

"I like the idea of a breakfast bar," I said. "Maybe that's something we can add to this kitchen when we get there."

"We can definitely look to see if that will work," she said.

Watching her talk about the plans, the ideas, and what would work well and what wouldn't, I grew more and more attracted to her. She seemed to really know her stuff, and the more she talked, the deeper I got in my head about all the things I wanted to do with her. She was animated, pointing things out, but all I could do was watch her mouth, watch her eyes light up, and see her in a whole new light.

"Spencer?" she asked, looking at me.

"Sorry," I said. "Must have gotten lost in thought."

"What do you think?" she asked.

"About what?" I asked.

"You weren't paying attention at all, were you?"

"Guilty," I said. "Last thing I know we talked about was a breakfast bar in the kitchen."

"Okay," she said, eyeing me carefully. "Why don't I leave these with you so you can look at them and see which ones have what you want. If you have questions about specifics, feel free to reach out."

When she moved to get up, I put my hand on her thigh. She froze, looking down at my hand, then up at me. We sat there, both staring at each other, neither of us moving.

CHAPTER TWENTY-TWO

A riana...

His hand was warm, even through the material of my jeans, which was thick. It sent jolts up my leg and down, filling me with a current that I wanted to dive into with everything I had. I knew we needed to wait and get everything figured out first. I didn't need to jeopardize my business with some fanciful dreams of a hot baseball player, but I was weak. So weak that I damn near exploded from the heat filling me.

Instead of pushing his hand away, walking out, and driving off, I moved closer. It was subtle at first, and I wondered if he even noticed, but then I saw him smile. It was a small change, but grew with each breath I took, stuttered as they were. What I should have done was ignore the fire building in my belly, but I wasn't smart enough for that.

No, I was pulled into him, drawn like Icarus to the sun, and I'd let that heat melt my wings, burn me to a crisp, if only I could have just a moment with him. Just one single time, I would be satisfied.

Even as I thought it, though, I knew it was a lie. If I did this, dove into the deep end, and gave myself over to him, I wouldn't look back. He held everything I wanted within him, and the thought of never having that nearly killed me.

"We should stop," he said, moving his hand away.

The absence of it was crushing, like he'd taken away my lifeline, and I needed it back. In a moment of pure weakness and stupidity, I stood up, slid my leg across his lap, and sat down facing him, placing my hands on his shoulders. It was bold, and not at all like me, but I needed him, and I needed him now.

"Are you sure?" he asked.

I could tell he wanted me, felt the need between my legs as I pressed down on him.

"Not at all," I replied.

"You say stop, we stop," he said, sliding his hands up my thighs, and every neuron inside me fired up, begging to be touched, to be held, to be turned into putty in his hands.

"I don't want to stop," I said, leaning forward.

The way we were sitting, my head was just slightly above his, so I actually had to sort of lean down to press my lips to his. Each movement was measured, giving him time to stop me if that's what he wanted. His hands were at the bend in my legs, right where they met my hips. He wasn't moving them, wasn't pushing, just holding them there, letting his warmth infuse me.

There was just a breath between us, barely any space between his lips and mine, and I waited, wondering if I should close the gap or make him do it. Every fiber within me was taught, wound tighter than a spring, just waiting to let go, to give in, and take that final plunge.

After hours or days or years, but what was more likely only a few seconds, he closed the gap, pressing his lips to mine in a soft, gentle kiss. He backed away, just enough that we were no longer touching, but I couldn't stand it. I needed him, had to have him, like a fish needs water, like the tide needs the moon. I could not exist without him, and I closed the gap, my hands coming up and around his head, threading through the short hair, holding him to me.

His own hands found their way to my back, up along my spine, and into my own hair, which I'd only put up in one of those claw holder things. I heard the plastic of it hit the floor, felt my hair fall around my shoulders, and his strong hands cling to the back of my head. We worked together, each taking turns in leading the dance of our tongues as they slid in and out of each other's mouths, tangling with each other in the most exquisite dance of passion.

When we finally pulled apart so we could breathe, I gasped, my eyes sliding open to look into his, the green flecks filtering through the darker browns. He was searching my face, looking for something, and I wanted him to see it. I needed him to know that I wanted him, wanted this, in whatever way it happened.

The way his nostrils flared as he caught his breath told me he was just as turned on as I was. His cock throbbing between my legs, even though there were two sets of clothes between us, gave me the same impression. I wanted him, needed him, and didn't even care if it would fuck up anything else. My desire was driving this ship, and I was but a mere passenger, going along in whatever way it flowed.

CHAPTER TWENTY-THREE

B illy...
My family was weird, but they were family, and I did actually enjoy spending time with them. It was good to be going home. As much as Spencer pissed me off sometimes, I did miss him when we were apart. He had family, too, but his sister just had a baby, so he was planning to stay home and get some shit taken care of so we could be ready to go whenever this remodel thing started.

Pulling into the driveway, I noticed that Ariana's car was there. It wasn't actually late, but it was late enough that it was past regular working hours. I wondered if she'd gotten the plans, and they were going over them. That was probably what it was. I parked in the driveway, climbed out, grabbed my bag, and headed up the walkway to the door.

The house was somewhat dark, but I could tell there were lights on in the kitchen. I unlocked the door, opened it, set my bag down, and looked at the kitchen table. Ariana was on Spencer's lap, and she had her shirt and bra off. Her back was to me, and I could see Spencer over her shoulder. He noticed me, but didn't say anything, so I was quiet as I headed in that direction.

Her hair was so fucking long it fell below her ass and halfway down Spencer's shins. It was this deep brown with some highlights of some other colors, but they were few and far between. Most people would probably have thought it was just plain brown, but there was more than that, and it was like a waterfall of hair. It took everything in me to keep from just grabbing a handful and yanking her head back to kiss her, because, my God, did I want to.

Spencer was working his mouth along her collarbone, and she was moaning in delight. I couldn't really see either of his hands but could tell that one was behind her. My guess was he was working her tit with the other one, the one behind her holding her upright as he did his due diligence in getting her going.

His hand slid up, sort of pushing her hair off to the side, giving me a spot where I could dive in as well. His lips moved up her throat until they reached her mouth, his hand at the back of her head, tilting it so that I had a clear shot to her neck. Instead of just diving in, though, I paused, watching as he worked her.

I stepped back, walking away from them and toward my room. I saw Spencer give a questioning look, but I just held up a hand, then mouthed that I'd be right back. I went into my room, walked to the nightstand, pulled out a box of condoms, then reached under the bed for my bag, the one that held my devices that kept me in check.

Opening the bag on the bed, I pulled out the cock cage, the one that I'd put on the last time I'd seen Ariana. I'd worn that fucker for three days, not taking it off at all. I knew it would be a bitch to put on, especially since Spencer was offering her up so sweetly, but I also knew that I had to keep myself away from actually fucking her, at least for now.

Stripping my clothes off, I strapped the cage around my cock, shoving it into the small enclosure of metal that forced my dick into the unnatural position while it was still hard. Grabbing the box of condoms, I stepped out of the room and headed back to the kitchen. She was still on his lap, and he had moved back to her shoulder. Her head was tipped to the side, but her eyes were closed. I knew he hadn't told her I was there.

When he saw me, he smiled, moving his mouth back up her neck so I had room to begin my ministrations on her as well. Instead of just diving in and kissing her, I sat on the chair behind her. Spencer must have shifted himself when she climbed on his lap, otherwise there wouldn't be a way for me to be behind her. Sitting on the chair, I slid it closer to her so I was just at her back.

My hand slid up her side, then around to the front of her until I reached her ample tit, which was more than a handful. I massaged it gently, tweaking the nipple between my finger and thumb, and the moan she gave was everything I wanted. I leaned in, pressed my lips against her shoulder, and she sighed. Fucking sighed. I kept at it, pressing kisses along her shoulder to her neck, then down the back. I think she finally realized that there were two mouths on her and she gasped.

"It's okay, baby," Spencer said. "We've got you."

She sort of craned her head around to look over her shoulder, and I smiled at her, squeezing her tit and pressing my cage up to her ass.

"We got all night," I said.

I slid my other hand beneath her hair and pushed it off to the side while my mouth touched the top of her spine. Spencer slid the hand he had on her back away, and I pressed my chest against her back as she leaned into me. I took the moment to capture her lips, pressing mine to them gently until she slid her tongue along my seam, seeking entrance.

Opening to her was everything I dreamed it would be, as she slid into me, tasting every bit of my mouth. Spencer had moved his head down, and she gasped when he wrapped his lips around her nipple. I knew what he was doing, as we'd shared enough to know how to push the woman to do what we wanted, when we wanted, and to make sure they got the best pleasure from our time together. We never did anything they asked us not to, and we stopped when they said so, but we were a pair that worked well together.

Her hips bucked on his lap, and I slid a hand to the front of her jeans, pressing against her clit to give her some friction. She sort of stuttered, like she'd touched something that shocked her, her body giving those pulsing motions it got when it was more than just a little excited. I could feel my cock weeping in the cage, and I scooted closer, just enough so that I was off the edge of the chair. Nothing was worse than cum stains on chair cushions.

"That's it," I said, pressing my hand firmly against her. "Ride it, baby. Get yourself all the way up."

"I need more," she whimpered.

Spencer let her move further onto me as he reached down and began to undo her jeans, starting with the belt. I didn't exactly move my hand, just shifted it over so he had full access to the things holding her hidden from us. My hands were around her, one on her tit, squeezing the nipple, the other pressed against her pussy through her jeans, giving her everything I had.

I felt the material slack, and sort of shifted to lift her hips as Spencer pulled on the jeans. We worked together, him doing the lion's share of the undressing while I held onto our little angel, making sure she kept climbing the peak. As he got her jeans moving down, I sort of stood, lifting her as he held the jeans, and then he was picking her up with me, her jeans wrapped around the lower half of her legs.

She should have been naked, but we'd get there. We set her on the table, like the perfect meal, and we both planned to feast on her as long as she'd let us. Moving from behind her, I let her down softly, the table-cloth a benefit, but there were papers strewn everywhere, and I didn't know if they were important.

"Shit," Spencer said, lifting her back up to shove the sheets onto the floor on the other side of the table. When he set her down again, he reached down and pulled her shoes off, then removed her jeans and thong. "So beautiful," he said, looking at her.

I sort of stood up as he pulled his shirt over his head, then he began to unbutton his jeans and remove them. Not wanting our girl to lose ground, I kept things up, kissing her and pinching her nipples. Her hand came off the side of the table and reached out to hold my cock. She sort of gasped at the feel of the metal around it.

"What the…"

She looked over the edge and saw it, then looked up at me. Her eyes were hooded, but I could still see the shock in them.

"Sometimes I need to be punished," I said, then leaned down and wrapped my lips around her nipple, pulling it into my mouth and setting my teeth into it just enough until I heard her gasp again.

"Can I taste you?" Spencer asked, and I pulled back to see that he was right next to her hip at the edge of the table.

She opened her legs, letting one sort of fall off the edge of the table. He pulled his chair up to her and picked it up, setting it on his shoulder. I loved watching him eat a woman out. It was like he could teach a master class on the art. He started with his lips at her knee, pressing them against her skin in soft kisses. As he moved further up, she held me in her hand, and thankfully, she couldn't squeeze too much because of the cage. When he got close to her pussy, he went right past it and on to the other side, pressing a kiss where her thigh met the trunk of her body.

Her hips lifted up, almost involuntarily, and she sort of let out a little whimper. The hand on the other side of her was pressed flat against the table, like she was trying to figure out how to hold on to the nothingness that was at her disposal. Where she was on the table, I figured she could take me into her mouth without it being awkward, so I stepped closer, and her hand naturally let go of me. I pressed my palm against her cheek, turning her head so she was looking at me.

"Will you taste me?" I asked.

She licked her lips, a slow and sensual movement of her tongue, and then turned her head further. The table was a bit too tall, so it wasn't gonna work the way we had it, so I sort of looked down at Spencer and he nodded. I reached under her and shifted her further down the table so that her head was sort of hanging off the end. I kept my hand underneath it and let it bend back slowly. I didn't want to hurt her, but I also knew that we had to get the angle right or she wouldn't be able to suck me.

Ever the one to please, she pressed herself further back, opening her mouth and sticking out her tongue, an invitation for me to step up and let her have me. It took a couple of seconds for her to get herself at the right height and angle, but then she had me inside her mouth.

The way her tongue slid between the bars of the cage, teasing my flesh, and making me painfully hard inside, was more than I could have asked for. I leaned over the table, my hands on either side of her body, as I felt her mouth on me. Watching Spencer slide over her pussy and feeling her suck in air around my wet cock was exactly what I needed, and I sort of lost myself, pulsing and coming without even meaning to.

"Shit," I said, trying to pull back so I didn't go down her throat, but she grabbed my thigh with one hand, and my balls with the other, and wouldn't let me go. "Fuck, fuck, fuck," I cried out as I spurted into her mouth.

CHAPTER TWENTY-FOUR

Ariana...

As Billy was coming in my mouth, Spencer stuck his fingers inside me, and it was all I could do not to bite down on Billy's cock. The spasm hit me hard, and I flexed my hips, but then felt Spencer bar his arm across me, holding me in place. Between the feel of the metal in my mouth, and the thrusts of fingers in my pussy, I was crashing on the rocks, wave after wave, until I was wrung dry.

Finally, I let go of Billy and relaxed my body, a shiver going through me as Spencer pulled his fingers out of me. I lay there, enjoying the afterglow of the orgasm I'd just been gifted. The way the two of them worked me, it was out of this world. I'd had enough sex to know when it was good, but I'd never had two men worship my body the way these two had. And it wasn't all that much, either. I mean, sure, there was penetration, but this was just simple, and now I wanted to know what it would be like when they went all out.

"How you doing?" Billy asked, his lips next to my ear.

"Good," I replied, though I wasn't sure I could actually get more words out.

"You did so good," Spencer said, his hand rubbing up my thigh.

"When you're ready, let me know. I'd like to get you to that high again."

I sort of nodded my head, but it was awkward because it was hanging over the end of the table. They'd been good about getting my hair out from under me when they'd shifted me up, and it was hanging on the floor beneath my head. I pulled my head up but couldn't quite get myself to a sitting position.

"Here, Angel," Billy said. "Let's get you upright."

He put one hand under my head and the other under my shoulder, and with Spencer reaching out to take my hands, they got me sitting up. Spencer had pulled his clothes off, so we were all naked at the table, and they'd just had me as their meal. Of course, I'd had some of that meal myself, which was so weird in so many ways.

"Can I ask you about that?" I said, looking at Billy's cock that was inside of some metal contraption.

"Sure," he said, his hands still on my shoulders.

"What is it?"

"It's a cock cage," he said. "It's for when I've been naughty. I mostly use it for myself when my thoughts go to places they shouldn't."

"So, why are you wearing it now?"

"I wanted to try to keep from coming," he said. "I guess you're too good, and I couldn't help it."

"Doesn't it hurt?" I asked because it looked painful.

"That's the point," Spencer said, stroking himself.

"You don't have one," I said.

"Don't need one," he said. "Billy's the resident bad boy, so he's the one who gets the punishment. Besides, he likes it."

"You do?"

"Yes," he said as he blushed.

God, he looked so young, I wondered where the fuck he'd gotten this idea that he needed to punish himself from. I did have to admit, though, that it was an interesting thing, and I wondered whether it could be used during actual sex, as in him fucking me. I didn't want to get that far, though. At least not yet. No, I wanted to get Spencer off, and something told me that a blow job wasn't gonna do the trick.

"I think we need to do something else," I said, and both men looked at each other. "Because I don't think Spencer will be satisfied with just my mouth."

"Don't sell yourself short," Billy said. "Your tongue is magic. Besides, I wanna taste you. You okay with that?"

I looked to Spencer, and he smiled, stepping back from beside the table, letting Billy slid down to take his place. He leaned in and kissed me, thrusting his tongue into my mouth just as he'd done with his fingers into my pussy earlier. I moaned, enjoying the feel of his tongue inside me, and nearly jumped when Billy sucked my clit into his mouth.

Spencer slid a hand under my hair, pulling it away from my body, then used the other to lower me back down onto the table. Again, my head was just over the end of it, but I didn't have to lean back quite as far as I had with Billy, since Spencer was taller by a few inches.

Billy wasn't quite as skilled as Spencer with his tongue, but he made up for it with his enthusiasm. I opened my mouth to take Spencer into me, his cock sliding along my tongue to the back of my throat. He was longer than Billy, at least when he was in the cage, so I had to work around my natural gag reflex. Fortunately, I'd had plenty of practice with that. It was one of the things I loved doing most, so had done it with men of most every size.

When Billy slid his fingers into me, I spasmed around them, holding them inside me as he worked my clit. Instead of just standing there and letting me suck him, Spencer started to move his hips. He must have realized that I was in a position that didn't give me much leverage, so he had to do more of the work. I used my hands on his balls to stroke the portion of his cock I couldn't take in, and he leaned forward, one hand beside me, the other on my breast, massaging me and tempting my nipple to a point.

All the sensations pushed me further and further, and I wanted to jump into the abyss, explode to a million pieces, and never come back to myself again. I was getting close, so close, and wanted it so badly, but couldn't quite get there. Billy slid a finger along my pussy, then pressed it against my asshole, and I almost convulsed.

"That's it, baby," Spencer said, his voice rough with strain. "Relax and let him in."

I did what he said and tried to relax, but it was foreign to me, and I was struggling. Spencer pulled out of my mouth and knelt by my head.

"Are you okay?" he asked, his eyes filled with concern.

"Yeah," I whispered. "It's just new."

"Okay," he said, kissing me. "I want you to relax your body, feel the way Billy is sliding in and out of that sweet pussy of yours. You feel him?" I nodded, the finger gone from my asshole. "Good girl," he said. "Now, he's gonna press against your asshole, just pressing against it. You ready?" Again, I nodded, and there he was, a finger right at that entrance.

"Good girl," Spencer said, and God, did I love hearing him say that. "Now," he continued. "He's gonna start pressing against you, and what I want you to do is sort of push out. That'll give his finger room to slide inside. You okay with that?" I nodded, but he looked at me, and I knew he wanted me to actually say the words.

"Yes," I whispered, and felt the pressure.

I did what he said, and Billy's finger slid just inside the opening, and damn if it didn't nearly knock me off the table.

"That's it," Spencer said, still next to my head. "Is that okay or is it too much?"

"It's okay," I said.

"Good girl," he replied. "Now, do you want me to stay with you like this, or would you like me to fuck that pretty mouth of yours?"

"Fuck me," I said.

He obliged almost instantly, standing up and offering his cock to me. I opened my mouth, and he slid inside, then I took a hand and reached underneath to stroke his balls. Between the cock hitting the back of my throat, Billy's mouth on my clit, his fingers fucking my pussy, and another in my ass, I was about as full as I could be, and it was absolute ecstasy.

As if they'd planned it, which they might have, Spencer pinched my nipple, Billy pressed his teeth into my clit, and then he shoved his finger further in, all while keeping up a brutal pace in my pussy. My entire body jolted, spasming around all the intruding bits, and then I felt Spencer come in my mouth, slamming against the back of my throat with each thrust. It was everything they'd promised and more, and I didn't ever want to give this up.

CHAPTER TWENTY-FIVE

S pencer...

The way she responded to us was magnificent. She showed some concern initially, but relaxed into the moment, letting us have her in every way imaginable. There would still be new things we could do with her but, for now, having all of us spent was a great place to be.

We'd helped her up, gotten her some water, and wrapped her in a blanket, before carrying her over to the couch. I'd pulled on some lounge pants, but Billy was still naked. His cock was red, and looked like he was hard again. I knew he was uncomfortable in that fucking cage, but it was what he liked, so who was I to yuck his yum.

Ariana had dozed off, slumped against Billy's shoulder, her body relaxed and exhausted. I wondered whether it was a good thing we'd done, or if I should have insisted it stop before we went too far, but it was a little too late to have those concerns now. We'd jumped into the deep end and were in this all the way.

"She was fucking amazing," Billy whispered over her head.

"Yes," I agreed. "She certainly was. I'm just worried about what she'll say when she wakes up."

"Not a now problem," he said.

"I think of the future," I said. "Can't help but look forward to what may happen next."

"I'm just worried about her brother finding out," he said. "He could pull the plug on the remodel and everything."

"Pretty sure she put him in his place," I said. "She pretty much said so when she got here."

"Good," he said.

Just then, her phone started ringing. She stirred but didn't move too much. I went to her purse, which she'd set next to the table, and pulled it out. It was her brother. I didn't want to answer it, but I knew if someone didn't, he might become suspicious.

"Hello?" I said, pretending I didn't know who it was.

"Who the fuck is this?" he said.

"I could ask you the same thing," I said, giving the same energy back.

"Look," he said. "Where's Ariana? Why do you have her phone?"

"She's unavailable right now," I said, not wanting to tell him anything else.

"You better not be fucking with me," he said, and I smiled.

"Tell me who you are, and I'll tell you where she is," I said, sounding cryptic as fuck, and having no problem with that.

"I'm her fucking brother," he shouted. "Now, where the fuck is she?"

"Oh," I said, as if realization had just dawned on me. "This is Spencer Adams. She's in the bathroom right now. I didn't want her phone to keep ringing, and figured it was someone important, so I answered it."

"Jesus, fuck," he said. "Tell her to call me when she's done."

"Okay," I said. "Anything else?"

"No," he said, all his bluster gone. "Just, don't answer her phone next time."

"What would you have done if I hadn't this time?"

"Called back until someone answered," he said.

"Well, then, there we go," I said. "I'll let her know you called when she's done."

"Fine, fuck, whatever," he said, then disconnected the call.

"You owned him," Billy said.

"But we gotta get her up," I said, and he looked sad. "I know, I don't want to, either, but she can't not call her brother back, so it's gotta be done."

"Can we wait five minutes?" he asked.

"Two," I said, then sat back down beside her.

As much as I wanted the night to continue, I knew she was probably gonna wake up, freak out, get dressed, and leave. I didn't want that, and didn't want to make her uncomfortable, so I looked at Billy, waiting for him to look back up at me.

"What?" he asked once he looked.

"You should probably put some pants on," I said. "It'll be bad enough that she's naked without you sitting there in that fucking cage monstrosity."

"She didn't seem to mind," he said.

"In the throes of passion, no," I agreed. "But now, after a light nap, when realization dawns on her, she might."

"Yeah," he said. "You're right. Give me another minute, then I'll get up. You can wake her up, and we can help her dress."

We waited, just for a little bit, then I slid my hand under her head and leaned her up and off of him. He got up and headed to his room while I held her, stroking her hair from in front of her face, just light touches to get her to rouse. I didn't want to startle her awake, but I had to get her back to this side of consciousness. I looked forward to the day when she could stay here, maybe even share a bed with both of us, where we could sleep, get rested, and get up to do it all over again come morning. But today was not that day.

CHAPTER TWENTY-SIX

riana...

I was warm, cocooned in something soft, strong arms around me, and I didn't want to leave. But the hands pressing my hair back were insistent, and I slowly came back from the dream world that held everything one could imagine in the ways of sex in it. Then it hit me, and my eyes popped open.

"Hey, Angel," Spencer said, his face close to mine, but not overtly so.

"Oh, God," I said, my hand going to my mouth.

"I wanted to let you sleep," he said. "We both did. But your brother called, so we thought it best you call him back before he became suspicious."

"Shit," I said. "Dee called?"

"Yeah," he said. "I answered it. Told him you were in the bathroom."

"When did he call?"

"Just a couple of minutes ago," he said.

"Where's my phone?" I asked and went to get up but noticed that I was completely naked. "Where are my clothes?"

"They're right here," Billy said, coming out from down the hall.

"Shit, shit, shit, shit, shit," I muttered over and over.

Billy picked up my shirt and brought it to me, letting Spencer help me pull it over my head. He then brought me my jeans, but my underclothes weren't with them. Truthfully, I didn't even care. I pulled my jeans on, letting Spencer hold the blanket they'd wrapped me in up and around me to give me some sense of privacy, but really, they'd already seen the whole fucking package, so what was the point at this juncture?

"I gotta call Dee," I said once I was covered. "Where's my phone?"

"It's right here," Spencer said, holding it out to me.

I unlocked it and pulled up the phone app, checking the time he'd called against the time it was then. Good, five minutes was definitely something I could explain. I punched the button and waited for it to ring.

"What the fuck happened to you?" he said.

"Well, hello to you, too," I replied.

"Seriously," he said. "You've been gone all afternoon. What actually have you been doing?"

"I've been looking over the plans," I lied. "We were also looking at the kitchen, the laundry room, and how we thought it might work to get everything fitted together. These things take time. Besides, what's up your ass? You don't normally check up on me like this."

"You also don't normally meet with clients in their homes alone," he said.

"I know," I replied. "This is something different, though. You wanted me to make sure we kept these guys, so you're gonna have to trust my judgment. I'm fine, everything is fine, and I'm still looking at the last bits for the bathroom remodel that I'll be starting soon. Satisfied?"

I needed him to believe me. If he knew what actually happened here, he would blow a fucking gasket, and I so did *not* need that. No, I needed him to believe that I was a fully capable woman who could handle herself alone with a couple of guys who were rich as fuck, and sexy as well. Dee likely didn't see the sexy bit, but that was beside the point. I knew what I was doing when it came to this, so I needed him to see that.

"I'm not," he said. "And I won't be until I see you back here."

"I'm heading straight home after I'm done here," I said. "I have some things I need to do tonight at the house. You know, boring things like laundry and dishes. I've been running the last few days and need to catch up. I'll be back in the morning, and we can talk then."

"I'm going to watch your location," he said.

"I'm not a toddler," I replied, pissed that he even thought of that. "I'm going to turn it off just because you're trying to micromanage me. If that pisses you off, too bad. You'll just have to get over yourself. You know what, on second thought, I'm gonna go find somewhere else to stay tonight, just so you can't stalk me at the house. I'll see you in the morning."

I hung up. I pulled up the tracking app we all had on our phones and turned it off, effectively shutting him out of my life for the night. Only issue was my car was parked outside the house, and I couldn't just turn a tracker off on that. No, I had to hide it somewhere.

"You wanna put your car in the garage?" Billy asked, and I could see he was hopeful that my bitching at my brother meant I was staying here.

"I probably should go," I said.

"You don't have to," Spencer said. "But if that's what you want, that's fine, too. There's room in the garage, though, if you'd rather stay the night. I know I wouldn't mind."

"Me, either," Billy said, a giant smile on his face.

"You're sure?" I asked, looking between the two of them.

"You, here with us, all night long," Billy said. "Yeah, that's definitely high on my list of good ideas. Hell, I'll even go move your car for you."

I put my hand over my mouth, looking between the two of them. Spencer kept his face pretty neutral, but his eyes clearly said he wanted me to stay. Billy was nowhere near as good at hiding his desires. Closing my eyes, I took a deep breath, let it out slowly, then nodded.

"Yes," Billy shouted and when I looked at him, he was pumping his arm up in the air. "Where are your keys? I'll go move the car now."

"I can't believe I'm doing this," I said as I walked over to my purse.

I reached into the side pocket and pulled the car key out, handing it to Billy. He nearly ran past me to the garage, and I heard the rumble of the door rising. I didn't know if this was a good idea or not, but I had had enough of my brother being a dick and trying to tell me what I could and couldn't do. I grabbed the company phone from my purse as well, turning the tracking app off on it before turning it off.

"You sure you're okay with this?" Spencer asked, and I looked up at him. "Because you can go any time you want. We won't make you stay, but we're happy you're here."

"I'm fine," I said. "Hungry, though. Do you have stuff I could make us for dinner?"

"Oh, no," he said. "I'm going to cook. You've had enough shit happen to you today. It's time someone did something for you for a change."

"Pretty sure you did that earlier," I said, and knew my entire face was that stupid bright red it got. "Thinking it might be nice for that to happen again."

"Oh, that's not a problem," he said, leaning down to kiss me softly.

I reached my hand up and wrapped it around his neck, pulling him closer, deepening the kiss. He wrapped his arms around my waist, holding me against him. I hadn't heard the garage door close, but I felt Billy at my back, his body pressing me into Spencer further.

He shifted a bit, sliding a hand into my hair, and moving it off to the side. When his lips pressed against my neck, I felt at peace. It was a weird thing to me, like they knew that I needed to be comforted, but that I didn't need to be babied. I could tell that Billy was still wearing that cage, because there was no denying the feel of it against my ass. Spencer was getting hard, and I could feel him between our bodies.

"This hair is gonna come in handy," Billy said, taking a firm grip of it at my scalp. "I could lead you around by it. Would you like that?"

Spencer still had control of my mouth, so I couldn't really answer him, but the thought of them using it turned me on, so much so that I couldn't help but moan. Sandwiched between the two men, their hard bodies both in front of and behind me, felt like heaven, and somewhere I didn't want to leave. After not nearly enough time, Spencer pulled away, looking down at me.

"Let's get you fed," he said. "After that, we can have another serving of our dessert."

"I like the sound of that," Billy said, still pressing against my back.

This was either the best or worst decision I'd ever made, and only time would tell which one it was.

CHAPTER TWENTY-SEVEN

Billy...

She was staying. She was fucking staying. I wasn't sure whether it was Spencer, me, her dick of a brother, or the combination of all three, but she said she'd stay. She'd been absolutely amazing the first time, and I couldn't wait to have her again. Oh, the things we could do with her tonight.

"Billy," Spencer said, and I realized that he'd been talking a while, and I'd just wandered off into my own little fantasy land.

"Sorry," I said. "What did you ask?"

"If you wanted more," he said, holding the dish up.

"Oh, no," I said. "I ate enough to keep my strength up, but don't want to overdo it."

He shook his head, then set the dish on the table. We'd cleared it of the tablecloth, tossing that into the laundry room to deal with later. Spencer was an amazing cook, and he'd fixed us chicken with a white wine sauce, asparagus, and small red potatoes. There was plenty to eat and would be enough for later on, or for lunch tomorrow. He tended to go overboard with his meals, making sure we had leftovers for days, but I didn't mind. I couldn't boil water without burning it, so I never cooked if I didn't have to.

"This was really nice," Ariana said. "Thank you."

"You are more than welcome," Spencer said.

"I'll get the dishes," I said, picking up my plate.

"I can help," she said, moving to stand.

"Nope," I said. "Guests do not do dishes. Angels don't, either. And you're both."

Her cheeks colored, but it wasn't quite as bad as it had been the first time she'd blushed around me. No, I think she was either getting used to us, or had figured out how to tone down the color somehow. I took her plate from in front of her, kissing the top of her head, before walking over and taking Spencer's.

Walking to the sink, I ran some water over the dishes, then placed them in the dishwasher. It wasn't much I was doing, but it was enough. I went back and picked up the serving dishes, making sure to kiss her head again. I couldn't stop touching her, and I wondered if that was gonna be an issue, especially if she was here when her brother was. If I couldn't figure out how to keep my fucking hands to myself around her, I'd have to always be gone or locked in my room when they were both here.

I boxed up the remainder of food into smaller serving-sized dishes so we could grab one dish and have all the parts of the meal. Made things easier, at least for me. Once all the food was put away, I rinsed the serving dishes and stuck those in the dishwasher, then dropped a pod into the cup, shut that, then closed the door and turned it on. It was one of those machines that you really couldn't hear when it was running, so we didn't have to try to talk over it.

"Would you like a shower?" Spencer asked her as he helped her to stand up.

"That would actually be nice," she said. "I kinda feel bad about just crashing here, but you guys heard my brother, or at least my side of the conversation. He's always been my big brother, and always made sure that I was taken care of, but this felt different. It was like he was trying to keep me from being me. Or tell me I couldn't do something because he didn't think I could, which, yeah, I don't know."

"Don't worry about him," I said. "He's just looking at you as his little sister, not the gorgeous woman you are. He sees you as younger, so you obviously can't make big decisions on your own."

"It did feel like that," she said. "Which is weird, because it's not like I've never gone out with a guy, or never had sex with them. It's like he doesn't trust me around you guys for some reason."

"It does feel like that," Spencer said.

We'd made our way down the hall and were walking into Spencer's bedroom. First, because he had the best fucking shower in the house at this point. And second, because mine was almost always dirty. He also had more room in his, whereas mine would be cramped if all three of us were to be in there.

"So," she said, sort of standing in the middle of the room. "I assume you guys have protection, right?"

"There's a bowl in the shower with plenty of condoms," Spencer said. "And one on the nightstand for later."

"Okay," she said, looking around the room more.

When her eyes landed on the spanking bench, they widened. She looked at me, then Spencer, then back at me again. I knew she wanted to ask what it was, how it was used, and who used it, but she wasn't willing to ask.

"Do you want to see how it works?" I asked her, and her eyes shot to mine. "Let me get undressed and you can tie me to it. Would that make you happy?"

Just the thought of it made my cock pulse, straining inside its cage. She nodded, but it was a barely there nod, so I didn't move. I looked at her, and Spencer placed his hand on her back, sort of guiding her toward it and me.

"He's gonna need you to tell him what you want," Spencer said.

"I want to see you on it," she said, and though it was low and soft, there was enough firmness to it that I simply shoved my sweats down and stepped over to it. "Do you want to do it, or should Spencer? Because I'd rather have you do it."

"I'll do it," she said, her face brightening.

Spencer had stopped after he got her moving, so he was far enough away that it was almost like we were alone. The straps were already undone, so all I had to do was climb up on it. Normally, Spencer and I would strap a woman to this, then we could take her from both ends without her having to be uncomfortable, but I'd been dying to try it.

I put first one knee up, then the other, leaning forward along the larger portion so my chest was pressed against it. It did have a cutout on that part, but we hadn't needed it until now. Thankfully, it was enough that my cock would be below the bench part, baring my ass to the entire room. She was tentative at first, sort of gently taking the straps to wrap around my calves, but that wasn't the way it was supposed to be used. I watched as Spencer came over and stood behind her.

"Strap it on tight," he said, and she shivered from his voice on her neck. "The tighter you put it, the less likely he'll be able to get out."

"I don't want to hurt him," she said.

I reached back and yanked on the strap she'd started. The way the leather bit into my skin felt amazing.

"Do this," I said, looking at her. "I want to feel the tightness. You won't hurt me. Promise."

"Okay," she said, taking the strap from my hand and threading it through the slot where it would buckle into place.

"Do the other one," Spencer said, and she moved over to the other side to put that strap onto my other calf. "Good girl," he said, and I swear she blushed even more.

Once my legs were secure, she sort of looked at me, then over at Spencer, then back at me, like she was wondering what to do next. Instead of telling her, he walked up behind her, wrapped his arm around her waist, and walked her up toward my head.

"Tell him what you want him to do," he said, his voice dropping low and intimate. "When he does what you tell him, reward him."

"Okay," she said, her voice at the same low level. "You should put your head there," she said.

I leaned forward, pressing my face down into the hole made for it.

"Good boy," she said, and my cock throbbed.

"Give him more," Spencer said.

I didn't know what more she could give me, but I was anxious to find out. She knelt in front of the bench, ducking down so I could see her face.

"You are such a good boy," she said. "Would you like a kiss?"

"I would," I said, and she leaned forward, pressing her lips to mine. Just that small press of her lips to mine was everything I wanted. "Strap me in," I said when she pulled away.

She smiled, then reached out and pulled the straps around my arms, one at a time. Once I was secure, she knelt in front of me again.

"Now what?" she asked, searching my face.

"Whatever you want," I said. "Unless you want to leave me here and do something with Spencer. You could make me watch."

"I don't want to punish you," she said. "You deserve to enjoy yourself."

"I would," I said. "I would love to watch you while Spencer fucked you."

"Really?" she said, her eyes wide. "You want to watch while I get pleasure and you're stuck here?"

"Very much so," I said.

Her smile told me she knew exactly what she was doing, and that playing coy was a game to her. Something about that just made her even sexier, and I couldn't wait to see what she did to and for me.

CHAPTER TWENTY-EIGHT

Ariana...

    While I'd never done a deep dive into the BDSM scene, I'd had my share of interactions to know how to play those types of games. The first time I'd met Billy, I'd realized he wanted to be submissive, simply by the way he reacted to my requests, simple as they were. I wasn't a true dominant, but I could fake it when the need arose, and Billy needed that from me.

Whether they'd done anything like this before, I didn't know, but Spencer was stone-faced, not reacting to anything except to nod, point, or give simple directions when needed. I didn't know if he knew that Billy was so submissive before I'd met them, but he had to have known after our initial encounter. I mean, I'd told him straight out that was what he wanted. Maybe he'd known all along, and they were testing me to see if I could read them. I didn't like to be tested like that, so when I stood up from kneeling in front of Billy, I walked away from them both and into the bathroom.

I took my time getting undressed, although all I had on was my tee shirt and jeans. Once I had my clothes off, I grabbed a couple of towels from the cupboard that was just inside the door, setting them on the end of the counter just outside the shower stall. I'd need them both for myself, so if Spencer was going to join me, he would have to get his own.

Instead of him coming right in, though, I could hear them talking in low voices outside, and wondered what they were discussing. I then heard a squeak, then wheels rolling on the hardwood floor. Spencer must have been moving Billy toward the bathroom so he could watch us, which was fine with me.

I wasn't exactly an exhibitionist, but I did enjoy putting on a show. Fuck, I had a boyfriend who would sit in a chair and watch me masturbate in front of him. He'd watch me strip for him, watch me fuck myself with a toy, then watch me shower. Always just the two of us, but it was fun to see him get so turned on by me. Too bad he ended up being a cheating asshole, although otherwise, I'd have never met the two men who were now watching me step into the shower.

The spray was warm, and I needed it to calm myself. I did tend to go off the handle occasionally, but more often than not, it was at my brother. He always seemed to bring out the worst in me. I didn't know how he did it, but it was annoying. Now, though, I didn't want to think about him. No, I needed to remember who I was with, and why I was here.

Two sexy baseball players wanted me and wanted to pleasure me. That was something that came right out of a fucking romance novel. It was one of those things that if I'd read it in a book or seen it in a movie, I would have called it fake. But this was what was happening to me, and it was most definitely real.

I turned myself around, so my back was in the shower and my front was on display for the men. Tipping my head back, I let the water run through my hair, feeling it slick down my body against my back and all the way past my ass. I'd always wanted to have long hair, but it didn't seem to want to grow when I was younger. When my mom got sick, though, she told me her secret. She'd had hair that was so long and pretty, and I loved brushing it, especially when she started slipping downhill toward the end. Since then, I'd promised myself that I would only trim the ends, nothing else, so I could have hair like my mom.

Once my hair was wet, I tipped my head back up and saw that both men were staring at me. Spencer hadn't taken his sweats off, but he was definitely hard. It was something that excited me. Billy was strapped on the contraption, but the place where his head was had been tipped up so that he could see me, and his smile was huge.

"You like this?" I asked, running my hands down my body.

Billy let out a little whimper, but Spencer didn't move. When I looked at him, he had some sort of emotion behind his eyes, but I couldn't read it. I stepped out from under the spray and closer to the entrance of the shower, watching Spencer closely. I couldn't tell if he was angry, turned on, or confused. He was turned on, for sure, as that was evident in his sweats, but there was something else there, and I wanted to find out what it was.

Spencer was close enough to the shower that I could reach out and grab ahold of the waistband of his sweats. I pulled him toward me and he came without resistance. I slid my hands inside the waistband and around to his back, shoving them down past his ass, letting myself lower along with them until I was kneeling in front of him.

Without hesitation, I leaned in and pulled his cock into my mouth, forcing it as far back as I could get it, then holding it there, shutting my breathing down until I felt him pulse inside before pulling back and giving myself space to breathe. I only took a momentary break before taking him in again, repeating the action several times until he held me off him when I'd pulled back.

"I need to fuck you," he said, his voice thick with strain. "If I don't get to it now, I won't last, and I need that. I need you."

He helped me stand up, then backed me into the shower before stepping in behind me. The way Billy was strapped in, and the way it was sort of raised up, he was looking right at me, but I could also see his cock, which was still in that fucking contraption. I didn't understand why he liked it, but whatever.

"I'm grabbing a condom," Spencer said. "You're not allergic to anything, are you?"

"No," I said. "I've never had any issues with condoms before, so I should be fine."

"Good," he said, and I saw him reach over toward the shelf that was in the shower to a small container and pull a condom out of it.

"You want me to stop at any point, you tell me," he said, his voice harsh and raspy. "I want you to enjoy this as much as I do."

"I want the same thing," I said, watching over my shoulder as he moved behind me.

I couldn't see all of him, which was a bit frustrating, but I could see his face, and he had this look of concentration that told me he was working hard not to lose control. When I looked back at Billy, I saw his smile grow with each movement Spencer made. I also looked down to see a small wet spot underneath him.

"Billy," I said, and his eyes snapped to me. "Did you come?"

"No," he said.

"Because if you did, that might mean you needed better control," I said. "And if you need better control, we might have to make sure you didn't get that pleasure."

"I didn't," he said.

"Good," I replied.

"You're good at that," Spencer said in my ear, the heat of his body at my back. "Have you done this before?"

"Some," I said. "But not to this extent. Why? Does that bother you?"

"Not in the least," he replied, running a hand down my side. "I just wanted to know how much you knew, and how much of it was just coming naturally to you."

"I'm a boss bitch," I said. "I know how to keep men in line."

"I can see that," he said. "Now, how would you like me to fuck you?"

My pussy clenched, and I wanted him inside me right that moment, so I sort of bent forward, setting my hands on the bench that was against the wall opposite the showerhead. I was pretty sure that Billy could see me, and see where Spencer was, and would be able to see the show once we got started. All of that just made me more than ready for Spencer to get on with it.

"You're so fucking beautiful," he said, his hand on my hip, just above my ass. "I need to taste you again, just to make sure to get that honey nectar you have going on. I didn't get nearly enough earlier."

With those words, his tongue swiped along my slit, from clit to cunt, then dove inside me with it before pulling it out again and starting all over. I'd been eaten out a few times, and some guys were good, but my God, did Spencer win the gold medal for it. It didn't take long before I was panting, moaning, and crying out my release once he'd added a finger and did that come-hither motion to scratch the itch inside me.

"That's it, Angel," I heard Billy say. "Come all over his face."

I'd barely had time to recover, let alone take stock of Billy's comment, before Spencer was sliding inside me, filling me slowly at first, getting me used to his size. Once he was fully seated, his hips meeting my ass, that pressure against my walls, he leaned over the top of me, pressing his chest to my back, his mouth next to my ear.

"How's that?" he asked.

The way I was standing, my feet were together, and I could see that his were apart, which meant he had to lower his cock so he could get it into me.

"Good," I said.

"Look at Billy," he said.

My head was turned, but not quite far enough, so I shifted. Billy was watching us, licking his lips, and straining against the restraints around his arms. I let my eyes slide down and saw that his cock was weeping, straining against the cage he wore.

"Is he gonna be okay?" I asked.

"I think he's in heaven," Spencer said, then stood up and began to move.

He slid out of me slowly, nearly pulling completely out, before surging forward with his hips, slamming into me, hitting my cervix in the process. Damn did that combination of pain and pleasure do something to me. I let out a guttural moan, and he pulled back and did it again. He held my hips, keeping me from hitting my head against the wall in front of me, keeping me safe in that regard. Each movement was precise, with measured control, and each time, he pulled from me some sort of moan.

I heard a whimper from Billy, and looked over at him to see that he was coming, dripping on the floor beneath him. He had this pained look on his face, like he knew he should have held off, but simply couldn't. I felt bad that he felt bad, until Spencer slammed into me again, and I groaned with pleasure.

Keeping the rhythm going, Spencer kept at me, pounding into me over and over, but I wasn't gonna get over the top. Something was missing, and I wasn't sure what it was. I nearly said something until he pulled out of me and stepped over to Billy, unlocking the straps around his arms.

"Get over here and work her with me," he said, and it was a command that Billy quickly followed.

I didn't know if they'd done this type of play before, where Billy had been set apart from Spencer and whatever woman they were with, but the dynamic was clearly built already. Billy was unbuckled from the bench and crawling over to me where I was still bent over. It was weird to see him so completely compliant, when, just a few days ago, he'd been the aggressor in pursuing me while my brother was at the house. I wasn't at all upset about getting two men to cater to me, but it was weird to see him act like an underling in this situation.

Once he was near me, he slid some sort of standing bench type thing back toward my feet, and I looked from him to it and back again.

"Step up on it," he said. "It'll give you more height, which will let you open your legs for me, so I can suck your clit while Spence fucks you."

I did as he said, with Spencer's arm around my waist to hold me up and keep me from falling over. Once my feet were up on it, they both helped to get them far enough apart that both men had access to me in the way they wanted. I didn't think either of them were bi, not that it mattered, but was surprised they had this sort of thing ready to go. I guess they had done this enough to know what they needed.

"God," Billy moaned as he looked up at me from below. "You are absolutely an angel sent here for our pleasure."

I sort of giggled at that until Spencer slid inside me again, and the laugh turned to a moan. With how I was positioned, my head was lower than my ass, and I had a clear view of both the men, well, completely of Billy, and of Spencer's legs. I saw him pull back, then slam into me again, and then Billy raised himself up and pulled my clit into his mouth. He was facing up, his ass on the floor of the shower, with his head high enough to reach my pussy.

"Oh," I said, as he sucked on me. "Oh, God."

"That's it, baby," Spencer said. "Let us make you feel good. You deserve it."

He kept increasing his speed with each thrust, getting faster and faster until I, once again, fell into the abyss, lost in the orgasm these men blessed me with. I spasmed over and over, completely blind to the entire universe, until I was pulled back together in Spencer's arms, Billy holding my head in his lap.

"Holy fuck," I gasped out.

"You are an angel," Billy insisted.

"A fallen one, maybe," Spencer said. "But, yes, you are divine."

He'd pulled out of me already and was tossing the condom into the trash can next to the shower. How they'd gotten me turned around and lying on the bench without my knowledge was beyond me, but I didn't care. I started to shiver, realizing that my skin was wet from the shower, and I hadn't been under the spray in a while.

"Come on," Spencer said, wrapping a towel around my body. "Let's get you dried off, warmed up, and tucked in."

The two of them sat me up and worked to dry me off, including taking my hair into a towel to pile on top of my head. They completely cocooned me in towels, then a soft robe once they'd gotten most of the water off me. Where it came from, or why they had it, didn't matter. I was warm, cared for, and swiftly moving toward the bed before I had time to think.

"I gotta dry my hair," I said.

"I got you," Billy replied. "We'll get it all dried and combed out before you go to sleep. Promise."

I believed him. Somehow, I figured out that, while he liked to be submissive, he also liked to be of use, and drying my hair was an easy task he could take on. I appreciated that about him.

CHAPTER TWENTY-NINE

S pencer...

Billy was combing through her hair, making sure he got all the tangles out while also drying it with the towel we'd wrapped it up in. I was on cleanup duty, which wasn't as bad as it sounded. Sure, there was cum on the bathroom floor, but it was in one spot, and a quick wipe up with a washcloth took care of it. The spanking bench went back out into the room against one of the walls, waiting for the next time we'd need it.

When I was done with all of that, I looked at my bed, bigger than a standard king-sized one, but not as big as they came. No, this was called a Wyoming king, which had enough room for both Billy and I to be in it with a woman between us. When I'd first moved in, I had the standard king-sized, but we found that there wasn't quite enough room for three to sleep in it comfortably.

That bed was now in Billy's room, and I'd gotten this larger one. Getting bedding for it was a bitch, but it was worth it when we had women stay. Now, though, I wish we'd never had anyone else in the bed with us. Not that we hadn't had fun, and not that I was ashamed of anything we'd done. It just seemed like it was tainted in some way.

I sort of felt bad for Billy, in that while he'd orgasmed, he hadn't gotten a chance to actually experience her in all her wonderful glory. Sure, he'd gotten to feel her mouth, taste her, and hold her as she finished her release, but not be inside her during that. And that was something he would definitely want to do.

"Come here," she said, reaching her hand out toward me.

I'd been standing in the doorway from the bathroom to the bedroom, watching them with each other, and it was a nice sight. Walking over, she took me in, her eyes raking down my body in a way I could almost feel. It was a good feeling. When her eyes came back up to mine, she was smiling at me, her arm still outstretched, reaching for me.

Sliding between the sheets, I scooted closer to her, reaching a hand behind her neck to pull her into a kiss. She leaned into it, opening for me so I could delve into her mouth, teasing her with the motion that mirrored what I'd done earlier. Her hands wrapped around my neck and she rose, scooting even closer to me as she did.

Her hair didn't fall onto my arms, so Billy must have held onto it as she rose. Sure enough, he moved behind her, her hair in his hand as he set it over his shoulder to kiss her neck. We moved together, the three of us, as if we were all listening to the same song, timing each touch, each kiss, each press of body against body, so that we were dancing in the bed.

When she released my mouth, I saw that Billy had his hand wrapped in her hair, his fist next to her scalp, pulling her head back so he could capture her mouth with his. As he did, I pressed my lips along her throat, moving down and down until I was at her breast, pulling her nipple into my mouth.

Her moan told me she was enjoying what we were doing, and she arched her back farther, her breast pressed into my mouth, my hand finding her clit, as she was raised on her knees, and sliding through the wet folds of her most intimate parts. She was so wet, ready to go again, her thighs opening to give me better access.

With her hands on my shoulders, her legs open, and her back arched toward me, I let go of her breast with my mouth to watch Billy with her. His hand was still holding her head, his other reached around her body, squeezing her breast, her nipple pinched between his thumb and forefinger. He'd taken the cage off earlier, so I knew he had to be hard against her ass.

I put my hand on her hip, pressing it back toward him, and Billy eased up on her head to allow her to lean forward, pulling his mouth from hers and turning her head to face me.

"Hey, beautiful," I said, and she smiled, her lids heavy with desire. "Let's see if we can get another orgasm or two out of you, shall we?"

"Oh, yes," she said, a rush of air from her mouth.

Billy still held her up some, his arm around her chest, but he eased back, reaching over to the nightstand to grab a condom. I kept my hand under her, stroking her clit, sliding through the slick folds as she leaned down and pressed her lips to mine. She slid her tongue along the seam of my lips, begging for me to open to her, and I couldn't disappoint her. She plunged into my mouth, taking charge of the kiss, and I enjoyed her enthusiasm.

Her sudden intake of air, and the feel of Billy's balls slamming into my hand, told me he'd simply pushed into her without much warning. She followed her inhale with a deep moan, and I loved that she was so vocal in her pleasure. It was an honest sound, and once she was over the shock, she again dove into my mouth, matching Billy's pace with her own, fucking my mouth with her tongue as he fucked her pussy with his cock.

She pulled back, resting her head on my shoulder, as he backed out and slid in, again and again, her breaths coming faster with each thrust, until she was keening, almost whining, like she was looking for something she couldn't quite find. I'd pulled my hand away from her clit when Billy started, so I reached down under her again, finding the bundle of nerves at the apex of her sex, teasing it in circles to work her up and over the ledge.

As she panted, she started saying, "Oh," over and over again, as if each thrust pushed a button to eject the word from her. I knew she was climbing, and I wanted her to get there. Billy was starting to strain, but he'd hold off as long as he could. I needed to get her to that release before he did so she didn't lose it.

With one hand on her pussy, I reached up with the other to take her nipple between my fingers, pulling on it and giving a twist, trying to find the right combination to get her to eclipse the top and tumble into the waiting arms of ecstasy. It didn't take much until she stiffened, her pussy clamping on to Billy's cock, stilling him as he was buried inside her.

"Oh, God," she cried, her body solid and frozen. "Oh. God, oh God, oh God."

Each word held a spasm of her body, one I could feel with my finger on her clit. It was like she was trying to pull away but didn't want to at the same time. As if all of this was almost too much for her, and I worried we'd broken her just as we'd begun.

Finally, she relaxed marginally, and Billy backed out a bit, only to have her stiffen up and moan again. When she'd softened again, he tried once more, only to have her become rigid again. After a couple of tries, Billy was finally able to pull out, holding the condom against his body as he did.

"Holy fuck," she said, her body sagging against me as she leaned forward. "How the fuck do you guys do that?"

"It's our pleasure," Billy said. "We aim to please, and we're glad we did."

She'd gone limp against me now, her body completely spent, and I kissed her forehead, brushing her hair from her face. Billy had let go of it, so it sort of fell along her body. As I pushed it back, he backed off the bed, taking his condom with him to toss away, and to get cleaned up.

He came back with a washcloth and set his hand on her hip. She jolted, but just enough for us to realize she'd completely relaxed.

"Just gonna clean you up a bit," he said.

Sliding the cloth softly along her, getting anything that might have been left behind from our escapades. Once that was done, he took it back to the bathroom to drop it in the hamper before coming back to the bed. By the time he was sliding between the sheets, I'd moved her around so she was under them as well, and had her up against my side, her head on my shoulder.

Billy took up her hair again, and started braiding it, dividing it into two sections to get all of it wound around and easier to handle. Once he had the side that was up done, I sort of turned her over, so she had her back to my front, pulling all the hair out from between us so he could braid that as well.

"There we go," he said once he'd tied the second braid off. "Now we can make sure it doesn't get tangled while we sleep."

"Mm-hmm," she hummed, her eyes closed, her body lax against my chest.

Billy shifted so he was facing away from her, then backed up so he was against her body, his back to her front. We'd already turned most of the lights off, so the only one that had been left was the one on his nightstand. He reached over and pressed the button on the bottom of it, plunging us into darkness as we settled into sleep.

CHAPTER THIRTY

Ariana...

I felt sore in all the right places. I was draped over a man, my head on his shoulder, my leg thrown across his. There was also a body behind me, tucked up against my ass. It was a nice place to be, so warm and safe.

"Shit," I said, my eyes popping open.

"Hey," Spencer said, brushing the loose hair out from in front of my face. "You're good."

"What time is it?" I asked, my memory slamming back into me.

"It's still early," he said. "Sun's not even close to coming up."

"I need to know the time," I said. "I have to work today."

He shifted, then Billy shifted behind me, rolling onto his back and away from my body.

"It's three," Spencer said, having looked at his watch. "You've got time, right?"

I sighed, thankful that it wasn't any later.

"Yeah," I said. "But I gotta pee."

"Okay," he said, sliding over and out of the bed.

"You don't have to get up," I said.

"It's fine," he replied. "I gotta go, too."

I climbed out of the bed and padded over to the bathroom. Thankfully, they had a night light of sorts so I didn't trip or fall on the way. Once I was in there with the door closed, I sat and peed, then flushed and washed before opening the door to let Spencer take care of himself. It was easy to get back to the bed, so I climbed back in, realizing that the thing was fucking huge. I either didn't notice or didn't care when we went in there, and I wondered whether I'd even paid attention to it when I was first in this room to look at his bathroom for the remodel.

Once I was up and in, I scooted over to Billy, snuggling up against his side, and he put his arm around me, pulling me against him. It had actually been nice to wake up between them, and I was glad they weren't weird about it.

Spencer slid in behind me, wrapping himself around my body, his hard chest against my back. How these two men handled me was remarkable, and I couldn't believe I'd done what I did with them. It wasn't that I was embarrassed or ashamed, but more like… It was like a fantasy that had come true, and I didn't even know it was something I wanted.

"Ari," Spencer said, his hand smoothing over my cheek. "It's six thirty. You should probably be getting up."

I stretched, arching my back like a cat, but not running into Billy on the other side of me. I blinked up at Spencer, who had a tee shirt on, and his hair was wet, like he'd showered.

"Where's Billy?" I asked. "And why are you up and showered so early?"

"He's in his own shower," Spencer said. "And we've gotta go to the gym today. Spring training is coming up faster than ever, so we've gotta get on our game before we're unable to."

"Oh," I said as I sort of sat up. "Where are my clothes?"

"Everything is here," he said, pointing to the end of the bed. "We have a spare key that we keep around, just in case. I've set it on your purse. I also put my garage door opener there as well, so you can use that to get in and out of the garage with your car."

"Hold on," I said, replaying the few words we'd shared. "You guys shower before you go to the gym?"

"We were both pretty messy from last night," he said. "Didn't really want to share that with everyone at the gym."

"Oh," I said. "I guess that makes sense."

"Hey, Spence," Billy said as he poked his head through the door. "Oh, good morning, Angel."

He said my nickname with a wink, his smile broad, his eyes bright. After his shower, he looked even better than he did the night before. The tousled hair having just a bit of curl to it and looking darker than the more blond color it had when it was dry.

"I was just giving her the run down," Spencer said.

"Good deal," Billy replied. "Hot water."

The words made sense but didn't in the context of what we'd been discussing, but then Spencer nodded and turned back to me.

"We're wondering what you think about getting the new hot water heater set up," he said. "We were good last night, but if we wanted to shower afterward, it might have run out. My guess is the house is older than we though, and the heater is on its last legs."

"I'll look into tankless ones," I said. "They'll be a quick and easy install, and not too expensive."

"You give us a cost and we'll get you the money," he said. "Cash, or however you want it. I don't know how your company works with that, so I'll let you figure that out."

"Okay," I said.

He leaned in, kissed me softly, then stood up. Billy was right there, waiting for his own kiss, so I gave one to him as well.

"See you tonight?" Billy asked.

"I think so," I said.

I wasn't quite sure whether that was true or not, but I definitely didn't mind spending the night with them. Billy's smile told me he wanted to make sure that happened.

"I have to check a few things," I added. "And I have to get some clothes if I'm gonna stay here."

"Whatever you want," Spencer said. "We're happy to have you."

"Very happy," Billy said, then blew me another kiss off his hand before walking out the door.

"Don't let him push you to something you don't want," Spencer said once Billy was gone. "If you don't want to stay, don't. I promise, we'll survive."

"Thank you," I said. "I appreciate that."

"Not at all a problem," he replied, leaning in for one more soft kiss before he went out the door after Billy.

I sat at the edge of this giant bed until I heard the door open and close, and a car start up out front. Only then did I breathe deeply, trying to figure out exactly what the fuck was happening with my life.

"You're never gonna figure shit out sitting here," I scolded myself, then pushed up and padded into the bathroom.

Whoever had been on cleanup duty had done a great job. I couldn't see anything on the floor from where Billy had been, and the shower nearly gleamed. There were a couple of towels set out on the bench for me, and a toothbrush in a package on the counter. I appreciated that they thought of that, because, yeah, gonna need to take care of that this morning.

I picked up the towels and set them on the counter, then stepped into the shower to turn it on. Once the water was running, I looked around to find the soap. I wasn't gonna bother with my hair, as they'd braided it up and it was still tightly in the braids, less some of the shorter hairs around my face. Instead, I pulled the braids up and around my head, tucking them into each other to keep the ends from getting wet.

Picking up the washcloth, I got it wet, then poured some of the shower gel that was on the shelf onto the soft material. Working it into a lather, I scrubbed myself clean, having to be careful around my pussy, as it had been worked over very nicely, and was still somewhat tender. Rinsing off, I thought about what I was gonna tell Demetri.

Obviously, I couldn't tell him the truth. I mean, how do tell your older brother that you've been fucking the customer? Not a conversation I want to have with him. Not today, and honestly, not ever. Once I was clean, I turned the tap off, realizing they were right about the longevity of their heater. They definitely needed a new one, and likely sooner rather than later, especially if I was going to be staying here. On average, ten to fifteen years was a good lifespan for a water heater. I didn't know how long they'd lived in the house, but if they bought it and hadn't changed the heater out, it was likely due.

As I dressed, I wondered whether I should go home first and change, or if I should go into the office wearing the same things I was yesterday. I opted to go straight in, make Dee feel bad that he'd been an ass and I didn't get to go home. I didn't do anything with makeup, because I didn't have anything with me aside from some lip gloss in my purse. I hadn't planned to be out overnight, so why would I have that sort of stuff with me?

I made the bed, making sure there wasn't a mess that would require the sheets to be changed, and felt both good and bad that there wasn't. I mean, it meant I didn't have to figure out where the sheets were, but it also meant that we weren't quite as sloppy as we could have been. Of course, most of the sloppiness happened in the shower, so I guess it made sense.

I could only avoid leaving for so long before someone, specifically my brother, got suspicious of my absence. Walking out of the room, I turned to check that everything was put in its place, then made my way to the kitchen where my shoes and purse were. I sat down and pulled my shoes on, one at a time, then picked up my purse. Reaching inside, I didn't feel either of my phones, which was not something I wanted to have happen. I looked around and there was a note on the table from Spencer.

Darlin'
I plugged your phones in so they would be fully charged. They're on the counter next to the coffee maker. Feel free to make coffee, cocoa, or whatever else you want or need. There are tumblers that fit in cup holders in the cupboard right above the maker, and pods in the drawer underneath.
We're taking Billy's Jeep to the gym so you can get out of the garage. Text me if you want to stay again tonight, and I'll have Billy park his Jeep on the street so you can get in and out easily.

*We'd both love to have you, but don't want to push if you're not
ready for that. You brought us both immense pleasure having
you with us, and would love to continue with that, if you're
interested.*

*If you want to pretend this never happened, we can do that as
well. We can discuss this at any point, and you can tell us to go
away. I want to continue with the remodel and will definitely
pay whatever price you think is appropriate.*

Yours,

Spencer

It was a nice letter and gave me a way to walk away without
having to deal with the aftermath of having fucked my clients. But I
didn't want to walk away. I wanted to keep seeing them. I just had to
figure out how to do that without making it a problem for our
company.

Not wanting to explain where I got a tumbler, or why I had to
return it, I opted to just grab my phones and drive through a coffee
stand on the way to the office. Once I got there, I'd turn back on the
tracking shit on my phones. I also wanted to have a talk with Dee and
remind him that what I did, and who I did it with, were none of his
concern, and the fact that I was at a client's house for longer than he
thought was necessary didn't concern him when it meant additional
revenue for the company.

I grabbed both phones, dropped them in my purse, and walked
toward the garage door from the inside of the house. Spencer had left
the key ring with a spare key, as well as the garage door opener on top
of the letter so they were easy to find. I pressed the opener, then pulled
the door shut behind me before climbing into my car.

As I pulled out of the garage, I eased around Spencer's car, and
down the driveway, pressing the button to close the door, waiting until
it solidly settled on the ground before driving the rest of the way down
the driveway and onto the street.

When I turned into the parking lot for the office, Dee's car was
there, along with Brad's and a few of the other guys. I parked, turned

the car off, and climbed out. When I got close to the building, Dee burst out the door and pulled me to his chest.

"Oh my God," he said. "What the fuck were you thinking? You scared the shit out of me."

"What are you talking about?" I asked, pushing him off me.

"You turned your location off," he said.

"Told you I was gonna do that," I replied.

"But I didn't know you would do it on both phones," he said. "I didn't know where you were, what happened to you, or anything. I thought about calling Dad but didn't want to freak him out. I drove over to your house, but you never came home."

"I told you I wasn't gonna go home, either," I reminded him. "I need you to understand that I'm an adult, and I can do whatever the fuck I want. I can stay at a hotel, sleep in the park, stay with some rando, or go home. All are fine."

"So, you stayed in a hotel?" he asked.

"That's none of your business," I said. "Just like what I had for breakfast or whether I'm wearing underwear. None of that has any effect on my work, so you need to remember that."

"Are you seriously not gonna tell me where you were?"

"Why the fuck should I?" I asked. "Are you my parent? No. Are you in charge of what happens to me? Also, no. Does what I do have any bearing on you at all, in the least? No. You can't pretend to care about me after telling me I'm doing something you don't like, just because you don't like it. Now, can you move so I can get to work?"

He stood there, starting at me like I'd lost my fucking mind, and it was insane. If I were a teenager, sure, but I was old enough to know better, and had probably done more than him, anyway. I mean, I was a rebel, had been my whole life, so why he thought pulling a dad move was a good idea, baffled me.

When he didn't move, I sort of just pushed past him, going to my office to fire up my computer. I needed to get some shit set up for a couple of the other things I was working on, and I also needed to see about getting a tankless water heater installed over at the guys' house. There were a ton of moving parts, and I couldn't just stand around and let my brother be butt hurt over the fact that I wouldn't let him know where I was.

After a good while, when I'd cooled off some, and figured that Dee had pulled his head out of his ass, I walked to his office.

"Hey," I said, and he looked up at me, then back at his desk. "You gonna pretend I don't exist?"

"I'm busy," he said, but his voice was rough, and he didn't quite look right.

"Dee, what's up?"

"Go away," he said.

"No," I replied, leaning against the doorframe, folding my arms over my chest.

He kept ignoring me, pushing papers around on his desk. It was something he did when he was pissed, and I had the patience to wait him out. Finally, after a good fifteen minutes or so, he looked back up at me.

"Listen," I said.

"No," he replied. "You need to listen. I'm your big brother. It's my job to make sure you're safe and not in a place where you can be hurt. You took that away from me last night, and it really isn't nice. I had no idea whether you even left their house last night, because I couldn't remember where they were, and you're the only one who has the address for them. I went to your house hoping you would come home and we could talk, but you didn't. I was really worried."

The last few words broke, and he was biting his lip to keep from crying, and I'd never seen him like this before. I shoved off the doorframe and went around his desk, wrapping my arms around him to hold him.

"I don't wanna lose you," he said. "I can't lose someone else."

"Hey," I said, my own eyes tearing up. "You're not gonna lose me. I'm right here, and I'm fine. I'm not stupid. I promise. I was just fed up with you trying to parent me. I'm an adult. Have been for a few years now. And I'm pretty good at taking care of myself."

"But you're a girl," he said. "And guys are gonna wanna take advantage of you."

"Oh, I know," I said. "But sometimes I wanna take advantage of guys, too."

"Eww," he said. "I do not need to know about that."

"I'm just saying," I said. "Sometimes I wanna do things that you might not approve of. Hell, you might think it's fucking insane. But I'm an adult, and I promise I will make sure that I don't do anything stupid. Besides, I'm a woman, not a girl."

"Okay," he said. "I guess I see your point. I'm still gonna worry about you, though."

"I appreciate it," I said. "But let's hold off on the stalker shit, okay. You don't need to track my movements or make sure I go home every night. How do you know I didn't already have a date lined up and was planning on bringing him back to my place? That would have been fucking awkward to come home and have my brother there waiting for me."

"I guess I see your point," he said. "I just didn't want you getting messed up with those guys. There's something wrong with that one dude, the one with the longer hair. He's got some seriously crazy eyes."

"I'm sure he's harmless," I said. "But if it makes you feel better, I'll make sure the other guy is there at the same time and I'm not left alone with him. Okay?"

"That would make me feel better," he said.

"And another thing," I said. "I am going to leave my work phone at the office from now on. I'll have my personal phone with me but will be turning the tracking off at five every night. I will happily text you that I am safe, but if you start with this stalker shit again, all bets are off, and I'll see if I can make a way to take my half of the business and walk away. We are partners, and I know for fucking sure that you wouldn't be doing this if I was a guy."

"Don't even fucking joke about taking your half of the business," he said. "That's not something I ever want to hear you say again."

"Then you best make sure you keep yourself out of my personal life," I said. "Besides, do you really wanna know how freaky I can get?"

"Okay, eww, eww, stop it," he said, and I had to laugh.

"I think you understand what I'm saying, right?"

"I do," he said. "Doesn't mean I'm not gonna worry, though."

"I know," I said. "And I'm glad you're concerned. But don't push it, okay?"

"Okay," he said.

"I gotta get," I said. "I'm heading over to the Simpson place to see if we can settle on what exactly that woman wants."

"Better you than me," he said, but I just shook my head and headed back to my office.

I already missed the guys, but I didn't dare think about them. Just thinking about them made me want them, and me wanting them just got me frustrated, and that was so not what I wanted right then.

CHAPTER THIRTY-ONE

S pencer...

We went to the gym, did our reps, and headed back home. The system notified me that the garage door had opened and shut, so I knew she was headed to work. Just thinking about her in our house, our space, was something I could definitely get used to. Would she want to stick around for the long haul? That was yet to be determined. But, from the way she responded to us, she was definitely interested. At least for the short term.

"What do you want for lunch?" Billy asked as we pulled out of the lot.

"Not sure," I said. "But I wanna go to the store and grab some stuff to have at the house for dinner and the like."

"Oh, and for play?"

"Let's not push her," I said. "If we want to add things, we can bring something in from the dresser in the garage. In fact, might not be a bad idea to grab a few things and get them cleaned up and ready to go. She may not even come back, though, so don't get too worked up and anxious. I'd hate for you to be disappointed."

"She'll be back," he said.

"You sound damn sure," I said.

"I am," he replied. "Didn't you see her? Like, when you woke her up, she was well fucked, and wanting more."

"But she might come to her senses," I said. "Realize we're a couple of fucking insane dudes and never want to be anywhere near us again."

Just as I said it, my phone buzzed, and I pulled it out to see a text from her.

I'll be back around six.

It was short, but so sweet, and I was more than happy she'd decided to come back.

I'll make dinner. Any preference?

I waited, knowing we were going to the store, and I had to see what she wanted before we got there and bought shit she wouldn't eat. Not that I think she'd turn down food, but I liked to make sure my guests were pleased with my offerings.

Whatever you want is fine with me.

I smiled, and Billy looked at me.

"Told ya," he said.

"Yeah," I replied, happy he was right.

When we got to the grocery store, we grabbed a cart and started our trip. I knew I wanted to make something decent but wasn't sure what I was feeling like. What I did know was that I didn't want anything super heavy. Dense foods tended to slow me down, and I didn't want to be slow when it came to our beautiful woman. I also didn't want her to feel bloated or uncomfortable, so I had to choose wisely.

I could go with a salad of some sort but felt we would definitely need protein to get us through what I hoped would be another night filled with just as much passion as we'd had the night before. Since we had chicken last night, I thought about something more in the red meat category, and decided to get some stew meat, along with some steak.

I found a couple of New York strip steaks and figured I could make steak au poivre. I pulled out my phone to check the recipe and make sure we had everything I'd need. Nothing like wanting to make a dish and not having all the ingredients. Billy had gone off to pick up whatever the fuck it was he wanted, and I knew I'd see him eventually.

Wandering through the aisles, I picked up the ingredients I'd need, both for a good stew I could make in the crock pot, as well as the steak dish I planned for that evening. I also grabbed a few staples, and some asparagus to make as a side. I grabbed some potatoes, carrots, and celery, along with the garlic and shallots I'd need for both dishes. I was sure there would be enough left over that we wouldn't have to make anything new for at least a day or so.

By the time I had all that I needed, I headed around to see if I could see Billy anywhere. I was surprised I hadn't seen him in the produce section, what with his penchant for using food as a toy, but he hadn't been there. Finally, after wandering through most of the aisles, I saw him near the pharmacy area.

"Hey," I said, and he turned to me.

"Wanna stock up," he said, tossing three boxes of condoms into the cart.

I picked one up and saw it was a jumbo pack that boasted there were thirty-six in the box.

"Don't think we'll be using them all up tonight," I said.

"No," he replied. "But it's better to be safe than sorry."

I just shook my head. He was ridiculous if he thought we'd even use up one box, but it was his money, and I had no issue if that's what he wanted to spend it on. He also dropped a couple things of lube into the cart. When we got to the checkout, I made him take his shit out and put it up first. Then I'd get the groceries, and we'd be on our way.

"I'm so glad she's coming back," he said when we climbed into the Jeep. "What do you think she'll wanna do?"

"Don't know," I replied. "When we get home, park on the street so she can pull into the garage. I don't know if she's told her brother where she was last night, and I'm also not sure if she wants him to see where she is tonight, either. I just want her to feel safe and secure in knowing we won't tell him until she does."

"For sure," he said as he started it up.

The drive home was relatively short, and he was pulling up next to the curb in front of the house. He pressed the button for the garage, and I watched as it rolled up while I walked up the driveway. Walking into the garage, Billy went to the storage room and unlocked it while I continued into the house, hitting the button on the wall to shut the outer door.

I set the groceries on the counter and started to put things away, leaving the steak out so I could get some marinade going on it. Most of the taste would come in the cooking, but I knew I would need to add things to it before I stuck it in the fridge to get ready. By the time I was opening the package, Billy came in, his bag much heavier than when he got out of the car.

"What the fuck did you get?" I asked.

"Just a few things," he said, setting the bag on the other side of the counter. "I gotta wash them all off so we can use them."

"If she wants," I added.

"Well, yeah," he said. "I know that. I just would rather have them ready to go and not need to delay than have to go find something and wash it."

He dumped the toys in the sink, and he was right. He'd gotten several items from the dresser, all of which would be fun to use with Ariana. As much as I wanted to believe that I wasn't a fucked-up individual, looking at the sink full of sex toys and thinking about using them on a woman sort of made it clear that I was about as fucked up as they came. But I always made sure I got consent before doing anything with anyone.

Billy turned the water on and waited for it to get hot before he started in on cleaning the toys. Reaching under the sink, he pulled out the bottle of soap we had especially for cleaning them, making sure to wash each item with care to get into any crevices or creases that might be there.

While he did that, I worked on getting our food ready to go, so that when she got here, we could either start dinner, or start playing. I was a fan of playing first, then eating after, although it would be up to her how she wanted to do things. She was our guest, and we always treated our guests right.

Just as I was putting the steaks into the fridge, my phone buzzed, and I pulled it out, shutting the door.

Still coming, just running late. Don't wait on dinner for me.

Well, if she thought we'd eat without her, she was mistaken.

We'll eat when you get here.

She sent a blushing emoji, so I guess she knew we wouldn't start without her.

Now that we knew she would be late, I went ahead and started cleaning up the bedroom. I wasn't a slob, but there were things that were left out that didn't need to be. I also started a load of laundry, got clothes put away, and even stripped and remade the bed. It hadn't exactly been dirty, but I wanted fresh sheets on there for tonight.

We got the toys cleaned up, dried them off, and placed them all on a towel on the edge of the bed. After I'd vacuumed the room, Billy helped me move the cross from the office in so we had another option if she was interested. The fact that she'd let us play, had been very compliant to our wants, and felt comfortable staying the night, told me that she was going to be with us for a while. I mean, her company was going to be doing a huge renovation, so that necessitated her being here. But she would likely stay with us, off and on, for the duration.

Once we headed south for spring training, she may have doubts, but while we were here, we would give her our undivided attention. Hopefully, we'd build enough of a relationship before we left that it wouldn't matter. On the other hand, we could also bring her down to stay with us there, too. Billy owned the condo we used while we were there, and there was plenty of room for her to stay. Of course, all that was jumping well ahead of what we were doing now, which was simply enjoying each other's company.

I flipped the laundry, started the sheets, and made sure there were plenty of towels in the bathroom. I also put condoms and a bottle of lube out and ready to go for when we got started. When I felt like the room was as put together as it could be, I headed to the kitchen to make sure it was ready to cook dinner, and that the table was set with everything we'd need to eat.

Billy was at the sink again, but I wasn't sure what he was doing. I walked over to see him washing another bunch of toys.

"Don't you think that's a bit of overkill?" I asked.

"It's one of those things," he said. "I never know what I want until I want it, and I don't know what she'll be comfortable with. We also don't know if she'll want to do anything at all, or if she'll just want us.

While I don't want to overwhelm her, I also want her to be able to pick anything she's interested in trying. Nothing wrong with expanding her horizons, giving her something new to try."

"You sure she hasn't tried some of these before?" I asked.

"Oh, I'm sure she has," he said. "She's played well. Of that, I have no doubt. The smirks she gave, the way she played coy, but knew what to do. Yeah, she's done some fun stuff. I just wonder how far she'll let us go, you know? Like, what all will she let us do with her?"

"Won't you overwhelm her?" I asked. "I mean, we have a shit ton of toys, and so far, we haven't used anything but ourselves."

"My guess is, she's wanting us to go all in," he said. "Did you not see her when she strapped me on that?"

"She was tentative," I said.

"Oh, no," he said. "She knew exactly what she was doing. She was playing shy and coy with us, luring us in so that we'd be suckered by her. I mean, come on. She didn't even bat an eye at the cage. You can't tell me she hasn't fucked a ton of guys and done a ton of fucked-up shit like we do."

"She was actually intrigued by the thought of both of us," I admitted. "So, yeah, I guess you're right. Maybe she is just waiting to see what we had to offer."

"Told ya," he crowed. "Now, come on and let's get the rest of these in the room before we start making dinner."

CHAPTER THIRTY-TWO

A riana...

I'd been stuck at the Simpson place, the husband and wife trying to figure out exactly what they wanted, which turned out to be the complete opposite of each other. It had taken all my strength to not just tell them to forget it and walk away. I didn't, obviously, but I wanted to. Instead, I told them to take a look at what I'd given them, decide which pieces they both liked, and we'd see if we could come to a compromise. I promised that I would definitely help with getting everything they both wanted, but that may end up being futile if they kept at it.

We'd done several designs for them, brought them in to make sure what we were doing would work for them, then they'd change something and ask us to redo it all. I wanted to throw in the towel, but with what Dee had said about needing the business, I opted to just give them false hope and deal with whatever happened later than sit there and deal with their talking over the other one without making any decisions. She'd say she wanted this, he'd say he wanted that instead, back and forth they went, and my God, all I wanted to do was take a big gulp from a bottle of damn near any alcoholic beverage I could get my hands on.

When I finally left, it was well after dinner time, and I felt bad that the guys might have waited to eat. I turned off my locator after sending a text to Dee to let him know I was running by the house to grab a couple of things before going to stay at a friend's place. I still wasn't over the fact that he was low-key stalking me, so I told him that if I saw him, or anyone else following me, I would pull into the closest stop and rob and get out and confront him. Thankfully, he'd told me that he'd stop worrying, and that as long as I was safe, being safe, and not doing anything that would put me in harm's way, he'd be fine.

Was what I was doing safe? Maybe. But the bigger question was whether it was the right thing to be doing. There's a reason for the saying, "Don't shit where you eat," and I was doing a whole lot of things that made that statement a problem. Was I shitting? No, but I was fucking, and that was just about as bad. There shouldn't have to be a rule that says to not fuck the customers, but I had jumped so far over that rule that it was not even a glimmer in my rearview mirror.

Instead of doing what was right, what was logical, and what was safe, I went home, grabbed a quick shower, making sure I was very clean in all the right places, then put on my sexiest bra and panty set under everyday clothes. It wasn't often I got the chance to wear something that made me feel pretty, but the guys had given me an incentive. Not only did I want to please them, but I also figured they'd want to please me, and would be happy I thought ahead and went the extra mile to make sure I was more than presentable when I showed up.

As I drove through the posh neighborhood, looking at the high-priced homes with their equally high-priced views, their expensive cars in their driveways, manicured front yards, and everything in its place, I wondered if I would fit in here. It wasn't the first time I was with a guy with money, but he'd been super secretive. Turned out, he was married, and I was a side piece. That's why I could never go to his place, and we had always gone to mine. I had figured he was still living with his parents, but turned out he was the parent.

My brother had known about my mistakes but hadn't pushed me on anything more than checking to see if I was safe. Now, though, he seemed to be wanting more information on my life outside the business. He wanted to know where I was, who I was with, and what I was doing. It grated on me when he started it, but I had to believe it was coming from a place of love and caring. Either that, or he was worried about the business, and deflecting that concern over to something he thought he could control. Me.

I saw the Jeep on the road, which meant they'd left me room to pull all the way into the garage. I was thankful for that, as it meant that even if my brother did suspect something, he wouldn't see my car on the street or in their driveway. Turning in, I reached over and grabbed the opener from my glovebox, which was where I'd stashed it after I left that morning. No need to leave it out where someone could see it, take it, or ask me about it. I didn't have one at my house, so if someone at the shop saw it, they'd ask, and that was a question I didn't want to answer.

The door rumbled up as I waited on the other side, and when it was up enough for me to see into the garage, the door to the house was open, and Billy was standing at the top of the handful of steps, leaning against the railing, waiting. I had to admit it gave me a sort of thrill to know that he was there and waiting. Knowing he wanted to see me, wanted to be with me, and was greeting me as I got there, was something I'd never felt, and hadn't really thought I would.

It wasn't that I was old, per se, more that I just felt like that part of me, the one that would find a guy, settle down, and start a family was over. Mom had Dee when she was still in college, and I was damn near right on his heels, just thirteen months later. I always thought I'd follow her in that regard, but that just wasn't meant to be. Not that I wanted kids and all that, at least not right now. No, now I wanted to play, and seeing Billy waiting for me, and knowing that Spencer was just inside, made my heart do that sort of pitter pat that it does when you're more than just a little happy.

"Hey, Angel," he said as I climbed out of the car. "We missed you today."

"Trust me," I said. "I would have much rather been here than with the people I was with."

"Work that bad?" he asked.

"Sometimes clients are a pain in the ass," I said as I went up the steps.

"Then we will feed you and pleasure you until you've forgotten all about them," he said, pulling me up to him and kissing me fiercely.

I melted into him, my arms going up and around his neck as his went behind my back, pulling me against his hard chest, and hard cock, that was definitely not caged. Was it weird that I was glad it was free? Probably. But that didn't matter right now. No, now I needed him, and Spencer, to get my mind off everything going on in my life.

"I'm going to enjoy you tonight," he said as he pulled away. "You taste like everything delicious in the world."

"Shit," I said, and he looked at me. "I forgot my bag."

"Get in there," he said, taking my keys from me. "I've got your bag, Spencer is waiting."

He smacked my ass as he went past, then grabbed it, rubbing where he'd spanked me before going down the stairs to get the bag from the back seat. I walked into the kitchen to see that there were candles set up on the table, and it was set for a feast. Whatever they were making smelled amazing, and my stomach rumbled at the scent.

"Hey," Spencer said, turning from the stove. "You're just in time."

"What did you make?" I asked, moving toward him.

"It's called steak au poivre," he said.

"Never heard of it," I replied.

"It's delicious," he said. "Just like you. It should be ready in just a minute or two. Why don't you sit down and relax while we finish up."

"What can I do to help?" I asked.

"Absolutely nothing," Billy said, setting my bag on the couch. "You are our guest and will be treated as the goddess you are."

I laughed because I was about as far from a goddess as they came. But when I went to sit down, they pointed to the head of the table, with them set to sit on either side of me. It was weird to sit there, because that's where my dad always sat at home when we were growing up. I always thought it was the place where the head of the family sat, and I was most assuredly not the head of any family.

"Billy," Spencer said. "Pull the wine out of the fridge and open it. It needs to rest a bit before we pour it. I'm sort of at the mercy of the food, or I'd do it."

"Of course," he replied, going to the fridge. "Which one?"

"The red," Spencer said. "It should be in the door. You can drink wine, can't you?" he asked me.

"Oh, yeah," I said. "I mean, I don't often, but that's because I'm cheap. But yeah, I can, and do drink wine."

"Then you are in for a treat," Spencer said. "This was something I picked up last year when we were in New York. Well, picked out and had shipped, but still."

"He's always finding things to ship home," Billy said as he pulled a bottle from the fridge. "Most of it's good shit, though, so I don't mind."

"I get that," I replied. "I mean, if I had the money, I'd be picking up a ton of things I wanted."

"Ask, and we shall find and deliver it," Billy said, doing a sort of bow thing before pulling open a drawer.

He pulled out a corkscrew that had a sort of knife thing on the edge of it. Taking the blade, he sliced open the foil around the top of the bottle, then pressed the screw into the cork, turning it down and down and down some more. Why the fuck was that turning me on? I mean, he's opening a fucking bottle and I'm getting wet. There's something definitely wrong with me.

"I think our lady is ready for her dessert," Spencer said, and my eyes flashed to him.

He'd pulled the pot off the stove and set it on the countertop next to the steak that had been resting there when I walked in. There were other dishes there as well, just waiting to be set on the table, was my guess. I hadn't noticed before, but he was wearing an apron. Nothing fancy or stupid, just a nice crisp white material that had a strap around his neck, and cords to go around his waist. As he walked toward me, though, he began to untie it, and damn if that wasn't sexy.

"Oh, yeah," Billy said, having pulled the cork out of the bottle. "I wonder whether she'd like to partake here at the table, or if we should go to the bedroom."

In the span of a few seconds, he'd already pulled his shirt off over his head, and was stalking toward me right behind Spencer. There was a feral look in his eyes that I hadn't seen before, and I wondered if it had always been there and I'd just never noticed it, or if this was something new.

"Well," Spencer said, drawing the word out and drawing my attention away from Billy and back to him.

"I don't know," I stammered, unclear exactly what they had in mind.

"We're happy with whatever you want to do," he said, kneeling in front of me having dropped his apron on the back of one of the chairs. "We can eat first, but I don't think that's what you want."

"No," I said, more a rush of air than anything else. "I want you. I want you both," I added, turning to include Billy in the conversation.

"That's what I like to hear," Billy said.

"But how do you want us?" Spencer asked. "On the table like the first time? Or in the bed like the most recent time? Or the shower?"

"Or anywhere else your mind might think up," Billy added. "We do have a collection of toys in the bedroom, if you're interested in seeing what might pique your interest."

"I don't know," I said, feeling the pressure of all the decisions being placed on me. "I just know that I want you, and sooner is better as far as I'm concerned."

Spencer reached out, hooking his hand under my shirt, and lifting it slightly. I went with the motion, raising my hands as he pulled it up and over my head. Billy was still in his sweats, but they were straining at the front, and I wanted him in me in some form or another. Spencer pulled off my shoes, then helped me to stand, undoing my belt, button, and zipper before pressing my pants down.

"Oh, goodie," Billy said, coming closer. "Looks like our little angel has dressed special for the occasion."

"Thought you might appreciate it," I said.

"Oh, I do," he replied, his eyes running over my body in a way I could feel. "I very much do appreciate a well-packaged gift."

I was down to just my bra and panties, and somehow the men were still mostly dressed. It reminded me of the first night, and how I was naked on the table and they were both mostly clothed. Well, Spencer was. Billy seemed to like to go without clothes, which was why I was surprised he hadn't gone that route, yet.

Spencer stood up after taking my jeans off and just sort of stood there, a small smile on his lips. I wasn't sure why he was just there, not moving in. In fact, they were both just standing and waiting on me. I didn't know what to do, but didn't want to disappoint either of them, so I reached out one hand and pressed it against Spencer's chest, pushing him back just a step before turning and heading down the hallway.

Billy had mentioned toys, and I was curious as to what they might have, so I wanted to see for myself. I could hear them following behind me but didn't bother to turn around. Instead, I stepped into the bedroom with its giant bed and large space for whatever else they wanted to put into it and had to stop in the doorway. I blinked for a minute or two, just staring at everything that was around. Off to the left there was the contraption that we'd hooked Billy up to the night before, but there was also this giant X shaped thing that had these sort of padded bracelet things at the top and bottom of each point. While I was sure I knew what that was for, I was also sure that I didn't want to be attached to it. Being completely helpless did not interest me at all.

On the end of the bed there were a couple of large towels, each of which had so many things on them I wondered how many women they had waiting in the wings, and it sort of made me pause. What was I doing? This wasn't just fun play, this was starting to feel like it was moving entirely too fast, and I sort of had to just sit down on the floor and think. I could feel them behind me, not moving, not too close, but there just the same. It was like all of a sudden I was prey, and they were the predators, and that terrified me.

"Darlin'," Spencer said, his voice so close I could feel the breath on my shoulder. "You don't have to do anything you don't want to. All of these are just options, but nothing is necessary. In fact, you don't even have to do anything with us. We enjoy being with you, whether or not it includes sex."

"Sorry," I said.

"Nothing to be sorry about," he replied. "We sort of rushed things, and that was our bad. You want to slow down, just get to know us better, we're cool with that. You want there to be no relationship outside of business, that's what it'll be."

"I just didn't expect all this," I said, still looking around the room. "It's just... It's a lot."

"That's on me," Billy said, and he was on the other side of me, both of them not touching me, but right there. "I sort of got a little enthusiastic. You're absolutely gorgeous, Angel, and I would do just about anything you wanted me to."

I turned to look at him over my shoulder and could see that he was telling the truth. He really did just sort of go overboard. When I looked over at Spencer, he had a look of concern on his face. But it was different from Billy's. Where Billy looked like he was sad that he'd done something wrong, Spencer had a look that he was worried he'd hurt me. They were so different from each other that I wondered how they had even started this insane thing between the two of them.

"Let's start simple," Spencer said, holding a hand out to me.

I took it, and he helped me to my feet. Billy rose with us, still not touching me, but so close I could feel his warmth. There was this electricity between us, a palpable thing I could almost touch. I was both terrified of it and fascinated by it in equal measures. God, I wanted this, but I also knew it was a slippery slope that might end in disaster. It could fuck us over, and not in the good way. The company's reputation could be trashed, and my brother, father, and everyone who worked with us could be caught up in some scandal that ran rampant through the area. I didn't want that, but I was called to them, like they were some sirens and I was the fucking captain of a ship, willing to sail into the rocks and die just to hear their song.

"Shower with me?" I asked, looking first to Spencer, then over to Billy. "Both of you?"

Billy's eyes lit up like it was fucking Christmas morning, and Spencer had that coy smile he had the night before. I think that was about as excited as he ever got. I aimed to change that, starting with the shower.

CHAPTER THIRTY-THREE

B illy...
    I was terrified we'd fucked up. Or rather, that I'd fucked up with my enthusiasm for bringing in all the things. I mean, I hadn't intended for us to use everything. I just wanted her to have choices. We were still new at this, and I didn't know what she did and didn't want to do. It's a good thing Spencer is so fucking smooth, cause he made sure she didn't rabbit on us and run. Instead, she'd invited us to join her in the shower, which, fuck yeah, I was down for.

As much as I wanted to fuck her while she was still wearing that sexy bra and panty set, her naked was better. She'd tied her hair up and out of the way, braiding it and wrapping it. She'd said it would take too long to dry if she left it down, which I understood.

"You guys need to get naked before me," she said when we got to the bathroom. "It seems unfair that I'm always less dressed than the two of you."

I didn't even hesitate. I had already taken my shirt off, so I just started on the jeans I was wearing, pulling the button from the eye first, then lowering the zipper. She seemed to be watching me, intensely, and then her pretty pink tongue poked out of her mouth as she licked her lips. Fuck, did that make me even harder. I slowed down, moving at a snail's pace, prolonging it as much as I could.

Spencer had pulled his shirt off and was watching her watch me. He got off on watching just as much as I did, and knowing he was enjoying her made it even better. Try as I might, I could only take so long before I was all the way to the bottom of my zipper. I opened the fly, letting my cock out, and her eyes widened. I think she'd only seen me in the cage, not out of it, because when I'd fucked her pussy the night before, she'd been looking at Spencer.

"You like it?" I asked and watched her lick her lips. "Oh, yeah. I think she likes it."

"She does," Spencer said, and she turned to him. "I can smell you, and my God, do you smell delicious."

She bit her lower lip, then looked down at Spencer's crotch and back up to him. I knew what she wanted, and I was sure Spencer did, too, but it was fun to see how she'd handle it. I couldn't see her face much, but knew she was staring into Spencer's eyes. When the tug came at the edge of his mouth, I smiled big, cause I knew she got to him, and he wasn't gonna wait any longer.

"You want these off?" he asked, and she nodded. "Oh, Darlin', that's not gonna work for me. I'm gonna need you to tell me what you want."

"Pretty sure I already told you want I wanted," she said, and damn was she feisty. "In fact, I said it pretty clearly just a couple of minutes ago." She turned back to me, her eyes light with amusement. "You didn't need to stop," she said to me. "You're just barely there. Get 'em off. You, too," she said when she turned back to Spencer.

"Well, well, well," Spencer said as he began to unbutton his jeans. "Looks like our girl's got a mouth on her."

"She knows how to use it, too," I said as I shoved my jeans down my legs, pulling them off by stepping on them. "I wonder what else she's good at doing with that mouth."

"You both know how good my mouth is," she said. "And neither of you are gonna get anything from it, or any other part of me, until you're naked. I'd suggest you get to going on that, cause I'm getting hungry, and that food smelled too fucking good to let it go to waste."

I'd finished pulling my jeans off and stood there naked as the day I was born. Spencer was making fairly good time with his own but made a show out of it because she was watching him. We were both assholes, and weren't afraid to make someone wait for us, so it didn't surprise me that he took his sweet time.

"Better?" he asked once he'd finally pulled his jeans off.

"So far," she said, then stepped back so she could see the both of us. "Damn, if you two aren't a sight. So hard, so ready. I fucking love it."

"You seem ready, yourself," Spencer said. "I can smell you from here, and I wanna have my dessert, and soon."

She sort of slid her feet apart, opening herself, and waited. When neither of us moved, she kind of did a little huff and stood back up, shoving her panties down before reaching behind her and undoing her bra, letting it fall to the floor on top of her panties.

"I'm wet," she said, stepping between us and into the shower. "You should join me."

With that, she turned the water on, letting it get warm before she stood under the spray. It didn't take me any time at all to be between her and the water, my arms wrapped around her from behind, holding her just under her breasts. Spencer stepped in, kneeling in front of her, and reached out to lift one of her legs up and over his shoulder.

"Didn't want to wash all that flavor away," I said in her ear. "Would be a terrible shame to waste it when we're right here and able to partake of your nectar."

"You're ridiculous," she said.

Whatever she was going to add was taken away when Spencer shoved his finger inside her and pulled her clit into his mouth. She moaned deep in her throat and relaxed into my arms. My cock was just above her ass, and I shifted, spreading my legs just enough so that I could get my dick in line with the crack of her ass. I wasn't gonna shove it in, or even slide it between her thighs. I just wanted to slide it up in the back of her crack, kinda like a hot dog in a bun.

Her little moans increased, and I think Spencer knew what I'd done, cause he sort of pressed her back further into me, then picked up her other leg so she could be spread even further. He was fucking her with his fingers, sucking her clit, and I felt him slide his other hand back toward her asshole.

We'd discussed that the night before but hadn't come to any sort of decision. Well, she hadn't said what she wanted, but I knew Spencer well enough that he'd press close, see what her reaction was, and if she told him to stop, he would. His fingers brushed my balls, which made my cock jump, which pulled a gasp out of her.

That's when he slid the finger in. I could tell because she tensed up a bit. I knew it wasn't in far, 'cause he didn't do that. Just enough for her to feel the pressure and make a response.

"Oh, God," she said, the words coming out in a moan. "Oh my God."

"That's it, Angel," I said in her ear. "We've got you. Relax and let it happen."

He must have slid out a bit, then in again, because she tensed up again, but then moaned deeply. God, she was so responsive, and all it did was make my cock throb. I wanted inside her so bad, but knew we needed to get her over the hill and falling to pieces before we got to that point. She wouldn't be ready for the both of us until she'd had at least a couple of orgasms.

"Come for us," I whispered in her ear, reaching one hand up and tweaking her nipple. "Fall apart and let us catch you."

And she did. She spasmed, her hands on my forearms, grasping and clenching as she exploded, and I held her up as Spencer continued to fuck her. Her thighs tightened against his head, and still he kept at it. Her little cries, her rasping voice, and finally, she called both our names.

"Billy," she cried. "Spencer. Oh God, please don't let it stop."

CHAPTER THIRTY-FOUR

Ariana...

I didn't know it was possible to come so hard, but my God, did these two pull everything from me. Once I was finished, Spencer was setting my feet on the tile, but Billy continued to hold me fast against his body. As he stood, Spencer moved in, sandwiching me between himself and Billy, lowering his mouth to mine.

I kissed him deep, tasting myself on his lips and tongue, and it was ecstasy. I didn't want the time to end, but they'd shut the water off and just held me until my breathing returned to normal. Once I was back to myself again, Spencer stepped back and reached for a towel, wrapping it around me as Billy let me go.

Picking me up, Spencer carried me across the tile of the bathroom, the carpet of the bedroom, and set me on the bed so he could dry me properly. The rhythm of the towel rubbing against my body made me relax even more, and it didn't take long for Billy to be beside him, a towel wrapped around his waist.

"Hungry?" he asked.

"Yeah," I said, and he nodded and left the room.

"Here you go," Spencer said, pulling the towel from around me and using it to dry himself. "Let's get you fed so we can have some more fun."

He helped me to my feet, then pointed me toward the door to the rest of the house.

"I should put something on," I said.

"Nah," Spencer replied. "We like to look at you."

"It kinda feels weird," I said. "I mean, I don't mind being naked, but sitting down to eat dinner without clothes on is just odd."

"Like I said, we like to look at you," Spencer said. "Is that a problem?"

"You guys aren't naked," I complained, but when I turned back to look at him, he was. "I mean, Billy's not. He had a towel on."

"I'm sure he's gonna use it to set on your chair," Spencer said. "We want you comfortable, but we also want you naked."

We stepped out of the hall, and Spencer had been right. The chair at the head of the table had been draped with the towel Billy took with him. He was pouring wine into three glasses, and there were plates already filled at each of the seats. My stomach growled at the smell, and I felt super self-conscious until Spencer wrapped his hand around my waist.

"Let's fill you up," he said. "Then, later, we'll fill you a different way."

He pressed his lips to the shell of my ear, and I shivered from the sensation.

"It smells so good," I said as I sat in the chair they had set up for me.

"Spencer is a fucking amazing chef," Billy said. "I can't cook nearly as good as him, but I'm learning."

"Like any skill, it takes time," Spencer said.

They both sat there, hands on the edge of the table, watching me.

"You should eat," Billy said. "He won't until you do. It's a thing with him."

"Why aren't you eating?" I asked him.

"Because I wanna see you use that pretty little mouth of yours," he said. "Shove that meat in there like the good girl you are."

I licked my lips, because the smell of the food was getting to me, and both men sort of leaned in. Smiling a little at their reaction, I picked up my fork and knife and sliced a small piece of the steak with its sauce on top of it, then put it into my mouth. Everything I did was in slow motion, moving the fork to my mouth, inserting it in, closing my lips, and slowly, so fucking slowly, I pulled it out, using my teeth and lips to hold the steak in.

The flavors exploded in my mouth, tastes I'd never had before, and I let my eyes slip shut, simply enjoying the food. There was a very peppery taste to it, but the sauce blended so well that it wasn't over-powering. While creamy, the sauce wasn't heavy, and it melded with the flavor of the meat itself, causing every tastebud in my mouth to sit up and take notice.

"I think she likes it," Billy said, and I opened my eyes and looked at him, then over to Spencer.

"I've never had anything this good in my entire life," I said.

"I just hope you make those sounds when we're together in the bed," Spencer said.

"Or anywhere when we're together," Billy added.

I felt the rush of blood to my face, heat rising from my breasts up and all the way over my face. Honestly, if we'd been eating lobster, I would likely have rivaled its color.

"Don't be embarrassed," Spencer said. "I'm glad you like it. I just hope you like us just as much."

"Oh, I do," I said after swallowing. "Now, will you both please eat? You're making me self-conscious."

"Your wish is my command," Billy said, picking up his fork.

They both did, and each took a bite of their own steak. Neither of them made any noise when they ate it, though, but watching them put the food in their mouth, the way their mouths moved, and how they swallowed, got my fire stoking again, and I had to press my thighs together to try and stave off the desire.

"I can still smell you," Billy said, and my face again brightened. "Don't stop. I love the way your fragrance melds with the food. Makes me want to use you as a plate. Put my food on you and lick it off."

He licked his lips after he said that, and it did nothing to quell my desire. I was such a fucking slut when it came to these two, doing things I'd never, even in my wildest dreams, thought I'd be doing. I didn't even know I wanted to do them, let alone fantasize about it.

"Dessert will be fun," Spencer said, and I looked at him. "Did you think we'd be done after this meal?"

"I didn't know," I said. "I mean, there's plenty of food."

I sort of shrugged, not really knowing how to respond to him. But his words tumbled in my brain, rolling around and making me wonder what they had in mind. I'd done some of the kinky stuff with some exes, whipping cream or chocolate flavoring, but they seemed to be planning something much more involved, and that made me both terrified and excited.

"Eat up," he said, pointing his fork to my food. "I slaved most of the day for that. You should enjoy it."

"I will," I said, carving another piece from the steak.

CHAPTER THIRTY-FIVE

S pencer...

She ate, and it was everything I had hoped for. The way she savored my food, the little moans she gave as she tasted it, and the desire I could smell coming from her, all made me stay hard the entire meal. I was sure Billy had been as well, but neither of us let her know. No, she'd find out how fucking hot she was once we stepped away from the table. At least we were in our own home, not at a restaurant where we'd have to hide our desire.

By the time she'd finished her serving and set her fork down, both Billy and I had long since cleaned our plates. As much as I wanted to just take her here, doing so would spoil all the effort we'd taken to open ourselves up to showing her who we were. No, we needed to hold out a little bit, see how she wanted to work this, and what she would be willing to do.

"That was amazing," she said, licking her lips, and fuck, did that make me want her. "But I think you said something about dessert."

The fire in her eyes told me she knew exactly what she was doing.

"You saying you're still hungry?" Billy asked. "'Cause there's plenty more. I can dish you up another plate."

She turned and looked at him. Watching him react to the same look I'd gotten was fucking hilarious, and I couldn't help but laugh.

"I think she was looking for something else," I said. "And I've got something very specific in mind."

I got up, and her eyes went right to my cock, which was standing out, just begging for her touch. She opened her eyes, shifted in her seat, and let her tongue roll out and over her lips. Everything was tempting me to just say fuck it and pin her to the chair and fuck her mouth. But I wanted to wait, wanted this to play out, see how much we could get from her.

Picking up her plate, I kissed her temple before taking my own and walking to the sink. I heard Billy get up and grab his plate as well, and when she sucked in her breath, I knew we were getting to her. She was a cute little mouse, and the two of us were definitely playing with our food.

"Can I help?" she asked, and we both turned to see her standing right behind us.

"Oh, Angel," Billy said. "*You* are a guest. We're here to serve you. Let us do that, please?"

She turned to me, but I just looked at her, unable to form words around the desire coursing through me.

"I feel bad that you guys cooked for me," she said. "I'd like to help at least clean up."

"You clean up just fine," Billy said. "In fact, why don't you head to the bedroom and see if there's anything you want to play with that we have out on the bed. That will give us a minute to clean this up and bring in dessert."

"You're sure?"

"Absolutely," I said. "Now, scoot."

I gave her a playful smack on her ass, and she yipped, fire rushing to her cheeks. She turned and walked away, and both Billy and I stared after her, watching her shapely ass sway as she sauntered across the kitchen and toward the hall.

"Holy fuck," Billy whispered when she was out of earshot.

"Yeah," I replied.

"So, dessert?"

"I have some chocolate mousse," I said. "I also have chocolate-covered strawberries, fresh whipping cream, and caramel syrup. I even pulled out some sparkling wine. There will be plenty for us to share."

"I wanna suck syrup from her pussy," he said, then licked his lips, his hand going to his cock to fist it.

"Dishes," I said, and he pulled the dishwasher open to start loading it.

I didn't bother to pack up the rest of the food, it was still too warm to be done. We would have time to do it later on. Now, I wanted to get what we needed ready and head into the bedroom to see what she'd chosen. Much as I wanted to strap her down and split roast her, I wasn't sure she would be into that, at least not yet. In time, maybe.

Pulling the mousse from the fridge, along with the strawberries, I placed them both on the island. The wine came out next, along with the whipping cream. I grabbed a tray from the cupboard, then set it all on top, before grabbing a handful of napkins and a couple of glasses. By the time I had everything loaded up, I turned to see that Billy had finished the dishes and was ready to go.

He went first, walking down the hall toward my room. I followed with the tray, taking my time, knowing that Billy wouldn't start anything without me. Especially since I had the food. He was a fucking nut when it came to food and sex. It was like they were symbiotic and needed to be enjoyed together.

When I turned the corner, Ari was standing next to the bed, her hands sort of hovering over all the toys laid out, and Billy was standing just inside the door watching her. I'm not sure if she heard us come in, or she might have stopped what she was doing. Instead, she picked up one of the toys on the towel, turning it over in her hand. I couldn't see what it was, but Billy sort of moved toward her.

"They're anal beads," he said when he got to her, and she jumped, turning and looking at him, holding the toy to her chest. "You can put them in me, or I can put them in you. Spencer won't use them, though, so don't ask."

She looked past him to me as I was setting the tray down on the nightstand, and her eyes went to all the food.

"Is all that for tonight?" she asked.

"We don't have to use it all," I said. "Just want to have enough to enjoy. The rest will keep for another time."

"Won't that make a mess?"

Her eyes were big, not overtly so, but big enough that she wasn't sure what we were planning to do. Billy walked up to the head of the bed and pulled down the comforter, blanket, and top sheet, opening it up so that there was room for us all to climb up. When he had it down enough to get to the side, he pulled the bottom sheet up a bit and showed her what was underneath.

"We're not new at this," he said. "We plan ahead. This will keep the mattress clean, catch anything that might fall off, and we can pull the sheets off when we're done and throw them in the washer. Don't worry about making a mess. Sex is better when its messy."

"Oh," she said, and that simple word wasn't enough. "I mean, I guess if you guys do this all the time, then you'd know."

"We don't do it all the time," I corrected. "In fact, we usually don't bring folks home. Only occasionally, and only with purpose and a plan."

I looked at Billy when I said the last, and hopefully he knew it was about the woman he'd brought home last time. I wasn't bothered about it, just needed to know in advance, and he knew that. It was a rule that we'd established early on in our relationship, strange as it was.

"Yeah," Billy said. "Sorry about that."

"What do you mean?" she asked.

"Let's not talk about that," he said. "Tonight is about you. I want to see how many times we can make you come. You up for the challenge?"

She took a deep breath, nodded, then looked at me and said, "Yes."

"Good girl," I said, glad that she'd remembered my comment about her needing to speak her words. "Shall we talk about rules?"

"Oh," she said. "I mean, I didn't know there were rules."

"There's always rules, Darlin'," I said. "Rules keep everyone safe and make sure that everyone has a good time. First question; do you have any hard limits? Anything you absolutely will not do?"

"I don't know," she said. "I mean, I've never thought about

anything like this before. Okay, I've thought about some of this, but never quite in this context."

"Consent is sexy," Billy said, sliding his fingers down her arm. "We'll start slow, work our way up, and anything you don't want to do, you just tell us to stop."

"If your mouth is full," I added, winking at her. "Then you just snap your fingers and we'll back off."

"You ready?" Billy asked, and she looked back at him, still holding the plug in her hands.

"Yeah," she said.

"You good with kissing?" I asked as I stepped next to her.

"I really like kissing," she said, turning to look up at me.

"Me, too," I said, lowering my mouth to hers.

She leaned into the kiss, turning her body toward me. One hand went around my waist while the other reached up to my neck. She either dropped the plug, or Billy had taken it from her, but she didn't have it in her hands. My arms were around her waist, holding her against my body. She pressed her body into mine, going up on her toes to gain some height. Her kiss was full of passion, and I could still taste dinner on her tongue.

I felt the pressure as Billy pressed into her from behind, my hand trapped between us, his hand sliding between my body and hers, sliding down toward the apex of her legs. We'd learned how to do this without actually grabbing each other's cocks. I was sure he wouldn't care, but I did. Nothing wrong with swinging both ways, but that wasn't me.

When she sucked in a breath, I knew he'd dipped his hand far enough to start moving along her pussy. She pulled back, gasping and leaning back against him, but looking up at me. I stepped back just a bit, pressing kisses down her neck, stopping at the hollow of her throat for a quick lick, then further down. I knew that Billy was holding her up, just as he'd done in the shower, so I didn't worry about her falling. Instead of going to her pussy, though, I pulled one of her nipples into my mouth, sucking hard to get it to peak, then pulling on it with my teeth just enough to get another intake of breath from her.

"Let's get you up on the bed," Billy said. "That way we can both reach more of you."

She nodded, then said, "Okay," before walking with Billy over to the side of the bed. He lifted her up, letting her feet go first onto the bed before sort of sliding her further over.

"Was there something you wanted to start with first?" I asked.

"Surprise me," she said. "Just tell me what you're going to do so I can be prepared."

"Absolutely," I said.

Snagging one of the vibrators from the stack at the foot of the bed, I crawled up to her, showing her the device I'd selected. It was one of the ones that had a sort of sucking thing on it, that if you positioned it right, it would pull the clit into it and add that extra sensation. Billy had grabbed the bottle of wine, pouring some into one of the glasses. Climbing onto the bed, he knelt next to her head, his cock almost touching her face.

"I want to suck this from your body," he said. "Can I pour some onto your belly and drink it from your navel?"

She sort of shuddered, then said, "Yeah."

He crawled over to her stomach, then gently poured some of the wine out. She flinched as it hit her skin but didn't move much more. He was smart in that he only poured a little out, so it all rested on her stomach. Leaning over, he let his tongue slide up from her side where some of the liquid had slid down, slurping it up until he got to her belly button, where he pressed his mouth around it and sucked the drink in.

"Oh," she said, her stomach flexing with the touch.

"I'm gonna get you a little more warmed up before I put this in, okay?"

"Okay," she said, her eyes still watching as Billy sucked on her stomach.

Sliding my fingers along her slit, I pressed against her clit, making a circular motion with my thumb. She flexed her body, her ass clenching and her pussy doing the same, but I didn't push anywhere but her clit. Just my thumb, going in circles, getting her warmed up.

Billy sat back up and poured a little more onto her, then lapped it up, causing her to clench again. When she did, I pressed my finger to her opening, sliding it into the center of her, pressing inside just enough that she could feel me, but not so far as to reach that ever elusive spot that would give her the ride she was looking for.

In and out, slow and steady, still keeping an even pressure on her clit. The more I moved, and the more wine Billy drank from her stomach, the wetter she got, until I was sure there was more than enough to keep her from having issues with the toy. On my next withdrawal, I swapped my finger for the toy, not having it on just yet. I slid it in, and she sort of sighed, her hips raising up just a bit from the mattress, like she was trying to get it into her further. When I got it all the way in, I shifted my hand and pressed the suction section against her clit, moving her lips out of the way so I could get a solid connection. When it was settled in place, I pressed the button on the bottom and it started to vibrate, the suction starting at the same time.

"Oh," she said, her stomach clenching, her hips rising from the bed, and her breathing increasing. "Oh," she said again, her body stiffening, as Billy moved from her stomach to her breasts, pulling one into his mouth.

He'd set the glass on the nightstand so it didn't get in the way, or get broken, which would be a huge issue. I increased the speed of the toy, both the suction and vibration moving faster, and she tensed up even more, her hips sort of bucking on the bed, so I put my arm across her hips to hold her still. Billy sat up, his hand still massaging her breast, but leaned forward to capture her mouth with his, her arm going up and around him.

Her hips increased in their desire to move, and her legs tried to close around my body, but I was too big, and they weren't going to make it. I kept pressure on the toy, not moving it in or out, but sort of holding it steady, letting it do all the work. She pulled Billy's hair, yanking him away from her as she cried out in ecstasy.

"Oh, God," she cried, over and over, as she spasmed under our care.

After she finally came back to herself, I shut the toy off, slowly pulling it out of her, and she sighed as it left her body.

"You did so good, Angel," Billy said. "You're so beautiful when you come like that."

I kissed the inside of her thigh, then raised up so I could see more of her face as well. She had a glow about her, not quite the embarrassed red she got when she was flustered, but more a sheen of complete bliss.

"Look at you, Darlin'," I said. "You're glowing. Makes me want to taste more of you."

She was languid, relaxed and sated, but she opened her eyes and smiled up to me, her tongue sliding out her lips and caressing them before darting back into her mouth.

"How you doing?" I asked.

"I feel good," she said. "But you guys need some relief, too."

"Watching you is more than enough," I said.

"I wouldn't mind some relief," Billy said, and then smiled down at her. "Should I put some mousse on my dick so you can lick it off?"

She giggled, her hand reaching up and stroking him, and he sort of settled back on his haunches, letting her do whatever she wanted to him. I slid back and climbed off the bed, walking over to the nightstand and picking up one of the spoons I'd set on the tray. Scooping up some of the mouse, I put it into a bowl and handed it to her. She took it, dipped her fingers into it, then slathered it onto his cock.

Turning onto her side, she moved so she could take his cock into her mouth, and let her tongue slide down the length, licking the mousse from it. I served up another bowl for myself, climbing back onto the bed and settling myself behind her. She was on all fours at this point, so I kissed her ass, then dipped my fingers into the mousse and spread it along her crack. Getting food into her was not my objective, so I was very careful as to how and where I let it slide.

Once I'd had some on her, I slid my tongue up her slit, taking all the chocolate with me. It was an art to use food near the openings and not end up with someone getting an infection. Once the food was off her, I went back with my tongue to work her more. She was bobbing up and down on Billy's cock, so I tried to time myself so that I was getting her as she backed off him.

With her hair all braided up and on top of her head, there really wasn't anything Billy could grab hold of, so he just had to sit there and take it, which wasn't exactly a hardship for him. He'd been mostly silent but started in with his encouragement.

"That's it, Angel," he said. "You're so good. Suck my cock like the good girl you are."

I never got into the dirty talk, just let things happen naturally. Not that I wouldn't encourage someone, but Billy always went well over the top. Saying something about him being what they wanted and shit like that. He knew I didn't like it, so when we were together, and were really into someone, he was careful about the words he chose.

"Oh, yeah," he said. "Oh, God. Oh, don't stop."

He spasmed, and she leaned all the way down onto him, and he had his hands on his thighs, holding himself up as she milked him dry.

"Oh, fuck, yeah, Angel," he said. "That was fucking awesome."

She pulled back and off him, and I backed away from her, giving her space to sit up, which she did. Shifting on her haunches, she sort of wiggled her ass, settling into a comfortable position, then turned and looked over her shoulder at me, her smile wide.

"Your turn," she said.

"Oh, no, Darlin'," I said. "It's still your turn."

I reached around her, pressing my front to her back, bending her back over and lifting her hips up again.

"First, I'm gonna get that toy started again," I said, and she let out a little moan. "Then, we're gonna see how much you can take. You okay with that?"

"Mm-hmm," she let out, and I sort of smacked her ass. "Yes," she added, getting my meaning.

I hadn't smacked her hard, just a slight stinging, but I rubbed the area to soothe it. Billy had laid back, sort of just watching us, since he'd already gotten his release. He liked to watch just as much as I did, but sometimes he wanted to jump in again. I looked at him, and he sort of gave me a nod, like he knew I wanted to do this alone. He knew I'd be fine with him watching, so he settled himself a bit better.

Sliding the vibrator I'd used before slowly into her, she sighed again, like she needed it or something. Her ass was up in the air, her shoulders down to the mattress, and it was picture perfect the view I had. Once it was in, and I'd gotten the suction part in the right place, I pressed the button and got it started.

She let out a little whimper, pressing her ass back toward me, like she wanted more contact than what she had. I put my hand on her ass, rubbing it over and over, just letting the toy do its job at getting her revved back up. Once she started really relaxing, I pressed it in a bit further, my palm against the base of it, moving my hand in a sort of circular motion so that the toy wasn't just sitting in there, but actually moving around.

When I looked up, Billy had picked up the toy that Ari had grabbed when she first came into the room. He'd been right in that they were anal beads, but these also had a vibrator function. Normally I wouldn't have gone for that, but we'd gotten these, and they were amazing to have in a woman while you were inside her pussy. The vibration from them against your cock as it slid in and out was something I hadn't realized I wanted until the first time I'd used them.

"I'm gonna slide something into your asshole," I said and she stiffened. "It's not very big. And if you don't like it, just say so and I'll stop. Okay?"

"Okay," she said.

The way she was lying, with her head on the bed so that her face was more away from me, I couldn't see her reaction, so I looked to Billy. He had this shit-eating grin on his face, so I knew she had a nervous look, but not a panicked one. I sort of glared at him, and he realized what I needed, so shifted and grabbed a bottle of lube. She took in a breath, and I guessed that she saw it and was concerned.

"It's okay," I said, running my hand along her back. "I'll go slow and easy. You just tell me to stop and I will. I promise."

"Okay," she said, her voice tentative.

I sat up a bit more, pressing my body against her so she could feel where I was. Then, I poured a little bit of the lube into my palm, setting the bottle next to me after flipping the cap closed. I pulled the beads through the lube, trying to make sure it was warm. Nothing shut shit down than cold lube, so I didn't want to stop this before we at least tried.

Billy reached out a hand and took hers in his, stroking his thumb across the back of it in a slow and steady rhythm. I could see she was tense, but I hoped that we could help her relax enough that this wouldn't be such a shock to her.

"Okay, Darlin'," I said. "This might still be a little cold, but I think it'll be good enough. You ready?"

"Yeah," she said, her voice strained a bit.

"Angel," Billy said, and I could see that she turned her head toward him. "I want you to look at me. Just watch me, and everything will be just fine. We won't do anything you don't like. I promise. I'm right here. Just look at me. I got you."

As he was talking, I pressed the head of the tiniest bead against her asshole, just enough that it was pressure, but not actually going in. The nice thing about this one was that the first bead was smaller than even my finger, so it wouldn't be too much pressure for her to start with.

"Push out," Billy said, and she shook her head. "Trust me. It's the easiest way to get things going in. I won't let anything happen to you. You can do this. Just relax and push out."

Sure enough, as soon as he told her what to do, her muscles relaxed and the first two beads slid inside. That was all I was gonna do at the moment, because I didn't want to overwhelm her. Her muscles were clenching and unclenching as I watched her handle the intrusion. She was doing so well, and I hoped we'd get to the point where we could both be inside her at the same time. Much as I wanted to fuck her myself, the two of us had become good at the sharing thing, and when we worked it well, we all got what we wanted in the end.

CHAPTER THIRTY-SIX

Ariana...

The sensation was an odd thing. It wasn't bad, per se, but it was definitely something I would probably have to get used to over time. Not that I didn't want to, it was just so different. Billy was so calm and comforting as he held my hand, and Spencer had been true to his word, going slow and not pushing too hard or too fast.

Now that I had them in me, though, I had to admit that it was honestly an amazing feeling. I mean, I'd already felt full with the vibrator in me, but when he put things in my ass, it gave a different kind of pressure. I'd read enough romance books to know that we would likely get to the point where they were both fucking me, one in each hole, but for now, this was actually pretty great.

I'd done what they said, relaxed myself as much as I could, and did the push out, which was fucking weird, but worked. Now, I had a toy in my pussy, with its sucking thing on my clit, and something else, probably the toy I'd picked up initially, in my ass. That fucker was long, though, so I was sure it wasn't all the way in.

"You okay?" Spencer asked, his body next to mine.

"Yeah," I said. "Just feeling full is all."

"Normal sensation," Billy said. "You'll get used to it once you practice enough."

"Practice?" I asked, looking up at him with my eyes.

"Sure," he said. "A lot of people do. It's not weird."

"Okay," I said, trusting him.

That was the thing. I trusted them. They'd been kind, had been completely comfortable to be around, and when we started the relationship, which I guess this was, they were patient with me, letting me go at my own pace with them.

"You ready for me to turn this back on?" Spencer asked.

"I think so," I said. "But slow, okay?"

"Sure thing," he said.

I felt him shift, then felt the vibration start up, and damn if it didn't just shoot me through the roof. I'd lost all control of my body, it was just reacting to the sensations, and I was along for the ride. Wave after wave rolled through me, my body convulsing around the intrusion, and it was beyond all comprehension, more than anything I'd ever experienced in my life, and I thought I'd die right then and there.

There was no way for me to know how long it lasted, because I was not in my right mind, but I guessed it was hours with how worn out I was when I came back to myself. The toys were out of me, that much I knew, but other than that, and the fact that I actually did know how to breathe, were the only things I was aware of.

"That's it, Angel," I heard Billy say.

"We've got you, Darlin'," Spencer added.

I was warm, wrapped in their arms, and I didn't know how I got there. The last thing I have any conscious memory of was the explosion inside me. Now that that had abated, I was aware that there was a puddle underneath me, and I was icked out so bad I tried to sit up.

"Hold on," Billy said. "Let us help you. You kind of went all the way to heaven, just to come back to us, Angel."

"What am I lying in?" I asked.

"Your orgasm," Spencer said, and I turned to look over my shoulder at him. "You squirted, Darlin'."

"Oh, God," I said, knowing exactly what it was.

"It's normal," Billy said. "Trust me, it's not gross."

"It's piss," I cried, trying to move from the puddle.

"It's not," Spencer said. "Used to think that, but it's been proven to be false."

"No," I said, shaking my head, trying to get up.

Billy helped me to sit, then helped me off the bed, and I nearly ran to the bathroom, slamming the door behind me. They fucking let me piss their bed and were trying to tell me it was something different. I knew what it was, and there was no way they were gonna get me to believe it was anything else.

"Hey, Angel," Billy said at the door.

"Go away," I said, sitting on the floor of the shower.

God, I was a fucking horrible, and they'd just let it happen. How the fuck did they let me piss all over, then let my lay down in it? It was disgusting. Completely gross. And they were totally fine with it.

I could hear that they were talking, and were moving about, probably taking the piss filled sheets off the bed. How had I let this get this far? I needed to get dressed and go home. This wasn't gonna work out. I had to stop it before it got any further along. I couldn't do this. This wasn't who I was.

Grabbing a washcloth from the closet they had in there, I got it wet and wiped myself up. Fuck, all my clothes were out there somewhere. I looked around and saw a robe hanging on a hook behind the door. I pulled it down and wrapped myself up in it, hoping they'd let me just go home and not try to make a big deal about it. Fuck. This could screw everything up. Like, my whole life could be ruined because I'd pissed in their bed.

CHAPTER THIRTY-SEVEN

pencer...

"Why is she freaking out so much?" Billy asked. "This isn't the first squirter we've had. We know what we're talking about."

"It must be her first time," I replied. "It's always intense for them, so the overwhelm is probably hitting her harder than we thought."

"I guess," he said.

We were pulling the sheets off the bed, well, mostly the bottom one, since we'd done a good job of making sure the pillows and other blankets were well out of the way. I took the wet material to the washer and threw it in, throwing a couple of the washing pods in with it, then started it up. When I got back to the room, Billy had already done a good job of wiping up the rest of it that I'd missed. He'd already pulled out a bottom sheet and mattress pad to replace the ones I'd taken to the laundry room.

"She said anything?" I asked.

"I heard the water run for a minute," he said. "I think she just sort of washed herself up, though. Haven't heard anything else."

The door to the bathroom opened slowly, and both of us froze. As much as I didn't want to gawk at her, and as much as she likely felt super self-conscious, I needed her to know that we were fine with what happened, and that we had no ill will toward her in the least. In fact, I was pretty fucking proud that we'd gotten her to that point, and so fucking quick, too.

"Hey, Angel," Billy said, and she looked at him, her eyes still wider than I'd have liked.

She was wrapped in one of the robes we had in there and was completely covered from her neck to her toes, no skin showing aside from her face. Even her hands were covered as she'd tucked them up in the sleeves, wrapping them around herself.

"You're good, Darlin'," I said.

"No," she said, but it was super soft. She cleared her throat and said it again. "No," she said. "I'm not good. I fucking pissed the bed."

"You did no such thing," I said, and I will admit, my voice was a bit firmer than I'd have liked. "You had an epic orgasm that resulted in your squirting. It was not piss, and it isn't wrong. I'm proud of it."

"How can you be?" she said, her voice rising higher. "I don't even understand this."

"Come sit down, Angel," Billy said, patting the edge of the bed.

She shook her head wildly, like we'd just been sitting there waiting for her and not cleaning up.

"We changed the sheets," I said. "They're in the washer now. This is fresh bedding. Let's talk."

I'd tried my best to have a low, even tone so as not to spook her any more than we'd already done. She was skittish, like a wild cat who'd been cornered, and we needed to tread lightly to keep her in our grasp. I didn't want to tame her, just needed her to know we were safe, and not about to harm her at all.

Billy backed off, walking around to the other side of the bed, and climbing up under the covers. I was standing at the foot of the bed, giving her plenty of room to come to it without being right next to me. She was still standing there, almost shivering.

"Should we put something on?" I asked. "Some pants or something?"

She nodded, and I let it go, not forcing her to say the words. I grabbed Billy's jeans and tossed them over to him, then pulled my own on. Once they were up, I went back to the foot of the bed, away from where she was, giving her plenty of space to come to us when she was ready.

When we'd pulled the sheet off, we'd also taken the toys and tucked them away, wrapped in the towels they'd been sitting on, and set under the spanking bench. If I'd have thought of it, I'd have had Billy help me pull the cross out and shove it back into the office, but it wasn't something that came to mind, so it was still there, looking ominous.

"Come talk," I said, again patting the edge of the bed.

She hedged a bit, then slowly moved toward us. I kept myself still and saw from the corner of my eye that Billy was doing the same. We both knew that look, the one where they were great for a moment, then all of a sudden freaked out. Neither of us wanted to scare her away, so we worked hard to give her that sense of security.

"Good girl," I said, my voice low.

Turning to me, she blushed that beautiful red that I knew covered her whole body, and I smiled. I didn't want her to be uncomfortable, but the thought that she had a little bit of fear was exciting. I'd never tell her that, nor show her if I could help it, but inside, my little devil was jumping up and down.

She climbed up onto the bed, scooting over just enough to not be on the edge, but not close to Billy. My guess was she was still nervous, which, if it was her first time, made sense.

"Can I climb up?" I asked. "Or would you prefer it if I stayed down here?"

Instead of answering, she scooted a little closer to Billy, who hadn't moved since he got back up after putting his jeans on. She was smack in the middle of the bed, so when I climbed up, there was still more than an arm's length of space between the three of us.

"I'm going to guess that was a first," I said.

"No shit, Sherlock," she said.

"It's not our first experience," I said. "In fact, if we can, we like to make it happen quite a lot. It's one of the signs that your experience was intense. I'm betting that, with the orgasm, and the realization that you'd squirted, you were a little overwhelmed?"

She nodded, looking down at her hands.

"It's okay," Billy said. "First time I had it happen, it freaked me out, too."

"It did?"

Her question was so quick, and so honest, like she was begging him to tell her she wasn't some kind of freak.

"It did," he said. "I had the same thought as you did, that the girl had pissed on me. It took a while before I was okay with even being around a girl for a bit. Wasn't until I did a little research on it that I realized it was just super intense for her."

"It really was," she said. "Like, I feel like I blacked out or something. Which, yeah, that was weird, too. And not the first time with you guys, either."

"Really?" I asked, excited at the prospect that we'd helped her get so far outside herself that she was purely existing in the space of pleasure.

"In the shower the first time," she said. "I remember the beginning, and how things progressed, but then, after I... Well, after that, I sort of forgot what happened next until you were holding me and drying me off."

"Is that a good thing?" I asked.

"Very much so," she said, and her blush had receded some, and she looked a bit more relaxed. "I just..."

She stopped, looked down at her hands, and it didn't feel like she was gonna continue. Billy and I had been around enough women who had that overload that we knew to just wait them out. They'd come to their own conclusions and decide what they wanted to say or ask. I was sure that Ari was no different.

"God," she said on a sigh. "I feel like it's the first time all over again. Like I didn't know what to expect, and everything just mashed together in this conglomeration of feelings and senses."

"Okay," I said. "So, you feel like it was too much?"

"No," she said, her voice sharp. "I mean, yeah it was, but not in the way you're thinking."

"So tell me," I said.

"I'm not sure I can explain it," she said. "It was good, don't get me wrong, I just feel like it was too good. Like, I'll never get there again, and that was the one and only time, and somehow, I fucked it all up."

"You didn't fuck anything up," Billy said. "It was intense. We get that. But that doesn't mean you did anything wrong. In fact, I'm pretty sure you did everything right."

"Except have a massive freak out and run away," she said with a laugh, and I was glad to hear that. Billy smiled, too, so I knew he was just as pleased. "I've just never had anything like this happen before, so I think it was a bit too much all at once."

"Where do we go from here, then?" I asked.

"I don't know," she said. "I've been having a really good time. Like, too good almost. But I also need to look at this from my business perspective as well. I don't want to fuck this up for my brother, but I don't want to walk away from something that is more than anything I've ever had, and everything I didn't know I wanted."

"So, we slow down," I said. "We take a step back, take some time apart, and figure out the business side of things."

"You don't want me?" she asked.

"That's not what I mean," I said.

"I want you all the time," Billy said, and she turned to him, like she'd forgotten he was there. "But I don't want you freaking out. I want you to want it, not because we do, but because it's what you want. There is nothing pleasurable about being with someone who doesn't want to be with you. We want you, but we want you to want us."

"Which I do," she insisted. "I just... God, this is so frustrating. It's like I know what I wanna say, but I can't put it into words. I feel stupid because I can't express myself."

"Darlin'," I said, using the term I'd come to think of as hers. "We understand the confusion you're going through. We both went through it when we first started sharing. It was complicated and confusing and full of so many things we didn't understand. It'll take time, which is fine, because I don't plan on going anywhere."

She was nodding as I talked, and I think it was finally filtering through to her that we understood her. Trying something new is complicated, and figuring out whether it's for you or not can take time. We'd only known each other a short time, and we were already having deep conversations about what we wanted and what we expected. I was considering that a good thing.

CHAPTER THIRTY-EIGHT

Ariana...

I just didn't understand why it had to be so fucking hard. They were amazing, and they showed me things I had never experienced before. It was amazing, but also terrifying. It was like I was running full steam down a hill, going faster than I anticipated, and couldn't figure out how to pump the brakes and slow myself down.

"Why don't we take a week off?" Spencer asked. "That will give you time to yourself, and to figure out what it is that's going through your head and will give us time to get this place ready for your crew to come in and get started."

I wanted to say no, that I didn't want time, but he was right. I needed to take some time away from them, get myself figured out, and try to see what it was I really wanted. Not just when it came to the two of them, but also for my future. Did I want to settle down? Think about a long-term relationship? Just fuck them for a while until I worked it out of my system?

None of the answers came to me, and I wasn't sure whether they would if I was away from them. The only thing I did know was that I had to separate from them and think about my job, my company, and what the next steps were when it came to that part of my life.

"That's not a bad idea," I said. "Not that I don't want to be with you, because I do. I just need… I don't know what I need."

"We get it," he said, looking to Billy to confirm. "We're here for you in whatever capacity you want us."

"For sure," Billy said. "You take whatever time you need."

Billy was trying so fucking hard to sound strong, but I could see it in his face. He didn't want to lose me. That, in and of itself, was something. What, I didn't know. I reached out a hand to him, and he scooted closer, across the giant bed toward me. I reached my other hand out to Spencer, and he mirrored Billy's movement, coming close to me as well. With them surrounding me, I felt more at ease. It was a weird thing, but they made me comfortable, made me whole, so to speak, and I knew in that moment that I would stay with them, for as long as they'd have me.

SIX WEEKS LATER…

"What are your plans for New Years?" Dee asked when I walked into the office.

"Not sure," I replied.

"Surprised you're not staying with your mystery man," he said.

"What's that supposed to mean?" I asked.

"You haven't exactly been keeping much secret," he said, and I flushed, feeling my whole body turning red. "Don't worry," he continued. "I don't know who he is, but I do know that you've been in a much better mood lately, and I can appreciate that."

"I have?"

"You have," Brad said, and I whipped around to see him sitting at my desk. "Prancing in here all high on life and shit. It's disgusting."

"Whatever," I said. "I'm just having some fun while I'm still young. Might go somewhere, might not. No need to rush anything."

"You ever gonna tell me who he is?" Dee asked.

"Not yet," I replied. "When I'm ready, and when… he's ready, then I'll let you know."

I almost slipped up and said when they're ready but caught myself just in time. Didn't need anyone to know it wasn't just one guy. Spencer and Billy had been so good to me that I never wanted to let them go. I also knew that no one in my family would understand my dating the both of them.

"We want to start on the baseball players' house right after the new year," Dee said. "Since you're running shotgun on it, I'll let you work with them to figure out dates to start the demo."

"Sure thing," I said. "You wanna move your fat ass out of my chair?" I asked Brad. "I have work to do, and you're in my way."

"Fuck you," he said.

"No thanks," I replied. "I'm getting plenty of that from people who appreciate me."

It was a low blow, especially since I knew he'd had a crush on me since I was like twelve. But the truth of the matter was, I never thought of him as anything other than my brother's friend, and now, an employee.

"You start the bathroom yet?" Dee asked, completely ignoring the comments Brad and I made.

"They said they wanted to hold off until we had dates for the big remodel," I said. "Besides, I think they'll be heading down for spring training at some point in the next month or two, so it'll be easier for us to do the work while they're away."

"You gonna riffle through their closets while they're away?" Brad asked.

"You really want me to answer that?" I asked, glaring.

"God," he barked. "I was fucking with you. Can't you even take a fucking joke anymore?"

"That's not something to joke about," Dee said, and I could see he was getting about as fed up with Brad as I was. "Now, I think you've got somewhere to be, don't you?"

"Fine," he said. "Great fucking way to treat your friend you've known since forever."

"Exactly," I replied, and he looked at me.

The look gave me a shiver I never thought I'd feel from him. I'd known him for as long as I could remember, and there had never been anything sinister about him, even when he first started hitting on me way back when. Now, though, he had size on him, and there was something in the way he was looking at me that gave me the willies.

"What the fuck was that?" I asked Dee when Brad had left.

"I think he was trying to make a go of something from that woman up in Bellingham," he said. "But when he tried to do anything, she kept shutting him down. He tried to pull the 'I saved you' card, but all that did was make her even more antsy about him."

"Does he not know how truly terrifying he can be?"

"He doesn't," Dee said. "He thinks he's just a giant teddy bear, but he's big, and that's something that will put everyone off. Besides, I think the woman from up there moved well away from here."

"Good," I said. "She doesn't need to be jumping from one toxic relationship to another."

"I wish he'd just fucking think before he acted," he said. "Like, that whole thing was probably terrifying for her, and he went and brought in a fucking biker gang to fix the problem. Word is, they got the woman out, but still. How would you feel if a whole ass gang of dudes showed up at your place and forced you out?"

"Is that what really happened?" I asked.

"From what I heard, yeah," he said. "I mean, Brad wanted to go with them, but they told him he was an added risk they didn't need or something. Really made him butt hurt. I guess he's been trying to get into the gang for a while, and they just don't want him, which is fucking hilarious to me."

"Dude's too dumb to get into a biker gang?" I asked.

"Dude's too dumb to know not to get into one," he replied.

"True that," I said. "Let me see if I can reach them and set up a start date. I'll also ask about when they're gonna be out of town so we can plan around that as well. I'll let them know we'll need to have access to the house, so see if they have a key or something they can give to me so we can get in and out."

"Oh, yeah," he said. "Good plan. Didn't think about that, but we definitely will need to get in and out of there while they're gone."

I sat down at my desk and started in on that project. I didn't need to actually borrow a key, because they'd given me one, but I was going to do my cover and ask for one anyway. No need for anyone in the office to know that I had full access to their house. That would just cause too many questions, and they were all ones I didn't want to answer.

CHAPTER THIRTY-NINE

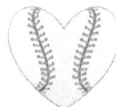

Billy...

"They're starting after the first of the year," Spencer said to me.

"Who all is gonna be here?" I asked. "Are they bringing in a whole crew? Or is it just gonna be her for a while?"

"The whole crew," he said. "She also said that they're gonna need access to the garage the whole time, so we're gonna have to figure out where to park our cars while we're in Arizona for spring training."

"Damn," I said. "I prefer them being here while we're gone."

"She offered to house them in her garage for us," he said. "It's not ideal, but we can think about it. I mean, she is kinda going out on a limb about that, cause it's not something normal."

"No shit, Sherlock," I said. "Who lets their clients park their cars at their house?"

"I'm just telling you what she said," he replied.

"Sorry," I said. "I'm just pissed that our time with her is going to stop. I don't want her to get away, so we gotta figure out a way for her to stay with us, even when we're gone."

"I know," he replied. "But it's the way the world works."

"We could marry her," I said, and he looked at me like I'd grown two heads. "Not both of us, obviously, but maybe you. You're the most presentable of us. Then, she wouldn't have to work."

"You really think she'd quit working if she married one of us?"

"I guess not," I said. "I just wish she'd come with us when we went down."

"We're still pretty early in this whole thing," he said. "Let's not try to rush it. We might scare her off if we push too hard."

"Still," I said. "The days she can't stay are the hardest for me. I miss her."

"I do, too," he said. "But we need to just be patient. She's come a long way in the last month and a half or so. I mean, she really has blossomed into the wild and crazy woman we knew she would be."

"Oh yeah," I said. "I'm loving seeing her freak flag fly."

"Of course you are," he said. "She also said that we should make sure that any of the toys we've got are well hidden while they're here and we're gone. She doesn't want her brother to find out about our stuff. She said it would make it awkward once she tells him that she's seeing us."

"Guess we need to get it all into the office, then," I said. "That seems the safest place to put it. No one should be going in there, right?"

"That's what I was thinking," he said. "We can just tell her where we put everything, and she can tell the rest of the crew that it's an off-limits room."

"What do you bet they still go in there?" I asked.

"I'm planning on locking the door," he said. "I've also got a camera coming that we can put in there to watch and see if anyone goes in the room while we're gone."

"You little spy, you," I said. "I like it. Can we keep the camera in the bedroom before we leave? To maybe give us some good things for the spank bank?"

"No," he said, and I waited. I knew he'd tell me why, and sure as shit, he did. "We are not going to record ourselves," he said. "I'm not going to tell you how horrible that could go if someone got ahold of the videos. And besides, Ari would never agree to it, so it's a moot point."

"You sure she wouldn't agree?" I asked.

"No," he said, and sort of just glared at me.

"Okay," I said, holding my hands up in surrender. "I was just asking."

"She is not one of our regular women," he said. "She is a partner to us, and not someone we are simply fucking. Do you understand the difference?"

"You're such an ass," I said.

"I'm not an ass," he replied. "I just want to make sure you know she is not some whore who we fuck. She's a woman, and a damn fine one at that. I don't want you to fuck this up for us, so I'm making sure you know what the deal is."

"I fucking know," I said, and was getting angry. "Do you think I'm a child or something?"

"Sometimes you act like one," he said.

"Fuck you," I said, and turned and headed into my room. "Fucking asshole thinks he knows every fucking thing there is to know about women."

I slammed my door, which is something I knew pissed him off, but I was petty, and didn't even fucking care. What I wanted to do was call her, ask her how she felt about it, but I knew he was right, that she wouldn't agree, and that if I asked her, she'd get skittish and maybe even bolt. That was not what I fucking wanted, so I didn't do it.

Instead, I stripped, climbed into the shower, turned the water on as hot as I could handle, and stood in the spray. Nothing calmed me down more than just getting in there and existing. I hadn't done it in a while, and I knew it was likely the result of all the shit my mom did, but I needed that to turn my brain off for a bit, undo whatever had been built up in me, and get it all washed clean.

I needed to get a therapist to deal with all the shit I went through but didn't want anyone else to know what it was. It was embarrassing, and disturbing, and I just sort of pretended it didn't happen. It's what I'd always done, and it had worked for me. Something about Ari, my little angel, brought up the feelings of inadequacy in me, and I didn't like it. She was absolutely perfect in every way, even with her little idiosyncrasies. She was good to us, and she let us be good to her.

I knew that eventually we'd have to have a talk about what the future looked like for us, but for now we were all content to just hang out, do our thing, and enjoy what time we had together. Once we were out of state, she may change her mind about us, and I had to get as much time with her before that happened as I could. I knew it would come, I just didn't want this to end. At least not yet.

CHAPTER FORTY

Ariana...

We'd already gotten some the framing parts of the project started, and they would arrive the second week of January, barring weather. I prayed for no snow. Rain wouldn't be great, but snow would be worse. Couldn't do a damn thing if it snowed. Thankfully, the winter had been pretty mild, but I was still worried. You could never tell what the weather would do in Seattle. It was one of those things where, if you wanted rain, all you had to do was either plan an outdoor event or wash your car.

We were set to meet with Spencer and Billy the Friday before the work was to start, and I'd let them know what to expect at that meeting. Dee would be with me, and we'd chat about what the crew would be doing, and what would need to be moved. All the things that logistically made a renovation work. I wanted them to know that Dee would be with me so they'd know to behave with respect to touching me. They were good about it, but I wanted to reiterate that it would need to not exist during that meeting.

When the date rolled around, Dee had been on another site, dealing with more Brad shit, and I'd let him know I'd meet him at the house. We really needed to start dealing with all the issues his friend had brought up, and maybe talk to him about it. The thing we didn't need was him fucking up a job, and us being left holding the bag when he did it. If he caused issues with a client, we needed to take a hard look at whether he was an asset, or just around because he was a friend. We didn't need him to be a friend, we needed him to do his fucking job.

I got to the house first, and when I went up to the door, Billy let me in. He looked behind me, and when he didn't see anyone else coming, he pulled me against him and kissed me, deep, long, and passionately. I didn't complain but did remind him that he needed to keep control once my brother arrived.

"But he's not here, yet," he said.

"I know," I replied. "And when he gets here, you need to back off. I can't let him know we're in a relationship, cause it would be an issue with the job, and I don't want that."

"I'll be a good boy," he said. "Does that mean you'll reward me later?"

I rolled my eyes but nodded. He loved the dynamic of a reward system, and he always did everything he could to make sure he played by the rules. It was honestly one of the things I loved most about him.

As soon as the thought entered my mind, I blinked and stalled, not moving further into the house. It was like a ton of bricks had just slipped off the roof and landed square on the top of my head.

"Hey," Spencer said as he came into the living room. "What's wrong?"

"What?" Billy asked, looking at him, then back at me. "Wait, what's wrong?"

"Nothing," I said, trying to compose myself. "Just a fleeting though."

"What did you think?" Billy pressed, just as the doorbell rang.

"Shit," I said, schooling myself, but failing miserably. "I'm going to the bathroom until I get my face under control. I can't let him see me right now, cause he'll know."

With that, I headed down the hall to the powder room that served as a guest bathroom. I knew the house well enough to know where everything was, so it wasn't hard to find a spot to get my shit together.

"Hey," I heard Billy say when he opened the door.

I shut myself inside and couldn't really hear anything they were saying, thankfully. I took deep breaths, closed my eyes, and tried to focus on the job that we were doing. I needed to get all thoughts of the guys out of my mind, because if anything showed, Dee would know, then he'd grill me once we were back at the office, and I didn't know if I could lie to him. Honestly, I didn't know if I even wanted to.

CHAPTER FORTY-ONE

S pencer...

"Hey," Billy said as he opened the door and let Ari's brother in. "She had to use the restroom, but should be out, I would guess, soon."

"No problem," her brother said. "Did she start talking about the project, yet?"

"No," I said. "She just got here, so I think she was preoccupied with needing the restroom to even think of anything else. She seemed kind of miserable, honestly. Has she been sick? Is she gonna be able to do this?"

"Did she look sick?" he asked.

"Not that I could tell," Billy said, glaring at me over the brother's head.

"It was probably nothing," I said, letting it go.

I didn't want to throw her under the bus, but I also didn't want her brother to know why she was in the bathroom. The fact that it had everything to do with the two of us and nothing to do with an illness was something I wanted to avoid discussing, especially with her brother.

"Hey," Ari said as she came down the hall.

"You okay?" her brother asked her.

"Yeah," she said, looking confused. "Why?"

"They said you rushed to the bathroom," he said. "He thought you might be sick."

"I'm not sick," she said. "Just one of those things where I drank too much soda and forgot to go before I left. I'm fine."

"Okay," he said, but was watching her. "Did you bring everything we need to talk about?"

"Sure did," she said. "Where can we sit to discuss?"

"Dining room or living room," I said. "Which would be better?"

"Having the table would probably be preferable," she said, so I held my arm out to indicate the dining room. "Hang on," she continued. "I think I left my phone in the bathroom."

She headed back down the hall, and her brother and Billy went into the dining room. I looked after her as she went down the hall, and she turned back, seeing the other two gone, she glared at me and I shrugged, so she motioned that I should go to her. I looked into the dining room and saw that Billy was getting some water, and Demetri was sitting with his back to me. When I got down the hall to her, she yanked me into the guest bathroom.

"You can't tell him I'm sick," she hissed. "You need to just act normal. We can't show him in any way that there is anything between us but the emails and occasional calls from the office. I can't have him knowing what's going on."

"I'm sorry," I said. "I didn't think."

"Well, you need to," she said. "If he finds out, I'm fucked six ways to Sunday."

"Then tell him," I said. "It's not a big deal. You're an adult, I'm an adult, why can't we be together?"

"You are a client first," she said. "After all the work is done, fine. But not yet. Not until after we're already well underway on this thing."

She shoved me out the door, pulled her phone from her pocket, and walked back down the hall.

"Found it," she said, as if nothing had just happened.

I walked into the kitchen and grabbed a bottle of water from the fridge. Billy had pulled out glasses and a pitcher of ice water from it, but I was needing something to occupy myself with, so I just grabbed the first thing that came to my mind.

"You okay?" her brother asked.

"Yeah," I lied. "Just thinking about the plan for when we head to Arizona in a few weeks."

"Which is one of the reasons we're here," Ari said, and just her voice made my heart skip. "We're gonna need to have access to the house while you're gone, so we will either need a key or whatever you use to get in."

"We've got a spare key and garage door opener," Billy said. "That way it'll be easier for you to get in and out of the garage. We've also set up a code on our security system just for the construction. That way we'll know when you're here as opposed to the friend we've got to come by and grab our mail and such."

The way he seamlessly put out the fire that I felt brewing, and answered the question with information that was relevant, made me glad we had joined forces so many years ago.

"There's one room we're asking that you don't go into," I said, turning to the table and walking that way. "We've given a key to our friend, but we'd prefer it if the construction folks can stay out of the office. We'll lock the door so it won't be a temptation, but wanted you to be aware, just in case. You can call us anytime if you need something, but know that we'll be working, and may not get back to you quickly."

"Obviously, if the house is on fire, we should probably know," Billy said with a sarcastic smile. "Otherwise, it'll probably have to wait. We're pretty busy during training camp."

"Since we're working above the garage, I'm assuming you'll make sure that we have full access to that," her brother said.

"Of course," I replied. "We've moved everything that doesn't need to be in there out. The only issue we have is that we'll need somewhere to leave my car. We'll be driving down with Billy's Jeep but would normally put my car in the garage while we're gone."

"I figured you guys would fly," Demetri said. "Thought you had a home and cars down there, so you'd just fly down and do your thing."

"I've got a condo down there," Billy said. "But having a car sit for most of the year isn't good for it, so we usually drive down. Either that or rent a car while we're there."

"So, how do you get the car home?" Ari asked. "I mean, don't you guys fly home to start the season?"

"Depends on where we're starting the season," I said. "Sometimes, if we're starting at home, we have a couple of days and can drive home. Most of the time, though, we have a service that either drives the cars up or puts them on a trailer to deliver them to the stadium."

"It's usually the trailer," Billy added. "But we get them back in plenty of time for the first game. They usually leave before we do, so it's not like we're without cars."

"So, can you leave your car at the stadium?" Ari asked.

"We could find a secure parking garage," I said. "But the stadium has too many events, and we can't leave them there, except on special occasions. Mostly for shorter out-of-town series."

"Yeah," Billy said. "We have always just left it in the garage, but can't do that this year, obviously."

"Do you want to put it in my garage?" Ari asked.

We'd talked about it some, but to hear her ask in front of her brother meant she needed him to hear us agree to it.

"I don't know," I said. "It feels like I would be taking advantage of your kindness."

"My garage is pretty much empty," she said. "There's room for my car and yours. I assume it's the sedan in the driveway, right?"

"It is," I said, even though we both knew which car it was. This was a performance for her brother, and I could play along with that. "If you're sure it's not too much trouble, I wouldn't mind at all. That doesn't mean you get to drive it, though."

The statement was said in jest, but she answered right away.

"I would never dream of it," she said.

"I know," I said, but then added another sentiment that would probably appease her brother. "I just wanted to joke with you. You seem like a pretty trustworthy person to me, so I'll trust you to take care of it while I'm gone."

"I'm not sure that's such a good idea," her brother said. "What if something happens? You would be on the hook for repairs."

"The only thing that could happen is something with the house," she said. "It'll be fine."

"Even if something happens," I said. "That's what insurance is for."

"But it would be her insurance that would take the hit," her brother said. "I just don't know that this is such a good idea."

"Dee," she said, and the way the word leaped out of her mouth, I knew it was the end of the discussion. "I can take care of a car, in my garage, while he's gone for a month or so. It's not that big of a deal."

He held his hands up in surrender and turned away from her.

"So," Billy said, cutting the tension. "We've got a little box here with the key, garage door opener, and the alarm code. We'd appreciate it if you didn't share the code with just anyone. We'd prefer it if just the two of you had it. Would that be okay?"

"Oh, absolutely," Demetri said. "One or the other of us will always be here when we have workers in the house. It's one of the things we make sure to have unless it's a job we've already got established and have a crew specifically for it. But if you want one or the other of us here, we can make that happen. Honestly, it'll probably be Ariana since she's the one that's running this one."

"Good," I said. "I appreciate it. We both do."

"Of course," Ari said. "We always want to make sure that the client is happy. It's how we get repeat business, and referrals."

Billy barked a half laugh, half cough, choking on the water he was just taking a sip of. I knew it was because of the comment she made, and I did my best to not show any outward emotion at what she said. She had definitely made us happy, and we'd like to keep it that way.

"Shall we check the garage to make sure there's enough room for our stuff?" Demetri asked.

"Sure thing," I said, standing and heading that way.

I felt her brother following me without seeing him, so I did my best to not reach out and caress Ari as I went past her. It was hard, but I managed. Opening the garage door, I walked down the few steps to the main floor, then headed a bit away from the steps so the others could follow.

"Is that room open?" Demetri asked, pointing to our little storage area.

"It is," I said. "We've emptied it out, too. We weren't sure whether you'd need the space and wanted to give you as much room as possible."

"Great," he said, walking over to it.

Truth be told, the dresser that had been in there had been moved to the office, along with the two larger pieces we had for playing. They would all be locked away while we were gone in order to keep them out of wandering eyes and hands. Didn't need Demetri or one of the others on the crew to stumble upon our goodies, especially when Ari had planned to let her brother in on our arrangement after the job was finished.

By the time Demetri was leaving, I was exhausted from keeping my hands to myself, and it looked like both Billy and Ari were having the same problem. I kept catching Billy looking at her, his eyes sliding up and down her body in a caress. She did much the same, although she schooled herself better. She'd come a long way since we started, and she'd learned to control that wonderful blush she got. It was one of those things that I was sad to see gone, but glad it didn't show up in moments like this.

"You coming?" her brother asked as he stepped out the door.

"I need to talk about the bathroom," she said. "There were some questions I had about the finishing touches for that project, so figured while I was here I could get those answered as well."

"Okay," he replied. "See you when you're back at the office."

"Thank you for coming out," I said, reaching a hand out to shake his. "I'll send the key, remote, and code for the security system with Ms. Carington when she leaves, if that's okay with you."

"Sure," he said, then went down the steps to the driveway.

I closed the door and turned around to find Billy wrapped around Ari, one arm around her waist, the other hand holding her head back and tilted toward him, his front to her back, and his lips on hers in a passionate kiss. I flipped the lock on the door, just to be sure that her brother wouldn't accidentally walk in on us. Leaning against the door, I watched my lover and my roommate as they devoured each other, my cock stirring in my pants with want.

CHAPTER FORTY-TWO

riana...

Dee was barely out the door before Billy grabbed me, pulling me against him, my back to his front, holding me with a strong arm around my waist. He turned my head around and kissed me deeply, delving his tongue into my mouth in what I hoped would be an action later explored with other parts of our bodies. I could feel his cock pressing into my ass, and I wiggled it just enough for him to groan into my mouth.

Spencer's hands were at the waistband of my pants before I realized what was happening, and he was quickly removing my clothing, at least so far as to gain access to my core. His tongue slid along my thigh, but my legs were still tightly together, having been trapped there with the jeans that were now at my knees.

When his teeth set into my thigh, just enough to push the pain level, I gave my own moan, trying desperately to give him access to where we both wanted him to be. Instead, he slid a finger between my thighs, working to find that spot he could work without much access, and when he did, my whole body relaxed. It was like they knew the pressure I'd been feeling with my brother in this space, a place I felt comfortable to be myself completely.

Billy's arm around my waist tightened, and he lifted me up. Spencer kept one hand working me, and the other went to my shoes to pull them off before stripping me from the waist down. I opened my legs once they were free, and he dove in, my thighs going over his shoulders as his finger slid inside me, his mouth covering my clit.

They had me trapped, and I couldn't be happier. The way my emotions had been strung so tight the last few days, I needed this release, and was beyond ecstatic that they'd picked up on it and were willing to help a girl out.

I damn near screamed when I heard a pounding on the front door. Thank God Billy had my mouth covered so it didn't come out. We all sort of froze, though, and Spencer set my feet on the floor, handing me my clothes while Billy let go of me to walk to the door.

"Fuck," he hissed, then waved us toward the bedroom.

I headed in that direction, Spencer hot on my heels, as we heard him open the door. Neither of us could really hear what he was saying, but we figured it was likely my brother coming back to check on me in some fashion, likely making up some mistake of leaving something here. I quickly pulled my jeans on, sliding into my shoes, and walking into the bathroom to check my appearance. With my hair having been in a ponytail, it was quickly fixed and adjusted to not look like it'd been used as a handle.

"...so I didn't want her to forget," I heard my brother say as I finished with the task. "Ari? You in here?"

"Oh," I said, stepping out of the bathroom, Spencer on my heels, as if we'd been discussing tile or paint or some other such nonsense. "What's up?"

"I wanted to let you know that I had a talk with Brad," he said, and I rolled my eyes.

"And this couldn't wait?"

"He's been given his walking papers," he said, and I looked at him, waiting for more. "I wanted you to know, so if he called you or something, you'd know what to say to him."

"Like I asked before," I said. "This couldn't wait?"

He sort of shuffled his feet, not looking at me, because we both knew what he was doing, and I was calling him out on it, in front of clients, and he was pissed, I could tell.

"I wanted to make sure you knew right away," he said.

"There's this magic thing called a cell phone," I said sarcastically. "You could have sent a text or called me. Either of those things would have been preferable to airing our dirty laundry in front of clients. Now, is there anything else?"

I knew it was a bitch move, but I pulled the words that Mom would often say out. She'd always told us to make sure that our laundry was clean before we started bitching about someone else's, and he was doing the opposite of that by bringing this up now.

"No," he said, and I could hear that I'd wounded him.

"Fine," I said. "So," I continued, looking at Spencer. "I think that keeping the tile in the shower where it is for now is the best course of action."

I'd effectively dismissed my brother without having to tell him to fuck off. I knew it, he knew it, and both Billy and Spencer knew it. I felt when he left more than heard it, but when I heard Billy come back into the bedroom with a low whistle, I knew he was gone, and I relaxed again.

"You think he suspects?" Spencer asked me.

"Don't know," I said. "And honestly, I don't care. At this point, I kind of want to flaunt it in his face, but I know that would be a dick move, and I try not to do that with him. Besides, it might fuck up the remodel, and I don't want to do that to you guys, so I'll just keep quiet for now."

"You need to do what will make you feel best," Billy said. "If you need him to know, then fine. If you need us to play it cool, that's fine, too. We both want you happy."

"It's true," Spencer said. "We're not just hanging around because you let us both fuck you. We're here because we like you. A lot."

"Like, a lot a lot," Billy added, wiggling his eyebrows up and down, and I burst out laughing.

"You guys are amazing," I said. "And I really like you guys, too. A lot."

"Good," Spencer said. "Now, I believe we were in the middle of something that got interrupted. I'd like to get back to that if you're willing."

"Oh, God, please," I said, pulling my shirt over my head and kicking my shoes off.

CHAPTER FORTY-THREE

S pencer...
       She began to relax as soon as she was in our arms, and I
       could tell that the secret she'd been keeping of us had weighed
on her heavily. I knew she wanted to keep her brother in the dark, and
I understood why that was important to her, but it certainly wasn't
doing her any good. The fact that she wanted to rub us in his face
made me concerned about the longevity of our relationship. It wasn't
something I would verbalize, but it still sat oddly in my stomach.

By the time she was naked, and we had her on the bed between us,
the thought had left, and was replaced by the feelings of love I had for
both her and Billy. I wouldn't call it a deep loving feeling, but things
were definitely brewing and bubbling in that direction.

"That's it," I cooed as I lined myself up at her entrance. "Relax for
me, Darlin' and let me in."

I was on the bed, propped up on the pillows some, and she was on
top of me, with Billy behind her. We'd done the double penetration a
few times, but she was always hesitant to go there. Even though she
said she liked it, and that she wanted to keep doing it, she still stiffened up when we moved that direction.

Finally, she slid down my length, settling at the base of my cock, still sitting up. There was no way for Billy to get into a position to enter her until she leaned forward. We were patient, never pushed her hard to do anything, but always told her what we wanted. The first time we had her between us, she cried from the pleasure she got, and I think that scared her a bit, which only made her more hesitant.

She'd always be down for being between us, one of us behind her, the other in front, with her sucking one while the other fucked her. Both of us had been in either position, so it wasn't like she had to choose. When we finally got around to this positioning, we made sure that I was in her pussy while Billy was in her ass. I was thicker, even though he was longer, but the thickness was what was hard for her.

I'd tried anal on her, but she couldn't take it. She said she felt bad that she couldn't do that for me, but I'd assured her it was fine, and that we would work around what worked best for her. And we'd stuck to it, too. We always made sure that our foreplay was intense, and that she was well relaxed by the time we moved to penetration of any kind, so the fact that she was holding back now was concerning.

"Talk to us," I said, brushing the loose strands of her hair behind her ear. "Tell us what you want, what you need. We're here to please you."

"It's our only goal," Billy added, still behind her, but just barely touching her.

"I'm afraid you'll think it's dumb," she said, not looking at either of us.

"Darlin'," I said, tipping her head up to look me in the eyes. "If you want to try something, or you want to not do something, that's fine. It won't hurt our feelings at all. I promise."

"He's right, Angel," Billy said, running a hand down her arm and kissing the side of her neck. "All we want to do is make you feel good. Give you the best high you can get simply by pleasure."

She looked from me to Billy, then back again, gauging our faces to see what our emotions were. I did my best to put on a supportive image, and Billy was honestly looking curious and eager to hear what she wanted.

Taking a deep breath, she finally said, "I want to try both of you in my pussy."

As soon as she said it, she flushed so red it was almost comical. From her hairline all the way down her body, she was bright. She started to duck her head, but I pulled her to me, pressing my lips to hers, sliding my tongue along the seam of her lips, hoping she'd open for me.

While I was doing that, I could feel Billy moving. He'd already put a condom on and had the lube ready to go, so he didn't need to get anything else. Instead of just shoving in beside me, though, I felt his hand slid along the edge of my cock until it slid inside. Her gasp opened her mouth, and I dove in, my tongue dancing with hers as I felt Billy slide another finger in.

Taking time, he worked her, slowly adding a third and fourth finger to her entrance, stretching her as he went. Finally, when he likely felt she was open enough to slid in, he pulled his fingers out and I felt the heat of him against my body as he positioned himself to enter her.

"You ready, Angel?" he asked, and I released my hold on her head, letting her answer him with a rushed, "Yes."

"I'm gonna go slow," he said. "You tell me if it's too much and you want me to stop."

"Okay," she said, her eyes pinned on mine, wide with a little bit of fear, but also a desire I'd seen in them many times.

As he slid in, just a little bit, she bit down on her bottom lip, sucking in a breath.

"Too much?" Billy asked.

"No," she said, but her voice was tight. "Keep going. Please."

She turned back to look at him behind her, and while I couldn't see her face, the reaction from Billy told me that she was begging him with her eyes. We'd learned her emotions and reactions in the last few months we'd been together, and it had been a pleasure to see her beg without actually saying anything. She'd do it all the time, and I didn't think she was even aware of it at the moment.

As he moved more, she sucked in her breath, allowing him to fill her against me. The sliding of him along my cock was challenging my control, but I held her tight, knowing that this was something she wanted, and was also something we were uniquely qualified to give her. When he was finally fully inside her, she sighed, and it was the most contented sound I'd heard in a long time.

"That feel good, Angel?" Billy asked.

"So full," she said. "But so very good."

We stayed there for a minute or two to let her get adjusted to the amount she had stuffed inside her pussy. Billy looked at me, and silently told me he was going to start moving, so I wrapped my arms around her, holding her in place. As he pulled out, I shifted my hips to do the same, both of us sliding just a little bit, then pushing back inside.

While we'd never actually done this type of double penetration, we'd done the other type enough to know how to move together as a team to keep us inside our partner, as well as give her the most pleasure. As we slid back in, she shuddered between us, and it was amazing to feel her enjoy us in this way.

"How you doin', Darlin'?" I asked.

"This is better than I imagined," she said. "Do it again."

"Yes, ma'am," I said, and Billy smiled.

We moved slow and steady, sliding in and out of her in a methodical rhythm in time with her heartbeat. Each time we slid back in, she would sigh, arch her back, and press back against us. I wasn't getting quite what I needed to go off, but that didn't matter at the moment. What mattered was that she was getting pleasure.

I felt her tighten up around us, the telltale sign she was close, and just a couple more thrusts sent her over the edge. She spasmed in my arms, and I felt her squirt, something we'd come to love.

"That's it, Angel," Billy said against her ear. "That's our very good girl."

The words made her shudder again, and as her pussy squeezed us, it shoved Billy out. Instead of just letting it go, he slid up and down against her ass, lubricating her up until he slid inside her slowly. With how relaxed she was, it was quicker than it had been previously, and she moaned, deep and guttural, in the most primal way, and the combination of her vocalizing her pleasure, the pressure of Billy in her ass, and the wetness that was all over me, pushed me over my own edge as I pumped in and out of her to find my release, Billy following quickly behind me.

We lay there, enjoying the bliss we'd created, simply existing in each other's company. While we all likely wanted to stay where we were, the need to clean up was clear. Billy shifted first, his hand sliding between his body and hers to hold the condom on him while he pulled out. I did the same, sliding my own hand between us to hold the condom in place until I could pull out.

Billy helped Ari slide over onto her side on the bed, kissing her temple and murmuring softly to her, and the way she looked was amazing. She was breathing soft, slow, even breaths, and she had this contented look on her face that told me we would likely be redoing this particular experience again in the future, and she'd get no argument from me.

Slipping the condom off myself, I rolled over and climbed out of bed, moving carefully to the bathroom to drop it and clean up. I grabbed a washcloth, wet it in some warm water, and went back to the bed to help clean our girl up. Handing it to Billy, I began the process of pulling the sheets off so we could swap them out with clean, dry ones.

"Sorry," she mumbled as she looked at me.

"Don't be," I replied. "I love it when you do that. Makes me realize we're doing something right. I will never be mad about it. Ever."

"He's right," Billy agreed. "When you squirt like that, all it does is reinforce our desire to keep on doing what we're doing."

"It's just a pain to have to change the sheets all the time," she said, and I could hear that she was seriously worried about it.

"I will change the sheets ten times a day if it means you're enjoying us," I said. "Hell, I'll go buy more sheets just so we can do that."

When she smiled at me, I knew she understood I was serious. While I likely wouldn't go out and get more sheets, I wanted her to know I could.

"Let's get you into the shower," I said, reaching over to her.

"Yeah," Billy said. "I could use another round in there if you're up for it."

Her smile went from sweet to sultry in just a second, and I knew she was going to be ready to go again. All that meant was we were going to be busy for most of the evening. I wondered whether her brother would check in with her, but when she started crawling across the bed at me, looking like a jaguar from the jungle, those thoughts just vanished, and all I wanted to do was bring her as much pleasure as I could manage.

CHAPTER FORTY-FOUR

Ariana...

After the bed, then the shower, and then the bed again, I wondered whether I was going to need to call in sick to work. They had done everything I'd asked them to, and even came up with more ways to make me come. I'd lost count early in the evening, and by the time they were laying me down in bed, I was exhausted and sore in all the right ways.

I was floating in a cocoon of warmth and muscle when I heard my phone going off. Hunkering down more, I tried to ignore it, but it just kept restarting. That's when I realized that it was morning, and I was still in bed with my two lovers. Billy groaned behind me, pressed himself against my back, slid his cock between my ass cheeks, and kissed my temple.

"Good morning, Angel," he said gruffly, sleep still in his voice.

"What time is it?" I asked, beginning to panic.

"Too early," Spencer said, pressing into my front and sandwiching me between them.

"Seriously," I said. "I need to know what time it is. I might be late for work."

"Then quit," Billy said. "We'll take care of you. You can be our kept woman."

I shoved backward, and he grunted, but gave me room to get up. Sliding over Spencer, who pulled my tit into his mouth and sucked hard before letting it pop out, I found myself entirely not ready for standing. I was definitely the good kind of sore, but almost too much. My legs didn't want to hold me up, and I wondered whether they'd broken me.

Finally, I found my phone in the pocket of my jeans just as the ringing began again.

"Hello?" I asked, not even paying attention to who was calling.

"Where the fuck are you?" Dee asked.

"What?" I asked.

"We were scheduled to meet with the Simpsons," he said.

"Oh, shit," I replied. "I completely forgot about that. I'm sorry. I got caught up with someone and completely lost track of time. I kinda also got a little drunk last night, so I'm not in the best shape this morning."

"Forget it," he said. "I'll do this. They've been giving you a hard enough time, so I'll come in as the big bad owner type to show them who's boss. And no, I don't mean that you can't do that. Just that, for these two, I think that I should be the one to lay down the law with them. They've been a headache for us for entirely too long, and it's gonna stop today."

"Damn," I said. "I'm impressed."

"Yeah, well, I'm also pissed," he said. "Brad fucked something up at the last job he was at, which is why I fired him. But now, he's trying to say it wasn't him that did it, and he wants to come back and fix it."

"Shit," I said. "I'll be at the office soon. Let me know if you need me somewhere else instead."

"Office is fine," he said. "I'll be back there before I go anywhere else. We do need to have a conversation, though."

"That sounds ominous," I said.

"It's not," he said, but was curt in the comment. "I'll see you soon."

He hung up before I could say goodbye, and I wasn't sure I really wanted to see him. The way he was talking made me think I'd done something stupid, I just didn't know what it was I could have done to set him off. Maybe it was just Brad being Brad that had him on edge, but I knew I needed to get out of here and to the office as soon as possible.

"Come back to bed," Billy said.

"I gotta go," I said, pulling my panties on and searching for my bra. "Something's up with Dee. He sounds off, and I don't know what it is. The fact that I completely forgot about a meeting this morning doesn't help, either. Shit, I need a different shirt."

"There are a couple of your shirts in my closet," Spencer said. He'd rolled over and was watching me try to put myself back together. "Here, let me help you."

He slid out of bed and walked toward the closet, completely naked and sporting his morning wood that I'd felt against my stomach just a few minutes earlier. God, I wanted to just say fuck it and let them keep me. I knew it wasn't what I really wanted, but I'd be lying if I said it didn't tempt me sometimes.

"Here you go," he said, handing me one of the business polos I'd left here for emergencies.

"Thanks," I said, hooking my bra in place.

I pulled the shirt over my head, pulled on my jeans, then socks and shoes, before heading out of the bedroom. On the way out, I grabbed my purse. When I turned toward the door, Spencer was there, looking like he wanted to say something, but unsure whether he should.

"What?" I asked.

"I think he knows," he said, and I didn't know what he meant. "About us. Or at least one of us."

"Why do you say that?" I asked, almost panicking.

"Your car is still outside," he said. "You didn't turn your locator off on the phone, either. Maybe that's what was in his voice that made you feel like something was off."

I took a deep breath and let it out slowly.

"Everything will be fine," he said.

"I want to believe you," I replied. "I'm just not sure that's what's gonna happen, though."

"Whatever happens," he said, pinning me with his stare. "We're here for you."

I bit my lip, trying to keep myself from getting emotional. How did I end up falling into this relationship with these two completely different men? It wasn't something I had an answer for and was too big of a question for me to puzzle out in that moment.

"Thank you," I said, finally. "I do appreciate it. More than you know."

"If we can help, let us know," he said, then pressed his lips to my forehead.

I inhaled his scent, which was actually all around me, and held him for a moment before letting go and heading out the door. I didn't know what I was heading to, but I hoped it wouldn't be as bad as my anxiety was telling me it was.

CHAPTER FORTY-FIVE

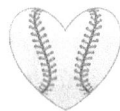

Billy...

"She's gone," Spencer said when he came back into the room.

I'd gotten up and pissed, but was back in the bed already when he walked in.

"She okay?" I asked.

"Don't know," he replied, walking into the bathroom, and shutting the door.

I got up and headed to my own room, picking up the clothes I'd taken off on my way. When I was dressed, I headed to the kitchen, which is where he was, already making coffee.

"What do you think is going on?" I asked.

"I think her brother knows," he said.

"About both of us?"

"Not necessarily," he said. "But one of us, probably for sure. She didn't turn off her location on her phone, and her car was on the street all night."

"Shit," I said. "We should have moved it."

"We were a little busy," he said, pouring milk in his cup. "Not that I'm complaining, just making a statement."

"Yeah," I said. "God, I hope her brother isn't a dick about it."

"I hope so, too," he said, before taking his coffee and heading back down the hall to his room.

Shit, this was just what we needed. And when we were set to leave in just a couple of weeks, too. Whatever it was, I hoped she'd let us know. The not knowing was the hardest thing about situations like this. When someone you care about isn't in a good spot, and you don't know what to do to help.

I went back to my room and changed into workout gear, pulling my shorts on first, then the sweats I had on back over top of them. Once I was dressed, I went into the bathroom to see what I could do about my hair. Should probably cut it before we headed south, but I liked it when my little angel grabbed it and used it for a handle to direct my mouth to where she wanted it. Shit, the six weeks of spring training were gonna be brutal if she didn't come down and break it up a bit for us.

When I walked out of my room, I saw Spencer had the same idea as me, so I just gave him a nod, then followed him down the hall. We each grabbed a jug to hold our water, filling it with ice first, then water on top. I grabbed a flavor packet and dumped it into mine, but Spencer stuck with just plain water.

It was like we had one mind, and we were working in unison. That worked well when we both had things on our mind and needed to figure them out. A workout was the best way to get out of our heads so our brains could just do what it needed. Snagging my keys, I opened the front door and hit the unlock button, knowing Spencer would lock up behind me. Neither of us said a word as I drove us down to the stadium, pulling into a parking spot in the mostly empty lot.

Working out did more than just build muscles and stamina; it helped to keep my mind occupied so I didn't worry about things I couldn't control. It was the one thing I could do to get away from everything that was happening around me when I was younger. I never took it to the extreme, but I would push myself as far as possible, and then just a little more. It was one of the few places my mom would leave me alone. That, and on the baseball field. Although, the field did have stands, and she'd be there all the time. It was like I could hear her, even now.

"That's my baby," she'd say. "My beautiful, sexy, powerful, brilliant little man."

Just the thought of it made me shudder, which was not what anyone wanted to do while they were holding a barbell above their body with entirely too much weight. I settled it back on the rack, with Spencer's help, and sat up, pulling the earbud out of my ear.

"What was that?" he asked.

"Nightmares from the past," I said.

"You've never talked about that," he said. "If you want to, I'll listen."

"I don't want to traumatize you," I said. "Besides, there are ears everywhere."

"I didn't mean now," he replied. "You ready to go? Or do you need more distractions?"

"Two more sets," I said, settling back against the bench.

He helped me as I struggled through the first set, and when I couldn't even get three reps, he pulled the bar up and set it on the stand.

"You're done," he said. "I don't want you injured before the season even starts."

"I know," I replied. "I'm just…"

I couldn't finish what I was about to say. He didn't need to live my nightmares. Hell, I didn't need to live them, but that was just the way my fucked-up life was.

"We're going to the cages," he said, turning to walk away.

"Good deal," I replied, getting up and heading in that direction.

The benefit of having the stadium be our training facility was that we could work on anything we needed to, without having to deal with the public. There were always trainers around, even in the off season, and we could work on most anything. With it being January, some had headed south already, but there were still a few that were here to help those of us who were local.

Stepping into the cages, I saw Huffman coming out.

"Hey," he said. "You guys ready for spring?"

"We're getting there," Spencer said.

"But it should be good," I added.

"Yeah," he said. "Can't wait to see the new guys."

"Can't even remember half of their names," I said.

"We've got all spring to learn that," Spencer said.

"True, that," Huffman said before heading out of the area.

"Is it me, or is he bigger than last year?" I asked.

"He's definitely bigger," Spencer said. "And he's got new ink, too."

"You noticed that, too?"

"Hard not to when it's all over his neck," he said. "Grab a bat."

I did as he said, snagging one of the many that were sitting near the cages. He headed to the other end of the space and poured a bucket of balls into the machine, setting it up and sending a test pitch from it to get it just right. Once he was done, he nodded to me, and I stepped up to the plate. It felt good to have a bat in my hands again.

CHAPTER FORTY-SIX

Ariana...

I headed straight to the office, not even stopping for coffee. When I pulled into the lot, Dad's car was there, so I knew it was something big.

"Shit," I said to myself as I turned the car off. "Might as well get this over with. I'm sure they're gonna rip me apart, but at least I have somewhere I can go to cry myself silly."

Climbing out of my car, I felt the oppression in the air, and it wasn't a feeling I liked. It was like there was a dark cloud over the entire place, and I didn't even realize it until I was halfway up the stairs. When I opened the door, I stopped dead in my tracks.

"Can I help you?" a police officer asked me as I walked in.

"I'm one of the owners," I said.

"Ari," Dad said as soon as he saw me. "She's my daughter."

The cop moved out of the way, and I stepped more fully into the space. Dee was sitting in a chair, a clipboard in his hands, and a scowl on his face that was full of so much vitriol that I didn't think I'd ever seen the look before. I hadn't really paid attention to anything as I walked in, my focus being solely on figuring out how I could explain why I'd spent the night with the guys, but now I wondered what I'd missed.

"What happened?" I asked.

"Brad happened," Dee said, and the words were like a punch with how much rage was in them.

"Come on," Dad said, pulling me back out the door. "Some of his fucking biker friends decided to pay us a visit last night. It was probably his initiation into their gang or something, but it had to have been him."

He walked me over to one of the buildings where we stored our equipment, as well as some of the supplies we kept on site. When I looked at the door, I realized it didn't have a handle on it anymore, and my stomach dropped.

"Fuck," I muttered as Dad pushed the door open.

The building was a mess. Shit strewn everywhere, and from what I could tell, there were many expensive tools missing. We had nail guns, compressors, drills, mixers, and about a million other small things that were easy to pocket and walk away with.

"Security footage?" I asked, looking at Dad.

"Nothing," he said. "Somehow, he got into the office and shut everything down, wiped it all clean from the last week, and disabled them so that even when Dee came in this morning, they weren't running. I think he fucked them up but good."

"Son of a fucking bitch," I hissed. "How do you know it was him, though?"

"Who else could it be?" Dad asked. "He was just fired, and he'd been on the edge as it was. Add in his obsession with that fucking gang, and you've got a recipe for exactly this."

"He's dumb," I said. "But I didn't think he'd be dumb enough to rip us off. He has to know we'd assume it was him, right?"

"Like you said," Dad replied as we walked back toward the office. "He's dumb."

"Fucking asshole," I mumbled.

"My sentiments, exactly," Dad replied as he opened the door for me.

"How long until we can get our equipment back?" I heard Dee ask as we walked in the door.

"Depends on if we find it with him," the officer said. "He may have hidden it, or the club could have shipped it somewhere else by now. They're quick with that."

"Get a copy of the report," I said. "I'll call the insurance company and see if they can wire us money so we can replace it."

"That's probably your best bet," another officer said. "This type of equipment can be fenced easily, so they've probably already liquidated it. Here's your copy," he added, handing the paper to me.

"Thanks," I said, taking it and heading to my office.

"I'll get the detectives working on this now," the officer said as I walked away.

"Just what I fucking wanted to do today," I muttered as I turned on my computer.

CHAPTER FORTY-SEVEN

S pencer...

We hadn't heard from Ariana since she left that morning, and I began to wonder whether there was something serious going on. I didn't want to bug her, didn't want to harass her, but I was worried, and there was no way around it. By the time we were ready to make dinner, Billy had asked about it as well.

"You should call her," he said.

"And say what?" I asked.

"Just ask if she's okay," he said.

"I don't know that that's the best thing to do," I said. "I don't want her to feel like we're controlling her or keeping tabs on her."

"But you're worried, too," he said. It wasn't a question, and it was something we were both thinking.

"The way she ran out of here…" I said. "And the fact that she said that something was wrong when she talked to her brother, yeah, I'm worried. But that doesn't mean it's anything dangerous."

"What if it is?" he asked.

"What are we supposed to do if it is?" I asked back.

"I don't know," he said, and I could hear the frustration in his voice.

"If she needs us, she'll let us know," I said. "We have to have faith in that."

"When will you call or text her?" he asked.

"Tomorrow afternoon," I said. "If she doesn't call or text before that, I'll reach out."

He took a deep breath, blew it out, then headed to his room. I felt the frustration as well, but instead of whatever it was he was going to do, I took food out of the fridge and began to prepare dinner. I needed to pound the chicken breasts to get them ready for the meal, so that's where I took my frustration out.

I'd plated the food before I saw Billy again, and he looked exhausted. As much as I'd like to pretend I didn't care about him, I did. He was as much a part of my romantic life as Ari was now, and the three of us had sort of built this relationship. None of us were less important than the others.

"What's going on?" I asked when he sat down.

"I'm trying to figure that out," he said.

"What were you doing in there?"

"You don't want to know," he replied, and I let it end there.

He had secrets and demons I didn't know about, and when he was ready, he'd share them with me. Since Ari had come into our lives, he'd been more open, but he still held things close to his chest. Especially his past. When he was comfortable, he'd share those things, but for now, he was closed off. Knowing that this was something he wouldn't budge on, I decided to talk about something I knew he was excited about, and that was the new addition and spring training.

"You sure you're good to drive down?" I asked after a few minutes of silence.

"Oh, yeah," he said. "Looking forward to it, actually."

"Because we could totally get a car while we're down there," I said. "Wouldn't be a bad thing to have a car that we left down there."

"Except that would fuck the car up if it sat for most of the year," he replied. "Can't do that to a car."

"We could have them ship it back up," I said. "It would mean we could stay here longer. Have more time with Ari."

He looked at me and actually thought about what I said.

"You want a new car?" he asked.

"Not really," I replied. "But it wouldn't be a terrible thing. Maybe I'd get a Jeep."

"Oh, yeah?" he asked. "Finally talked you into one?"

"We'll see," I said.

"Let's do that," he said. "Start checking flights, though, cause they're gonna be spendy this late in the game."

"I'll look tomorrow," I said.

"You booking us together?" he asked.

"If you want," I replied.

"First class, my dude," he said, and he seemed to be more himself.

I heard my phone ringing from the kitchen counter, so I got up and grabbed it.

"Hey," I said, answering. "We were worried about you."

"Is that her?" Billy asked.

I nodded as I waited for her to talk.

"We had a theft at the business," she said.

"Oh, no," I replied. "What happened?"

"We think it was a former employee," she said.

"The guy you just fired?" I asked.

"Yeah," she said. "But we can't get in touch with him at all. He disabled the cameras, erased everything for the last week, and made them so they can't record anymore. I've spent the entire day contacting our insurance and working to get new security set up. It's been a nightmare. I didn't even get to do anything I wanted to on any of the projects that are coming up due."

"Sounds like you could use something to distract you," I said.

"As much as I want to come over and get lost between you two," she said, and I heard in her voice before she said it, that she wouldn't be here. "I just need to get some actual sleep. If I go there, I'll not get the kind of rest I need. I want to, don't get me wrong, but I need sleep."

"I understand," I said. "We'll miss you, for sure, but we've decided to fly down to Arizona, so we will have at least another week here before we have to go."

"Nice," she said. "I might need a little vacation at some point."

"We'd love to have you come with us," I said.

"Please tell me she's coming with us," Billy said, but I waved my hand at him.

"I'll let you know," she said with a laugh. "Tell Billy hello from me."

"You can tell him if you want," I said.

"Sure," she replied, so I handed the phone to Billy, who had gotten up and was standing in the kitchen with me.

"Hey, Angel," he said. "We will miss you, that's for sure, but you're welcome any time. We'll keep the bed warm." He hummed a couple of times, smiling at whatever it was she said. "Okay," he said. "Let us know if we can help with anything. Seriously, we're here for you." Another humming, another smile, then he said, "Love you," and handed the phone to me.

"Hey, Darlin'," I said when I got back on the phone.

"Did he just say he loved me?" she asked, and I smiled, because I didn't think he even realized what he'd said.

"I think so," I said. "But let's not hold that against him."

"What?" Billy asked, looking at me very confused.

I again waved him away and turned from him so I could listen to the rest of the call. As much as I wanted her to come over, I knew we wouldn't let her sleep much if we could help it.

"I just don't know if I'm ready for that level of a relationship," she said.

"I'm sure it was an accident," I replied. "Rest well, and like Billy said, if you need us, at all, let us know. I'll also let you know when we're ready to leave, so you know when to plan to have my car in your garage."

"Will Billy need to leave his car somewhere, too?" she asked.

"I'll check with him," I said. "We'll miss you tonight, but I understand your need for sleep."

"Thanks," she said. "I will miss you, though. If we could guarantee no sex, I'd be there, but I know that wouldn't be fair to either of you. And I'm sure I'd willingly give in if either of you gave even half an effort to start something."

"We can behave," I said.

"I'm sure you can," she said. "But Billy would have a hard time."

"I could come to you," I said, and could feel the scowl from Billy at my back.

"I can't do that to you," she said. "I also wouldn't want to do that to Billy. It wouldn't be fair to him."

"I'm sure he would agree," I said.

"Either way," she said. "I plan to be there tomorrow night. I'm sure I'll need you both by then."

"I'll make dinner," I said. "What do you want?"

"That steak you made the first night was delicious," she said.

"Consider it done," I replied. "What time do you think you'll be here?"

"Not really sure," I said. "I might need to get a bunch of equipment to replace what was stolen."

"Not my idea of a good time," I said.

"Mine, either," she agreed. "How about I call you when I have an idea?"

"Are you going to want food first?" I asked. "Or would you rather be ravaged by two very capable men to work up your appetite?"

"The second one is my choice," she said with a laugh.

"Your wish is our command," I said. "Do you have anything special you want us to set up before you get here? Any specific toy? Something else?"

"I'm going to let you surprise me," she said. "But please be sure that you both are taking part in making me come so hard I can't see straight. I'm gonna need to be so drunk on orgasms I won't know who I am, where I am, or why I'm not still being fucked."

"Darlin'," I said. "I do believe we can make that happen."

"Good," she said, then mumbled, "Shit."

"What's wrong?"

"I'll call you back," she said before disconnecting the call.

"What was all that?" Billy asked as I looked at my phone.

"She's sleeping tonight," I said. "But tomorrow, we have been given orders to fuck her so hard she can't see straight, and she doesn't want us to stop. She's given us free rein, too, so I think we need to figure out how to make the most of the night."

"It's Friday tomorrow, right?" he asked.

"Yeah," I said.

"Does that mean she won't have to leave in the morning?" he asked.

"Let me check, because that would make things much easier," I said, shooting a text over to her asking exactly that. "She said she's free on Saturday and Sunday, so we can continue to pleasure her all weekend long."

"Fuck, yeah," he said, pumping his fist. "I'll start making plans, pulling out toys. We should get her on the rack."

"I think we'll find plenty to do," I said.

"I intend to wear her out," Billy said. "I want to have her so mellow she forgets all her worries."

"Yeah," I said. "That's the goal I'm going for as well."

CHAPTER FORTY-EIGHT

Ariana...

The insurance guy didn't want to give me any leeway, but I pushed hard, and he said he'd see if he could get a check out to us by Monday. I told him that wouldn't work because we had jobs that were relying on the equipment that was stolen, and we had a police report. I didn't understand why they were holding the money up.

I was still pissed when I went home, and I climbed into the shower, determined to scrub the day away. While it would have been nice to lose myself with Spencer and Billy, I knew I needed the sleep more. The fact that they'd asked about the weekend was nice, so I had something to look forward to. Just thinking about it made me want to start early, but I knew I wouldn't want to leave once I was there.

Sliding between my sheets, I thought back over the last couple of months, at what had started as just a fantasy of mine, and how they'd made every sexual experience I'd ever thought of, and more, come true. I'd read plenty of books that had the ménage trope going, but to experience it firsthand was more than I could have asked for.

As I dozed off, I heard my phone ring. While I wanted to ignore it, I figured it was likely Dee calling with an update. Maybe he'd found

Brad, talked him into returning the stuff he'd taken, and that tomorrow we'd go back to business as usual.

"Hello?" I asked, noting that the number read *private.*

"You're a naughty girl," a man said. "The things you've been doing are bad, and you're going to be punished for it."

"Who the fuck is this?" I asked, wide awake now.

"I'm so disappointed in you," he said. "You will pay for your transgressions. For the things you've done that were not what you should have been doing."

"I don't know who the fuck you think you are," I barked. "But this is not any way to gain my confidence. Now, kindly fuck all the way off and never contact me again."

I disconnected the call before he could say anything else, but I was shaken. As much as I tried, though, I couldn't place the voice. The fact that the number came in as private didn't help, either. Hoping against hope, I sent a text to Spencer.

Can you come over?

The little dots showed up right away, and I was hopeful.

Give me the address and I'll be there. Alone?

I was glad he asked, because, as much as I loved having the two of them, I felt the need for Spencer's stronger, more stable emotions.

Please. I need stability, not chaos.

I sent the address and wasn't sure what to expect in response. The dots came back, and then the text I hoped I'd see came in.

On my way.

I sighed with relief, climbed out of bed, and threw on a pair of panties and an oversized shirt, then headed down the hall to the front of the house. I didn't know how long it would take for him to get here, but since it was the middle of the night, I was hopeful it wouldn't be long.

Instead of going to the front door, I went into the kitchen, filling the teapot on the stove with water, and setting it on the stove to get warm. Pulling down a couple of mugs, I opened another cupboard and pulled down my collection of tea bags, shuffling through them to find the chamomile I knew was in there.

Not knowing whether he'd want any, and not knowing what kind he might want, I left the whole box there for him to choose. When the pot started to boil, I pulled it off the burner, turning the stove off as I did. I poured the water over my bag, letting the flavor come out of the bag, the smells rising to start the relaxation process.

When a knock came on my door, I headed over, then paused. There wasn't enough time for Spencer to get to my place, yet, so it couldn't be him. I wanted to be brave, call out to ask who it was, but I was also smart enough to know that if it was someone I didn't know, or someone who meant me harm, I didn't want to be dumb enough to open the door to them.

"Ari, it's me," I heard, and pulled the door open.

"What are you doing here?" I asked my brother.

"There was a really weird message on my phone," he said, pushing past me and walking in. "Oh, are you expecting someone?"

"Yeah," I said, praying that Spencer wouldn't pull up while my brother was here.

"You're not hooking up with a stranger, are you?" he asked.

"No," I said. "It's someone I've known a while."

"Good," he said. "Because I was worried about you."

"I'm fine," I said. "So, can you go, now?"

"I suppose it's because you don't want me to see who's coming over," he said.

"Exactly," I said.

"I'd feel better waiting until he got here," he said.

"Demetri," I said, and put as much force as I could muster behind his name. "I know who's coming over. I trust him. I don't need my brother to babysit me. Can you let me be an adult, please?"

Just then, I heard a car come up the street.

"Shit," I muttered.

"That must be him," he said.

"Go," I said, shoving my brother toward the door.

Unfortunately, Spencer hadn't seen, or recognized, that someone else was here. Either that, or he thought that whatever threat I had going on had shown up, and he was there to protect me. Whichever it was he was thinking, he strode up to the door, determination in his step. When he saw my brother, he faltered, but then kept coming.

"Really?" Dee said, looking at me. "I thought you said you weren't doing that."

"Dee," I said. "It's not what it seems."

"The fuck it's not," he said, his voice raising.

"Hey," Spencer said. "Don't talk to her like that. She's an adult, and capable of making her own decisions. If you wanna be pissed, fine, but don't talk that way to her."

"I'm not going to let our company be fucked up because she decided to fuck a client," he said.

"Dee, please," I said.

"No," he said. "The remodel, the addition, it's all off. You can find your own way on that, but Carington Construction isn't gonna do it."

"Are you serious?" Spencer asked. "You're gonna fuck up your company because your sister decided to call me when she was in need. Were you the one who freaked her out? Because I'm here as a friend. Someone she trusted to make sure she was safe."

"Wait, you're not…" Dee said, looking between us.

"Dee," I said, unsure exactly what Spencer was doing.

"Mr. Carington," Spencer said. "Your sister has my number in her phone because we've been working together to get everything set up for the remodel of the bathroom and kitchen. When she sent me a text asking me to come over and stay here because she was afraid, I was willing to do that. It's what you do for friends, and I feel like we've reached that point in our relationship. Now, if you think that little of your sister, maybe I'll offer to fund her own company, and let her do my remodel and addition with the new business."

"Hold up," Dee said, and I was looking at Spencer like he'd grown a third head. "You're saying that you guys have become friends?"

"We've been spending quite a bit of time together," Spencer said. "There is a lot to planning everything we've requested. Why wouldn't I become friends with her?"

"Fuck," Dee said, shaking his head.

"Yeah," I said, unsure how I was going to explain this when it came out that I'd been fucking both Spencer and Billy. "You should check yourself. This isn't something you'd accuse a guy of, but to think that you think this little of me is rather disappointing."

"I'm sorry," Dee said. "I just, I've kind of been pushed to the limit today."

"No need to take it out on your sister," Spencer said.

"I guess you're right," he said. "I'll see you in the morning. I'm going to need you to hear this voicemail, though."

"Let's listen to it now," I said. "Having the door open is really not good for my energy bill."

"Sorry," Dee said, stepping back into the house.

Spencer shut the door behind him and looked at me over my brother's head. I sort of just shook my head, not wanting to have this conversation at any point in time, but right now, I was terrified from the phone call. And if Dee had a voicemail that was anything like the call I got, I didn't know what I needed to do.

CHAPTER FORTY-NINE

S pencer...

I hadn't expected her brother to be there and didn't even think when there was another car in her driveway. But when I saw him, I fucking freaked. I had to think quickly and try to do what I could to keep the secret we were sharing, so I let whatever fell out of my mouth happen.

When Ari looked at me, I could tell she was freaked, but it was more than just the fact that one of her lovers showed up when her brother was there. She moved into the kitchen and came out with a steaming mug. I didn't know what was in it, but that didn't matter. It could have been damn near anything, and I wouldn't have faulted her.

"Are you gonna play it or just stand there?" she asked.

"Yeah, right," her brother said, pulling his phone out.

"Your sister is a whore," the male voice said from his phone. *"She is fucking clients and is selling you out. You better get her in check, or the whole world is going to know the name Carington Construction, and not in a way that will be helpful for your future."*

"That's why I was suspicious," her brother said, looking at me. "Sorry, man."

"I get it," I replied. "Do you recognize the voice?"

"It's the same voice that called me tonight," Ariana said.

"Do you recognize it, though?" I asked, looking at her.

She was standing there in nothing but an oversized shirt, and all I wanted to do was pull her next to me, let my hands run over her skin, and tell her I would protect her from the entire world. That wouldn't solve the issue right now, though. No, I needed to keep my cool, stay the friend who was there to support her, and let her brother believe that was why I was here.

"I don't think so," she said.

"I'd say it's someone who either knows you, or has seen you somewhere," I said.

"That's what I think," her brother said.

"Could it be a former boyfriend?" I asked.

"I don't think so," she said.

"Is it the guy who was just fired?" I asked, looking between the two of them.

"It's not Brad," he said.

"Definitely not," she added. "But it could be someone from that gang he was trying to get into. Maybe they're trying to intimidate us."

"I didn't even think about that," he said.

"What gang?" I asked.

"It's a local motorcycle gang," she said. "Brad's been trying to get into it for a while. We think that's who put him up to stealing the stuff from the business."

"But that didn't sound like him to you?" I asked.

"No," her brother said. "It's not him. I've known him for years, and there's no way he could figure out how to disguise his voice like that."

"Okay," I said. "What did the voice on the call you got sound like?"

"Just like that," she said.

"Okay," I replied. "What did he say?"

"He said I did things I shouldn't have been doing," she said. "Said I'd pay for it."

"Okay," her brother said. "I don't like this. Not one bit. You need to stay with someone, or at a hotel or something."

"Like he couldn't figure that out?" she asked.

"Then what are you gonna do?" her brother asked.

"I'm going to take a vacation," she said, pointedly not looking at me. "I'm going to go away somewhere that no one knows where it is. I'm leaving my phones here, getting another one that I'm not swapping my shit over to, and I'm going to ghost the whole area."

"Do you think that's wise?" I asked.

"It's the only thing I can think of that will get me away from whoever the fuck this is," she said, and the determination was strong in her voice.

"Can you afford it?" her brother asked.

"I'll figure it out," she said. "In the meantime, I'm not telling anyone where I'm going. Not even you."

"How are you going to get anywhere?" her brother asked. "He might have something tracking your car. I mean, if he knows something he thinks he can hold over your head, how do we know he hasn't tapped your phone, stuck some sort of recording device in your house, any of that."

"I'll take her to a place she can rent a car," I said. "Whoever is following her or whatever won't think she'd go somewhere with me. Why don't you go pack a bag? I can take you tonight to a hotel. Your car will be here, so they may not realize you're gone."

"Unless they're listening to us right now," her brother said.

"Doesn't matter," I said. "They're not going to know which hotel I drop her at. I'll go to several, stay long enough for her to check in, then we can drive to the next one. I'll pay, too. It's the least I can do. I feel like I might be the reason this is happening."

"Why would you think that?" her brother asked, and I wondered whether I'd gone too far.

"Because of my high profile," I said. "People tend to latch on to people who are famous and want to either bring them down a notch or cause them problems."

"But how would they know you're connected to her?" he asked.

"Because you're doing my remodel," I said. "It isn't something that we like to talk about, but people will stalk us online, even in person, and try to figure out what we're doing, and how they can bring us down. It's the price we pay for being in the limelight."

"But it's not like you're some superstar," he said. "Nothing wrong with what you do, but you aren't exactly a household name."

"Yeah," I said. "But that doesn't usually matter. I'm in the same position, being a professional athlete. I wish it weren't that way, but it is."

"Can you keep her safe?" he asked me.

She'd gone down the hall. I think he was really scared for her, because he'd lowered his voice and was taking me at face value, someone who had decided to befriend his sister.

"I will do my best," I said.

"I'm ready," Ari said when she came back down the hall. "You guys figure out who it is?"

"I have no idea," her brother said.

"Well," she said, dragging a suitcase behind her. "I'm leaving. Everything is on your shoulders for the next week or so. My phones are in my room, car keys are on the hook by the door. You've got a key for the house, so I'm going to let you lock up."

"I can't believe this is happening," he said.

"Me, either," she said. "But it is, so I'm not gonna deal with it. My brain hurts, my heart hurts, and I just need to run away."

"Where are you going?" he asked.

"I'm not telling you," she said. "I haven't decided, yet, but I don't want you to know. You might accidentally say something, and that would fuck everything up. If you don't know, you can't say anything."

"This doesn't feel right," he said.

"I know," she replied. "I just know that I can't stay here and be safe, so I'm going to trust my friend to take me somewhere else."

Her brother looked at me, and I nodded to his unasked question. I would keep her safe. There was no doubt about it. Whatever I had to do, she'd be safe with me.

CHAPTER FIFTY

Ariana...

When we pulled up to a nondescript motel in the middle of nowhere north of Seattle, I started to feel just a little better. I don't know what Spencer and my brother talked about while I packed a bag, but whatever it was, it was enough to put my brother at ease, which was good. It was bad enough that someone was possibly stalking me, but I didn't need my brother to be freaked out by what was going on between me and Spencer, too.

"Is Billy gonna join us?" I asked. "Not that he has to, just wondering."

"I think it's best if he doesn't know," he said as he got out of the car. "I'll be right back. Lock the doors."

His car was much nicer than mine, but that's because he could afford it. I had a beater that got me where I was going, but his was sleek and quiet. I pressed the lock button on my door and heard the click of the lock engaging as I watched him walk into the lobby of the motel. I didn't know who it was that had called me, or Dee, but it was definitely the same guy. The more I thought about it, the more I realized I'd heard the voice before. By the time Spencer came back out, I knew when.

"He called me last year," I said as he slid into the car.

"Who?" he asked.

"The guy who called tonight," I replied. "The same guy who called and left Dee the message. I knew I'd heard the voice before, but I just now placed it."

"Who is it?"

"I still don't know that," I said. "But he called right after I sent out the email to architects for your job. It was weird, 'cause I specifically asked everyone to email me. When I called him on it, he sounded off. Not bad, just weird."

"Yeah," he said. "I don't like that you've been dealing with this for months."

"I haven't," I replied. "It was the one call right at the start. Nothing since then, until tonight."

"I mean that he's been watching you for months," he said. "Are you sure you don't recognize the voice?"

"If I knew who it was, I'd tell you," I said. "Fuck, I'd tell the cops. I don't take stalking lightly, at all."

"Good," he said.

He started the car, pulled it up into the lot, then turned around and headed back out onto the street.

"Aren't we staying there?" I asked.

"Nope," he said.

Taking a few back roads, he ended up winding through the little town, following the main drag until he came up to another side road. This one lead up toward the mountains more. He seemed to know where he was going, but I wasn't sure. He finally pulled off the main road and off onto a gravel one that transitioned to dirt just a bit down the way.

I wasn't sure where he was taking me, or if this was even planned, but he pulled up to a tiny little cabin nestled in the woods. It was a two-story, but super small and very rugged.

"Come on," he said, opening his door.

This was not what I was expecting, but I undid my seatbelt and went to open the door. When it opened on its own, I jumped and shrieked before covering my mouth with my hand.

"Sorry," he said, holding a hand down to me.

He had my suitcase sitting next to him, which surprised me. I didn't think it'd taken me that long to get my head around, but it must have. I got out of the car with his help, and he led me to the cabin. He pulled his keys out of his pocket and pressed it into the dead bolt on the door, turning it so the tumblers unlocked. Then he did the same with the knob, opening it up to this amazing little space.

"Welcome to my sanctuary," he said as the door opened.

I stepped into the space that was dark and heard him close and lock the door behind him. There was no light, so I couldn't really see much of anything, until I heard the flick of a lighter and light started to glow from behind me. Turning, I saw him putting the chimney onto one of those old lanterns that you put oil in. I was surprised at how much light it gave.

"It's rustic," he said. "But it's well out of the way, and no one knows about it but me. Well, now you, too."

"Your secret is safe with me," I said, turning to take the space in more.

He didn't strike me as the outdoorsy kind of guy, but the more I looked around the space, the more I realized it suited him. It was rugged, that was for sure, but the log walls were lined with bookshelves as well as paintings. They all looked like cowboys and western-themed images. I walked toward the fireplace that was set in the side wall to look at the image just above the mantle. It wasn't clear, with so little light, but what I could make out was fascinating.

"I'll get some wood and start a fire," he said, and I saw that he'd moved to the other side of the cabin where another door opened to a small deck that was covered.

This was a side of him I didn't know existed, and I kind of liked it. Basic, simple, settled. He even seemed more relaxed than at any other point in our encounters. When he came in with a small satchel type thing full of small logs, I stood transfixed by this image I never saw before. It brought out a side of myself I'd never experienced, either.

"What?" he asked when he looked up at me.

"Nothing," I said, stepping away from the fireplace so he had somewhere to put the wood.

"Not what you expected?"

"Not at all," I said.

"I'll get this going," he said, pulling the screen back from the fireplace and beginning his process to get the fire going.

I walked over to where he'd left my suitcase, just a handful of steps, and turned to really take in the whole cabin. It was tiny, just a small loveseat in front of the fireplace, the kitchen barely anything more than the stove, sink – small as it was – and a tiny ice chest sort of thing.

"Do you have electricity up here?" I asked, realizing that I couldn't hear any of that kind of background noise.

"No," he said as he struck a long match and set it to the paper in the hearth.

I watched as the flames began to dance, slowly at first, then catching the wood that was in there. It didn't take much time for it to be going, and I was impressed with him even more. If I'd tried to start a fire, I'd probably manage to burn myself. Either that or catch the entire structure on fire and burn it to the ground, along with half the forest around us.

"Bathroom?" I asked, realizing I hadn't seen one in the tiny space, unless it was tucked under the staircase at the side.

"Outhouse," he said. "Sorry. It's not luxury, but it's hidden, and no one knows about it. I figured it was the safest place I could bring you."

"What was with the hotel?" I asked.

"Red herring," he said. "I checked in under my actual name, so if anyone goes looking, that's where they'll think we are."

"You don't have to do this," I said.

"I know," he replied, standing from his crouched position in front of the fire. "I wanted to. Besides, this way, you're safe, your brother is off your back, and I can have a couple of days with you all to myself."

"You're not gonna bring Billy up here?"

"He doesn't know about this place," he said. "I texted him that you were in danger and that I was going to take care of you. He already replied that he was fine with it. He'll carry on at the house as if I'm there, or away, or whatever. He doesn't mind. Did you want me to invite him?"

"No," I said, almost too quickly. "I mean, you don't have to."

"I get it," he said, closing the space between us. "We haven't done anything with just the two of us, so it's new. We don't have to do anything, either. I'm fine if you want to just sleep upstairs in the bed for the whole weekend. I'll make sure you have food, and that you're warm and safe. This is just a good place to be."

"If I said I wanted to do something?" I asked, knowing he would understand the full question.

"Your wish is my command," he said, sliding his hand around my waist and pulling me to him. "I'm yours to do with as you please."

I reached a hand up and ran it along his jawline, feeling the stubble that was there from more than just a couple of days growth. I liked the friction against my palm and wanted to feel it on other parts of my body as well.

"Take me," I said, pressing up on my toes. "Do with me anything you want. I am yours."

Pressing my lips to his, I told him with my body that I wanted him. He was the one who intrigued me initially, so the thought of having him alone was something I was looking forward to. It wasn't that I didn't like having the both of them, just that it was sometimes so much I felt overwhelmed.

His arms pulled me closer, and I raised my leg, hooking it around his hip as he deepened the kiss, a hand sliding down to grip my ass and press me to him, his cock hard against my core, and the angle we were at made it just miss hitting me in the right spot. I whined, shifting my hips to try to get some friction going, and he lifted me, stepping to the counter and setting me on the edge.

Tearing his mouth from mine, he loomed large over me, and if I didn't know him, it would be an intimidating thing. But this was Spencer, my Spencer, the one who teased me and tantalized me. The man who had shown me things I'd never experienced and taught me to expect the unexpected. To desire everything I could imagine. To want him, to want them, and to let them play me like the beautiful instrument they'd created.

"You're so beautiful in this light," he growled. "I've wanted to bring you up here for a while, and while this isn't the ideal condition for it, I am glad you're here."

"I've wanted to be with only you for a while, too," I said, confessing my desire for some one-on-one. "This is a beautiful place, and I can't wait to share it with you."

Again, his lips crashed to mine, his hands pressing at my back, his hips rocking in a way that made his length slide against me, and the movement gave me enough contact to push me near the edge. But it wasn't enough, not in any way. I needed to be next to him, my skin against his, and I pulled my hands to the front of him, working to remove his jacket.

Pulling back, he flung the offensive garment off and onto the floor. I followed suit, getting my jacket, then my hoodie off, both ending up on the floor as well. When he'd pulled his shirt over his head, I was mesmerized. While I'd seen him without a shirt many times, I hadn't taken in the tattoo that ran from on top of his shoulder halfway down his arm. There was a sunburst of sorts on the shoulder, and some lettering in a script font lower down on his bicep. Everything was in black and white, with shades of gray blending it all together.

Reaching out, I traced a finger over the letters along his arm, wondering what they stood for. I didn't want to ask, didn't want to hurt him for not knowing, and for not even caring before now.

"My grandfather," he said.

"Oh," I replied, not knowing what else to say.

"He's the one who taught me about baseball," he said. "Well, baseball and life. He really was an amazing man, and I miss him all the time."

"I'm sorry," I replied. "I didn't mean to cause you pain."

"It's fine," he said. "I think he'd be proud of the man I've become. Well, minus all the sex. He was definitely of the mindset that you should be married before you have sex, so I guess I messed that one up."

"What would he think of you and Billy?" I asked. "Of your arrangement?"

"Yeah, he'd not be pleased," he said. "But he was a rebel in his own way, so I guess I'm following in the spirit of his footsteps."

"And me?" I asked, unsure why it was important.

"Oh, he'd have loved you," he said, his eyes bright in the flicker of lamplight. "You are absolutely the kind of woman he'd want me to be with."

"Really?" I asked.

"Definitely," he said, stepping back up to me.

He lifted my shirt off, and I raised my hands to let him remove it. When he saw that I wasn't wearing a bra, he sucked air in through his teeth, which just made me want him even more.

"Didn't want anything extra to distract us," I said.

"Fuck," he sighed. "You are about the most beautiful woman I've ever known."

His hands came up and cupped my breasts, his thumb rubbing across each nipple, pebbling it from his touch, and I sighed, letting my head fall back, just allowing him to touch me, tease me, and enjoy my body. When he pulled one of my nipples into his mouth, I arched my back, pressing it further, allowing him to bring it taught, setting teeth just barely into it to give me that fine razors edge of pain and pleasure.

"Oh, God," I sighed.

There was space between us, and he used it to his advantage, sliding his hand into the waistband of my sweats. I hadn't dressed glamorous, just covered myself until I could get to a place to figure out what was going on. Now, though, I was glad I had been minimal in my attire. It gave him enough room to slide his hand all the way down to my pussy, slicking his fingers in the arousal he brought about, and sliding a finger inside me.

Bucking against his hand, I held onto his shoulders, as he fucked me with his fingers, while sucking my tit. It was a combination that he knew worked on me, and I let go of everything but his touch as he sent me flying into the stratosphere, exploding into a million pieces.

CHAPTER FIFTY-ONE

S pencer...

She was putty in my hands, meant to be teased and treated like the goddess she was, and I intended to give her as much pleasure as possible. I wanted to make her forget about all the worries she'd been dealing with and just enjoy herself, and we were off to a wonderful start.

Billy had never been interested in my cabin when I'd first got it a few years ago, and I knew that he would understand my taking her here and not telling him. He knew that something was wrong, or at least he would once he woke up, so I didn't anticipate him worrying. He might, and he might try to reach me, but where the cabin was, cell service was spotty at best, so I doubted I'd even get a text from him.

Instead, I planned to enjoy Ariana to the fullest. The fact that she'd said she had wanted to do something just with me gave me a thrill I wasn't sure I wanted. She'd insisted that she loved being with the both of us, but wanted to experience me alone, too, and I was happy to oblige.

Her first orgasm came on the counter of my kitchen, tiny as it were, and then we moved to the couch. She'd asked about condoms, and I'd been somewhat prepared. I had thrown a box in the trunk, so I went out and grabbed it while she waited. When I got back, she was staring into the fire, but not seeing it.

"Hey," I said when I sat next to her. "You okay?"

"I don't know," she replied. "Who could be doing this?"

"Doesn't matter," I said. "You're safe, now."

"I don't want to live like this, though," she said, turning to look at me. Her eyes were bright with unshed tears. "I can't live my life looking over my shoulder, just waiting for someone to come and get me."

"We'll figure it out," I said. "This weekend, you're safe here with me. Nothing will come to get you, no one will find you, and we'll be able to enjoy ourselves as much as you want."

"I know that logically," she said. "I just wish my brain would stop with the serial killer reel that's running through it. All I can think about is how someone I know, or don't know, is stalking me, looking for me, and wants to hurt me."

"You're safe," I said, again. "If you want to leave, we can do that. If you want to stay, we'll do that, too. If you want, we can fly to Arizona early and give you a very nice vacation prior to our starting spring training."

"I don't want to run away," she said, and the steel in her voice was back. "I'm not going to let some jackass threaten me and scare me into hiding."

"For tonight, though," I said, letting her answer the rest of it.

"Tonight, we'll hide," she said. "But I want to go back tomorrow. I know I said I'd stay with you guys, but I need to figure this out."

"Will you let me distract you?" I asked, and she turned to look at me.

"Please," she said. "Turn my mind to mush. Let me forget the rest of the world exists. Just for tonight, I want to pretend that it's just you and me and nothing else."

"With pleasure," I said, pulling her toward me.

She moved easily, straddling my lap, and leaning in against my chest. The cabin had warmed up enough that she was warm against me, and my arms were likely cold around her body. She shivered a bit, but then settled in, letting me hold her as she relaxed. Her head was on my shoulder, and I knew she could feel my erection against her core, but she relaxed so fully, that it wasn't long before I heard the soft sound of her snores.

As much as I wanted to get myself off, her comfort and rest were more important. I held her until I was sure she was in a deep sleep before shifting and laying her down on the sofa. I wanted to take her up to the bed, but I didn't want to chance hitting her head on the walls, or tripping while going up, so I opted to leave her here. I found a blanket in the trunk behind the sofa, and set it over her, tucking her in. When that was done, I pulled my shirt back on, and settled onto the overstuffed chair that was next to the couch. It wouldn't be the first time I'd slept in it, and while it wasn't comfortable, I didn't want to leave her down here alone, either.

CHAPTER FIFTY-TWO

Billy...

Spencer had sent a text that he was going to get Ariana, but then sent another one a little bit later that said he was taking her to his cabin. He didn't say what was going on, but the way he worded the texts indicated something was up. Much as I wanted to see her, I knew that if he was taking these measures to get her away, there must be something he didn't need me to know about.

I was hurt that he hadn't woken me up, but figured it was the middle of the night, and he didn't feel like dealing with my cranky ass. He knew I hated it when he had to get me up, so figured it was easiest to just let me sleep. Couldn't fault him for that.

Saturday, I spent the day cleaning up the kitchen, as well as my own room. I wanted to make sure that everything was ready for the weekend. The toys we'd recently used were thoroughly washed, as well as the ones I wanted to try out with her. Everything was put into a safe spot where we'd have access to them when the time came. I couldn't move the rack by myself, so I left it in the office.

As the day wore on, I headed to the gym to get my workout in. Walking into the stadium without Spencer wasn't completely unusual, but it was fairly rare.

"Where's your buddy?" Hennings asked when I showed up.

"Busy," I said.

"I didn't know you could function without him," he replied.

"Fuck you," I said.

"No thanks," he said with a laugh. "I've got someone I like to do that with."

"Then go get fucked by him," I said, knowing it would piss him off.

I was right, too, cause he got up and glared at me, making like he was gonna come at me, but Huffman put a hand on his shoulder to calm him down.

"Yeah," I said. "Keep that dog away from me."

"I could take you," he said.

"Whatever, Becky," I replied, then turned my back on him.

Was it a smart move to give him my back? Maybe not, but I knew that Huffman wouldn't let it get too out of hand, so I trusted him. I heard a scuffle, Hennings grunting, and turned to see that he was sat down on a chair, Huffman standing over him. It was comical, and I couldn't help but laugh.

"Keep it up, buttercup," Huffman said. "You're next."

"I got shit to do," I said, grabbing a towel and heading to the cages.

The machine was already set up, and our hitting coach, Sandoval, was in there. There were some new faces of players I hadn't met, yet, but I also saw some I hadn't seen since the season ended.

"Hey, dude," Matsui said. "You look like you've been keeping up with shit."

"You know it," I said, taking the hand he offered and pulling him in for the half hug, back slap we usually did. "How was the off season?"

"Good," he said. "Got married."

"Really?" I asked. "I didn't know you were even dating anyone."

"High school sweetheart," he said. "We've been working toward it for a while. We finally just did it, cause I ain't getting any younger, and she wants kids."

"You make babies while you were off?" I asked.

"We gave it the old college try," he said, smiling.

"Good on you," I said.

"How about you?" he asked.

"We've got a steady girl," I said. "But it's still new."

"Ah," he said. "I don't get that sharing thing. I couldn't imagine wanting anyone touching Rachel. It just pisses me off thinking about it."

"It's not for everyone," I said. "But we make it work."

"Where is he?" he asked, looking behind me.

"He had something he had to take care of," I said.

"Well," he said, slapping my shoulder. "See ya round."

"See ya," I said, then went to grab a bat to get to work.

I took some swings to get myself set up, then stepped into an open cage. Digging myself into the box, I squared up to take the first ball from the machine. It came at me, and I swung, cutting just underneath it, bouncing it straight up into the net above my head.

"Fuck," I muttered.

"Do it again," Coach said. "Focus on the seams."

It was what he'd taught us over the last several seasons and was something that had improved all of our vision when it came to the plate. I settled myself again, slowing my breathing, and stared at the machine, waiting for it to send me a ball. It came, and I watched as time seemed to slow down. The turn of the ball was simple, tumbling over and over, and I knew exactly where it was going to be when I pulled the bat off my shoulder.

Thwack.

I connected on the sweet spot, drilling it right back at the machine. If it'd been a pitcher there, he'd have either had to duck or get hit in the chest. The way most of them fell off the mound, though, it would have sailed right over his back. Only a lucky thrust of his mitt in the air would have caught it.

"Nice," Coach said. "You've been listening."

"You told me last season that I was pulling the ball too much," I said. "I took that to heart and worked on it. I'm glad it's paying off."

"Glad you listened," he said.

I spent the next half hour switching out with the new guys, and the handful of veterans who had shown up, until I was hot and tired. After that, I headed to the weight room, wanting to bulk up more. It had helped when I started toward the middle of last season, and with what I've done since September, it's shown up in my swing. I just need to make sure it doesn't mess with my fielding.

CHAPTER FIFTY-THREE

riana...

It was so quiet it was eerie. Dark and quiet, and it smelled like the woods. There was smoke in the air, too. Something else was filtering through all of that, though, and I stretched, pulling the blanket off my head, blinking at the brightness of the space.

"Mornin', Darlin'," Spencer said, and I sighed.

"Good morning," I said through a yawn. "What time is it?"

"No clue," he said, and I peered over at him in the little kitchen space. "Doesn't matter. We're not going anywhere today. It's just you and me and the great outdoors. Nothing's gonna come between us."

"You sure it's not you that was stalking me?" I asked, sitting up.

"I wouldn't be so subtle," he said, turning to me, and I could see this little stove type thing he had on the counter. "Want some coffee?"

"Do you have any sugar?" I asked.

"Sugar, yes," he said. "No cream, though. Didn't get a chance to grab anything on the way and didn't want to leave you here alone."

"Afraid I'd run away?" I asked.

"Didn't want to freak you out," he said, pouring coffee into a large mug. "Let this warm you up while I dig out the sugar."

He handed the mug to me, and the warmth was nice in my hands. I was naked from the waist up, but it was warm enough in the space that I didn't really need anything else on. There was a fire going in the fireplace, which was crackling away just a few feet across from the sofa I was sleeping on. He was shirtless, wearing a pair of sweats, and by my guess, nothing underneath. I licked my lips, wanting to taste him, anticipating all the things we could get up to alone in the woods.

"Shit," he said as he opened a tin. "Fucking ants."

Opening the door, he stomped out and disappeared from my sight.

"Take that, fuckers," I heard him shout, and then he was walking back into the cabin without the tin.

"What did you do?" I asked.

"Tossed the whole fucking thing down the side of the mountain," he said. "Sorry. No sugar until I can get to a store."

"Aren't we going back today?" I asked.

I knew we'd talked about it, about me not wanting to run away from whoever the fuck it was that thought it a good idea to threaten me, but now I doubted myself.

"We can," he said, sitting next to me with his own cup of coffee. "But it might be nice to just not be anywhere for a while. Off grid, out of the limelight, away from the hustle and bustle of society. What do you say?"

"I mean," I said, inhaling the aroma of the coffee in my mug. "I don't want to run away. I've never run from a fight, and I don't intend to start now."

He dropped his head, took a deep breath, then let it out slowly.

"How about we spend today here," he suggested. "We can head home tomorrow morning. You good with that?"

"I think I can live with that," I said, and he smiled so big it looked like it hurt.

He leaned over, kissed my forehead, then took a drink of his coffee, only to spit it back in the cup.

"Gimme that," he said, taking the cup from my hand.

"Hey," I complained.

"Trust me," he said, opening the door and tossing the liquid out of both mugs. "It was bitter. No, it was bad. Seriously bad."

"Why?" I asked.

"I haven't been up here in a while," he said, setting the mugs on the counter. "Maybe a year or more."

"You have this beautiful cabin and you don't come up here?" I asked.

"It's better in the summer," he said. "And I'm usually working the whole summer. So, no cabin for me. Getting up here in the winter can be challenging, especially when it snows."

"I mean," I shrugged, not sure what else I could say.

"I know," he said. "It's stupid to have something you don't use. But I loved it the first time I saw it, and I wanted to have a place to run away to when the city was giving me grief. Now, though, I'm glad I have it."

"Me, too," I said. "Thank you."

"For what?"

"For rescuing me," I said. "I usually like to take care of myself, but I was actually afraid. Seriously afraid. The shit he was saying was bad, and I didn't know how he knew about you and Billy, but it pissed me off, too."

"I thought you said you were gonna go away for a week," he said. "Did that change somehow overnight?"

"I don't want to run away from a fight," I said. "I hate being afraid, but I hate backing down more."

"There's a little shop down the way," he said. "Glen and Tracy are good people. We can get a signal there and you can check in with your brother if you want while I pick up some staples."

"Do they have coffee?" I asked.

"I'm sure I can talk them out of a cup for you," he said. "Let's get some clothes on and head down. Won't take more than an hour to get there, get some stuff and head back."

"Okay," I said, shoving the blanket off me.

He sucked in a breath and stared at me, eyes wide with desire, and I really just wanted to have him hold me. But I had to pee, and that wasn't exactly a good thing if you wanted intimacy. Not that it was bad, just something to take into consideration.

"Bathroom?" I asked.

"Outhouse," he said.

"Shit," I said. "I forgot."

"You put clothes on," he said. "I'll go make sure all the bugs are gone."

"Thank you," I said.

CHAPTER FIFTY-FOUR

S pencer...

I cleaned out the outhouse, then handed her a roll of toilet paper as she went out, reminding her to bring it back with her when she was done. While she was gone, I got myself dressed, banked the fire so it would die down some and not run the risk of burning the whole damn place down, and got everything else ready to go to the store. I hadn't seen either Glen or Tracy in a bit, but I was sure that they were still at the store. I noticed it when we drove by on the way up and figured it would be good to see them again.

If we were only gonna be here for another day and night, I wasn't gonna get anything perishable, just a couple of staples. Coffee was a must, but I'd be taking it with me when we left. I would also be taking the sugar, cause I fucking hate ants. Those little creepy things can get fucked.

"That was... Interesting," she said when she came back in.

"You've never used an outhouse?" I asked.

"I'm a city girl," she said. "With how quiet it is, it's kinda freaking me out. Not gonna lie, it's weird."

"I love the quiet," I said. "It feels like I'm the only person in the whole world."

"Me, too," she said. "The only person in the world thing. But I think that's why it freaks me out. I like to have alone time, but I need to know I'm not too far from another person."

"I get it," I said. "Billy's the same way."

"So," she said, scuffing her shoe on the floor. "Do you think it's right that I go back?"

"That's not something I can answer," I said. "This is happening to you, not me, and I don't live in your head, so don't know how it's affecting you. If you think it's a good idea to go back, then we can do that. If you want to hang out longer up here, I'm down with that, too. Or," I added, waiting for her to look at me. "I could take you on a trip somewhere out of state. We can go pretty much anywhere. Billy's got a condo in Phoenix, and we can stay there. Or Hawaii, or anywhere else you want to go."

Her smile grew with each destination I mentioned, and I was pretty sure she was gonna take me up on it, until she shivered and frowned.

"Hey," I said, going to her and tipping her head up with my finger under her chin. "Tell me what's going on."

"It's like this fight is going on inside me," she said. "One part of me wants to run away, let you whisk me off my feet to some unknown destination where I can hide from everything. But the other part is pissed that someone drove me from my home, called my brother, and said terrible things about me and my life. I've never run from a fight, and I don't want to start now."

"Let's get some food," I said. "And coffee. I'll check in with Billy to make sure he knows we're alive, then you can call your brother to see what's going on there. After that, we'll decide what we want to do. Sound good?"

She nodded, smiling at me, hopefully knowing that I would do anything for her. Just then, her stomach growled, and we both laughed.

"I guess I better take you to get some food," I said. "Otherwise, the bears in the woods might want to run for cover. Your stomach sounded like it could give them a run for their money."

"Pretty sure they're hibernating," she said.

"Never can be too careful," I replied, pulling her against me to kiss her forehead.

"I could stay in your arms forever," she sighed.

"I would hold you until you wanted me to let you go," I replied.

We did stay there, just for a few minutes, but then her stomach rumbled again, and she pulled back.

"Let's get food," I said.

"Do they have a restaurant or something?" she asked as I locked up the cabin.

"They live above the store," I said. "They always have something freshly made available, so we'll see what's what when we get there."

The drive from the cabin down to the store was nice. We just sort of let the world around us rush by, holding hands, and enjoying the quiet. When I pulled into the little lot, she gave a sort of, "Oh," sound, and I wasn't sure whether it was a good sound or not.

"It's so tiny," she said as I put the car in park. "And they live here?"

"Yeah," I said. "They're a really nice couple. Not sure what they did before, but they told me when I first got the cabin that they wanted to get out of the rat race and do something simple with their retirement."

"So, they're older, then," she said.

"Not really," I replied as I opened my door.

I helped her out of the car, shutting the door behind her, then hooked my arm around her waist as I guided her into the store. The little bell above the door tinkled as we walked in, and Ari was mesmerized by the whole thing. Watching her see it just squeezed my chest tight. God, I wanted her to stay in my life for a long damn time, and I'd do whatever it took to make that happen.

"Welcome in," Tracy said, then looked up to see me. "Spencer. It's so nice to see you again. Hey, Glen. Spencer's here."

"Spencer," I heard from the back of the room, and then I saw the man come forward. "Damn, man, it's good to see you again. How've you been? I've been watching you."

"Been good," I said. "Still reaching for the playoffs, but we'll get there."

"Some of the guys you got this winter should help," he said.

279

"Let's hope so," I replied. "I need just a few things, cause we're only here for today and tonight."

"Sure thing," he said.

"This is my friend, Ariana," I said, looking at her standing near me with eyes wide. "It's her first time up to the cabin. Tried to make coffee, but it was bad. Ari, this is Glen and Tracy."

"Hi," she said, her voice somewhat quiet. "Nice to meet you."

"I gotta go make a call," I said. "I told her you might have some-thing for breakfast. If not, no biggie, but if you do, I'll need some, too."

"We have all sorts of things," Tracy said. "We'll take good care of her."

Ari looked at me, eyes wide, like she was terrified I was leaving her alone with them.

"I gotta call Billy," I said. "Won't be long. Promise."

"Okay," she said, but I knew I had to be really quick, so I stepped outside and turned my phone on, waiting for it to power up so I could make the call.

CHAPTER FIFTY-FIVE

Ariana...

I didn't want him to leave me alone, but I also didn't want to be rude.

"I don't think I've ever seen Spencer bring anyone up to the cabin with him," Glen said, and that was actually a relief to me. "Have you?"

"Not that I remember," Tracy said. "Ariana, is it?"

"Yeah," I said. "Sorry. I'm still tired. It was kind of a sudden trip, and we came up sort of in the middle of the night, so I'm a little out of my element right now."

"Doesn't surprise me that he didn't plan ahead," she said, a knowing smile on her face. "Sometimes men don't think of all the things we might need. Now, he said you might be hungry."

Just then, my stomach growled, and I mean growled. It was embarrassing, and I wanted to just run from the store, but she smiled at me and moved down the counter.

"I've got some orange and cranberry scones," she said, stepping up to a little open counter thing. "I might have something more substantial upstairs, though, if you don't mind waiting."

"I think the scones would be fine," I said. "I wouldn't want to put you out."

"Trust me," she said, lowering her voice. "It would be no trouble at all. You and I can go upstairs and leave the guys to talk their sports and such."

"So," Glen said as he came back from wherever he had gone. "How long have you and Spencer been together? I haven't seen anything about him finding someone."

"Um…" I stammered.

"Glen," Tracy said. "Knock it off. You don't need to know everything about everything. Go find some coffee and sugar for them. Maybe some of that powdered creamer, too."

"I just wanted to be polite and ask," he said.

"Well, you're being an ass," Tracy said, shaking her head.

"Hey," Spencer said as he came in. "Billy didn't answer. My guess is he's at the gym working out. I left him a message, though. You wanna call your brother?"

"I probably should," I said. "He's gonna want to know where I am."

"You can tell him whatever you want," he said. "Here," he added, handing me the car key. "It's cold out there, so feel free to get into the car to keep warm."

"Thanks," I said. "It was nice to meet you," I called out to the couple.

"Pleasure to meet you, too," Tracy said, but Glen wasn't anywhere that I could see.

Spencer was right when he said it was cold, and I was glad he gave me the key. I climbed into the passenger seat, shutting the door to keep the cold at bay, and dialed my brother. I didn't know if he'd answer, though, since the call was coming from someone else.

"Carrington Construction," he said when he answered.

"Hey, Dee," I said.

"Ari," he replied, and I could hear the relief in his voice. "Thank God. Are you okay?"

"Yeah," I said, confused. "I told you I was going off grid. What happened?"

"I got another call," he said. "I answered it, though. Guy was telling me that he had taken you and was holding you for ransom. Said that he was gonna get your boyfriends to pay, since they were rich. I tried to get him to tell me something, anything that would indicate that he was telling the truth, or to figure out who he was, but he never let me get a word in."

"I'm sorry," I said. "Spencer has a cabin in the mountains. That's all I want you to know, other than it is very rustic and there's no signal up there. We're coming back tomorrow."

"You're still with him?" he asked.

"Yeah," I said. "I'll come to the office when we get back."

"Why don't you come to my place?" he said.

"Because your place is a mess," I replied. "The office would be better."

"Okay," he said. "I'm really glad to hear your voice. I was getting worried."

"Thanks," I said. "I'm fine. I'll see you tomorrow."

"You figure out who it was?" he asked.

"Not yet," I replied. "But I do have an idea."

"Who?" he asked.

"I'll talk to you tomorrow," I said.

"Okay," he replied. "I love you."

"Love you, too, ya goober," I said, then disconnected the call.

I looked up and saw Spencer coming out of the store. I was actually glad he was, because the couple were nice, but I just didn't want to meet new people at the moment. What I wanted was to get back up to the cabin and have Spencer blow my mind, get me out of my head, and help me forget about everything that was happening to me.

CHAPTER FIFTY-SIX

Billy...

The message Spencer left was short, basically saying they were at his cabin, and that they'd be back the next day. I knew when he went up there, there was no reaching him. Hell, I didn't even know where it was, other than in the mountains somewhere. Didn't matter, though. He had our girl, and she was safe. What was weird was that it came in now but showed that it was sent before I even left the house.

"Hey," one of the new guys said as I was stuffing my phone into my pocket. "We're heading out for food. Wanna come?"

"Where you guys going?" I asked.

He looked over at another new guy, and the other guy looked back.

"We're not sure," the first guy said. "I'm Dallas, and this is Ricky. We were kinda hoping you could suggest somewhere."

"Sure," I said. "I'm sure we can find somewhere to get some good grub."

The guy beamed, and I was glad to help them out. I offered to drive, and they gladly accepted, so we climbed into my Jeep and I pulled us out and into the light rain that had begun to fall.

"It rains a lot here, huh?" Dallas asked.

"Mostly cloudy," I said. "I mean, we get plenty, don't get me wrong. It's why the roof is retractable. But there's more in Boston as far as total inches."

"No way," Ricky said. "It's gorgeous in Boston."

"Yeah," I said. "We get more clouds, but as for rain, it's usually light, like this."

I drove away from the stadium and headed north along First, heading toward the Market and where Huffman's girlfriend had a shop. Finding parking on the weekend was usually hard, but with the rain it was easier. Regulars would come out, but tourists tended to not like being in the wet, which was nice for those of us who didn't mind.

Parking in one of the paid lots, I went to the kiosk and paid for my space, dropping the ticket onto my dash.

"Let's go," I said, heading down the sidewalk toward Post Alley.

The guys looked around as we went, checking out all the sights as we went down the hill toward the waterfront.

"Are we going to the Pike's Place Market?" Ricky asked.

"First of all, it's Pike Place Market," I said. "If you're gonna live here, you need to know the right way to say it. And no, we're going to a pub just a half block before we get there."

"A pub?" Dallas asked. "As in, a bar?"

"It's an Irish pub," I said. "Good food, good beer, and not someplace that will draw attention to us."

"Okay," Dallas said.

"But first," I said, stepping into the tea shop next door to our destination.

"Welcome in," the woman behind the counter said.

"Skye in?" I asked.

"Yeah," she said, stepping to the doorway at the back of the shop. "Skye, you got company."

She came out the door and smiled.

"Hey," she said. "Did John come with you?"

"No," I said. "He's still working out. Looks like he's been doing that a lot in the off season."

"Oh, yeah," she said, coming to give me a hug. "He said he needed more power."

"Dude hits like a cannon," I said. "I wanted to introduce you to a couple of the new guys. This is Dallas and Ricky. Guys, this is Skye. She's dating Huffman."

"Nice to meet you," Ricky said, sticking his hand out.

"Pleasure," Skye replied, taking his hand, then shaking Dallas's.

"I'm taking them to Kell's," I said. "Figured I'd give them a good meal today, then work their asses off tomorrow."

"They have really good food," she said.

I was watching Dallas as he was wandering around the shop, pretending to look at the things Skye had in here, but he wasn't really looking at them. He was watching the woman behind the counter. Raising my chin, I sort of pointed over to him, and Skye turned to see what he was doing, and how the woman was reacting.

"You like tea?" she asked him.

"I'm not sure," he said, and he was blushing like a teenager.

"Be nice," Skye said, slapping my arm just as I was about to say something.

"What?" I asked.

"I know how you guys get," she said. "Mai's nice and could use a nice guy in her life."

"Not sure he's nice," I said.

"He's super naïve," Ricky said. "I'm pretty sure he's a virgin."

I looked at him like he'd grown a second head.

"How the fuck has he not been laid?" I asked, a little too loud because Dallas turned to me, eyes wide. "His brother," I said, hoping like fuck that Ricky had one.

"It's my nephew, and he's sixteen," Ricky said, covering well, which, thank fuck for that.

"Now I'm worried," Skye said. "Mai might chew him up and spit him out."

"I think he's due," I said. "Hey," I said louder. "We gonna eat or what?"

"Oh, um, yeah," Dallas said, fumbling with his words.

"Mai," Skye said. "Why don't you go with them?"

"Sure," she said, and the way she looked at Skye told me that they had some sort of girl telepathy going on.

"You guys should get your own table," I said. "Way in the back, away from prying eyes. You know, so you can get to know each other better."

Skye slapped my shoulder, and I shrugged and smiled.

"You're an asshole," she said, but she was smiling as they walked out the door.

CHAPTER FIFTY-SEVEN

Spencer...

Tracy had packaged up some of her famous orange cranberry scones, Glen had brought out a small bag of ground coffee, some sugar, and one of those tumblers with powdered creamer in it. I also grabbed a couple cans of stew and a small sourdough roll that Tracy had made up, figuring that could be for our late lunch or early dinner. We could stop on the way home and grab food tomorrow, but I didn't want to have to leave the cabin any more today.

"She seems nice," Tracy said.

"She is," I replied.

"Are you sure she's not after your money?" Glen asked.

I smiled, because we'd actually had a handful of conversations over the years about how hard it had been for me to find someone who was interested in me as a person rather than the bankroll from the team I earned.

"She owns half of a construction company," I said. "Her and her brother are equal partners. That's how I met her, actually."

"Oh," he said. "I guess she doesn't need your money, then, does she?"

"It's not about that," I said. "We actually get along pretty well."

"That's good," Tracy said. "It's always important to be friends as well as lovers."

"That it is," I replied, dropping a hundred-dollar bill on the counter.

"I don't have change for that," Tracy said, opening her cash register.

"Consider it a tip," I said. "And advanced payment on watching the cabin. I do appreciate that you keep your eye out."

"I do what I can," Glen said. "Now, go enjoy yourself."

"That's the plan," I said, taking the paper bag Tracy had packed my items into.

Ari looked like she was just hanging up the phone when I stepped out, so I went to the driver's side and opened the back door, setting the bag on the floor behind my seat, before shutting it. I climbed into the driver's seat and shut the door, turning to look at her.

"What's wrong?" I asked as soon as I noticed the look on her face.

"I think I know who the stalker is," she said.

"Is that a good thing?"

"Maybe," she said. "But I don't want it to dampen our day. I want this day with you, just the two of us. Can we do that?"

"Of course we can," I said, starting the car.

The relief that seemed to wash over her as I didn't question her further was what I was going for. My plan was to make her forget absolutely everything else in the world for the rest of the day. Tomorrow would get here soon enough, and we'd be heading back to town to deal with the ramifications of what had been going on then. Today was about her, and only her, pleasure.

When we pulled up next to the cabin, she tensed a bit, and I wasn't sure why. I looked to the cabin, but nothing seemed out of place, so I looked back at her.

"What is it?" I asked.

"I don't know," she said. "It's a gut thing. I'm not sure, but something isn't right."

"Stay here," I said, moving to open the door.

"No," she said, grabbing my arm.

Just then, I saw someone come from the back of the cabin. I didn't recognize him until he came into the light. I opened the door and climbed out of the car, walking over to my brother.

"What are you doing here?" I asked.

"I could ask you the same thing," he replied, pulling me into a hug. "Did you forget I was gonna come up and use the cabin?"

"Obviously," I replied, smiling up at him.

I was tall enough for baseball, but my brother was taller than me by almost five inches. Elliott played basketball for a while, but said he wasn't cut out for the lifestyle. He and his wife, Beth, have three kids and a home back in Georgia. Elliott comes out here every year or so to have a week to himself to refresh his soul. Beth does the same thing, just somewhere else.

"I'm glad you're here," I said, turning to look at the car. "I have someone I want you to meet."

"Really?" he asked, his smile bright.

I walk to the passenger side of the car and open the door.

"Ari, this is my brother, Elliott," I said as I helped her out. "El, I'd like to introduce you to Ariana Carington. She's become an important part of my life."

"It's nice to meet you," she said.

"Pleasure is all mine," my brother replied, taking her outstretched hand. "I didn't know anyone would want to hang around my little brother."

"He's been nice to get to know," she said, her face blushing.

"Oh, I'm sure he has," my brother replied. "I brought some stuff to make breakfast, if you haven't eaten."

Just then, her stomach growled again, and her blush just brightened.

"Come in," he said. "It's cold out here, and I've got some breakfast cooking."

CHAPTER FIFTY-EIGHT

Ariana...

I hadn't known what was going on when we pulled up, but there was a sense that something was off. When a literal giant walked out from behind the cabin, I froze. I wanted desperately to keep Spencer in the car, but he walked out and hugged the man who was nearly a head taller than him.

When he introduced him as his brother, I relaxed somewhat, but was still uneasy around him, and I couldn't put my finger on what it was. Introductions were made, and we went inside to eat some of the food that Elliott had cooked. I relaxed marginally as I listened to the brothers talk about family and back home, which was Georgia for them.

"Where is your car?" I asked after a while.

"Took an Uber," Elliott said. "I didn't want to have to rent something and have it sit here while I fiddled around at the cabin. It was an expense I just wasn't willing to put out."

I nodded, as if that made all the sense in the world, except for the fact that I had no idea how he'd get a ride back when he was ready, since there was no service.

"Are you guys here for a while?" he asked after the dishes were rinsed.

"We're planning to go home tonight," I said, not wanting to stay anymore.

"I thought it was tomorrow," Spencer said.

"No," I said, and felt guilty about taking Spencer away from his brother, but I needed to be away.

"Okay," Spencer said.

I could hear the questions in his voice but was thankful he didn't ask them out loud. I excused myself and went out to the outhouse, wanting to be away from them, but with how cold it was outside, I didn't want to just be on the porch. The small space was overwhelmingly rank smelling, but it was basically a hole in the ground filled with shit, so I had to expect that. I wanted my own home, my own bed, and my own shower. I felt like I still had the ick from the call the night we left on me, and I wanted it off.

By the time I walked back into the cabin, Spencer had my bag by the door. I knew he wanted to stay longer, but I needed to get out of here. I needed civilization and to not feel so isolated and out of touch with the world.

"Ready?" he asked as I shut the door behind me.

"Yeah," I replied. "It was nice to meet you," I said to his brother.

"You, too," he said. "Keep him in line for me, will you?"

I stuttered a bit but nodded in agreement.

"Call when you get back to the city," Spencer said. "We can grab a bite to eat."

"My pickup is scheduled to take me straight to the airport in time to get on my flight," his brother said. "But I'll come see you when the team goes to Atlanta."

"That works," he said, then pulled his brother in for a hug.

We climbed into the car, and he started it up, backing around to drive down the path to the paved road. He was quiet as we went, and it wasn't until we were well on the way that he spoke up.

"What's going on?" he asked, not looking at me.

"I don't know," I said. "I just need to be at home."

"Okay," he said, and it sounded forced, like he was trying not to say something.

"What?" I asked, and he pulled off the side of the road we were on, putting the car in park.

"You're acting weird," he said. "I know you've got stuff going on, and that you're a little skittish, but I want to help you, and I don't know how."

I could feel tears welling in my eyes, my throat was dry, and I couldn't figure out how to articulate what was going on inside me.

"Come here," he said, reaching over and unbuckling me, pulling me across the space between the seats. "Let it out," he continued, holding my head to his shoulder.

The position was awkward, but not uncomfortable, and the smell of him, the way he held me so tight, just unlocked whatever it was that was holding me back and I did as he said, letting everything out. I cried like I hadn't cried in years. Like I hadn't cried since…

"I'm sorry," I said, trying to pull away.

"Nope," he replied, keeping me against him. "You let it out, and when you're done and ready, we'll talk."

I took a deep breath and let it out, then leaned back some and looked into his dark eyes.

"I had a stalker in high school," I said. "It didn't start out that way, but that's where it ended up. He was one of the popular kids, and even though I wasn't exactly one of the outcasts, I didn't quite fit into that group, either. A bunch of the guys made a bet on who could get me to sleep with them first. It was stupid, and I didn't even realize it wasn't real until he finished and started laughing."

I swallowed, trying to recall all the things that were going on at that time in my life.

"My mom had just gotten sick," I continued. "She wasn't near the end, it was at the very beginning. I felt lost, like I didn't matter that much, and needed someone to reassure me that I was valuable. Caden started the whole thing as a tutoring session, one that his parents were paying for. He kept the thing up until I finally slept with him."

"Is this the guy you told me about?" he asked.

"I told you?" I asked.

"Yeah," he said. "But you didn't mention the stalking part."

"I try to block that part out of my brain," I said. "Once I slept with him, he wanted to go public. At least, that's what he told me. I told him he had to make a grand gesture, make it clear that we were together, and not just a matter of convenience for his grades. I thought he was gonna do it, too."

"He started rumors, right?" he asked.

I'd shifted back to the passenger seat, because sitting across the divide in the front was too uncomfortable. He was watching me, holding my hand, stroking his thumb across the back of it, and I could tell he wanted to just hold me. It's what I wanted, too, but I didn't want to go anywhere else. I didn't want to be out in public sharing this story.

"Yeah," I said after taking a big breath. "He said I gave him the clap, that I didn't know what I was doing, and that I let him fuck me every way imaginable, well, at least at that time in my life. It was awful, and everyone believed him, too. I mean, he was the well-known person in the school, and I was just a nobody."

"You're not a nobody," he said, squeezing my hand.

"I know that, now," I said. "But tell that to fourteen-year-old Ariana."

"Wait, you were fourteen in high school?" he asked.

"Skipped a couple of grades," I said. "Sucks being smart, but it is what it is."

"That's cool," he said. "Okay, back to the story."

"Fourteen-year-old me had no idea that what someone says can be taken as the truth if they say it loud enough and to enough people," I continued. "My brother was the one who came up with the idea that I should talk about how small his dick was. I had someone ask me something about what he said, and I laughed, looked at her, and asked if she'd seen his dick, cause it was kinda hard to find if you weren't looking for it."

"You were brutal," he said. "But it was well deserved."

"Unfortunately," I said. "He figured out what I was saying and started stalking me. I didn't know it, but he'd had a camera in his room to record his exploits. When I saw the video, I about died. It was terrible. I looked like a stupid girl who was excited to get her cherry popped by the popular guy. I did what he asked me to do, and watching it when it came out, it was clear that he knew where the camera was and played to it."

"I'm so sorry," he said.

"Yeah," I said, sucking in a breath. "My dad found out and went to the cops. They wanted to say there was nothing wrong with people consenting to being recorded. It wasn't until my dad pointed out that Caden was eighteen and I was only fourteen that they actually paid attention. He basically got a slap on the wrist, told to delete the video, and a restraining order against him to keep him away from me. Because he was a star athlete, I was made to change schools. It fucking sucked, but I did it because I didn't want to be anywhere near him."

"I hate that the system screwed you," he said.

"Me, too," I said. "I hadn't thought about him in years, and when the calls started coming in, I didn't even put the pieces together."

"You think it's him?" he asked.

"Makes sense," I replied. "I haven't kept the restraining order in place because I didn't think he'd be that stupid."

"How does he know about us, though?" he asked.

"Not sure," I replied.

"Why did you freak out when we got back to the cabin?" he asked, and he was genuinely asking.

"I have a sort of sixth sense now," I said. "It's something I developed. When your brother came around from behind the cabin, all I saw was Caden. He was big like your brother, and I figured he'd just gotten bigger in the years between when I saw him last and now."

"Do you know where he is?" he asked.

"No clue," I replied. "I just know that he was given community service because it would be a shame to let one little misunderstanding ruin a perfectly good life."

"Someone actually said that?" he asked.

"The judge," I replied. "And his dad. I mean, the coach from the school would have probably said it, too, given the chance. But when the judge said it, I just lost all faith in the system. It's been a decade, give or take, since it happened, and not a damn thing has changed. If you're powerful enough, you can get away with anything."

"I wish I could say you were wrong," he said. "But I know how it is. I've seen it up close and personal."

"So," I said, after taking a deep breath and letting it out. "I just had to be out of there. I know he's your brother, but I don't know him."

"It's fine," he said.

"I feel bad that you don't get to hang out with him," I said.

"It wouldn't have happened anyway," he replied, lifting my hand, and pressing his lips to my knuckles. "He likes to do these things solo. If I want to spend time with him, I do it with his whole family."

"I still feel bad," I said. "I know it's a me thing, and you don't have to try to convince me not to, 'cause it won't work. But I care about you, and I don't want to get in the way of you getting what you want."

"Darlin'," he said, and the southern drawl came out hard with that one word. "I want you. I want to play baseball. And I want to be happy. I've got all of that right now."

I blushed, from the tips of my toes to the roots of my hair. I'd been better about keeping it to a minimum, but there were still times when either he or Billy would say something and I'd just go bright red. Thankfully, I didn't feel like that was a problem for them. He kissed my hand again, then put the car in drive and pulled back out onto the road. I'd be back to civilization soon enough.

CHAPTER FIFTY-NINE

Billy...

When I turned into the drive, Spencer's car was there, and I was confused. He said they were staying another night up at the cabin, so I didn't expect to see him or my little angel until Sunday. I wondered if something had happened and went into the house unsure of what I'd find.

"Hey," Ari said as I walked through the door. "Where were you?"

"At the gym," I said. "You're here early."

"Elliott was at the cabin," Spencer said. "I forgot it was that time of year."

"No brother sharing?" I asked.

"Not on my life," he said. "That man is about as conservative as they come. I think even the mention of more than one man and one woman would fry his brain."

"You good?" I asked Ariana.

"Yeah," she said, but there was uncertainty in her voice.

"Talk to us," I said, and she looked at Spencer who was in the kitchen getting something fixed for dinner.

"We'll talk over dinner," he said.

"Okay," I replied. "I need to shower. Want to join me?"

"Not this time," she said, and I was sad, but understood.

"See you when I'm out," I said. "Any preferences on tonight? I can get something ready for us if you want."

"I actually have something in mind," she said, and there was a bit more confidence in her voice. "I'll get things set up, but you have to promise not to go into Spencer's room."

"But of course," I said. "I wouldn't want to spoil the surprise. Although, I do have a few things set out that I'd be interested in using. You know if you need a direction."

"I'll take that into consideration," she said.

The whole time we were talking, I was walking toward her. Slow and steady, not rushing, but not staying back, either. When she said the last, I was right in front of her, and she placed her hands on my shoulders and pressed up onto her toes to kiss me. Spencer was taller by a few inches, but I was still tall enough that she couldn't kiss me flat footed.

My arms wrapped around her waist, holding her against my body as I deepened the kiss, sliding my tongue along the seam of her lips until she opened for me. She tasted of coffee and cranberries and citrus, and I wondered what she'd eaten. My cock was also very much aware of how close we were and decided to stand at attention and press into her.

"Should I take care of that," I said. "You know, so I will last longer?"

"I won't say no to stamina," she replied. "But I thought you liked the delayed gratification."

"Five minutes without you is more than enough delay," I said, pressing my lips softly to hers. "I'll let you tell me what you want. You're in charge."

She bit her lip, pulling it into her mouth as she thought about what I said.

"Just know," I added. "If I delay, I won't last long. But I can recover pretty quickly, which you know."

"Oh, I know," she said, her eyes bright. "Why don't you take care of yourself in the shower. By the time you're out, I should be ready to put my ideas to work."

The way her eyes danced with humor made me desperate to get ready. She'd become more daring, asking for things outside of what we'd done, and willingly participating in our fantasies as well. The fact that she had some ideas as to what she wanted to do made me so proud of her, and wanting to give her everything she asked for, without question.

Kissing her once again, I headed to my room, stripping along the way, and turning the water on so I could be ready for whatever she had in mind.

CHAPTER SIXTY

Ariana...

I'd been on my way down to Spencer's room, which is where we'd decided to keep all the toys until they left for spring training, when Billy had come in. I hadn't lied when I told him I had some ideas for what we could do. It hadn't been the whole truth, though, either.

The phone calls had really gotten to me, pulled me back to when I wasn't nearly as self-confident as I had become, and I wanted to be the one in charge. The one to tell them what to do, how to please me, and not just do what I knew would work for them. I wasn't gonna deny them their pleasure, and I knew that pleasing me would be high on their list of things to do, but I really just wanted to not let them run the show.

Our entire time together had been beneficial for all of us, but sometimes I felt like I bent to their will too much. That was going to change tonight, and I hoped that they would both be receptive to what I wanted from it.

Seeing the toys that Billy had set out made me shiver with anticipation, and almost made me back down on what I wanted, but I figured I could use some of what he'd set out, as well as the things I knew were available, and we could all have a wonderful night. In fact, I wouldn't be opposed to having our fun last through the next several days. Dee didn't know I was back, and I was sure my lovers would be thrilled to have unlimited access to me for more than just the night.

Grabbing a couple of the toys that I preferred, I set them on a hand towel on the bench in the shower. I also grabbed a bottle of lube to put with them. I'd found that water was very much a detriment to lubrication and having that extra available would make things work better for everyone. Moving back to the bedroom, I looked closely at what was set out, pulling ones I either didn't know what they were, or wasn't interested in using off the bed and setting them back in the box in the closet.

We'd done some bondage, but it had been fairly tame so far, and I wanted to sort of ramp that up. I knew Spencer would never allow me to restrain him, but Billy loved it. I wanted to use that to my advantage as much as possible, so I pulled the restraints out from under the mattress so we had easy access to them.

The container next to the bed was full of condoms, so I didn't have to worry about that, but I did set another bottle of lube next to them, just in case. Tonight would be the first time I really took control, and it was starting to make me doubt myself. I heard the shower turn off, so knew that Billy would be ready soon. I just had to make sure that Spencer was in the right frame of mind for what I wanted to do.

I'd made a point to throw some sexy clothes into my suitcase before I left home the night before, so I pulled them out and started to get changed. They loved my body without any decorations – they'd said as much – but I wanted to do something special for them, something to show them that I cared about them just as much.

There were times when I wore something special, like at Christmas and New Years, but this was something that I wanted to do up extra. I'd been saving it, and it just felt right to throw it into my bag. I had plenty of other things that were still here, but I bought this a while ago and now was the perfect time to wear it.

It wasn't anything super fancy, just a babydoll style top that buttoned in front with just one clasp between my breasts. The thong underneath was barely there, but I always liked it when they peeled my panties off me, so I went ahead with putting it on as well. They loved it when I wore purple, so that was the color I'd ordered. I had to use a different account than the one I normally did, because my brother knew that information, and I didn't need him knowing I was ordering sexy things.

I'd shut the door when I came in, not wanting to chance them sneaking a peek before I was ready. I double and triple checked all the things I'd set out, then pulled a couple of extra towels from the cupboard in the bathroom and set them on the bed. The first time I'd squirted, it freaked me out. But the more time I spent with these men, and the more they showed me how amazing sex could be, especially when it was messy, the more I felt at home letting myself get lost in their touch, their arms, and completely consumed by them.

Once I was dressed, I went to the closet and grabbed a couple of the candles that we had that were specifically for using during our play. They melted at a lower temperature, so the wax didn't burn our skin when it touched it. I'd been hesitant to using them initially, but they'd been patient, allowing me to go at my own pace, taking their time to show me the pleasure that could come from the heat of the wax dripping along my skin.

There was one that I loved the most, and it wasn't just the scent, or the fact that it was black. No, it was because the wax had some sort of moisturizer in it, and after playing, my skin felt amazing. So soft and smooth that I had been tempted to use it regularly, just for those properties. Spencer had gotten several of them because I enjoyed them so much. I grabbed two of them to take with me, along with the electronic lighter thing they had. Setting them on the dresser right by the door, I stepped back to look at what was before me in the room.

Feeling like I was good to go, I went back into the closet and pulled down the robe that they'd gotten me for Christmas. It was oversized, but so soft that I simply wanted to curl up inside it. I wrapped it around my body, pushing my arms through the sleeves, and tightening the belt around my waist to keep it closed, holding the secrets I wore underneath in check until I was ready to reveal them to my men.

That thought made me pause. They really had become mine, and I theirs, over the last few months. It wasn't a property kind of thing, or any kind of real ownership. No, it was the fact that we worked well together, cared about each other, and only wanted what was best. It hit me, square in the middle of my chest, that I loved them both. Loved them so deeply that I didn't want to hide any longer. I wanted the world to know that they were mine, and I was theirs.

The knock on the door startled me, and I gave a little yip.

"Hey," Spencer said. "You want to eat first?"

"Um," I hummed. "I think I'd like to have my dessert first, if that's all right with you guys."

"Yes," I heard Billy shout, and I had to smile.

"You guys need to go sit down at the table," I said, trying to sound strong, but not sure it came across that way. "I'll be out in just a minute."

"Your wish is our command," Billy said, and I could hear the laugh under his words.

"Whenever you're ready," Spencer said.

I gave them time to move down the hallway, then a minute longer so they could get settled at the table. Finally, when I figured they were both ready, I opened the door, just a bit, and peeked out. Not seeing either of them, I opened it further, leaving it open so we could move in without anything between us once we were done in the rest of the house.

Tonight was going to be something we would not soon forget, and I couldn't wait to get started.

CHAPTER SIXTY-ONE

S pencer...
We'd sort of settled on who sat where at the table, with the number of nights she was over, so both of us sat in our usual spots, leaving the head of the table, the open chair between us, empty. She'd been spooked the night before, and that had been ramped up with my brother being at the cabin when we came back. The fact that she didn't want to just sleep meant that she felt safe with us, and I would do whatever it took to make sure that trust was not put in jeopardy.

"Close your eyes," she said from my doorway.

I looked at Billy and he grinned about as big as I'd ever seen him before, then slowly closed his eyes, sitting back in his chair, ready to accept whatever it was that she was going to give us. I trusted Ari, with more than just the secret of our relationship, so I did what she asked and closed my own eyes, though I was nowhere near as relaxed as Billy.

She came down the hallway. I heard it, but also knew she was getting close, simply by the way my body reacted. It was like she was my true north and would guide me to herself at every moment. The heady knowledge that she could ruin me barely washed through my mind as I smelled the unmistakable scent that was her arousal.

"Thank you," she said next to my ear, and I shivered.

I wanted to open my eyes, look at her, and see what she was wearing. Or, perhaps, what she wasn't wearing. She'd been in the room long enough to change several times if that was her plan, but she was much simpler than that. It wasn't something that was a dig on her, just something that I noticed. She liked things easy, smooth, simple. Couldn't fault her for that because those were wonderful things to know.

The table creaked a bit, and I almost opened my eyes, wanting to make sure she was safe, but decided that she'd let us know if she needed help. Waiting was torture, but I endured, knowing that we would all get to enjoy the fruits of her labor eventually. Billy and I had talked about bringing out the cross but hadn't had a chance to get it moved from the office. Now, with us gearing up to be heading out for spring training, we might not get a chance.

"Are you ready?" she asked.

"Yes," Billy said.

"More than you know," I said.

"I don't think you are," she said, and I wanted to argue, but held my tongue. "I probably should have said something first, but you both have entirely too many clothes on. Can you undress without opening your eyes?"

"I can," Billy said, and I heard the rustle of cloth.

"Of course," I replied, pulling my shirt over my head.

"Mmm," she hummed, the sound rushing through me and straight to my cock, which throbbed against the zipper of my jeans.

I toed my shoes off and stood, shoving the chair back some with the motion. I didn't want to bump the table, so had purposefully moved in a way that kept me away from it. If I got too close, I was afraid I'd open my eyes and ruin whatever surprise she had in store. Stripping wasn't my thing, but I went as slow as I could, trying to make sure she knew I was doing what she'd asked.

"Should we sit?" Billy asked, and I hadn't even thought about what we were going to do after we were naked.

"Yes," she said, her voice breathy.

God, it was torture being this close to her, but keeping my eyes closed. As much as I wanted to see her, I wanted her trust more. Keeping my eyes closed was the smallest thing to ask, and I wouldn't give her a reason to doubt me.

My cock was hard, standing up against my stomach, and it longed for her touch. I could hear movement, but it was such a foreign thing to not be able to look. I mean, I could, but that would ruin it for her, and that was the last thing I wanted to do. I could be patient and wait for her. Hell, I knew how to be patient in damn near everything. It was something I prided myself on. There was a tearing noise, and I guessed it was a condom she was opening. I guess we would be starting at the table, which was fine by me.

"Eeny, meeny, miny, moe," she said, and I could hear that she was between us, so guessed she was on top of the table. "You both look so tantalizing, I don't know which to choose first."

"Both," Billy said, and I had to bite the inside of my cheek to keep from laughing.

"Oh, you'll both get some," she said. "I'm just trying to decide which flavor to start with."

"Chocolate," I said, and she laughed.

"Oh, I hadn't thought about that," she said. "Might have to add to my ideas."

"We've got all night," I said.

"And all day tomorrow," Billy added.

"We could also go into next week," I said. "We don't have to leave for spring training for a few weeks. Even when we go, you could come with us."

"Mile high club could be ours," Billy said.

There was no way that we could fuck on a plane unless it was a charter. Even then, it likely would have several other people on it as well. I wasn't exactly one for exhibitionism, but I knew that Billy was. Commercial airlines had small bathrooms, so that just wasn't gonna happen.

She was moving again, and I wasn't sure where she was going, but the anticipation was building. My breathing increased, my cock throbbed, and my ass was not happy about sitting on this chair.

"You don't hurry up," I said. "I just might open my eyes and take you where you stand."

Her mouth captured my cock, her wet tongue sliding on the underside of it, and I hadn't even felt her touch me. I let out a groan, couldn't stop it if I tried, as she masterfully sucked on me. Her hands settled on my thighs to hold herself where she was and pulled me all the way back to the back of her throat, swallowing around the head, and I shuddered, that build up starting at the base of my spine.

"I'm not gonna last long," I muttered.

Keeping my hands on the edge of the chair to keep myself from gathering her long hair in my hand to guide her. She popped off of me, letting out a sigh, and then rolled the condom along my length.

"Don't move," she whispered against my ear.

Feeling her move away, I wanted so badly to see her, but did as I had been told and keeping my eyes closed. I heard Billy moan, and figured he was getting the same treatment I did and waited until I heard her move again before I let my breath out.

"Gentlemen," she said, and I could tell she'd moved back up on the table. "Open your eyes."

I waited half a second, wanting to give Billy the first glance, and I was glad I did, because his moan was what I wanted to hear before opening my eyes. When I did, I saw her lying on the table atop her robe. She had on a cute little purple outfit that left absolutely nothing to the imagination. The fabric was so thin it might as well not have been there.

"Can we move?" Billy asked, and I looked across her to him to see that he was straining.

"Yes," she said, and it rushed out of her on a breath. "I want you to each stand next to me, but don't touch. Not yet."

Not one to dismiss an invitation, I stood up, getting closer to the table, my cock falling forward some, pointing directly at her. It was like it had a homing beacon or something and was searching out its release of its own accord. Her hand went to it, stroking it within the condom that was wrapped around it. Billy had done the same thing, and she had her other hand working him.

"Spencer," she said, looking up at me.

"Yes," I said, the word strained from my attempt at control.

"Will you undo my top?"

I didn't even hesitate. Reaching toward her, I slid my hand under the clasp between her breasts, unhooking it without trouble. The fabric parted but didn't fall completely away. Unsure whether she wanted me to do more, I pulled my hand back to my side.

"Billy," she said, turning to him.

"Yes, ma'am," he said, his eyes not leaving hers.

"Pull that side of the fabric away for me, please," she said.

"Whatever you say," he said, his hand gripping the thin material and pulling it off her, letting it settle next to her.

"Spencer," she said, turning to me.

"What can I do for you, Darlin'?" I asked.

"Pull that side off," she said, and it was a stronger command than she'd used with Billy.

Doing her bidding, I did as he had, pulling the fabric up and off her body, letting it settle next to her. She was bare to us on top but had a tiny scrap of material covering the apex of her thighs, the place I got lost in any chance I could. She took a deep breath, her breasts heaving toward the ceiling, before she let it out. Her hands hadn't stopped moving, and I was wondering what she had in mind next.

"Those should be ready," she said, tipping her head up and looking above her.

There were two candles on the table, and they were both lit. I didn't know how she'd done that without me noticing, but I didn't fault her. It was my inattention that was the problem, not anything she did. Neither Billy nor I moved, waiting for her to tell us what to do with them. The more we played together, the braver she got, and we'd introduced wax play to her a few weeks earlier. When we first started, she was hesitant, not wanting to burn herself.

Billy had simply shown her how it worked, used himself as the receiver of the wax. She'd watched in fascination as the melted wax pooled on his stomach, even dipping her finger into it. After realizing that it truly was a low temperature, she agreed to let us pour some on her. She insisted it always stay on her stomach, though, not wanting to burn the more sensitive areas of her body.

"You want us to get a towel?" I asked, since she was on her robe on the table.

"No," she said, turning to me.

Looking across her body, I saw that Billy had already grabbed one of the candles in his hand, holding it out and over her stomach.

"You ready?" he asked, and she turned back to him.

"Do it here," she said, taking her hand from his cock and pointing to the spot between her breasts.

"That's gonna sting," I said, not wanting her to be hurt.

"I know," she said, looking at me. "You should grab the other one."

Reaching above her head, I picked up the other candle. She'd pulled out the black ones that were made with soy. I knew she liked the way they made her body feel, so was glad I'd stocked up.

"Here we go," Billy said.

Tipping the candle so that the melted wax would drip from the little spout at one edge of the top, he was careful to make sure that it had plenty of time to cool down on the drop from about a foot or so above her body. Just a couple of drops came out, and he tipped the candle back upright. As they hit her chest, she sucked in a little bit, but her smile was wide.

"Oh, that's nice," she said.

CHAPTER SIXTY-TWO

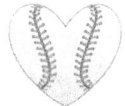

Billy...

"Oh, that's nice," she said.

I'd only let a little bit of wax out of the candle. She'd liked it fine when we dripped it lower on her body, along her stomach as well as along her thighs. Even her ass was fair game when we used the wax. But she was pushing the limits of tenderness when she asked me to put it between her tits.

"Want some more?" I asked.

She nodded, but I stood still. There were rules we'd set up in the very beginning, rules that said that she had to use her words, had to tell us what she wanted, what she needed. She had a safe word for when we pushed it to a point she was uncomfortable, but it had been weeks since she'd used it. I was so proud of how far she'd come, and so thrilled that she wanted to take charge today.

"Should I go in the same spot?" I asked, unsure how brave she was.

While I'd never use it on her pussy, nipples could be fun. I enjoyed it on mine, but hers were likely more sensitive. Didn't know it for sure, but figured they were. I didn't want it on my cock, so wouldn't put it on her pussy. The globes of her ass? Absolutely. The sides of her tits? Sure. Nipples would be a test, though, and I didn't want to hurt her.

"How about here?" she asked.

She'd stopped stroking me, both of us, actually, and pointed to the edge of her breast on my side, just inside the nipple. I moved the candle slightly toward me, making sure it was well off her nipple, then tipped it again. A few drips came out, and I turned it upright again.

"Oh," she said, arching her back and sucking in a breath.

"Is that a good oh?" Spencer asked, and she turned to him with a smile.

"Very much so," she said. "Your turn. Same spot, but this side."

Spencer didn't let the wax get on him. It wasn't anything he was interested in at all. But he was always willing to use it when the woman we were sharing was willing. Now, though, we only used it, or did really anything else, with Ari, my angel, my beautiful woman who filled my heart as much as I filled her.

"Ooh," she sighed as the few drops came from his candle.

He'd been closer to the nipple than I was, but his aim was better. I watched as she shifted, just a little, and the wax slid down the side of her tit, into the pool that I'd started her with.

"Let's get dangerous," she said, a wicked smile on her face. "I want both of you to drip right here," she said, pointing to her nipple on my side, "and here," she added, pointing to the one on Spencer's side of her.

"You sure?" I asked. "It's intense."

"Yes," she said. "I want this."

I looked over to Spencer, and he was smiling with a wicked grin of his own. His cock was sticking straight up, which meant he was very turned on. Mine was matching energy with his, too, and I could smell that our little angel was getting wetter by the minute.

"Together?" Spencer asked, looking between her and me.

"Together," she said. "One, two, three."

At three, we both tipped the candles, both of us only letting a couple of drops out before righting them. She sucked in a breath, her hands in fists next to her, and I worried we'd hurt her.

"You okay?" I asked.

"Oh, yeah," she said, sliding her hands up and over her stomach to slide between her thighs. "That was good."

"You want us to work your pussy?" I asked her. "One of us could do that while the other did the wax."

"Not yet," she said, her arousal filling the air. "I want to do it one more time, first. Then I have something else planned."

"Ready?" Spencer asked, a strain in his voice matching the one I felt at not being able to touch her.

"Yes," she said.

He looked at me and we tipped, at the same time, letting more of the wax fall to her skin, not just the few drops.

"Oh, God," she said, arching her back again, her hand at her cunt working herself.

"You're so fucking hot," I said, my cock desperate to find relief.

She hadn't said we couldn't touch ourselves, just that we couldn't touch her, so I began to stroke my cock with my other hand, needing to get more relief.

"Naughty boy," she said, and I immediately stopped. "You need to wait for me. It won't be long."

I stopped as soon as she said the first word, knowing that she never let us wait long, and that she was looking forward to being in control.

"Why don't you put those down," she said. "You can blow them out, too. I think we're done with them for now."

I did as she asked, blowing the candle out before setting it back on the table. Spencer did likewise and set his next to mine. Waiting for her to decide what was next, I realized that I never wanted to be with anyone else, that she was it for me. I just hoped that she and Spencer felt the same way.

CHAPTER SIXTY-THREE

Ariana...

While I hadn't done a ton of planning, there had been things I'd been desperate to try for several weeks. Knowing that Dee thought I was out of town, out of touch, and that he wouldn't likely contact either of my guys, I felt free to let myself be creative. Using the wax on my breasts was just the first of several things I wanted to try, and it had been so worth it.

I'd asked them to get me a towel to wipe the wax from my body before I got up and clipped my top back together. The rough of the lace against my sensitive skin shot straight to my pussy, giving a low and steady throb in time with my heartbeat.

They would be leaving in a few weeks, and I felt like I wanted to get everything I could out of the time they were still here to hold me over until they returned. I'd already decided I was going to tell Dee about us, but not until I was back in the office. It could wait, and I didn't want anything to spoil the weekend.

When they walked into the bedroom behind me and saw everything I had set out, Billy gave a low whistle.

"You're not messing around," he said.

"I didn't think you'd complain," I replied. "Some of them were what you had out, but others were ones I'd been wanting to try."

"I can see you have a very wide variety," Spencer said, his voice low and rough.

"But first, let's shower," I said.

Climbing up onto the bench, I turned to see them both looking at me a bit confused.

"You're gonna have to help me out," I said. "Can't seem to figure out how to get these things off me. You don't mind, do you?"

"Not in the least," Spencer said.

"I will strip you anytime you want," Billy added.

Spencer stepped into the shower first, moving to the side wall and giving Billy room to join him. It wasn't exactly a small space, but they were both big enough that it made it feel that way.

"First my top," I said.

"You can start," Billy said. "I got to do it once already."

Reaching up, Spencer slid his hand under the clasp, unhooking it swiftly, allowing the sides of the piece to slip away from my body, giving me another thrill as it slid along my nipples. I held my arms down, and they each reached up and slid the sleeves off, Billy taking it from Spencer and setting it outside the shower stall.

"Give me your hand," I said, reaching out to Spencer. "And yours," I said, turning to Billy.

They both gave me their hands on the inside next to each other. I pulled them each up, cupping my breasts with their hands, moving their thumbs to stroke the peak of my nipples. They knew what I liked, and how I liked things, and it showed in how they responded to my requests.

My hair was still in braids wrapped around my head, so I reached up and pulled the pins, letting the braids fall along my back. They liked it when I wore my hair down, giving them a way to hold me, and I liked letting them control me at times, too.

"You smell delicious," Billy said, pinching me between his finger and thumb. "I want to taste you."

"You're going to have to unwrap me first," I said, watching them both watch me.

Billy reached out the hand that wasn't on my breast, and Spencer did the same, both of them peeling down the thong I had on. I stepped out of it, one leg at a time, and Billy added it to the top that was outside the shower. Spencer's hand was on my hip, massaging the muscles beneath the surface, and I loved it.

When Billy turned back to me, he reached behind, sliding his hand around my ass, dipping his hand between my cheeks, and sliding toward my pussy. Instead of diving right in, though, he let it move lower, along my thigh, and pulled my leg so that I was standing in a more straddled position. Pulling the hand from my breast, he stepped closer to Spencer, sliding his hands up the inside of my thighs until he reached the apex. I let my head fall back and just felt what he was doing.

Spencer's hand slipped from my breast, but I didn't pay much attention to it, as Billy was sucking my clit, sliding a finger into my pussy, and scratching that rough spot inside that made me see stars. I could feel that Spencer was getting up onto the bench, but I didn't even care. They were now in control, and I let them do what they wanted, just enjoying their touch.

"You good with us taking over?" Spencer asked, his body against my back, his voice in my ear.

"Very much so," I said, relaxing into him.

"You're so fucking sexy," he whispered, his hands sliding around and under my arms to come back up and cup my breasts from behind.

With his palm against my back, he angled me downward so that he had easier access to my most intimate parts. Billy was still going at my clit, his finger plunging in and out of me in rapid strokes, and my muscles began to tighten around his finger. My knees were growing weak, but Spencer had wrapped an arm around my waist, keeping my ass pressed against his body, his cock sliding up and down the slit.

Pulling back, Spencer slid his cock right next to my opening, and Billy pulled his finger out as Spencer shoved his cock in. Billy hadn't let go of my clit, and I was getting closer and closer to my release. As Spencer pulled back, I felt his hand slick through my arousal, then slide up toward my ass. He slid a finger slowly into me, and I relaxed and pressed back to give him the space to enter.

The onslaught of touch, the rising emotions, and the letting go of the stress of the last few days all came together in an exquisite burst of light, exploding behind my eyelids, lighting through my veins, and coming out in a low and deep moan from my throat. Wave after wave ran through me, and as much as I wanted to stay in control, I relished the fact that they took over.

Coming back to myself, I was still held in the strong arms of Spencer, but Billy was standing in front of me, and I was no longer on the bench. They'd moved me down to the floor of the shower and had switched the water on. As we moved toward the downpour, I realized that I couldn't keep my feelings in any longer.

"I love you," I said, looking Billy in the eye. "Both of you," I added, craning my neck around to look up at Spencer.

"I love you, too," Spencer said, pressing his lips to my temple. "Have for a while now, too. Just didn't want to scare you off so soon."

"Yeah," I agreed, then turned back to Billy.

He was standing still, just looking at me with this odd expression on his face. It was like I had said something odd or out of character, but it was more than just that. I think he was actually taking in what I'd said, and what Spencer had said. It was like he was afraid we were gonna continue on without him.

"Hey," I said, reaching a hand up to cup his cheek. "You aren't going anywhere. I need both of you."

It was like a damn had been burst, and he just let out this little sob. He tried to hold it in, tried to keep himself in check, but he just couldn't. I knew he had some trauma in his life, and that he was very careful as to what he said and how he said it, but I hadn't expected this.

"Come here," I said, pulling him to me.

He came without resistance, pressing his body against my front, his arms going around my neck. Spencer pulled his arm out from between us and wrapped it around Billy as much as he could, while I held him close. Sob after sob escaped him, and I held him, brushing his hair back from his face as he let everything out. Spencer was rubbing his back while helping me to hold him up. Finally, he slowed his sobs, swallowed hard against my shoulder, and sniffled until he'd regained composure. He went to pull back, to let go of me, of us, but I held him fast, and Spencer did the same.

"We got you," Spencer said above me. "I always have."

"And I'm here, too," I added, hoping he knew that we both cared about him.

"I'm such a fucking mess," he said, though he stayed against me.

"Doesn't matter," Spencer said.

I felt Spencer move from my back, and watched as he went around to the side and pulled Billy to him. They weren't lovers, never had been, but Spencer cared, hell, he loved Billy, the way you love a partner. It wasn't romantic between them in the sense one would think, but they truly were partners. I was just the piece that held them together, and I was good with my role in the relationship.

"I'm sorry I'm such a fucking mess," he said as he pulled away from Spencer.

"Wouldn't have you any other way," Spencer said, and I could see he meant it.

I didn't know Billy's story, and I didn't know if Spencer did, either, but we both loved him, and would do whatever it took to make sure he was happy.

CHAPTER SIXTY-FOUR

S pencer...

We showered and then headed to the bedroom where we climbed into bed and cuddled. It was still early, but I knew that Billy was exhausted by the way he was acting, and that Ari was equally tired because of the ordeal of the past few days. It was nice to just snuggle down into bed with the two most important people in my life, and I soon drifted off to sleep along with them.

When I woke up, I was alone in bed, and was surprised that I hadn't heard or felt them move. I wondered what they were doing, so I got up and pulled on some pants before heading down the hall toward the main area of the house. I could hear them talking and thought about just standing out if sight to listen but felt that wouldn't be a good way to build on our relationship, so I stepped out of the hall.

"Hey," Ari said, and her voice was light and flirty. "We were wondering when you'd get up."

"You could have woken me," I said.

"You needed sleep," Billy said. "Besides, we've been chatting, and it's been nice for me to get some things out."

"Oh," I said, not sure how I felt about that.

I'd known him for several years, and he'd never shared anything deep with me other than to say his family was messed up. It felt a bit like a betrayal, but not so much that I wanted to bring it up. Instead, I walked to the coffee maker and started a cup for myself.

"I'm telling my brother today," Ari said. "He needs to know about us. I'll tell him that I'm still doing your work, and he can either deal with it or not be involved. I also have to contact someone about Caden."

"How are you feeling about that?" I asked.

"Creeped out," she confessed, and I could tell that she and Billy had already discussed it.

"Are you going to the police?" I asked.

"I think I'm going to talk to his parents," she said. "They were horrified at what he'd done and were so apologetic to me when everything came out, so I feel like I can get what I need by making sure they know that he's back and up to his old tricks again."

"Why do you want to tell your brother about us, though?" I asked.

"Because of what Caden said," she said. "I'm sure my brother suspects something, but I need him to know that I went into this with my eyes open, fully on board with who you are and who I am in the mix. I don't think it'll freak him out too much, but he needs to know."

I just nodded as my coffee finished brewing. I pulled the pod out of the maker and dropped it into the trash, then went to the fridge to pull out some milk, pouring it in and watching the color soften. They were watching me, I could feel it, but I didn't know what they were thinking.

"Hey," Ariana said as she placed a hand on my shoulder. "Talk to us."

"About what?" I asked.

"How you're feeling," she said. "What you think of what I'm planning to do."

"It's not my decision," I said. "You know your brother better than we do, so you're the one who will know how he will react. I have no problem with him knowing, I just want to make sure you're going to be okay."

"I'll be fine," she said. "What about Caden?"

"That's something else that I can't make a decision on," I said. "You know what happened, and you know him and his family. If you think the best thing to do is start with them, then I'll back you up."

She looked at me and nodded, seeming sure of her decisions. It wouldn't be what I'd have done, but I'm not her, so she had to make that decision. Billy was suspiciously quiet, leaning against the island, his arms folded across his chest.

"How about you?" I asked, looking at him pointedly.

"Our little angel is in charge," he said. "I'm good with her making those decisions."

"You doing okay?" I asked him.

"Fine," he said.

"Good," I replied, knowing that they had likely talked about whatever it was that happened the night before. "If you need someone, I'm here."

"I know," he said, and this time there was more emotion in his voice. "Look," he continued, letting his arms drop. "I am a fucked-up mess. I know that, and you guys know that. I need therapy, but don't feel like I can do it right now. Maybe at some point I will, but for now, I need you guys to just let me exist."

"We can do that," Ari said, then turned to me. I nodded, and she said, "See, we're here for you. Whenever you're ready, we'll listen."

He nodded but didn't say anything. I watched as he swallowed, and guessed he was trying to maintain some sort of image, but we knew who he was, and loved him. Eventually, he'd probably unload, but until then, we'd just keep being there for him.

"I gotta go," Ari said. "I told Dee I'd be there in an hour to talk to him."

"You sure you want to go alone?" I asked.

"I actually kinda need one of you to drive me," she said. "Either to my house or to the office. My car's at my house, remember?"

I felt like an idiot not remembering that I'd picked her up and taken her away, but so much had happened in such a short amount of time, that it completely slipped my mind.

"I'll take you," Billy said, and I wanted to argue, but he was already dressed. In fact, they both were, so they'd likely been up a while.

"You want us both to go with you when you tell your brother?" I asked.

"Pretty sure that would just make things more awkward," she replied. "Billy can take me home, and I can drive into the office. I have to go talk to Caden's parents, too. They're not gonna be happy, and neither will Dee."

Much as I wanted to argue, wanted to go all caveman on her, I knew she was right. Her talk with her brother would need to be done without us around. If we were there, he'd likely want to punch us, and no one wanted that to happen.

"Call us or text us when you get to places," I said. "We need to know you're safe."

"I will," she said. "Billy can take me home, and I'll drop my bag off, grab my phones, and head out. He can stay while I do that. I'll be fine. I promise."

She pressed up on her toes and kissed me, and my arms naturally went around her waist, holding her to me as she deepened the kiss. When she pulled away, she held my hands in hers, squeezing them before letting go.

"Trust me," she said.

"I do," I replied, and it was the truth.

"Come on," she said to Billy, then headed toward the door.

Much as I wanted to argue, to make her stay, I knew I had to let her handle this on her own. We'd be fine. I was sure of it. I just didn't want her to get hurt, either by her brother's reaction to our relationship, or by the guy who'd been stalking her. All of that was out of my control, though, and it pissed me off.

Instead of just waiting, I did what I usually did when I needed to let off steam or get outside my own head. I went to my room, changed into my workout gear, and headed to my car. I shot a text to Billy to let him know where I was going and also sent one to Ari so she'd know as well. Then, I took my unhappy ass to the stadium to let my anger out.

CHAPTER SIXTY-FIVE

riana...

Billy took me home, went into the house first to check it out, then waited while I grabbed my phones and car keys. Spencer had texted that he was going to the gym, and Billy said he'd be joining him after he knew I was safely at my office. He followed me all the way, then headed away after I was in the lot.

"About time," Dee said.

"I'm here," I replied. "And I know who called."

"You do?" he seemed surprised. "How do you know?"

"First," I said, sitting down in a chair in his office across the desk from him. "I need to tell you something."

"You're fucking him, aren't you," he said.

He didn't sound pissed, though. No, he sounded almost proud. Like I'd done something impressive or something, which just pissed me off.

"Actually," I said and waited for him to look up. "All three of us are in a relationship."

"I'm sorry, what?" he asked.

"Spencer, Billy, and I are together," I said.

"Wait, like one of those..." he paused, like he was looking for a word. "Threesome? Throuple? I think that's the word I've seen used. You three fuck each other all at once?"

"You don't need to be crass," I said. "We work together well, and we all have fun and enjoy ourselves."

"So, they're gay?" he asked.

"No," I said. "I'm the filling in that sandwich. I'm between them, always."

"I do not need to hear this right now," he said, and he looked completely grossed out.

I laughed. Couldn't help it. The face he had on was hysterical, and with everything else that had been going on, it was like something inside me just burst, and it all came tumbling out in a laugh.

"Okay," Dee said when I'd settled. "Let's not talk about sex and you in the same sentence, okay? I don't need that mental picture, especially when you tell me that you're some fucked-up ice cream in the middle of an ice cream sandwich. That's just too much for me."

"Sorry," I said, and meant it. "Caden."

I let the name hang in the air, waiting for him to catch it, and the connotation that came with it. It took a good couple of minutes, but then realization hit him. It was like the lights were turned on and everything fell into place, all the pieces fitting together.

"Fuck," he said.

"Yeah," I replied. "But it gets worse."

"How?" he asked.

"When we were first getting started on the project," I said. "I sent out that email asking about architectural firms. Do you remember?"

"Vaguely," he said.

"I got a call on the way home," I said. "I didn't recognize the voice, and it was a private number. He said he was with an architectural firm and wanted more details. I told him he had to email, like I'd asked, then hung up on him. When he called the other night, it all fell into place, and I realized that he'd been the one to call then, too."

"I'm confused," he said.

"I started seeing the guys fairly early on," I said. "I know you said not to, and I really tried, but things just sort of clicked with us. They said we should wait, but I wanted them. I think Caden started stalking me again right after I sent that email. How he knew, though, is what's been bugging me."

"Hang on," Dee said. "Let me go back through some stuff. When did you send that email out to the architects?"

"Mid-November," I said. "Before Thanksgiving, for sure."

He was scrolling through something on his computer, searching for something. My heart was hammering, wondering if he'd been following me all the way back then, because if he was, he'd have seen that I stayed at their house regularly.

"Yeah," he said, and sounded pissed. "I didn't even think about it, but we had a breach. It was small, and I checked it out with our tech guy, who said that our outgoing emails had been captured, but that the leak fixed itself. Now I'm wondering if it really did."

"Shit," I said, knowing that this was bigger than just what we thought.

"Let me reach out to Ryan and see what he says," he said. "It shouldn't take long."

He picked up the phone and started dialing. I sat and waited, hoping that it was a quick fix and nothing else was in jeopardy. I only heard Dee's side of the call, and it was a whole lot of humming yes and no after the initial explanation. When he hung up, I sat and waited, hoping that it was going to be good news.

"He's going to run another test and call me back," he said. "Should be quick, though."

As if by magic, the phone rang, and he answered it.

"Carington Construction," he said. "Hey, what did you find?"

Another half conversation with nothing more than a 'yeah' or 'no' on Dee's part.

"Thanks, man," Dee said before hanging up. "He's tapped into your stuff specifically."

"Everything?" I asked.

"Maybe," he said. "Right now, I think we need to shut you out of everything, turn it all off, and wait for Ryan to get back to me."

"I'm calling his mom," I said.

"You're what?" he asked.

"His mom always liked me," I said. "She was the one who really made sure things fell into place. Sure, his dad was all bravado, and when Dad told him what was what, he started to settle. But his mom? She's the one who had the balls in that family. She made sure that Caden was kept in check, kept away from me."

"I had no idea," he said.

"No one did," I replied. "I think she liked to stay behind the curtain and pull the strings. I really liked her."

"If you're sure that's what you want to do," he said, and I could tell that he wasn't sure whether it was best or not, but I'd made up my mind.

"I'm gonna call from my office," I said, standing up. "I'll let you know what I find out."

I headed out of his office and down to my own, shutting the door once I was in. I contemplated using my cell but was afraid that Caden would have access to it and be able to listen to the call. Instead, I picked up the office phone and made the call. It rang a couple times, then she answered.

"Hello," she said.

"Hi, Mrs. Whittman," I said, and she paused.

"Who is this?" she asked, and I could hear fear in her voice.

"It's Ariana Carington," I said and waited.

"What's he done now?" she asked, and I could hear her anger.

"I think he's stalking me again," I said. "He called me in November, then again this last week. He was saying some pretty terrible things to me this last week, and also left a voicemail on my brother's phone. He indicated that he was going to spread rumors around and try to damage our business."

"He came home at the end of October," she said. "He'd been working for a security company, but said that he didn't like the work, so was looking for something closer to home. Then, he said he got a job that was all online and he didn't need to go into an office. I'd been skeptical, but he's been paying us rent, so I assumed he was working."

"Is he home now?" I asked.

"No," she said. "He left a few minutes ago. Said he had an errand to run, and that he should be back before dinner. I'm so sorry."

"You didn't do anything wrong," I said, but inside I was fuming. "What kind of car does he drive?"

"He's still driving the same car he had in high school," she said. "He has always driven that car."

I thought back, trying to remember what the car was, but for the life of me, I couldn't, so I asked her.

"It was his dad's Nova from his high school days," she said, and it all came back.

"Thanks," I said. "I need to go, but if you see him, please don't tell him that I called you. I need him to not know that I know. Okay?"

"Your secret is safe with me," she said. "It always has been."

"Thank you," I said, then hung the phone up. "Demetri," I shouted, getting up from the desk.

I walked to the door and opened it to see Caden standing on the other side.

"What the fuck are you doing here?" I shouted, hoping that my brother was still around and would come out.

"I've come to take back what's mine," he said.

His voice had deepened, but it was unmistakably the voice that had called me both times. It was also the voice on Dee's voicemail. The place was quiet, and I wondered what he did to my brother, but I had to be smart. We had cameras in the building, but he could've shut them down. If he'd been able to hack in and get information from my emails, he likely knew how to get around that shit, too.

"You don't have anything here," I said, stalling, hoping that I could think my way out of this situation. "Whatever you think is yours, it's not me."

"You're the reason my life got fucked up," he said. "If you hadn't been such a little bitch, things would've been fine for me. I'd have gotten my scholarship, gotten to go pro, and would have had you as my little plaything. Now, you're out there fucking some dicks who don't even care about you."

"Really?" I asked. "That's the way you think about it?"

"It's true," he said. "You were smart back then. I can see you've dumbed down since."

"And I see you've done nothing but become dumber," I replied.

I was stalling, praying to whatever god I could think of, that Dee was fine, would hear this, and would come out of his office and deal with this dick with a tiny dick for me. But I couldn't just wait. I had to do something. He was clenching his fists against his sides, his breathing had increased, and I was doing nothing but pissing him off even more than he already was. Thing was, he wasn't thinking. He was reacting, which gave me the upper hand.

"I heard you ran back to mommy's house," I said, backing into the office, my ass hitting my desk. "I talked to her," I continued, feeling behind me and finding my phone. "She isn't very happy with you right now."

"Don't fucking talk about my mom," he said, closing the distance between us.

"Why not?" I asked, pressing my thumb onto the side, and getting the phone to open up. "She doesn't like you talking to other girls? She jealous?"

It wasn't true. His dad was the dick, but his mom was nice. I just needed something to push him over the edge, and I figured this would do it.

"Siri, call nine-one-one," I said, and heard the phone respond.

"You little bitch," he said, lunging toward me.

I knew it was coming, and skirted away from him easily, sliding out into the hallway and slamming the door behind me. Instead of running to my brother's office, which was further into the building, I ran toward the front, pulling the door open and seeing Spencer and Billy in the lot, coming toward me.

"What are you doing here?" I asked as I ran down the steps.

The door crashed open behind me as I hit the parking lot and saw both Billy and Spencer break into a run toward me. Billy flew right past me, and I crashed into Spencer's chest as I went to turn around. He put me behind him, blocking my view of what was happening, but I could hear flesh slamming into flesh, and then the crash of the door as it opened again.

I shoved Spencer out of my way, wanting to protect Billy, but didn't need to worry. He stood over Caden, who was out cold. When he turned to me, I could see every emotion he had rushing over his face.

First was fear, then pure rage, and finally, so much caring it made me want to cry.

Running up the stairs, I flew into his arms, holding him to me and muttering my thanks for the rescue. Spencer came up the steps as well but went past me to go inside. I heard a woman's voice asking what was going on and realized that I still had my phone in my hand.

"Hello?" I asked.

"This is nine-one-one," she said. "I heard fighting. Are you okay?"

"Sorry," I said. "I am, but can you send the police and an ambulance? There's a man who's been hurt, but he's the one who attacked me."

"What's your address?" she asked.

I gave her the name of the company, as well as the address, and she assured me that both police and aid were on the way, then asked if I needed her to stay on the line until they arrived. I declined, letting her know that the person was subdued and I had other people with me to make sure he stayed that way.

"Ariana," I heard my brother shouting, and turned to see him run to the door, then stop cold. "What the fuck happened?"

"He came in," I said. "Didn't you hear me scream your name?"

"I had my headphones on," he said. "I was working with Ryan to try to figure out what happened. Holy shit, is that him?"

"Yeah," I said.

"He got fucking huge," he said, looking down at the prone figure on the ground.

Just then, Spencer came back out with zip ties from somewhere and pulled Caden's hands behind his back, hooking them together with the ties to keep him where he was until the cops got there. Demetri looked at me, then up at Billy, then down at Spencer and Caden, then back at me. It was clear he had no idea what had happened, or what the fuck was going on with the three of us, but he didn't look like he cared, either. Just then, we heard sirens, and I turned to see a couple of cop cars pulling into the lot.

"Thank God," I said.

"Hey," one of the cops said as he got out of the car.

"That guy," I said, pointing to Caden. "Came into our office without permission. He stalked me when I was in high school, came back, and started up again. Decided he didn't want to wait for me to make what he considered the right decision, so he came to me. My boyfriend hit him, but it was to keep him from getting to me."

"All right, then," he said, as the other cop got out of her car.

"What's up?" she asked as she came up to us.

"You can take her," he said, pointing to me. "I'll take you guys, one at a time."

"Sure," Billy said, then kissed the top of my head. "You okay?" he asked me.

"Yeah," I said, but could feel the adrenaline crash pouring over me. "I think I need to sit down, though."

An ambulance pulled into the lot just then, and I turned to watch as they came out of the vehicle and toward us.

"Punched guy," the male cop said. "He's restrained, though. Use caution."

"Sure thing," one of the medics said, coming up the steps to stand over Caden. "Does he have any underlying issues we should be aware of?"

"Other than being an asshole, not that I know of," I said, and the cops and medics did their best to hide their smiles, but I think they understood where I was coming from.

Billy helped me over Caden's body and into the office. The cops followed, and we were all separated so they could get the truth, likely, without us checking our stories. The female cop came with me to my office, where I sat on the chair behind the desk and she sat across from me. I saw Dee walk down to his office with the other cop and assumed that Billy and Spencer were left out in the lobby area.

I told her the entire story, or at least what I knew about it. About my history with him, what had happened in high school, how things went to shit after he decided to be a dick, and how he ended up getting shipped off to somewhere else by his family after he graduated. I told her I hadn't seen him since the court date where I got the restraining order against him but did confess to not having renewed it.

The calls were discussed, and I said that I'd been dating Billy for a few months. I wasn't gonna out either of my lovers and our unusual relationship, so I stuck with Billy being my guy for now. Since I'd said it out loud, I was sure that they knew how to keep things simple. They'd been doing this for entirely too long to not know how to answer questions without answering questions.

Finally, when I had finished my entire story, the cop checked her notes, asked a couple more questions, then asked me to stay in my office until she came to let me know I could come out. My guess was that she went out to talk to the guys, and I just let everything from the past week flood through me until I broke down and cried.

I don't know how long I was there, my head on my arms, crying my eyes out, before Billy came in. He was quiet enough that I didn't hear him. Either that, or I was so loud it overpowered the noise from him coming in. Didn't matter, though, because he simply pulled me up from the chair, sat down, and pulled me back onto his lap where he held me until I got it all out.

When I'd finished, I was more than just a hot mess. I was snotty and red-eyed and all the things that are so ugly you never want anyone you care about to see them. But he was there, holding me, kissing the top of my head, and rocking me back and forth.

"I know it's not the time," he said, his voice pitched low so it didn't carry past my ears. "But you are fucking gorgeous when you cry."

I laughed at that and shook my head.

"I don't ever want you to hurt like this again," he added, running a thumb under one of my eyes. "But I can't help but love you more when I see you like this."

"You were pretty fucking brave," I said, my voice scratchy from the crying. "Why did you do that?"

"Because he was fucking with my woman," he said, and this time he wasn't nearly as quiet.

"Our woman," Spencer said from the doorway.

I turned and looked at him, motioning for him to come into the room. He sat on the desk, his legs apart, and I slid off Billy's lap and up onto my feet. Raising myself up, I pressed my lips to his, just a soft touch before pulling back.

"Cops are gone," he said. "So is the ambulance. He's being

detained at the hospital until they sort things out. I guess your brother has some sort of proof of his stalking, so that's good."

"Yeah," I said. "I mean, I guess. Fuck. I don't even know what to think right now."

"You don't have to," Billy said, and I turned to look at him. "Just let us take care of you. No need to think about anything else."

"Did they look at your hand?" I asked him, seeing it wrapped.

"Yeah," he said. "Fucker cut my knuckles with his teeth, but it's all good. I'll probably have to get rabies shots, but I'd do it again in a heartbeat."

"Hey," I heard my brother say from the door, and I turned to him. "Are you okay? Do you need anything?"

"I'm fine," I said, moving from between my lovers to go hug my brother. "Thank you for getting the information for them."

"It was Ryan who figured it all out," he said. "Dude was a fucking cyber genius or something because of the way he hid his tracks. But there was enough information there to prove it was him. At least that's what the cops said."

"Good," I said. "I don't ever want to see him again."

"Me, either," he said. "Right now, though, I think you need to go get some rest. You were supposed to go on vacation."

"Yeah," I said. "I don't think I want to go anywhere right now."

"Well, you should take some time off," he said. "I've got everything handled here. We should have the permits for the remodel for your guys in the next week or so, and we'll be able to start on the project as soon as they're ready for us to."

"I think you should start when we head to Arizona for spring training," Spencer said.

"We can definitely do that," my brother replied. "Now, take her away from here. I don't want to know what you guys are doing, so long as you're making her happy."

"Thanks," I said, hugging my brother again.

We walked out the door, down the steps to the lot, and Spencer took my keys to drive my car to his place while I rode with Billy. I was actually looking forward to not thinking for a while and knew they would be the best people to help me accomplish that.

EPILOGUE

TWO MONTHS LATER...

B illy...

"Look at you," I said, smiling in the sunshine.

"Here I am," Ariana replied as she came out of the airport. "You didn't have to book a first-class ticket, though. I would have been fine flying coach."

"Nonsense," I replied. "You're our girl, and we'll make sure you're treated like the queen you are. Now, come here so I can tongue fuck your mouth."

She laughed, but came to me anyway, pressing up on her toes and wrapping her arms around my neck. Spencer had stayed at the condo, making us all something to eat once we'd finished with all the other things we'd planned to do.

"You taste like chocolate," I said when I finally pulled away.

"They served me some on the plane," she replied.

"Come on," I said, picking up her suitcase and dropping it in the back seat of my Jeep.

We'd gone ahead and driven down for spring training, leaving Spencer's car at Ariana's house. It was a three-day drive to get there, but that's because we made a handful of stops. We'd tried to convince her to come with us, but she said she had some things she wanted to get done before she came down. Now, we had just a couple of days before the first games, and we intended to spend as much time as possible with each other.

When I pulled into the condo's parking lot, she gave a low whistle, and I turned to look at her. She was looking up at the building, assessing everything about it, and I just had to marvel at the way her mind worked. She knew the building trade well, and she was so fucking smart it was ridiculous. Like, she could have chosen to be damn near anything she wanted, but I was so glad she went into business with her brother. Otherwise, we'd never have met, and I'd be a fucking loser without her.

"Come on," I said as I helped her out of the car.

We walked over to the elevator in the garage, pressing the button to call it down. When it opened up, she went in, and I followed her, pressing the fob on my keys to the panel.

"That's cool," she said as the elevator started its rise.

When it stopped on our floor, she stepped out, looking around.

"Come on," I said, pulling her suitcase behind me, wrapping my other arm around her waist. "Spencer's making us dinner, but we don't have to eat right away."

"Good," she said, and I looked at her. "I'm in the mood for dessert, first."

"Me, too," I said, pressing my lips to the top of her head.

The door opened just as we got to it, and Spencer pulled her from my arms, wrapping his around her. I pushed them further into the condo, then shut the door behind, coming up to sandwich her between us. He'd lifted her up, and she had her legs wrapped around his waist, her mouth on his.

She was wearing a sundress, and I couldn't resist the temptation that was before me. Spencer had his hands under her ass, but the skirt was short enough that it wasn't caught between them, so I lifted it, crouching behind her, and sliding my tongue along her slit. Spencer's hold on her shifted, and he used his hands to open her up more for me, and I slid a finger inside her, twisting so that I could find that spot that set her off, my tongue teasing her asshole as I did.

As much as we were enjoying ourselves, there was no way for us to keep this position up, so I stood up, keeping my fingers inside her, and guided them toward the table that was just left of the entrance. Thankfully, Spencer and I had talked about this, and he'd made sure that it was completely cleared except for a tablecloth to keep her from being stuck onto the cold marble surface. There was also a pile of condoms on the table, just so we wouldn't have to go searching in the moment.

I slid my fingers out just before he laid her down, moving so that I was near her head instead. She reached up above herself, working my shorts down so that she had access to my cock while Spencer let himself out of his own shorts.

"I've missed you both," she said, pulling me closer to slide into her mouth.

Spencer rolled a condom on, hiking her legs up, her dress falling to her waist, and slid his fingers along her slit. She hummed her approval, which only made me ache more, until he slid inside her and she gasped. I took that moment to press further into her mouth, and she swallowed around the head of my cock, threatening my control.

"You're so tight," Spencer said, and I could hear the strain in his voice, too.

His thrusts increased, and the way he was pumping into her shoved her onto my cock even more, and before I could even control myself, I was coming down her throat, hearing my friend losing his own fight with control and following suit.

"Oh, God," I groaned as I slid from her mouth.

"Exactly," Spencer echoed.

"My turn," she said, sitting up and pulling her dress off.

She was wearing a tiny little thing that had a strap that tied around her neck, swooping down her body with a band just under her breasts, and sliding down to her waist. There was a ring at her belly button, and it was attached to this sort of contraption that went around her thighs. The lace that went across her breasts was barely there, and couldn't really contain her tits, and the bottom was open so we had easy access to her pussy and ass. It was like it was built for fucking, and I loved it.

To add to the appeal, it was a deep purple, and just fucking suited her. She reached up to undo her hair, letting the waves fall from the bun she'd had it tied up in, and it was just as I'd remembered it; long, wavy, and so damn soft.

"I assume you have some toys here, right?" she asked, and I smiled.

"You need to not move," I said, turning and heading into my bedroom.

I opened the drawer in my closet where I kept all the things we usually used when we were here, and pulled out a couple that I knew she liked, marching my happy ass back out to the table.

"Close your eyes," I said, and she smiled and did as I asked.

Bringing one of the toys to the front of me, Spencer smiled. We both liked to work her, and we both liked to make her come as hard as possible, and this was the thing that seemed to work best on her. She was on her ass on the table, but that wasn't gonna work for what we had in mind, so I waited for Spencer to situate her. Like the good girl she was, she kept her eyes closed the entire time he moved her, turning her so she was on her hands and knees on the table facing me.

I handed the toy off to Spencer, then slid a mask over her eyes, just so she didn't have to think about that. Pressing my lips to hers, she opened to me, allowing me to slide my tongue into her mouth, tasting myself on hers as Spencer slid a hand along her sex. I held her face in my hands, but pulled away so I could watch as he slid the double dildo into both her pussy and ass at the same time.

"Oh," she moaned, arching her back.

"You like that?" I asked in her ear.

"So much," she said, her chest lowering toward the table.

He slid the toy in and out of her in a slow and methodical manner, nice and even strokes, as she arched herself lower and lower until her shoulders were touching the table. As much as I liked watching him work her, I knew I wanted to add to her pleasure. Her head was near the edge of the table, so I shifted her so that she was facing me, then slid my softened cock into her mouth.

She pulled it in, pushing my balls in with it, and holding me in her warm mouth. I reached around her upper body, sliding my hands under the lace, finding her nipples, and pinching them between my finger and thumb. The way she was situated, I couldn't do much more than pinch, even though what I wanted to do was pull.

I'd grabbed some clamps, not really sure whether she'd be comfortable with them, but decided to work to get at least one clipped onto a nipple and see how she reacted. I'd unscrewed them so there was plenty of give, but knowing they'd still grasp, and squeezed the pincher, opening them. When I slid them onto her nipple and slowly released the grip, she sucked in a breath around me, and then let me fall from her mouth.

"That's new," she said.

"Is it okay?" I asked.

"Very much so," she said, and I could hear the smile in her voice.

"Push up and I'll do the other one," I said, and she did as she was asked, pressing her palms to the table.

"Hang on," Spencer said, and I looked over at him. "You should turn over on your back."

She did as he asked, turning herself carefully so she didn't slip off the table, then lying back, where I helped to make sure she was safe. The whole time, he kept pumping that toy in and out of her. How he did it without it slipping out, I had no clue, but he was a master. When she was settled, I moved to attach the other clamp to her nipple, and she reached up, shifting herself so she could have her head sort of hanging off the edge of the table, then pulled my cock and balls back into her mouth. I shuddered, feeling myself growing hard again, and all I wanted to do was fuck her.

Spencer gave me a sort of nod and I pulled myself from her mouth. I went to the other side of the table and took over with the toy, sliding it in and out of her in the same even motions he'd been doing. He was stroking himself before sliding into her mouth, his used condom sitting on top of his shorts to take care of later.

We'd talked about the possibility of what we were going to try, but hadn't actually executed it, yet. She'd given us permission to try it when we were ready, and she had said that if she wasn't comfortable, she would tell us, so we knew we had her permission. I grabbed a condom, ripped it open with my teeth, then slid it on my hardening cock. Once it was in place, and Spencer was positioned to slid into her mouth, I stepped forward, lining myself up with the toy that was sliding into her pussy.

Pulling the toy almost all the way out, I set myself on top of it, used my hand to guide me, and slid inside her pussy with the toy, the other part of it in her ass. She shuddered, letting a low moan out before Spencer slid into her mouth. Her knees were wide open, her arms wrapped around Spencer's thighs, and I was pumping in and out of her pussy with the toy, my thumb on her clit running in circles.

There was no way we were going to be able to keep this up for long, so I pressed as hard as I could, working all the thing I knew got her off, and after just a few strokes, she was spasming around me, working Spencer's cock in her throat, and holding him and me in place as she soared to the heavens like the angel she was.

Finally, she relaxed her grip on me, and pulled her hands back from around Spencer, and let him pull from her mouth as I pulled myself and the toy from her pussy and ass. She was panting, short and shallow breaths, and I worried that we'd pushed her too far.

"We're gonna have to do that more often," she finally said, and I smiled.

"Anytime you're ready," I said.

"Whenever you want," Spencer added.

She blinked, looking up at Spencer, then down her body at me, and her smile brightened the entire world.

"I love you guys," she said. "And I don't ever want to be without you."

"I'm not going anywhere," I said.

"Me, either," Spencer agreed.

NOTE FROM AUTHOR

Images and Blurbs available upon request.
I would ask that you obtain high quality headshots and cover art images directly through me, rather than taking them from either my website or Amazon, however, blurbs are readily available through both places.

ABOUT THE AUTHOR

Born and raised in the Pacific Northwest, CM Kane was fed a steady diet of sports, particularly baseball. Having this love of the game instilled in her at an early age, she found that nothing was better than getting lost in the game. Storytelling was another gift that was encouraged in her youth, and she's taking to the written word to explore a new aspect to the game she loves.

Social Media and Website Links:

Website:
https://www.authorcmkane.com

Facebook:
https://www.facebook.com/AuthorCMKane

Instagram:
https://www.instagram.com/authorcmkane/

Amazon:
https://www.amazon.com/author/cmkane

BlueSky:
https://bsky.app/profile/authorcmkane.bsky.social

ALSO BY C.M. KANE

A Switch in Time